心智圖神記憶

初級英文文法

作者 Alex Rath Ph.D.
心智圖製作 Yang Wei-Xin
譯者 謝右／丁宥榆
審訂 Dennis Le Boeuf／Liming Jing

U0025386

MP3

寂天雲 APP

如何下載 MP3 音檔

❶ 寂天雲 APP 聆聽：掃描書上 QR Code 下載「寂天雲－英日語學習隨身聽」APP。加入會員後，用 APP 內建掃描器再次掃描書上 QR Code，即可使用 APP 聆聽音檔。

❷ 官網下載音檔：請上「寂天閱讀網」（www.icosmos.com.tw），註冊會員／登入後，搜尋本書，進入本書頁面，點選「MP3 下載」下載音檔，存於電腦等其他播放器聆聽使用。

心智圖神奇記憶
初級英文文法

作 者	Alex Rath Ph.D. / Yang Wei-Xin（心智圖製作）
譯 者	謝右／丁宥榆
審 訂	Dennis Le Boeuf & Liming Jing
編 輯	楊維芯
校 對	歐寶妮／陳慧莉
主 編	丁宥暄
內文排版	蔡怡柔／林書玉
封面設計	林書玉
製程管理	洪巧玲
發 行 人	黃朝萍
出 版 者	寂天文化事業股份有限公司
電 話	+886-(0)2-2365-9739
傳 真	+886-(0)2-2365-9835
網 址	www.icosmos.com.tw
讀者服務	onlineservice@icosmos.com.tw
出版日期	2024 年 02 月 初版四刷

* 本書內文取材自《彩圖初級英文文法 Let's See!》一書。

心智圖神奇記憶初級英文文法 / Alex Rath, Yang Wei-Xin 作；
謝右，丁宥榆譯 . -- 初版 . -- [臺北市]：寂天文化，2024.02
　　面；　公分
ISBN 978-626-300-240-1 (25K 平裝)

1. 英語 2. 語法

805.16   113000953

用圖解秒懂英文文法重點，破解文法盲點！
心智圖文法說明 + 例句 MP3 = 文法記憶再強化！

豐富試題
- 有效檢視學習成效
  書中附有題型多元的練習題，
  並為貫徹圖像化學習的精神，
  融入大量**看圖作答題**，有效檢視學習成效。

圖像式文法
- 一圖習得文法要點
  心智圖建立有系統的文法架構，
  運用**圖像記憶**搞定難懂的文法，
  擺脫冗長文法說明，不再一知半解！

詳盡補充
- 幫助延伸學習
  補充相似文法概念間的**比較**、**例外**情況，
  一次習得最全面的文法內容。

**秒懂
文法心智圖**

精美彩圖
- 逗趣的彩色插圖輔助學習
  書中圖表穿插許多精美逗趣的
  彩色插圖輔助學習，讓學文法
  有趣又好玩！

道地例句
- 清楚點出文法運用
  每單元附有專業外師精心撰寫的例句，
  難易適中，清楚點出文法運用，
  無痛習得文法要點！

多元圖表
- 系統歸類文法更好學
  除了心智圖，還針對文法主題特性設計有不同
  的**圖解**、**表格**，看圖表秒懂抽象的文法規則！

例句 MP3
- 專業外師錄製 MP3，文法記憶再強化
  書中單字、片語及句子皆有專業外師錄製音檔，
  用聽力加深文法規則的記憶，好背好用超難忘！

使用導覽

1 ▸ 先閱讀前導主題，熟悉先備知識

根據文法性質，有些單元會有多個主題，並以粉紅色核心
表示需先閱讀的前導主題，先熟悉基礎先備知識的前導主題
後，再進入中心主題，以利快速理解學習。

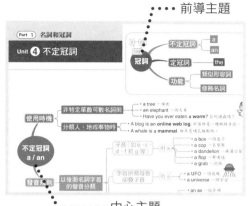

前導主題

中心主題

2 ▸ 由上 → 下，右 → 左順時鐘閱讀

心智圖有向右延伸型及放射型。向右延伸型由上到下依序閱讀；放射型則請由右上角起始，順時鐘閱讀。

閱讀順序

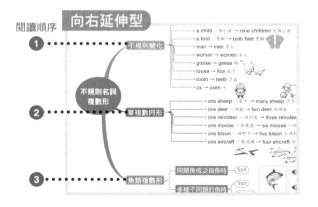

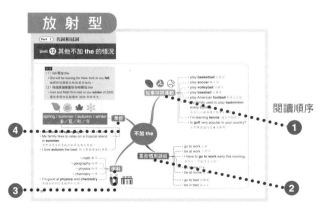

閱讀順序

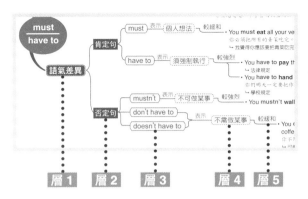

3 ▸ 不同層級以不同格式區分

心智圖以不同格式區分每條分支的不同層級，
清楚區分文法概念，理解更容易。

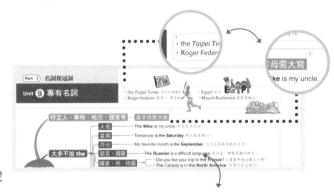

4 ▸ 心智圖外範例以編號方便對照

部分片語、例句等範例會放在心智圖框外，並以編號
來與心智圖中的文法概念做對應，方便對照學習。

5 ▸ 每單元例句 MP3 搭配文法規則更好記

除總複習單元，每單元例句皆錄有 MP3，
搭配文法學習，使記憶更加牢固，自然學
會文法！

6 ▸ 章節後皆有自我檢測練習題

每 Unit 和 Part 結束後分別有
Practice、**Review Test** 可供練習，
即學即用，幫助檢視學習盲點及成果。

目 錄

Unit **1** 可數名詞（1）

001 ▶ 每個 Unit 一個音軌。（註：單元總複習無音軌）

Practice

① 請將下列單數名詞改成「複數」形態。

1. cat	....	**11.** group	....
2. car	....	**12.** picture	....
3. loss	....	**13.** orange	....
4. tax	....	**14.** hike	....
5. flush	....	**15.** kick	....
6. match	....	**16.** dive	....
7. tux	....	**17.** tree	....
8. push	....	**18.** branch	....
9. punch	....	**19.** tick	....
10. star	....	**20.** clock	....

③ 將下列名詞改為複數形，並依字尾 s 或 es 的發音填入正確的空格內。

wish	brother	aunt	class	roof	card
job	box	park	shop	watch	idea

/s/	/z/	/ɪz/

② 選出圖中各種物品或身體部位所對應的名詞，並寫出它們的複數形。

shoe
hand
tree
path
shirt
plant
leg

1. ....
2. ....
3. ....
4. ....
5. ....
6. ....
7. ....

Unit ❷ 可數名詞（2）

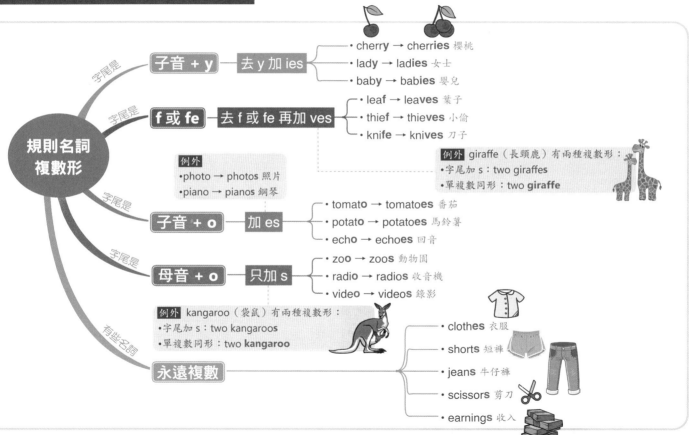

規則名詞複數形

字尾是 **子音 + y** → **去 y 加 ies**
- cherry → cherries 櫻桃
- lady → ladies 女士
- baby → babies 嬰兒

字尾是 **f 或 fe** → **去 f 或 fe 再加 ves**
- leaf → leaves 葉子
- thief → thieves 小偷
- knife → knives 刀子

例外
- photo → photos 照片
- piano → pianos 鋼琴

例外 giraffe（長頸鹿）有兩種複數形：
- 字尾加 s：two giraffes
- 單複數同形：two giraffe

字尾是 **子音 + o** → **加 es**
- tomato → tomatoes 番茄
- potato → potatoes 馬鈴薯
- echo → echoes 回音

字尾是 **母音 + o** → **只加 s**
- zoo → zoos 動物園
- radio → radios 收音機
- video → videos 錄影

例外 kangaroo（袋鼠）有兩種複數形：
- 字尾加 s：two kangaroos
- 單複數同形：two kangaroo

有些名詞 **永遠複數**
- clothes 衣服
- shorts 短褲
- jeans 牛仔褲
- scissors 剪刀
- earnings 收入

Practice

❶ 請將下列單數名詞改成「複數」形態。

1. kitty ....
2. cargo ....
3. calf ....
4. piano ....
5. strawberry ....

6. fly ....
7. wolf ....
8. hero ....
9. scarf ....
10. doggy ....

❷ 找出必須以複數形表現的物品，並寫出正確的名稱。
其他的請打 ✕。

1.

2.

3.

4.

5.

❸ 將錯誤的句子打 ✕，並寫出正確的句子。
若句子無誤，則在括弧內打 √。

1. I took some photos of the lake yesterday.

( ) ....
....

2. The scissors are in the drawer.

( ) ....
....

3. Be careful. Those knives are very sharp.

( ) ....
....

4. Leafs keep falling from the trees.

( ) ....
....

5. People say cats have nine lifes.

( ) ....
....

6. I can't find the cloth I wore yesterday.

( ) ....
....

7. I'd like to express my thank to every one of you.

( ) ....
....

8. You can find three librarys in this city.

( ) ....
....

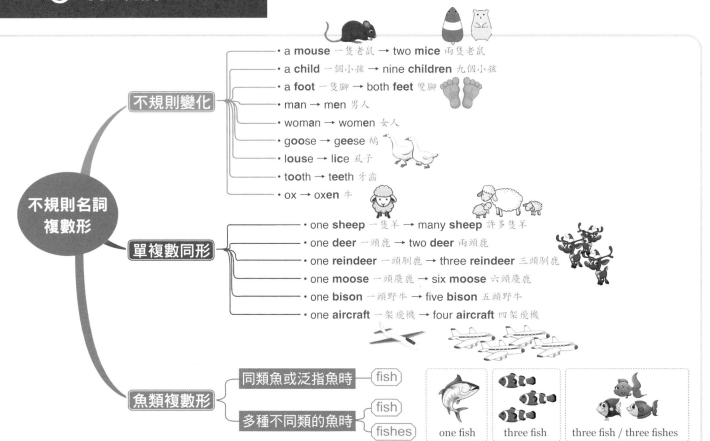

不規則名詞複數形

不規則變化
- a **mouse** 一隻老鼠 → two **mice** 兩隻老鼠
- a **child** 一個小孩 → nine **children** 九個小孩
- a **foot** 一隻腳 → both **feet** 雙腳
- man → men 男人
- woman → women 女人
- goose → geese 鵝
- louse → lice 蝨子
- tooth → teeth 牙齒
- ox → oxen 牛

單複數同形
- one **sheep** 一隻羊 → many **sheep** 許多隻羊
- one **deer** 一頭鹿 → two **deer** 兩頭鹿
- one **reindeer** 一頭馴鹿 → three **reindeer** 三頭馴鹿
- one **moose** 一頭麋鹿 → six **moose** 六頭麋鹿
- one **bison** 一頭野牛 → five **bison** 五頭野牛
- one **aircraft** 一架飛機 → four **aircraft** 四架飛機

魚類複數形
- 同類魚或泛指魚時 — fish
- 多種不同類的魚時 — fish / fishes

one fish　　three fish　　three fish / three fishes

Practice

❶ 寫出下列各種動物的複數名詞。

1

2

3

4

5

❷ 選出正確答案。

1. Bob used to count _____ to get to sleep.
   Ⓐ a sheep   Ⓑ sheeps   Ⓒ sheep

2. Who are those _____ standing in front of the gate?
   Ⓐ woman   Ⓑ women   Ⓒ womans

3. Mom told me to brush my _____ twice a day.
   Ⓐ tooth   Ⓑ tooths   Ⓒ teeth

4. Rhinos and pandas are two of the endangered _____.
   Ⓐ species   Ⓑ specieses   Ⓒ specy

5. Sometimes _____ are not afraid of cats.
   Ⓐ mouse   Ⓑ mouses   Ⓒ mice

6. Some _____ in that remote village do not have enough food to eat.
   Ⓐ children   Ⓑ child   Ⓒ childs

7. Jim likes to jog in bare _____.
   Ⓐ foot   Ⓑ feet   Ⓒ foots

8. The airline bought six _____ from France.
   Ⓐ aircraft   Ⓑ aircrafts   Ⓒ aircreft

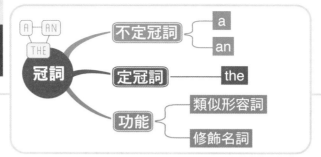

冠詞
- 不定冠詞
  - a
  - an
- 定冠詞 — the
- 功能
  - 類似形容詞
  - 修飾名詞

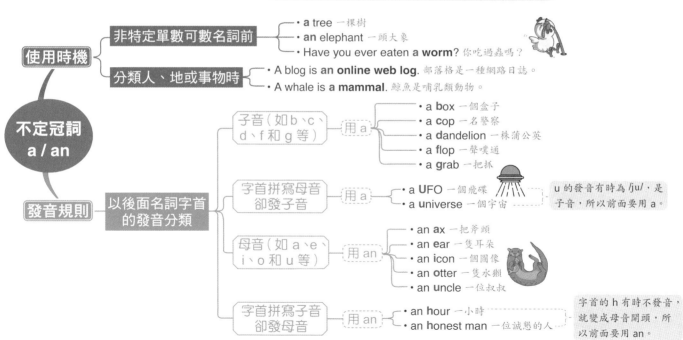

不定冠詞 a / an

使用時機

非特定單數可數名詞前
- **a** tree 一棵樹
- **an** elephant 一頭大象
- Have you ever eaten **a worm**? 你吃過蟲嗎?

分類人、地或事物時
- A blog is **an online web log**. 部落格是一種網路日誌。
- A whale is **a mammal**. 鯨魚是哺乳類動物。

發音規則 以後面名詞字首的發音分類

子音(如 b、c、d、f 和 g 等) 用 a
- a **b**ox 一個盒子
- a **c**op 一名警察
- a **d**andelion 一株蒲公英
- a **f**lop 一聲噗通
- a **g**rab 一把抓

字首拼寫母音卻發子音 用 a
- a **U**FO 一個飛碟
- a **u**niverse 一個宇宙

> u 的發音有時為 /ju/,是子音,所以前面要用 a。

母音(如 a、e、i、o 和 u 等) 用 an
- an **a**x 一把斧頭
- an **e**ar 一隻耳朵
- an **i**con 一個圖像
- an **o**tter 一隻水獺
- an **u**ncle 一位叔叔

字首拼寫子音卻發母音 用 an
- an **h**our 一小時
- an **h**onest man 一位誠懇的人

> 字首的 h 有時不發音,就變成母音開頭,所以前面要用 an。

Practice

❶ 用 a 或 an 寫出 Lydia 和 Trent 在超市裡購買的商品名稱。

light bulb

orange

newspaper

umbrella

candle

fish

ice cube tray

Lydia bought . . .

Trent bought . . .

❷ 自框內選出適當的詞彙，加上 a 或 an，完成下列句子。

1. I could walk home, but I would rather take ....
2. We don't have any wine. Do you want .... ?
3. I'm having an espresso. Would you like .... ?
4. Have you ever been to .... ?
5. She spent more than 5 years composing .... based on a novel about Africa.
6. Let's eat dinner at .... tonight.
7. In her dream she saw .... sitting on a branch of a tree.

art museum

glass of beer

owl

cup of coffee

opera

cab

restaurant

17

Unit 5 不定冠詞和定冠詞

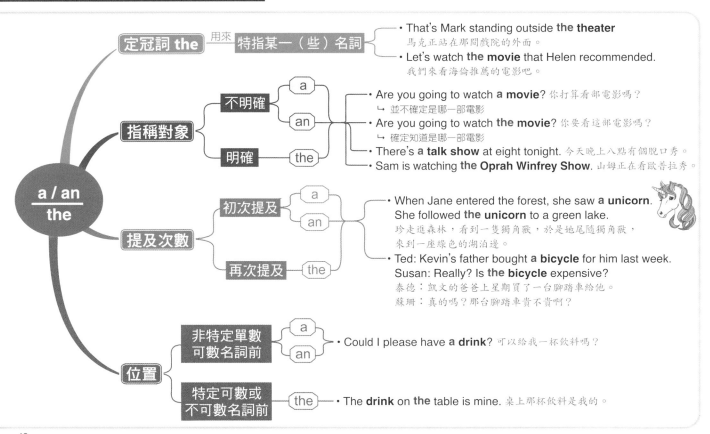

定冠詞 the ── 用來 ── 特指某一（些）名詞

- That's Mark standing outside **the theater**
  馬克正站在那間戲院的外面。
- Let's watch **the movie** that Helen recommended.
  我們來看海倫推薦的電影吧。

a / an
the

指稱對象
- 不明確 ─ a / an
- 明確 ─ the

- Are you going to watch **a movie**? 你打算看部電影嗎？
  ↳ 並不確定是哪一部電影
- Are you going to watch **the movie**? 你要看這部電影嗎？
  ↳ 確定知道是哪一部電影
- There's **a talk show** at eight tonight. 今天晚上八點有個脫口秀。
- Sam is watching **the Oprah Winfrey Show**. 山姆正在看歐普拉秀。

提及次數
- 初次提及 ─ a / an
- 再次提及 ─ the

- When Jane entered the forest, she saw **a unicorn**.
  She followed **the unicorn** to a green lake.
  珍走進森林，看到一隻獨角獸，於是她尾隨獨角獸，
  來到一座綠色的湖泊邊。
- Ted: Kevin's father bought **a bicycle** for him last week.
  Susan: Really? Is **the bicycle** expensive?
  泰德：凱文的爸爸上星期買了一台腳踏車給他。
  蘇珊：真的嗎？那台腳踏車貴不貴啊？

位置
- 非特定單數可數名詞前 ─ a / an
- 特定可數或不可數名詞前 ─ the

- Could I please have **a drink**? 可以給我一杯飲料嗎？
- The **drink** on **the** table is mine. 桌上那杯飲料是我的。

Practice

❶ 用 a、an 或 the 填空，完成對話。

1. **David:** Is there .... public library in town?

   Janet: Yes, there is one.

   David: Would you like to go to .... library tomorrow?

   Janet: OK.

2. **Joe:** Where is .... remote control?

   Kay: .... remote control is on .... table.

   Joe: Where are .... DVDs?

   Kay: .... DVDs are in .... carrying case.

3. **Nancy:** Did you see that woman?

   Phil: What woman?

   Nancy: .... woman who is looking at .... cellphone.

   Phil: Oh, yes.

4. **Amy:** Where is Mom?

   Tony: She's in .... kitchen.

   Amy: What is she doing in .... kitchen?

   Tony: She's making .... sandwich.

5. **Jim:** How do you like your new office building?

   Kelly: I like it. It has .... big conference room.

   Jim: Do you use .... conference room a lot?

   Kelly: Yes, I use it every day.

❷ 請選出正確的答案填入空格。

1. a channel   the channel

   ⓐ Please change ....

   ⓑ Please find .... with something good on it.

2. a movie   the movie

   ⓐ Do you want to watch .... on cable?

   ⓑ Do you want to watch .... we rented at the video store?

3. a sandwich   the sandwich

   ⓐ Do you want to eat .... ?

   ⓑ Are you going to eat .... I made for you?

4. a soda   the soda

   ⓐ Do you want .... with your sandwich?

   ⓑ Do you want .... you bought at the store?

19

Unit 6 不可數名詞

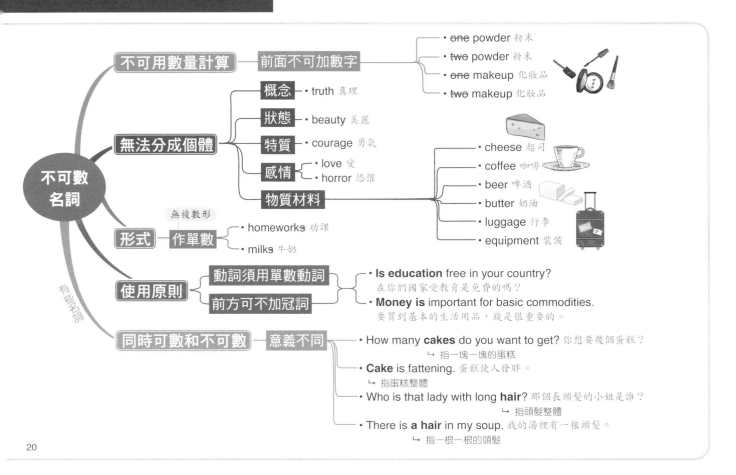

- ~~one~~ powder 粉末
- ~~two~~ powder 粉末
- ~~one~~ makeup 化妝品
- ~~two~~ makeup 化妝品

不可用數量計算 — 前面不可加數字

無法分成個體
- 概念 · truth 真理
- 狀態 · beauty 美麗
- 特質 · courage 勇氣
- 感情 · love 愛 · horror 恐懼
- 物質材料

- cheese 起司
- coffee 咖啡
- beer 啤酒
- butter 奶油
- luggage 行李
- equipment 裝備

不可數名詞

無複數形
形式 — 作單數
- homework~~s~~ 功課
- milk~~s~~ 牛奶

有些名詞

使用原則
- 動詞須用單數動詞
- 前方可不加冠詞

· **Is education** free in your country?
在你們國家受教育是免費的嗎?
· **Money is** important for basic commodities.
要買到基本的生活用品,錢是很重要的。

同時可數和不可數 — 意義不同

· How many **cakes** do you want to get? 你想要幾個蛋糕?
↳ 指一塊一塊的蛋糕
· **Cake** is fattening. 蛋糕使人發胖。
↳ 指蛋糕整體
· Who is that lady with long **hair**? 那個長頭髮的小姐是誰?
↳ 指頭髮整體
· There is **a hair** in my soup. 我的湯裡有一根頭髮。
↳ 指一根一根的頭髮

Practice

❶ 將下列單字歸類為可數或不可數名詞，並在可數名詞前正確的加上 a 或 an，不可數名詞則不用加。

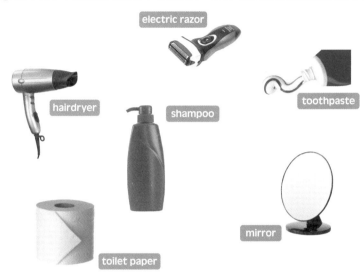

electric razor

hairdryer

shampoo

toothpaste

toilet paper

mirror

可數 | 不可數

❷ 在第一格填上正確的動詞（is 或 are），並在第二格填上正確的冠詞（a 或 an），若不需要冠詞請打 ✗。

1. There _____ _____ some water in the bottle.
2. There _____ _____ some cream rinse in the bathroom.
3. There _____ _____ jar of cold cream on the sink.
4. Those women _____ _____ buyers for the company.
5. That man _____ _____ sales representative.
6. That _____ _____ beautiful bottle.
7. That _____ _____ inexpensive makeup case.
8. There _____ _____ sale on eyeliners.

❸ 改正下列句子的錯誤，若句子無誤，則在後面寫上 OK。

1. How often do you cut your ~~hairs~~? __hair__
2. I am thinking of buying some jewelries. _____
3. Where do you buy your makeups? _____
4. How much skin cream do you use? _____
5. It takes a lot of courages for Tom to do this.

    _____
6. Beauty is only skin deep. _____

21

Unit **7** 計算不可數名詞

比較		
a **bottle** of glue	a **tube** of glue	a **stick** of glue

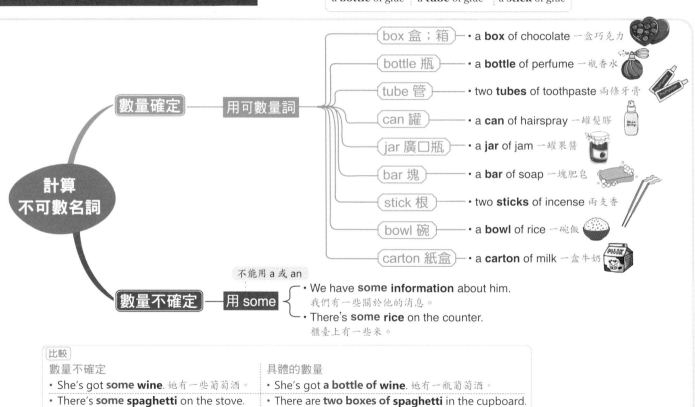

計算不可數名詞

數量確定 ── 用可數量詞

- box 盒;箱 ── · a **box** of chocolate 一盒巧克力
- bottle 瓶 ── · a **bottle** of perfume 一瓶香水
- tube 管 ── · two **tubes** of toothpaste 兩條牙膏
- can 罐 ── · a **can** of hairspray 一罐髮膠
- jar 廣口瓶 ── · a **jar** of jam 一罐果醬
- bar 塊 ── · a **bar** of soap 一塊肥皂
- stick 根 ── · two **sticks** of incense 兩支香
- bowl 碗 ── · a **bowl** of rice 一碗飯
- carton 紙盒 ── · a **carton** of milk 一盒牛奶

數量不確定 ── 用 some （不能用 a 或 an）

- We have **some information** about him.
  我們有一些關於他的消息。
- There's **some rice** on the counter.
  櫃臺上有一些米。

比較

數量不確定	具體的數量
· She's got **some wine**. 她有一些葡萄酒。	· She's got **a bottle of wine**. 她有一瓶葡萄酒。
· There's **some spaghetti** on the stove. 爐子上有一些義大利麵。	· There are **two boxes of spaghetti** in the cupboard. 櫃子裡有兩盒義大利麵。

Practice

① 請將物品正確的數量搭配表中量詞填入空格，不需要使用 **of** 片語的，請填入 **some**。注意量詞的單複數。

| bowl of | stick of | jar of | tube of |
| bar of | carton of | bottle of | some |

1. *two bottles of* wine
2. _____ chocolate
3. _____ jam
4. _____ ketchup
5. _____ spaghetti
6. _____ soup
7. _____ juice
8. _____ gum

② 改正下列句子的錯誤。

1. Where can I buy a chocolate?

2. How many luggages do you have?

3. It's too quiet. I need a music.

4. How many bowls of perfume did you get?

5. Can you buy me two breads?

6. My brother wants to buy a new furniture.

Unit 8 名詞的泛指

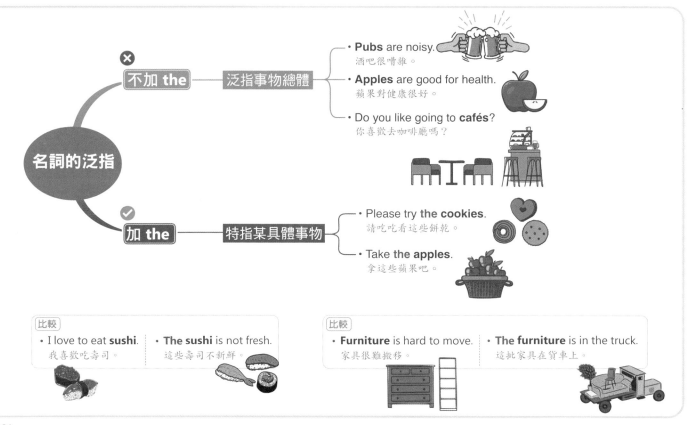

名詞的泛指

❌ 不加 the — 泛指事物總體
- **Pubs** are noisy.
  酒吧很嘈雜。
- **Apples** are good for health.
  蘋果對健康很好。
- Do you like going to **cafés**?
  你喜歡去咖啡廳嗎？

✅ 加 the — 特指某具體事物
- Please try **the cookies**.
  請吃吃看這些餅乾。
- Take **the apples**.
  拿這些蘋果吧。

比較
- I love to eat **sushi**.
  我喜歡吃壽司。
- **The sushi** is not fresh.
  這些壽司不新鮮。

比較
- **Furniture** is hard to move.
  家具很難搬移。
- **The furniture** is in the truck.
  這批家具在貨車上。

Practice

① 狗狗都喜歡些什麼？根據圖示，並利用框中提示，造句解釋狗狗喜歡什麼和不喜歡什麼。

| balls | showers | cats |
| water | dogs | vets |

Dogs like . . .

Dogs don't like . . .

1. ....
2. ....
3. ....
4. ....
5. ....
6. ....

② 選出正確的答案填入空格中。

1. Coffee   The coffee

   ⓐ .... keeps you awake at night.

   ⓑ .... is in the pot next to the cups.

2. money   the money

   ⓐ You need .... to live.

   ⓑ I gave .... to the landlord.

3. Rice   The rice

   ⓐ .... is the most important grain crop.

   ⓑ .... is cooked with butter and parsley.

4. attendance   the class attendance

   ⓐ The class has low ....

   ⓑ I entered .... into the computer.

25

Unit ❾ 專有名詞

- the *Taipei Times* 《台北時報》
- **R**oger **F**ederer 羅傑・費德勒

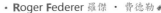
- **E**gypt 埃及
- **M**ount **R**ushmore 羅斯摩爾山

特定人、事物、地方、國家等 ── **首字母需大寫**①

專有名詞

大多不加 the

| 人名 | • ~~The~~ **Mike** is my uncle. 麥克是我叔叔。 |

| 星期 | • Tomorrow is ~~the~~ **Saturday**. 明天是星期六。 |

| 月分 | • My favorite month is ~~the~~ **September**. 九月是我最喜歡的月分。 |

| 語言、國籍 | • ~~The~~ **Russian** is a difficult language. 俄語是一種很困難的語言。 |

| 國家、州、地區 | • Did you like your trip to ~~the~~ **France**? 你喜歡那趟法國之行嗎？
• ~~The~~ Canada is in ~~the~~ **North America**. 加拿大在北美洲。 |

| 村、鎮、城市 | • ~~The~~ **Toronto** is the biggest city in Canada. 多倫多是加拿大最大的城市。 |

| 街道 | • I have a friend who lives on ~~the~~ **Washington Street**. 我有個朋友住在華盛頓街。 |

| 地點 | • I know a student at ~~the~~ **Seattle University**. 我認識一名西雅圖大學的學生。 |

| 湖泊 | • ~~The~~ **Lake Michigan** is located entirely within the United States. 密西根湖完全位於美國境內。 |

有時加 the

| 飯店、餐廳、酒吧 | • **The Ritz Carlton** is a famous hotel. 麗池卡爾登度假酒店是間知名的飯店。 |

| 電影院 | • *Joker* is showing at the **New Art Cinema**. 《小丑》正在新藝術電影院上映。 |

| 劇院 | • How do I get to the **Goodman Theater**? 我要如何到古德曼劇院？ |

| 海、洋 | • Is the **Mediterranean** a sea or an ocean? 地中海是海還是洋？ |

| 河流 | • The longest river in South America is the **Amazon**. 亞馬遜河是南美洲最長的河。 |

| 名稱含有「...of...」 | • I studied at the **University of Michigan**. 我在密西根大學念書。
• I went on vacation to the **Bay of Fundy**. 我到芬地灣度假。 |

Practice

❶ 請在必要的地方，填上 the；若不必要，則劃上「✕」。

1. ＿＿＿＿ University of Paris
2. ＿＿＿＿ Joseph
3. ＿＿＿＿ Tuesday
4. ＿＿＿＿ January
5. ＿＿＿＿ Four Seasons Hotel
6. ＿＿＿＿ Spain
7. ＿＿＿＿ Europe

8. ＿＿＿＿ Whitewater Pub
9. ＿＿＿＿ German
10. ＿＿＿＿ Budapest Café
11. ＿＿＿＿ Osaka
12. ＿＿＿＿ Santa Barbara
13. ＿＿＿＿ East River
14. ＿＿＿＿ Indian Ocean

15. ＿＿＿＿ Los Angeles County Museum of Art
16. ＿＿＿＿ Lake Michigan
17. ＿＿＿＿ Century Cinema
18. ＿＿＿＿ Michigan Avenue
19. ＿＿＿＿ Ireland

❷ 將下列句子改寫為正確的句子。

1. "What are you reading?" "I'm reading *china post*."

   → ＿＿＿＿＿＿＿＿＿＿＿＿＿＿＿＿＿＿＿＿＿＿

   ＿＿＿＿＿＿＿＿＿＿＿＿＿＿＿＿＿＿＿＿＿＿

2. Is mary going to japan with you?

   → ＿＿＿＿＿＿＿＿＿＿＿＿＿＿＿＿＿＿＿＿＿＿

3. jane has a project due in the october.

   → ＿＿＿＿＿＿＿＿＿＿＿＿＿＿＿＿＿＿＿＿＿＿

4. Why don't we see the latest movie in miramar cinema?

   → ＿＿＿＿＿＿＿＿＿＿＿＿＿＿＿＿＿＿＿＿＿＿

   ＿＿＿＿＿＿＿＿＿＿＿＿＿＿＿＿＿＿＿＿＿＿

5. Is the yellow river the longest river in china?

   → ＿＿＿＿＿＿＿＿＿＿＿＿＿＿＿＿＿＿＿＿＿＿

6. Excuse me, how do I get to the maple street?

   → ＿＿＿＿＿＿＿＿＿＿＿＿＿＿＿＿＿＿＿＿＿＿

Unit ❿ 加不加 the（1）

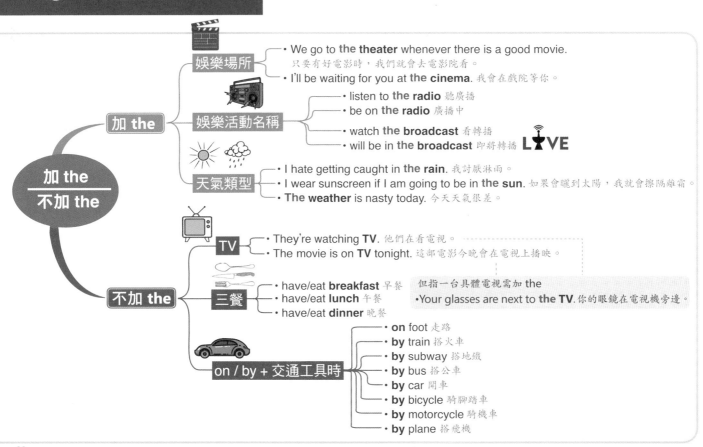

加 the / 不加 the

加 the

娛樂場所
- We go to **the theater** whenever there is a good movie.
  只要有好電影時，我們就會去電影院看。
- I'll be waiting for you at **the cinema**. 我會在戲院等你。

娛樂活動名稱
- listen to **the radio** 聽廣播
- be on **the radio** 廣播中
- watch **the broadcast** 看轉播
- will be in **the broadcast** 即將轉播 L**I**VE

天氣類型
- I hate getting caught in **the rain**. 我討厭淋雨。
- I wear sunscreen if I am going to be in **the sun**. 如果會曬到太陽，我就會擦隔離霜。
- **The weather** is nasty today. 今天天氣很差。

不加 the

TV
- They're watching **TV**. 他們在看電視。
- The movie is on **TV** tonight. 這部電影今晚會在電視上播映。

> 但指一台具體電視需加 the
> - Your glasses are next to **the TV**. 你的眼鏡在電視機旁邊。

三餐
- have/eat **breakfast** 早餐
- have/eat **lunch** 午餐
- have/eat **dinner** 晚餐

on / by + 交通工具時
- **on** foot 走路
- **by** train 搭火車
- **by** subway 搭地鐵
- **by** bus 搭公車
- **by** car 開車
- **by** bicycle 騎腳踏車
- **by** motorcycle 騎機車
- **by** plane 搭飛機

Practice

❶ 依據圖示，自框內選出適當的詞彙，完成下列句子，並視需要加上 **the**。

breakfast
plane
radio
rain
theater
foot

1. What's that music you're listening to on
   ....?

2. On their first date, Tom and Patti went to
   ....

3. It'll take longer if we go on ....

4. Every morning we have cereal and milk
   for ....

5. The laundry got all wet because of ....

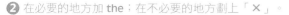

6. We could take a train, but going by
   .... is faster.

❷ 在必要的地方加 **the**；在不必要的地方劃上「✕」。

1. This morning I got caught by .... rain.
2. When was the last time you went to .... cinema?
3. I'm so busy that I don't have time to eat .... lunch.
4. While I was driving, I heard a beautiful song on .... radio.
5. We could go on .... foot, but going by .... cab will be faster.
6. There is a fashion show on .... TV tonight.

Unit ⑪ 加不加 the（2）

①
- go to court 上法庭
- be at court 在庭上
- be in court 在庭上

- go to jail 進監獄
- be in jail 進監獄
- go to prison 進監獄
- be in prison 進監獄

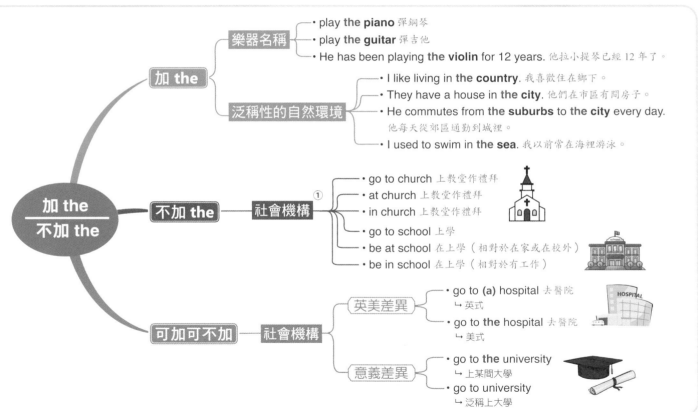

加 the / 不加 the

加 the

樂器名稱
- play **the piano** 彈鋼琴
- play **the guitar** 彈吉他
- He has been playing **the violin** for 12 years. 他拉小提琴已經 12 年了。

泛稱性的自然環境
- I like living in **the country**. 我喜歡住在鄉下。
- They have a house in **the city**. 他們在市區有間房子。
- He commutes from **the suburbs** to **the city** every day. 他每天從郊區通勤到城裡。
- I used to swim in **the sea**. 我以前常在海裡游泳。

不加 the

社會機構 ①
- go to church 上教堂作禮拜
- at church 上教堂作禮拜
- in church 上教堂作禮拜
- go to school 上學
- be at school 在上學（相對於在家或在校外）
- be in school 在上學（相對於有工作）

可加可不加

社會機構

英美差異
- go to **(a)** hospital 去醫院　↳ 英式
- go to **the** hospital 去醫院　↳ 美式

意義差異
- go to **the** university　↳ 上某間大學
- go to university　↳ 泛稱上大學

Practice

❶ 依據圖示，自框內選出適當的詞彙，完成下列句子，並視需要加上 the。

city
school
flute
prison
hospital
sea

1. Do you prefer to swim in a pool or in
....?

2. She wants to learn to play ....

3. I grew up in the suburbs, but I always wanted
to live in ....

4. What time do you go to .... in
the morning?

5. The criminal was convicted and will go to
....

6. Grandma is sick and has been in
.... for a week.

❷ 在必要的地方加 the；在不必要的地方劃上「✕」。

1. I love the beach, but I don't like lying in .... sun.

2. They go to .... church once a year on Christmas Eve.

3. He can play .... guitar, ... bass, and .... piano.

4. He is studying electronics in .... college.

5. First he was in .... jail and now he is in .... prison.

6. Are you going to show your guest around .... town?

7. Terri and Craig love riding bicycles in .... countryside.

8. They are going to .... court for a murder case.

Unit 12 其他不加 the 的情況

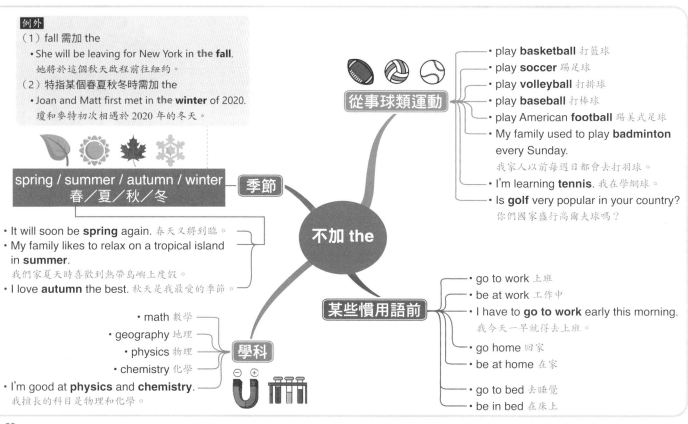

例外

（1）fall 需加 the
- She will be leaving for New York in **the fall**.
她將於這個秋天啟程前往紐約。

（2）特指某個春夏秋冬時需加 the
- Joan and Matt first met in **the winter** of 2020.
瓊和麥特初次相遇於 2020 年的冬天。

spring / summer / autumn / winter
春／夏／秋／冬　　【季節】

- It will soon be **spring** again. 春天又將到臨。
- My family likes to relax on a tropical island in **summer**.
我們家夏天時喜歡到熱帶島嶼上度假。
- I love **autumn** the best. 秋天是我最愛的季節。

- math 數學
- geography 地理
- physics 物理
- chemistry 化學
【學科】

- I'm good at **physics** and **chemistry**.
我擅長的科目是物理和化學。

【從事球類運動】
- play **basketball** 打籃球
- play **soccer** 踢足球
- play **volleyball** 打排球
- play **baseball** 打棒球
- play American **football** 踢美式足球
- My family used to play **badminton** every Sunday.
我家人以前每週日都會去打羽球。
- I'm learning **tennis**. 我在學網球。
- Is **golf** very popular in your country?
你們國家盛行高爾夫球嗎？

不加 the

【某些慣用語前】
- go to work 上班
- be at work 工作中
- I have to **go to work** early this morning.
我今天一早就得去上班。
- go home 回家
- be at home 在家
- go to bed 去睡覺
- be in bed 在床上

Practice

❶ 依據圖示，自框內選出適當的詞彙，完成下列句子，並視需要加上 the。

bed
ping-pong
home
work
winter

1. Call his office because he said he is going to be at _____ all day.

2. Hey, why not play _____ with me this afternoon?

3. Birds will fly south before _____ comes.

4. You are up past your bedtime, and it's time to go to _____.

5. He decided to cancel his date and just stay at _____ and read.

❷ 在必要的地方加 the；在不必要的地方劃上「×」。

1. If I'm tired, I go to _____ bed and sleep 12 hours straight.

2. She will be going to _____ college in _____ fall.

3. I love _____ autumn better than _____ summer.

4. Billy had surgery this morning, and he has to stay in _____ bed for the next two days.

5. Is _____ soccer popular among the students in your class?

6. Are you good at _____ English grammar?

❸ 依據事實，回答下列問題。

1. What's your favorite sport?
   → _____

2. What's your favorite subject?
   → _____

3. What's your favorite season?
   → _____

4. What subject do you dislike the most?
   → _____

5. What season do you dislike the most?
   → _____

33

① • "Whose coffee is this?" "It's **Jim's**." 「這是誰的咖啡？」「吉姆的。」
    ↳ Jim's coffee
• "Whose cake is this?" "It's **Jan's**." 「這是誰的蛋糕？」「是珍的。」
    ↳ Jan's cake

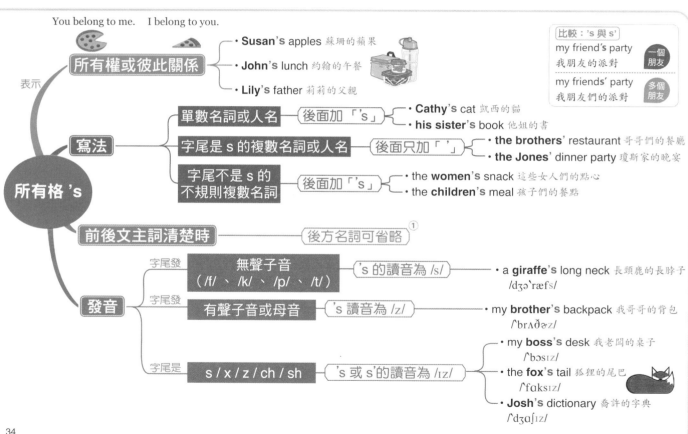

You belong to me.　I belong to you.

所有格 's

表示

所有權或彼此關係
• **Susan's** apples 蘇珊的蘋果
• **John's** lunch 約翰的午餐
• **Lily's** father 莉莉的父親

比較：'s 與 s'
my friend**'s** party 一個朋友
我朋友的派對
my friends**'** party 多個朋友
我朋友們的派對

寫法
單數名詞或人名 —— 後面加「's」
• **Cathy's** cat 凱西的貓
• **his sister's** book 他姐的書

字尾是 s 的複數名詞或人名 —— 後面只加「'」
• **the brothers'** restaurant 哥哥們的餐廳
• **the Jones'** dinner party 瓊斯家的晚宴

字尾不是 s 的不規則複數名詞 —— 後面加「's」
• the **women's** snack 這些女人們的點心
• the **children's** meal 孩子們的餐點

前後文主詞清楚時 —— 後方名詞可省略 ①

發音
字尾發　無聲子音（/f/、/k/、/p/、/t/）—— 's 的讀音為 /s/
• a **giraffe's** long neck 長頸鹿的長脖子 /dʒəˋræfs/

字尾發　有聲子音或母音 —— 's 讀音為 /z/
• my **brother's** backpack 我哥哥的背包 /ˋbrʌðəz/

字尾是　s / x / z / ch / sh —— 's 或 s'的讀音為 /ɪz/
• my **boss's** desk 我老闆的桌子 /ˋbɔsɪz/
• the **fox's** tail 狐狸的尾巴 /ˋfɑksɪz/
• **Josh's** dictionary 喬許的字典 /ˋdʒɑʃɪz/

Practice

❶ 下列物品可能會是誰的？請依圖示，分別用完整句子和簡答來回答問題。

 Jody
 my father
 Momo
 the wizard / Vince Carter

1
Whose key is it?
It is _Jody's key_ .
It is _Jody's_ .

2
Whose collar is it?
It is _____ .
It is _____ .

4
Whose magic wand is it?
It is _____ .
It is _____ .

3
Whose briefcase is it?
It is _____ .
It is _____ .

5
Whose basketball is it?
It is _____ .
It is _____ .

❷ 將框內的名詞改為所有格，並依字尾「 's 」的發音填入正確的空格內。

Michael	teacher
lion	brush
Alice	ant
mouse	kid
ape	Frank
ox	Jeff

① /s/
_____
_____
_____
_____

② /z/
Michael's
_____
_____
_____

③ /ɪz/
_____
_____
_____
_____

Unit ⑭ 所有格（2）

所有格 the . . . of . . .

通常作為 → **無生物所有格**
- **the** window **of** the room 房間的窗戶
- **the** end **of** the road 路的盡頭
- **the** cover **of** the magazine 雜誌的封面

有時也可作為 → **有生物所有格**
- **the** smile **of** the dog = the dog's smile 狗狗的笑容
- **the** leaves **of** the tree = the tree's leaves 這棵樹的葉子
- **the** son **of** Tim = Tim's son 提姆的兒子

但有生物所有格以「's」或「'」較常見、自然

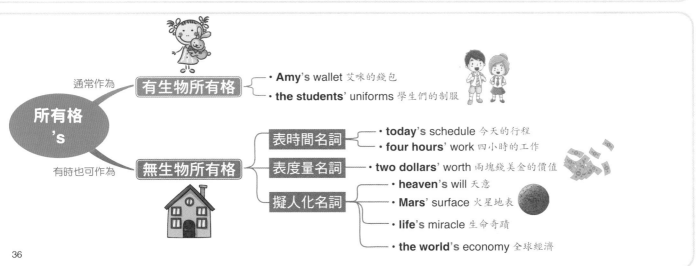

所有格 's

通常作為 → **有生物所有格**
- **Amy**'s wallet 艾咪的錢包
- **the students**' uniforms 學生們的制服

有時也可作為 → **無生物所有格**

表時間名詞
- **today**'s schedule 今天的行程
- **four hours**' work 四小時的工作

表度量名詞
- **two dollars**' worth 兩塊錢美金的價值

擬人化名詞
- **heaven**'s will 天意
- **Mars**' surface 火星地表
- **life**'s miracle 生命奇蹟
- **the world**'s economy 全球經濟

Practice

❶ 將下列「of ...」的用法改寫為「's」或「'」的所有格。

the pen of the teacher
1. *the teacher's pen*

the pillow of my mother
5.

the iPhone of Jennifer
2.

the telephone of the manager
6.

the umbrella of Grandpa
3.

the PlayStation of my brothers'
7.

the lunch of Jane
4.

the purse of Liz
8.

❷ 自紅框和藍框中各選出相關的詞彙，並用「the ... of ...」
描述它們之間的附屬關係。

1. _the light of the sun_

2. _____

3. _____

4. _____

5. _____

the sun
trash
the computer
the president
Beethoven

pile
light
ninth
symphony
keyboard
speech

Unit 1, 6
重點複習

1 下列物品名稱，哪些是可數名詞？哪些是不可數名詞？
請在可數名詞的空格內寫上 C（countable），不可數名詞的空格內寫上 U（uncountable）。

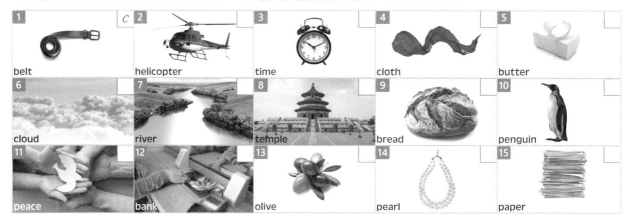

1 belt C	2 helicopter	3 time
4 cloth	5 butter	
6 cloud	7 river	8 temple
9 bread	10 penguin	
11 peace	12 bank	13 olive
14 pearl	15 paper	

Unit 1–3
重點複習

2 依據題意，自圖片中選出正確的單字，並改成複數名詞來填空。

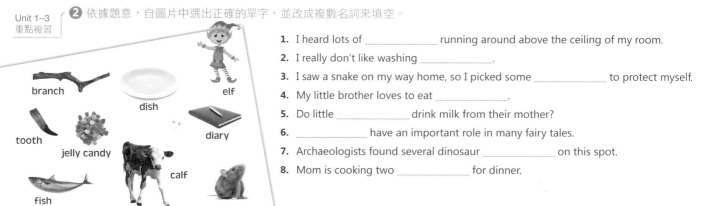

branch
dish
elf
tooth
jelly candy
diary
calf
fish
rat

1. I heard lots of .... running around above the ceiling of my room.
2. I really don't like washing ....
3. I saw a snake on my way home, so I picked some .... to protect myself.
4. My little brother loves to eat ....
5. Do little .... drink milk from their mother?
6. .... have an important role in many fairy tales.
7. Archaeologists found several dinosaur .... on this spot.
8. Mom is cooking two .... for dinner.

❸ 運用提示字填空，並根據內文做正確的單複數形變化，或加上 a、an、the。

carrot

1. Give the rabbit _____.
2. I left _____

   on the grass for the rabbit.
3. _____ are a healthy food.

banana

9. Would you like _____?
10. Who gets _____?

lion statue

4. They have a statue of _____.
5. The statue of _____

   is very old.
6. _____ are a symbol of power.

video

11. Did you buy _____

    at the video store?
12. Denzel Washington is in _____.

sugar

7. I like _____ in my tea.
8. Where is _____?

music

13. _____ distracts me when I am

    studying.
14. What is _____ you are playing?

❹ 選出符合題意的詞彙，以正確的形式（加上 a、an、the，或改為複數名詞，或完全不需要冠詞等）來填空完成句子，同一詞彙可能用於不同空格。

Johnny lives in ❶＿＿＿＿＿＿＿＿＿＿. He commutes from his place to work by ❷＿＿＿＿＿every day. He loves playing ❸＿＿＿＿＿＿＿＿. Tonight there is going to be a football game on ❹＿＿＿＿＿. So he plans to go ❺＿＿＿＿＿ early. He will also buy two cheeseburgers and some French fries for ❻＿＿＿＿＿＿＿. He will not go to ❼＿＿＿＿＿ until the game is over.

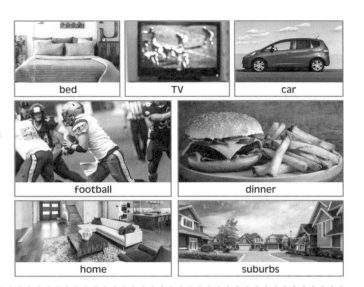

bed   TV   car

football   dinner

home   suburbs

scientist

Amazon River

tourist

Egyptian

Brazil

Nile River

Muhammad is ❽＿＿＿＿＿＿＿＿. He told me that ❾＿＿＿＿＿＿＿＿＿＿＿＿, the longest river in the world, plays an important role in the life of all ❿＿＿＿＿＿＿＿. However, some geographers from ⓫＿＿＿＿＿ and Peru are claiming that ⓬＿＿＿＿＿＿ is the longest river in the world by now. They are claiming that they've found new sources of the river, and the length of the river makes it the longest one. Debates between ⓭＿＿＿＿＿ go on. No matter which river is the longest one on earth, they are popular sites for ⓮＿＿＿＿＿ from all over the world.

Unit 4, 5, 8 重點複習

❺ 圈選正確的答案。完成句子。

1. Do you have camera a camera an camera some camera ?

2. We are having potatoes a potatoes an potatoes
some potato for dinner.

3. She has long hair a hair an hair hairs.

4. Please help me carry a boxes a box an box some box.

5. We already have a loaves a loaf an loaf some loafs
of bread.

6. There is lots of snow a snow an snow snows in the
mountains.

7. Where is are your watch?

8. How many people is are coming?

9. Is Are this rice expensive?

Unit 13–14 重點複習

❻ 根據題目所提供的內容，以「 's 」和「the . . . of . . .」這兩種形式來表達所有格；若該題目不適合以某一形式表達，則劃上「✕」。

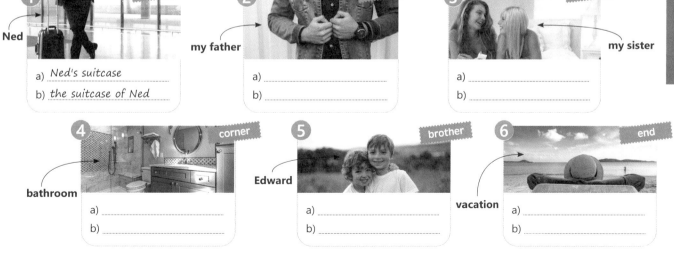

1 suitcase

Ned

a) *Ned's suitcase*

b) *the suitcase of Ned*

2 jacket

my father

a) ....

b) ....

3 room

my sister

a) ....

b) ....

4 corner

bathroom

a) ....

b) ....

5 brother

Edward

a) ....

b) ....

6 end

vacation

a) ....

b) ....

❼ 將下列圖中的各項物品名稱，依據其適合的量詞，填入正確的空格內。

 sardine	 soy sauce	 cherries	 alcohol	 baggage	 shaving cream
 cheese	 watercolor	 potato chips	 jewelry	 pickles	 cleansing foam
 tea	lotion	 peanut butter	 soda	 coffee	 salad
 boiling water	 facial cream	 ketchup	 soup	 cookies	 ointment

1 a bottle of

2 a can of

3 a bowl of

4 a piece of

5 a tube of

6 a jar of

7 a pot of

8 a packet of

❽ 下列名詞類別是否需要加「the」？在需要 the 的類別上將「With the」打勾；在不需要 the 的類別上將「With the」打叉，並各舉兩個例子。

1. place names

☑ With the

the Shed Aquarium

the Field Museum

2. hotels, restaurants, and pubs

☐ With the

3. days of the week

☐ With the

4. theaters

☐ With the

5. seas, oceans

☐ With the

6. countries and continents

☐ With the

7. cinemas

☐ With the

8. street names

☐ With the

9. months of the year

☐ With the

10. languages and nationalities

☐ With the

11. rivers

☐ With the

12. villages, towns, cities, and regions

☐ With the

Unit 16 人稱代名詞（1）

①
- Tim is English. **He**'s from London. 提姆是英國人，他是從倫敦來的。
  ↳ 人稱代名詞，代替 Tim。
- The cell phone on the desk is **mine**. 桌上的手機是我的。
  ↳ 人稱代名詞，等於 my cell phone。

人稱代名詞 → 代指人或事物 ①
人稱代名詞 → 分為三類

主詞代名詞		受詞代名詞		所有格代名詞	
I	我	me	我	mine	我的
we	我們	us	我們	ours	我們的
you	你	you	你	yours	你的
you	你們	you	你們	yours	你們的
he	他	him	他	his	他的
she	她	her	她	hers	她的
it	他；它	it	他；它		
they	他們	them	他們	theirs	他們的

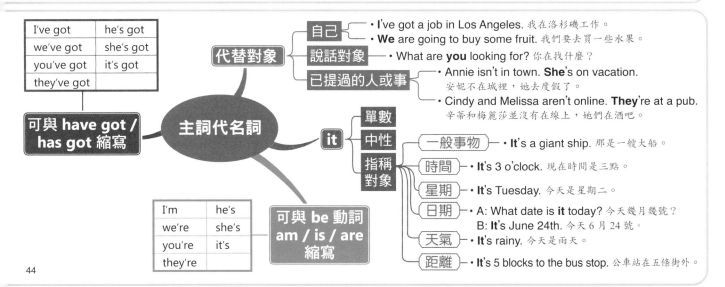

I've got	he's got
we've got	she's got
you've got	it's got
they've got	

可與 have got / has got 縮寫

主詞代名詞

代替對象
- 自己
  - **I**'ve got a job in Los Angeles. 我在洛杉磯工作。
  - **We** are going to buy some fruit. 我們要去買一些水果。
- 說話對象
  - What are **you** looking for? 你在找什麼？
- 已提過的人或事
  - Annie isn't in town. **She**'s on vacation. 安妮不在城裡，她去度假了。
  - Cindy and Melissa aren't online. **They**'re at a pub. 辛蒂和梅麗莎並沒有在線上，她們在酒吧。

it
- 單數
- 中性
- 指稱對象
  - 一般事物 · **It**'s a giant ship. 那是一艘大船。
  - 時間 · **It**'s 3 o'clock. 現在時間是三點。
  - 星期 · **It**'s Tuesday. 今天是星期二。
  - 日期 · A: What date is **it** today? 今天幾月幾號？ B: **It**'s June 24th. 今天 6 月 24 號。
  - 天氣 · **It**'s rainy. 今天是雨天。
  - 距離 · **It**'s 5 blocks to the bus stop. 公車站在五條街外。

I'm	he's
we're	she's
you're	it's
they're	

可與 be 動詞 am / is / are 縮寫

Practice

1 請依圖示，在空格處填上 I、you、he、she、it、we 或 they，完成句子。

1. _____'m on the phone.

2. _____'re taller than me.

3. _____'s got cool hair.

4. _____'s raining hard.

5. _____'m going surfing.

6. _____'re going to jump.

7. _____'s running.

8. _____'s got a new car.

2 請依圖示，在空格處填上 I、you、he、she、it、we 或 they，完成句子。

1. These are my parents. _____'re both in excellent health.
2. My dad is retired. _____'s 75 years old.
3. My mom helps take care of our kids. _____'s a big help.
4. My son is Sam. _____'s a very good student.
5. My daughter is Mary. _____'s learning to play the violin.
6. My dog is Fred. _____'s cute.
7. We just bought a summer house. _____'s in Hawaii.
8. That's us. _____'re a happy family.

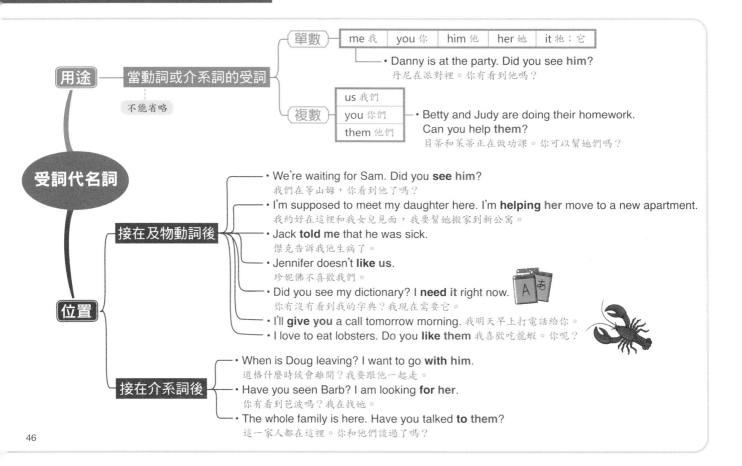

受詞代名詞

用途 ── 當動詞或介系詞的受詞

不能省略

單數：me 我 ｜ you 你 ｜ him 他 ｜ her 她 ｜ it 牠；它

• Danny is at the party. Did you see **him**?
丹尼在派對裡。你有看到他嗎？

複數：us 我們 ｜ you 你們 ｜ them 他們

• Betty and Judy are doing their homework.
Can you help **them**?
貝蒂和茱蒂正在做功課。你可以幫她們嗎？

位置

接在及物動詞後

• We're waiting for Sam. Did you **see him**?
我們在等山姆，你看到他了嗎？
• I'm supposed to meet my daughter here. I'm **helping her** move to a new apartment.
我約好在這裡和我女兒見面，我要幫她搬家到新公寓。
• Jack **told me** that he was sick.
傑克告訴我他生病了。
• Jennifer doesn't **like us**.
珍妮佛不喜歡我們。
• Did you see my dictionary? I **need it** right now.
你有沒有看到我的字典？我現在需要它。
• I'll **give you** a call tomorrow morning. 我明天早上打電話給你。
• I love to eat lobsters. Do you **like them** 我喜歡吃龍蝦。你呢？

接在介系詞後

• When is Doug leaving? I want to go **with him**.
道格什麼時候會離開？我要跟他一起走。
• Have you seen Barb? I am looking **for her**.
你有看到芭波嗎？我在找她。
• The whole family is here. Have you talked **to them**?
這一家人都在這裡。你和他們談過了嗎？

Practice

1 請依據事實，用右邊框內的句型來回答問題。

| I like him/her/them/it. | I don't like him/her/them/it. |

1. How do you like Cristiano Ronaldo?
   I like him.

2. How do you like hiking?
   _____

3. How do you like ice cream?
   _____

4. How do you like washing clothes?
   _____

5. How do you like flowers?
   _____

6. How do you like Ariana Grande?
   _____

2 在空格處填上 me、you、him、her、it、us 或 them 來完成這篇日記。

Dear Diary:

I went to a café with my best friend tonight. Becky brought her camera and got a cute guy to take our picture. That's ❶_____ in the picture. The guy seemed to like ❷_____. After he sat down at the table with his friends, I spent a lot of time watching ❸_____. He looked back at ❹_____. Becky waved at ❺_____ and he smiled back at ❻_____. I told Becky that we should go sit with ❼_____. She liked the idea, but said we should not do ❽_____. Becky said we should make ❾_____ come and sit with ❿_____. The guy left before we could decide how to get ⓫_____ to come over. I felt like it was over for ⓬_____ and wanted to go home. So we left. I liked the café and wanted to go back again.

Unit **18** 人稱代名詞（3）

①
- Where's my newspaper? Is this **mine**? 我的報紙呢？這是我的嗎？
  ↳ 代替已經出現過的 my newspaper
- I found my coat. Where is **yours**? 我找到我的外套了，你的呢？
  ↳ = your coat，避免重覆 coat。
- These are our tickets. Did you bring **yours**? 這是我們的票，你們的有帶來嗎？

所有格形容詞

表示 → 物品所有權

單數		複數	
my	我的	our	我們的
your	你的	your	你們的
his	他的	their	他們的
her	她的		
its	牠的；它的		

- Where is **his** car?
  他的車子在哪裡？
- These are **our** roller blades.
  這是我們的直排輪溜冰鞋。

放在 → 其他名詞前
- Brenda and **her twin sister** are playing.
  布蘭妲和她的雙胞胎姊妹正在玩耍。
- This is **my lovely dog**. **Its name** is Michael.
  這是我的寶貝狗狗，牠的名字叫麥可。

所有格代名詞

表示 → 某人所屬的人／物

單數		複數	
mine	我的	ours	我們的
yours	你的	yours	你們的
his	他的	theirs	他們的
hers	她的		

- Rita: This is **my coffee**. 這是我的咖啡。
  Andy: Where is **mine**? 那我的呢？
- George and Annie have been served **their food**, but we are still waiting for **ours**.
  喬治和安妮已拿到餐點，但我們的還沒。

用來 → 代替出現過的名詞 — 等於 → 所有格形容詞 + 名詞 ①

可視為 → 完整名詞片語 — 單獨存在
- A: Are these **ours**? 這些是我們的嗎？
  B: Yes, these are **yours**. 是的，這些是你們的。

Practice

1 一對兄妹的媽媽正在做簡短的家庭介紹。請在空格處填上 **my**、**your**、**his**、**her**、**our** 或 **their**，幫她完成這段簡介。

1. _____My_____ name is Jane. My husband is Jerry.

2. These are _____ two kids, Jimmy and Sara.

3. Jimmy is eight years old. Those are _____ trains and cars.

4. Sara is six years old. Those are _____ dolls and stuffed animals.

5. They don't play with _____ blocks anymore.

6. Jimmy and Sara don't like cleaning up _____ room.

7. _____ house is usually a mess, but today it is clean.

8. I made Jimmy pick up _____ side and Sara cleaned up _____ side of _____ room.

2 請依圖示，在空格處填上所有格代名詞或所有格形容詞，完成句子。

Dad: Amy, it's not _____ doll. It's Nancy's doll.
Amy: I'm sorry. I didn't know it's _____ (=her doll). I'll give it back to her.

Joe: Have you seen _____ dog? I can't find it anywhere. It's a black Labrador.
May: No, I haven't seen _____ dog.

Jessica: Is this _____ watch?
Nick: Yes, that's _____ (= my watch).

The dog is chewing _____ bone.

Mr. Anderson, that's not your office.
_____ (= your office) is down there.

49

Unit 19 不定代名詞與不定形容詞（1）

不定代名詞

指未知的人或事物

some	一些
any	任何
few	一些
one	一個
many	許多
much	許多
something	某物
everywhere	到處
nobody	沒有人

某些也可當形容詞

some / any

可當

形容詞 — 修飾不確定數量的名詞

- There are **some** squirrels in the tree. 樹上有一些松鼠。
- There aren't **any** squirrels in the tree. 樹上沒有任何松鼠。

用法 — 後接

複數名詞
- **some** apples 一些蘋果
- **any** carrots 任何胡蘿蔔

不可數名詞
- **some** beer 一些啤酒
- **any** wine 任何酒

適用句型

some
- 肯定句 — We have **some** rice. 我們有一點白飯。
- 疑問句 — Could I have **some** rice, please? 可以盛點飯給我嗎？
- Would you like **some** rice? 你要不要吃點飯？

用於表示禮貌性詢問，希望得到肯定回答時。

any
- 否定句 — We don't have **any** soft drinks. 我們沒有飲料。
- 疑問句 — Are there **any** potato chips in the cabinet? 櫃子裡有洋芋片嗎？

後接名詞可省略 — 作代名詞

用於已知所指名詞為何時

- Linda: He is selling lottery tickets. Would you like **some** (lottery tickets)?
  他正在賣樂透彩，你要買一些嗎？
  Bob: No, I don't want **any** (lottery tickets).
  不，我不想買。

no 可替代 not any

no 的語氣較 not any 強烈
- There isn't **any** room in the car.
  = There is **no** room in the car. 車上沒位子了。
- There isn't **any** time.= There is **no** time. 我們沒時間了。

no 常放在句首來加強語氣
- **No** one likes his new hairstyle. 沒人喜歡他的新髮型。

Practice

❶ 冰箱裡有什麼、沒有什麼？依據圖示，自框內選出適當的句型造句。

> There's some . . .   There're some . . .
>
> There isn't any . . .   There aren't any . . .

eggs

1. There aren't any eggs.

leeks

2. ....

ice

3. ....

kiwi juice

4. ....

lemon

5. ....

wine

6. ....

❷ 利用括號內的字，改寫下列的否定句。

1. There isn't any space. (no) → There's no space.

2. We've got no newspapers. (any) → ....

3. She hasn't got any money. (no) → ....

4. There are no boxes. (any) → ....

5. I've got no blank disks. (any) → ....

6. He has no bonus points. (any) → ....

❸ 用 some、any 或 no 填空，完成句子。

Would you like .... cookies?

There isn't .... tea.

Can I have .... nuts, please?

Hurry up! I've got .... time.

We need .... rock and roll.

Have you got .... chocolate chip ice cream?

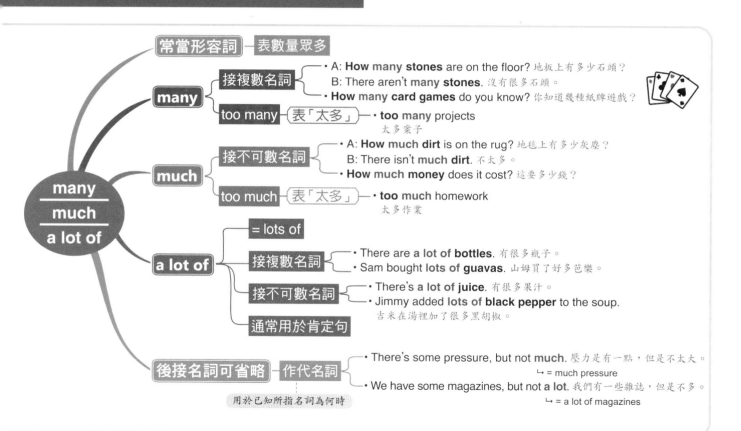

常當形容詞 — 表數量眾多

many

接複數名詞
- A: **How many stones** are on the floor? 地板上有多少石頭？
  B: There aren't **many stones**. 沒有很多石頭。
- **How many card games** do you know? 你知道幾種紙牌遊戲？

too many — 表「太多」
- **too many** projects
  太多案子

much

接不可數名詞
- A: **How much dirt** is on the rug? 地毯上有多少灰塵？
  B: There isn't **much dirt**. 不太多。
- **How much money** does it cost? 這要多少錢？

too much — 表「太多」
- **too much** homework
  太多作業

a lot of

= lots of

接複數名詞
- There are **a lot of bottles**. 有很多瓶子。
- Sam bought **lots of guavas**. 山姆買了好多芭樂。

接不可數名詞
- There's **a lot of juice**. 有很多果汁。
- Jimmy added **lots of black pepper** to the soup.
  吉米在湯裡加了很多黑胡椒。

通常用於肯定句

後接名詞可省略 — 作代名詞
- There's some pressure, but not **much**. 壓力是有一點，但是不太大。
  ↳ = much pressure
- We have some magazines, but not **a lot**. 我們有一些雜誌，但是不多。
  ↳ = a lot of magazines

用於已知所指名詞為何時

many
much
a lot of

enough

表示足夠的數量 — 固定量的最低限度

用法 — 後接 — 複數名詞 — • We have **enough paint brushes**. We don't need any more.
我們已經有足夠的油漆刷子，不需要更多了。

不可數名詞 — • I can't paint the house. I don't have **enough time**.
我沒辦法油漆這間屋子，我的時間不夠。

與 **a lot of** 的差別 — enough — 固定量的最低限度 — • **enough** tea
足夠的茶

• **enough** apples
足夠的蘋果

a lot of — 固定量的較大限度 — • **a lot of** tea
很多茶

• **a lot of** apples
很多蘋果

後面名詞可省略 — 作代名詞 — • We don't need any tissues. We've got **enough**.
我們不用面紙，我們有的已經夠了。   ↳ = enough tissues

用於已知所指名詞為何時

Practice

❶ 假設你在下列電器與相關用品部門工作，你會如何詢問顧客的需求？自框內選出適當詞彙，依照範例句型造句。

air conditioners

cellphone batteries

detergent

cameras

light bulbs

televisions

microphones

water filters

1	Video Equipment 影音設備部	*How many televisions do you want?*
2	Video Accessories 影音部門	
3	Telecommunications 電信通訊部	
4	Cameras and Accessories 攝影器材部	
5	Washing Machines and Accessories 洗衣機及相關用品部	
6	Lighting 照明器材部	
7	Heating and Cooling 冷暖器材部	
8	Water Treatment 水處理設備部門	

❷ 用 **too much**、**too many** 和 **enough** 描述圖中情境。

He eats ___too much___ junk food.

She buys _____ clothing.

He has _____ caps.

She has _____ teddy bears.

She eats _____ dessert.

He buys _____ shirts.

She watches _____ TV.

She doesn't have _____ money for the giant teddy bear.

He has _____ cans of soda.

Unit 21 不定代名詞與不定形容詞（3）

表示數量的形容詞
- a little sugar 少許糖
- little food 沒什麼食物
- a few cups 幾個杯子
- few things 沒多少事

a little / little
a few / few

a little 後接 不可數名詞 表示 一些
- We have **a little food**. 我們有一些食物。

little 後接 不可數名詞 表示 幾乎沒有
- Jack got **little help** from his brother. 傑克的哥哥沒有幫他什麼忙。

a few 後接 複數名詞 表示 一些
- We have **a few meatballs**. 我們有一些肉丸。

few 後接 複數名詞 表示 幾乎沒有
- There are **few people** she likes. She loves only herself. 她沒有什麼喜歡的人。她只愛她自己。

反義字
- few ↔ many ・ few apples 沒有幾個蘋果 ↔ many apples 很多蘋果
- little ↔ much ・ little tea 沒有什麼茶 ↔ much tea 很多茶

作代名詞用時
與「 of + 名詞」連用
- Only **a few of the students** agreed to participate in the charity event on Sunday. 只有一些學生願意參與週日的慈善活動。
- **Few of us** can speak German. 我們沒幾個人會說德文。

若前方已提及欲指稱對象 再次提及時可單獨存在
- Ted drank **a little of the wine** on the table, so there is **little** left. 泰德喝了一些桌上的酒，所以所剩不多了。

Practice

❶ 依照圖示，描述各種水果和相關物品的數量。請從框內挑出最適當的用語，完成句子。

There are a few . . .
There are a lot of . . .
There are many . . .
There isn't much . . .
There's a little . . .
There's a lot of . . .

1 bananas

There are a lot of bananas.

2 lemons

3 watermelons

4 guavas

5 pears

6 orange juice

❷ 依據圖示，用框內詞彙完成下列段落。

little
a little
few
a few
much
many

There is not ❶............................ furniture in this room. There are only
❷............................ chairs and a cushion. ❸............................ dirt can be found
on the floor. The curtains are open, and the large window allows
❹............................ light to come into the room.

There are ❺............................ tables and chairs in the square. It's
getting dark. I think we're expecting ❻............................ rain later,
but the weather broadcast says there won't be much rain.

Unit 22 不定代名詞（1）

① · My **house** is the small **one**. 我家是小的那間。
　　　　　　　↳ = house；單數可數名詞
· I am getting **a glass of orange juice**. Do you want **one**? 我要去拿一杯柳橙汁，你要嗎？
　　　　　　　　　　　　↳ = a glass of orange juice；單數可數名詞

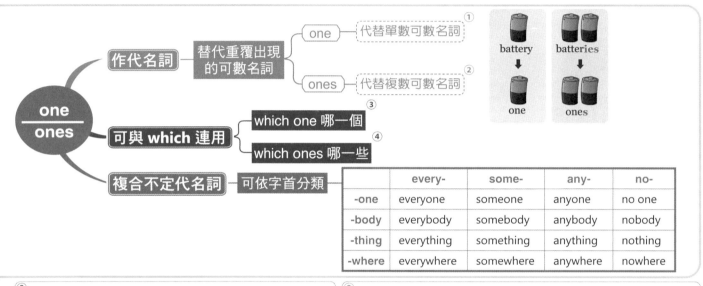

one / ones

作代名詞 ── 替代重覆出現的可數名詞
- one ── 代替單數可數名詞 ①
- ones ── 代替複數可數名詞 ②

可與 which 連用
- which one 哪一個 ③
- which ones 哪一些 ④

複合不定代名詞 ── 可依字首分類

	every-	some-	any-	no-
-one	everyone	someone	anyone	no one
-body	everybody	somebody	anybody	nobody
-thing	everything	something	anything	nothing
-where	everywhere	somewhere	anywhere	nowhere

battery → one
batteries → ones

③ · We have lots of **soft drinks**. **Which one** would you like, 7 Up, Pepsi, or Coke?　↳ = Which soft drink
我們有很多種飲料，你要哪一種，七喜、百事可樂還是可口可樂？

④ · We have many **online games** here at the cyber café. **Which ones** do you like to play?
↳ = Which online games
我們網咖有很多線上遊戲，你想要玩哪幾種？

② · Do you like large **cars** or small **ones**? 你喜歡大車還是小車？
　　　　　　　　↳ = cars；複數可數名詞
· Where did you take those **photographs**, the **ones** on the wall?
牆上的那些照片，你是在哪裡拍的？　↳ = photographs；複數可數名詞
· We have lots of **snacks**. Try the **ones** on the table. 我們有很多點心，吃吃看桌上這些吧。
　　　　　　　↳ = snacks；複數可數名詞

Practice

❶ 請依照圖示，在空格填上 one 或 ones 完成對話。

Mother	Sweetheart, which .... would you like?
Girl	I want the small ....
Mother	Wouldn't you like the big .... ?
Girl	No way! That's for big girls.

Jane	Which .... did you catch?
Joe	I caught the little ....
Jane	You should buy the large .... from that guy or you'll go hungry.

Mia	How much are the .... on the left?
Peter	They are extremely expensive.
Mia	Oh. How much are the .... on the right?
Peter	They are very expensive, too.
Mia	Do you have a cheap .... ?
Peter	No, madam. I am sorry. We don't have any cheap .... in the store.
Mia	OK. Thanks. I guess I can't get .... here.

Unit 23 不定代名詞（2）

①
- **Somebody** left an umbrella. 有人留下了一把傘。
- **Someone** claimed the lost umbrella. 有人說遺失的那把傘是他的。

②
- **Anybody** could have entered the contest. 任何人都可以參加這場比賽。
- **Anyone** who enters the contest needs to pay $100. 任何參加這場比賽的人都要繳 100 元。

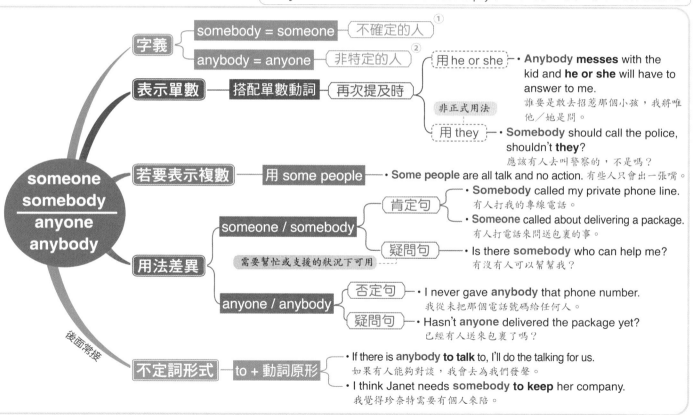

字義
- somebody = someone — 不確定的人 ①
- anybody = anyone — 非特定的人 ②

表示單數 — 搭配單數動詞 — 再次提及時
- 用 he or she — • **Anybody messes** with the kid and **he or she** will have to answer to me. 誰要是敢去招惹那個小孩，我將唯他／她是問。
- 非正式用法
- 用 they — • **Somebody** should call the police, shouldn't **they**? 應該有人去叫警察的，不是嗎？

若要表示複數 — 用 some people — • **Some people** are all talk and no action. 有些人只會出一張嘴。

用法差異
- someone / somebody
  - 肯定句 — • **Somebody** called my private phone line. 有人打我的專線電話。 • **Someone** called about delivering a package. 有人打電話來問送包裹的事。
  - 疑問句 — • Is there **somebody** who can help me? 有沒有人可以幫幫我？
  - 需要幫忙或支援的狀況下可用
- anyone / anybody
  - 否定句 — • I never gave **anybody** that phone number. 我從未把那個電話號碼給任何人。
  - 疑問句 — • Hasn't **anyone** delivered the package yet? 已經有人送來包裹了嗎？

不定詞形式 — to + 動詞原形
- If there is **anybody to talk** to, I'll do the talking for us. 如果有人能夠對談，我會去為我們發聲。
- I think Janet needs **somebody to keep** her company. 我覺得珍奈特需要有個人來陪。

someone somebody anyone anybody

後面常接

Practice

❶ 用 someone 或 anyone 填空，完成句子。

1. **Helen:** I saw _____ in the alley last night.

   Peter: Oh?

   Helen: Did you see _____ in the alley last night?

   Peter: I didn't see _____ in the alley last night.

2. **Ray:** You don't look good. What's the matter?

   Elain: I lost my job. I'm so helpless, and there isn't _____ who can help me.

   Ray: There must be _____ who can help. Don't worry.

3. **Jack:** What is Sandy doing?

   Bella: She is talking to _____ on the phone.

   Jack: Is it _____ we know?

   Bella: No, it's _____ we've never heard of.

❷ 圈選正確答案。

1. Some people never **go/goes** out on the weekend.

2. Is there someone **talk/to talk** to about your problem?

3. **Someone/Anyone** mailed a box to me last week.

4. Jack wouldn't tell **someone/anyone** about his decision.

5. Kim is an orphan. She doesn't have **someone/anyone** to rely on.

6. I can go by myself. I don't need anyone **to keep/keeping** me company.

7. I talked to **someone/anyone** in the personnel department about my job.

Unit 24 不定代名詞（3）

①
- **Something** is wrong with my car.
  我的車子有點毛病。
- At this point, I am willing to try **anything**.
  到了這個時刻，我願意做任何嘗試。

something
somewhere
anything
anywhere

something / anything

表示 不特定狀況或事物 ①

視為 單數
- 作主詞用時搭配 單數動詞
  - **Something is** walking towards us. What is it?
    有什麼東西往我們這邊走來，到底是什麼？
- 再次提及時使用 it
  - I will eat **anything** if **it** is good for my health.
    只要對健康有益，我什麼都吃。

後面常接 to + 動詞原形
- Would you like **something to eat**?
  你想吃些什麼嗎？

somewhere / anywhere

表示 非特定地點
- She lives **somewhere** in Florida. 她住在佛羅里達州的某處。
- I don't want to go **anywhere** today. 我今天哪裡都不想去。

用法差異

something / somewhere
- 肯定句
  - There is **something** in my left shoe. 我左邊鞋子裡有東西。
- 疑問句
  - Is there **something** I can help you with while you wait?
    你在等的時候需要我幫什麼忙嗎？
  - Is there **somewhere** safe in this town?
    這個鎮上有哪裡是安全的嗎？

需要幫忙或支援的狀況下可用

anything / anywhere
- 肯定句
  - If you need **anything**, just let me know.
    你如果需要任何東西，就告訴我。
  - My family would love to live **anywhere** in this city.
    我們家想住在這城市裡，哪裡都好。
- 否定句
  - We haven't had **anything** to drink for two days.
    我們已經連續兩天沒東西喝了。
- 疑問句
  - Is there **anything** wrong with you? You look sad.
    發生了什麼事嗎？你看起來很難過。

表示「無論是什麼／在何處」時可用

Practice

❶ 利用下面框內的**不定代名詞**和**動詞**來完成句子。

| anything something anywhere somewhere | to eat to go to do to drink |

1. Sam doesn't have

....

3. They don't have

....

2. Does he have

.... ?

4. He still has

....

❷ 選出正確的答案。

1. **Don:** Is there **something/anything** in your drawer?

　　Lee: There isn't **something/anything** in my drawer.

2. I know somewhere for us **hide/to hide**.

3. Is there **somewhere/anywhere** we can go for a swim?

4. I want to give you **something/anything** for your birthday.

5. You can sit **somewhere/anywhere** in this room.

no one / nobody

搭配 — **單數動詞** — · We looked everywhere, but **nobody was** there.
我們到處都找過了，但是那裡一個人也沒有。

意義相同 — 表示 — **沒有人**

後面常接 — **to + 動詞原形** — · There's **no one to talk** to. 沒有人可以跟我說話。
· I have **nobody to turn** to for help. 我求助無門。

帶有否定意味 — **不可搭配否定詞** — · ~~I don't want to see nobody now.~~
→ I don't want to see **anybody** now.
我現在誰也不想見。

nobody / not anybody — nobody 語氣較強烈 — · **Nobody** can help.
完全沒有人可以幫忙。
↳ 語氣強烈
· There **isn't anybody** who can help.
沒有人可以幫忙。
↳ 語氣緩和

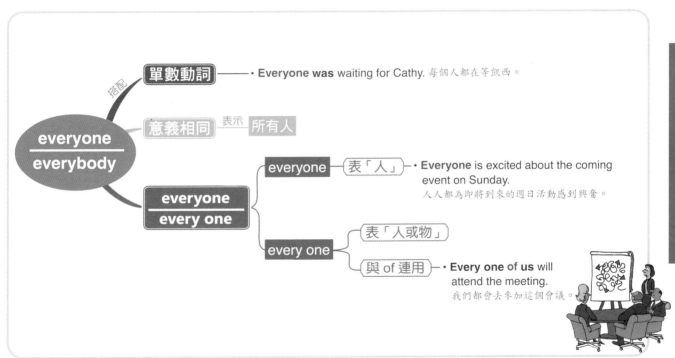

單數動詞 —— • **Everyone was** waiting for Cathy. 每個人都在等凱西。

搭配

意義相同 表示 所有人

everyone / everybody

everyone / every one

everyone — 表「人」 • **Everyone** is excited about the coming event on Sunday.
人人都為即將到來的週日活動感到興奮。

every one — 表「人或物」

與 of 連用 • **Every one of us** will attend the meeting.
我們都會去參加這個會議。

nothing / everything

搭配 — 單數動詞 —— • **Everything is** under control. 一切都在掌握之中。

nothing — 表示 — 沒有事／物

後面常接 — to + 動詞原形 —— • I have **nothing to lose**. 我沒什麼好失去的了。

帶有否定意味 — [不可搭配否定詞] —— • ~~I never said nothing about this to Kenny.~~
→I said **nothing** about this to Kenny.
我沒有對肯尼提及此事。

nothing / not anything — [nothing 語氣較強烈] —— • **Nothing** can be added.
完全沒什麼可以補充了。
↳ 語氣強烈
• There isn't **anything** that can be added.
沒有什麼可以補充了。
↳ 語氣緩和

everything — 表示 — 所有事／物

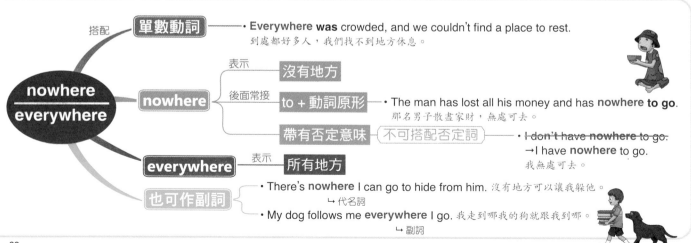

nowhere / everywhere

搭配 — 單數動詞 —— • **Everywhere was** crowded, and we couldn't find a place to rest.
到處都好多人，我們找不到地方休息。

nowhere — 表示 — 沒有地方

後面常接 — to + 動詞原形 —— • The man has lost all his money and has **nowhere to go**.
那名男子散盡家財，無處可去。

帶有否定意味 — [不可搭配否定詞] —— • ~~I don't have nowhere to go.~~
→I have **nowhere** to go.
我無處可去。

everywhere — 表示 — 所有地方

也可作副詞 — • There's **nowhere** I can go to hide from him. 沒有地方可以讓我躲他。
↳ 代名詞
• My dog follows me **everywhere** I go. 我走到哪我的狗就跟我到哪。
↳ 副詞

Practice

1 請利用括弧內的單字，改寫下列各句。

1. There isn't anybody at the office. (nobody)

→ *There is nobody at the office.*

2. There isn't anyone leaving today. (no one)

→

3. There isn't anything to feed the fish. (nothing)

→

4. There isn't anywhere to buy stamps around here. (nowhere)

→

5. There is nobody here who can speak Indonesian. (anybody)

→

6. There is no one that can translate your letter. (anyone)

→

7. There is nothing that will change the director's mind. (anything)

→

8. There is nowhere we can go to get out of the rain. (anywhere)

→

2 將下列句子改寫為正確的句子。

1. I don't have nowhere to go.

→

2. Noone believed me.

→

3. Everything are ready. Let's go.

→

4. There is nothing eat.

→

5. I never want to hurt nobody.

→

6. Every one in this room will vote for me.

→

7. Have you seen my glasses? I can't find them nowhere.

→

8. Any one who doesn't support this idea please raise your hand.

→

Unit 26 指示代名詞與指示形容詞

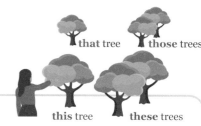

that tree   those trees

this tree   these trees

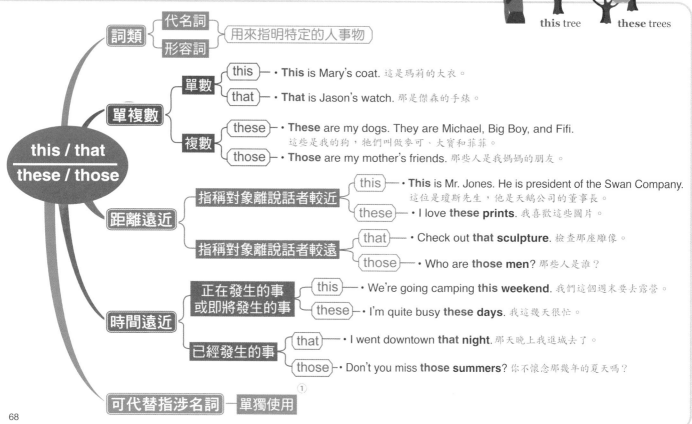

this / that
these / those

- 詞類 ─ 代名詞 / 形容詞 ─ (用來指明特定的人事物)

- 單複數
  - 單數
    - this ─ • **This** is Mary's coat. 這是瑪莉的大衣。
    - that ─ • **That** is Jason's watch. 那是傑森的手錶。
  - 複數
    - these ─ • **These** are my dogs. They are Michael, Big Boy, and Fifi.
      這些是我的狗，牠們叫做麥可、大寶和菲菲。
    - those ─ • **Those** are my mother's friends. 那些人是我媽媽的朋友。

- 距離遠近
  - 指稱對象離說話者較近
    - this ─ • **This** is Mr. Jones. He is president of the Swan Company.
      這位是瓊斯先生，他是天鵝公司的董事長。
    - these ─ • I love **these prints**. 我喜歡這些圖片。
  - 指稱對象離說話者較遠
    - that ─ • Check out **that sculpture**. 檢查那座雕像。
    - those ─ • Who are **those men**? 那些人是誰？

- 時間遠近
  - 正在發生的事或即將發生的事
    - this ─ • We're going camping **this weekend**. 我們這個週末要去露營。
    - these ─ • I'm quite busy **these days**. 我這幾天很忙。
  - 已經發生的事
    - that ─ • I went downtown **that night**. 那天晚上我進城去了。
    - those ─ • Don't you miss **those summers**? 你不懷念那幾年的夏天嗎？

①

- 可代替指涉名詞 ─ 單獨使用

①
- **This** is **the book** I want.
  - ↳ = this book
    這本正是我想要的書。
- **That** is not **the book** I want.
  - ↳ = that book
    那本不是我想要的書。
- **These** are **the books** I was looking for.
  - ↳ = these books
    這些正是我之前在找的書。
- **Those** are not **the books** I was looking for.
  - ↳ = those books
    那些不是我之前在找的書。

Practice

❶ 看圖用 this、that、these 或 those 填空，完成句子。

1. _____ pencil is Johnny's.

2. _____ tomatoes are sour.

3. Whose hand cream is _____?

4. Whose hair pins are _____?

❷ 選出正確的答案。

1. Is **this/these** the book you want?
2. Do you recognize **that/those** man in the blue shirt?
3. Does our dog love **that/those** toys?
4. What are you up to **these/those** days?
5. We had a lot of snow **that/those** year.
6. We're going to have heavy rain **this/that** year.
7. **That/Those** children are hungry.
8. Will you move **this/these** boxes for me?
9. **This/That** was the end of the vacation.
10. Schoolchildren used chalk and slate boards in **these/those** days.

Unit 27 反身代名詞

- **You** are feeling sorry for **yourself**. 你在自怨自艾。
- The **kids** built the tree house by **themselves**. 這群小孩們自己蓋了間樹屋。
- Let **me** introduce **myself**. 我來自我介紹一下吧。
- My **aunt** is looking at **herself** in the mirror. 我姑姑正在看鏡中的自己。
- My **cat** likes to lick **itself**. 我的貓喜歡舔自己。

反身代名詞

與人稱代名詞對應
- 單數 ─ -self 結尾
- 複數 ─ -selves 結尾

	人稱代名詞		對應的反身代名詞	
單數	I	我	myself	我自己
	you	你	yourself	你自己
	he	他	himself	他自己
	she	她	herself	她自己
	it	牠；它	itself	牠自己；它自己
複數	we	我們	ourselves	我們自己
	you	你們	yourselves	你們自己
	they	他們	themselves	他們自己

使用時機 ─ 主詞和受詞一樣時①

反身代名詞片語 by oneself ─ 表示 獨自 = alone ─ 強調 無他人幫助或參與
- I always go off **by myself** during lunch.
  = I go places alone for lunch.
  午餐時我總是自己出去。
- Do you always eat lunch **by yourself** in your office?
  = Do you always eat lunch alone?
  你都自己在辦公室吃午餐嗎？

作用 ─ 強調「自己」
- I finished the report. 我把報告完成了。
  → I finished the report **myself**. 我自己把報告完成了。

類似功能的字詞 ─ 相互代名詞 each other ─ 表示 彼此相互關係
- They are taking a picture of **themselves**.
  她們在為她們自己拍照。
  → They are taking pictures of **each other**.
  他們在幫彼此拍照。
- Dogs like to sniff **each other**.
  狗狗喜歡互相聞來聞去。

Practice

❶ 請看圖並填入適當的反身代名詞。

1.

I am brushing my teeth by
myself .

2.

Can you carry that box by
_____ ?

3.

This book is not going to
read _____ .

4.

The little boy cannot dress
_____ .

5.

She always eats lunch by
_____ .

6.

Are you going to drive
_____ to the
toy store?

7.

I guess we have to get the
food by _____ .

8.

Micky and Lucky can find food
by _____ .

❷ 請用 themselves 或 each other 造句說明圖中的情況。

1. They are going to hug
_____ .

2. They are videotaping
_____ .

3. They are painting the wall by
_____ .

71

Unit 16–18
重點複習

① 自框內選出正確的第一人稱單數代名詞填空，完成句子。

| me | I | mine | my |

1. That's _____ notebook computer.
2. This morning _____ sent an email message to the boss.
3. The funny flash animation was _____.
4. If you see someone in the chat room named Monster, that's _____.
5. _____ computer has a wireless connection to my cellphone.
6. _____ use a bluetooth connection from my computer to my cellphone.
7. Wireless Internet access is better for _____.
8. That laser mouse is _____. It's also wireless.

Unit 16–18
重點複習

② 在空格內填入正確的人稱代名詞。

1. _____ first name is Kevin. What's _____ name?
2. My husband and _____ have two children. _____ children are John and Grace.
3. Jeanie is going out to get dinner. I am going with _____.
4. Here's a photo of _____ family. That's me on the left.
5. Winnie is in love with Arthur, but _____ doesn't love _____.
6. This is your hat. _____ can't find _____. Have _____ seen _____?

7. The Jones have _____ air conditioner on. Let's turn on _____.
8. I bought a new car. I like _____ very much.
9. My cat caught two mice. _____ is playing with _____ now.
10. Kim and Tim have moved to a new apartment. _____ new apartment is rather big. _____ really love _____.
11. **Linda:** Where is _____ car?
    Anne: _____ is broken.
    Linda: Then how will you go to school tomorrow?
    Anne: I don't know.
    Linda: Would you like to borrow _____?
    Anne: That would be great.

3 下列各句的空格中，應填入可數名詞、不可數名詞還是兩者皆可？請選出正確答案填入空格內。

wine
green peppers

1. Do you have any
<u>wine/green peppers</u> ?

bread
cookies

2. Please have some
_____ .

sugar
ice cubes

3. There's no
_____ .

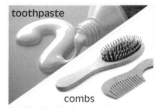

toothpaste
combs

4. There isn't any
_____ .

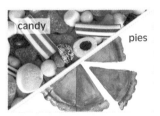

candy
pies

5. How much _____
did you get?

juice
grapes

6. Did you get many
_____ ?

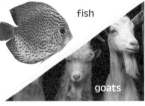

fish
goats

7. I saw a lot of
_____ .

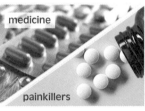

medicine
painkillers

8. Get me a little
_____ .

rice pudding
fruit tarts

9. How about a few
_____ ?

soup
juice

10. Did you get enough
_____ ?

garlic
lamb chops

11. How much _____
did you buy?

homework
notebooks

12. We have many
_____ .

❹ 檢查各句 **any** 和 **some** 的用法是否正確。在正確的句子後寫 OK；
不正確的請將錯誤用字畫掉，並於句後更正。

1. We have any rice. ....

2. Are there any spoons in the drawer? ....

3. There isn't some orange juice in the refrigerator.

....

4. Are there any cookies in the box? ....

5. Could I have any coffee, please? ....

6. Would you like some ham? ....

7. We have lots of fruit. Would you like any? ....

8. I already had some fruit at home. I don't need some now.

....

9. There aren't some newspapers. ....

10. There are any magazines. ....

❺ 請用 **one** 或 **ones** 重寫以下句子。

Who are these boxes for,
the boxes you are carrying?

→ ....
....
....

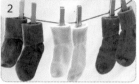

Do you like the red socks or the white socks?

→ ....
....
....

My cubicle is the cubicle next to the manager's office.

→ ....
....
....

4 I like the pink hat. Which hat do you like?

→ _____

_____

_____

_____

5 Our racquets are the racquets stored over there.

→ _____

_____

_____

_____

Unit 20 重點複習

6 選出正確的答案。

___ **1.** We haven't got _____ time.

   Ⓐ many   Ⓑ much

___ **2.** We don't have _____ milk left.

   Ⓐ many   Ⓑ much

___ **3.** _____ information do you have?

   Ⓐ How many   Ⓑ How much

___ **4.** _____ people agree with you.

   Ⓐ Many   Ⓑ Much

___ **5.** He has _____ homework.

   Ⓐ too many   Ⓑ too much

___ **6.** He has _____ sandwiches.

   Ⓐ too many   Ⓑ too much

___ **7.** Do we have _____ DVDs?

   Ⓐ lots of   Ⓑ little of

___ **8.** There are _____ gifts for your family.

   Ⓐ many   Ⓑ much

___ **9.** You have _____ things to do.

   Ⓐ too many   Ⓑ too much

___ **10.** Do you have _____ experience with this?

   Ⓐ many   Ⓑ much

7 從框內選出適當的字首搭配標籤裡的提示字根，填空完成以下句子。

some-
any-
no-
every-

-where

1. I've looked for my wallet _everywhere_, but I can't find it.
2. My wallet is _____ to be seen.
3. It must be in the house because I haven't gone _____.
4. I have to go _____, and I need my wallet.

-one

5. I called Joe's house about the party, but _____ answered.
6. Do you know if _____ is going over there tonight?
7. _____ should answer the phone.
8. _____ else intends to go there tonight except me.

-thing

9. Sue tried to tell me _____ about a problem.
10. Have you heard _____ about Sue's problem?
11. There is probably _____ I can do, but I want to help.
12. Is _____ OK with her now?

-body

13. Hello. I'm home. Hey, where is _____?
14. Is _____ home? I am here.
15. There must be _____ here because the lights are on.
16. Well, if _____ is here, then I am going to leave. Bye-bye.

8 請看圖並利用框內的不定代名詞，完成下列對話。

someone

no one

anyone

everyone

1. In the Musical Instrument Store

Woman I am looking for **❶**⸻⸻⸻ to give opera lessons to my son.

Man We just sell musical instruments.

❷⸻⸻⸻ here teaches opera.

Woman Do you know **❸**⸻⸻⸻ who teaches opera?

Man **❹**⸻⸻⸻ likes rock and pop.

❺⸻⸻⸻ likes opera.

Woman Maybe my son should try gospel singing.

somewhere

anywhere

everywhere

nowhere

2. In the Airport Parking Lot

Woman Your car is **❻**⸻⸻⸻ close by, right?

Man I think so, but it could be **❼**⸻⸻⸻ in the parking lot.

Woman It's **❽**⸻⸻⸻ to be seen. That's for sure.

Man We haven't looked **❾**⸻⸻⸻. It could be **❿**⸻⸻⸻ else.

Woman You keep looking. I am waiting here.

something

anything

everything

nothing

3. In the Principal's Office at School

Woman You must have done **⓫**⸻⸻⸻ wrong for your teacher to send you to the office.

Man I didn't do **⓬**⸻⸻⸻.

Woman Are you sure there was **⓭**⸻⸻⸻ going on?

Man The teacher blames **⓮**⸻⸻⸻ on me.

9 選出正確的答案。

.... **1.** .... is not my cellphone. That is mine.

Ⓐ This   Ⓑ That   Ⓒ These

.... **2.** We are going to the beach .... weekend. Would you like to join us?

Ⓐ this   Ⓑ that   Ⓒ these

.... **3.** Can you pass .... glasses to me?

Ⓐ this   Ⓑ that   Ⓒ those

.... **4.** Can you pass .... bottle of black pepper to me?

Ⓐ this   Ⓑ that   Ⓒ those

.... **5.** We had a lot of fun on .... Christmas.

Ⓐ this   Ⓑ that   Ⓒ those

.... **6.** .... suitcase belongs to Heather.

Ⓐ This   Ⓑ These   Ⓒ Those

10 下列各句若正確，在句後寫上 OK。若句子有誤，劃掉錯誤的字並寫出正確的反身代名詞或 **each other**。

1. My brother made himself sick by eating too much ice cream. ....

2. My sister made himself sick by eating two big pizzas. ....

3. The dog is scratching itself. ....

4. I jog every morning by me. ....

5. You have only yourself to blame. ....

6. We would have gone there us but we didn't have time. ....

7. He can't possibly lift that sofa all by himself. ....

8. Do you want to finish this project by yourself or do you need help? ....

9. I helped him. He helped me. We helped ourselves. ....

10. Don't fight about it. You two need to talk to each other if you are going to solve this problem. ....

Unit 19–21 重點複習

⑪ 選出正確的答案。

1. I have **a little/a few** business to do here.

2. You need to give **a few/a little** examples in your essay.

3. Let's not start now. I don't have **enough/a little** time.

4. He has **a lot of/many** courage.

5. Don't buy more food. We have **many/enough**.

6. Buy some new clothes, but not **a lot/much**.

7. There is **little/few** we could do.

8. **Little/Few** people would have done as much as you did.

9. There is **enough/few** salad for everybody.

10. He bought **much/many** games.

11. You had **a few/a little** telephone calls.

12. There are **a lot of/much** boxes in the garage.

13. There were **too many/too much** people in line.

14. I checked the batteries. We have **enough/much**.

Unit 29 be 動詞現在時態

①
- My name **is** Yuki. 我名叫雪。
- **Are** you both Japanese? 你們兩個都是日本人嗎？

②
- Cathy **is cleaning** her dog's house. 凱西正在清理狗屋。
- **Is** Dad **fixing** the broken pipe? 爸爸正在修理壞掉的水管嗎？

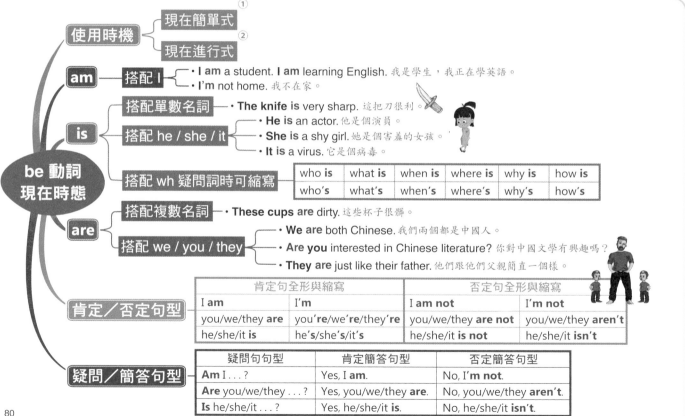

be 動詞現在時態

使用時機
- **①** 現在簡單式
- **②** 現在進行式

am — 搭配 I
- **I am** a student. **I am** learning English. 我是學生，我正在學英語。
- **I'm** not home. 我不在家。

is
- 搭配單數名詞 — **The knife is** very sharp. 這把刀很利。
- 搭配 he / she / it
  - **He is** an actor. 他是個演員。
  - **She is** a shy girl. 她是個害羞的女孩。
  - **It is** a virus. 它是個病毒。

搭配 wh 疑問詞時可縮寫

who **is**	what **is**	when **is**	where **is**	why **is**	how **is**
who**'s**	what**'s**	when**'s**	where**'s**	why**'s**	how**'s**

are
- 搭配複數名詞 — **These cups are** dirty. 這些杯子很髒。
- 搭配 we / you / they
  - **We are** both Chinese. 我們兩個都是中國人。
  - **Are you** interested in Chinese literature? 你對中國文學有興趣嗎？
  - **They are** just like their father. 他們跟他們父親簡直一個樣。

肯定／否定句型

肯定句全形與縮寫		否定句全形與縮寫	
I am	I**'m**	I am not	I**'m** not
you/we/they **are**	you**'re**/we**'re**/they**'re**	you/we/they **are not**	you/we/they **aren't**
he/she/it **is**	he**'s**/she**'s**/it**'s**	he/she/it **is not**	he/she/it **isn't**

疑問／簡答句型

疑問句句型	肯定簡答句型	否定簡答句型
Am I...?	Yes, I **am**.	No, I**'m** not.
Are you/we/they...?	Yes, you/we/they **are**.	No, you/we/they **aren't**.
Is he/she/it...?	Yes, he/she/it **is**.	No, he/she/it **isn't**.

Practice

1 利用 be 動詞的現在時態（am、is 或 are）填空，完成下列段落。

My name **1**_____ Eizo. I **2**_____ the singer in a band called the Rockets. My best friend **3**_____ Haruki, and he **4**_____ the guitar player. Ichiro **5**_____ the bass player. Kiyonobu **6**_____ the drummer. Ichiro and Kinonobu **7**_____ brothers. We **8**_____ a rock band.

I **9**_____ trying to get the band a gig playing at a pub. The place **10**_____ called the Beer Bar. We **11**_____ not making enough money from our music, so we **12**_____ all working day jobs. That **13**_____ the life of a musician. We **14**_____ used to it.

2 依照提示和範例，描述圖中人物的國籍和職業。

drummer
policeman
waiter
chef
violinist
singer

Karl

Karl is Canadian.

He is a violinist.

Dominique

Huyuki

Italian
American
Japanese
Russian
Canadian
Chinese

Lino

Jane

Mike

Unit ➌ there is / there are

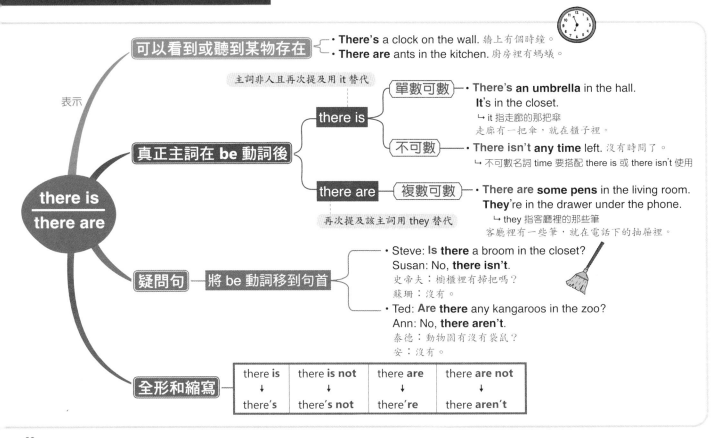

there is / there are

表示

- **可以看到或聽到某物存在**
  - **There's** a clock on the wall. 牆上有個時鐘。
  - **There are** ants in the kitchen. 廚房裡有螞蟻。

- **真正主詞在 be 動詞後**

  主詞非人且再次提及用 it 替代

  - **there is**
    - 單數可數
      - **There's an umbrella** in the hall.
        It's in the closet.
        ↳ it 指走廊的那把傘
        走廊有一把傘，就在櫃子裡。
    - 不可數
      - **There isn't any time** left. 沒有時間了。
        ↳ 不可數名詞 time 要搭配 there is 或 there isn't 使用
  - **there are**
    - 複數可數
      - **There are some pens** in the living room.
        They're in the drawer under the phone.
        ↳ they 指客廳裡的那些筆
        客廳裡有一些筆，就在電話下的抽屜裡。

  再次提及該主詞用 they 替代

- **疑問句** — **將 be 動詞移到句首**
  - Steve: **Is there** a broom in the closet?
    Susan: No, **there isn't**.
    史帝夫：櫥櫃裡有掃把嗎？
    蘇珊：沒有。
  - Ted: **Are there** any kangaroos in the zoo?
    Ann: No, **there aren't**.
    泰德：動物園有沒有袋鼠？
    安：沒有。

- **全形和縮寫**

there **is**	there **is not**	there **are**	there **are not**
↓	↓	↓	↓
there**'s**	there**'s not**	there**'re**	there **aren't**

Practice

❶ 依據圖示，並使用框內提供的文字，完成下列句子。

| there is | there isn't |
| there are | there aren't |

1. _____ any broccoli on the top shelf.

2. _____ some tomatoes on the bottom shelf.

3. _____ any meat in the refrigerator.

4. _____ a lot of grapes in the refrigerator.

5. _____ still some room on the shelves of the refrigerator door.

6. _____ a bottle of mineral water on the bottom shelf of the refrigerator door.

7. _____ some cheese on the top shelf.

8. _____ a carton of milk on the bottom shelf of the refrigerator door.

9. _____ any chicken in the refrigerator.

10. _____ some grapes on the bottom shelf.

11. _____ an apple on the bottom shelf.

12. _____ two oranges.

13. _____ three guavas.

14. _____ some watermelon.

15. _____ any milk on the bottom shelf.

16. _____ some vegetables on the bottom shelf.

❷ 用下列詞彙完成句子。

1. There _____ some orange juice. _____ in the refrigerator.

2. There _____ any rice wine in the kitchen. Can you go buy some? You can buy _____ at the grocery store on Tenth Street.

3. There _____ a bottle of mouth wash in the bathroom. _____ beside the sink.

4. There _____ many stray dogs in the streets. _____ very hungry.

5. There _____ some fantastic programs on TV this weekend. _____ on Channel 6.

6. There _____ a lot of homework tonight. _____ too much.

| is |
| isn't |
| are |
| aren't |
| it is |
| they are |
| it |
| them |

Part 3 現在時態

Unit 31 have got / has got

①
- I **have got** a new boyfriend.
  = I **have** a new boyfriend. 我有一個新男友。
- He **has got** blue eyes.
  = He **has** blue eyes. 他有一雙藍色的眼睛。

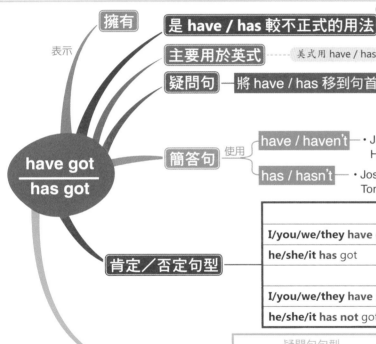

表示 擁有

have got / has got

① 是 have / has 較不正式的用法

主要用於英式 — — 美式用 have / has

疑問句 — 將 have / has 移到句首

- Tim: **Have** you **got** a pencil, Sam?
  Sam: No, I have only got an eraser.
  提姆：山姆，你有沒有鉛筆？
  山姆：沒有，我只有橡皮擦。
- **Has** she **got** blonde hair? = Does she have blonde hair?
  她有一頭金髮嗎？

簡答句 使用 have / haven't
- Jason: Have you got a cellphone? 你有手機嗎？
  Helen: No, I **haven't**. 我沒有。

has / hasn't
- Josh: Has your wife got a job? 你老婆有工作嗎？
  Tom: Yes, she **has**. 她有。

肯定／否定句型

肯定句全形與縮寫	
I/you/we/they have got	I've/you've/we've/they've got
he/she/it has got	he's/she's/it's got
否定句全形與縮寫	
I/you/we/they have not got	I/you/we/they haven't got
he/she/it has not got	he/she/it hasn't got

疑問／簡答句型

疑問句句型	肯定簡答句型	否定簡答句型
Have I/you/we/they got ...?	Yes, I/you/we/they have.	No, I/you/we/they haven't.
Has he/she/it got ...?	Yes, he/she/it has.	No, he/she/it hasn't.

Practice

❶ 根據圖示，找出相符的寵物名，並利用框內的句型造句。

hamster
pig
cat
snake
big dog
parrot

She's got a hamster.

❷ 利用 have/has got 和題目所提供的詞彙，寫出問句。

1. your family / cottage on Lake Michigan
   Has your family got a cottage on Lake Michigan?

2. you / your own room

3. you / your own closet

4. How many pets / you

5. How many TVs / your family

6. How many cars / your brother

Unit 32 現在簡單式

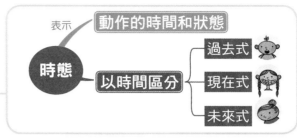

時態 —— 表示 動作的時間和狀態

以時間區分 —— 過去式 / 現在式 / 未來式

現在簡單式

表示

習慣及重覆發生的事 —— 常搭配 —— **頻率副詞**

every day 每天	usually 通常	often 通常	sometimes 有時
never 從不	yearly 一年一次	rarely 鮮少	

動詞形式

動詞原形 —— 主詞是 —— | I | you | we | they | 複數名詞 |

- **I cook** dinner every Thursday.
  我每個星期四都會做晚餐。
- **My grandparents like** oatmeal.
  我的祖父母喜歡燕麥粥。

加 s / es / ies —— 主詞是 —— | he | she | it | 第三人稱單數名詞 |

- **My dog loves** chasing a ball.
  我的狗狗喜歡追著球跑。
- **She** sometimes **goes** jogging in the evening.
  她有時傍晚會去慢跑。
- **Jackson studies** hard for exams.
  傑克森為了考試努力讀書。

否定句

加 do not / don't —— 主詞是 —— | I | you | we | they | 複數名詞 |

加 does not / doesn't —— 主詞是 —— | he | she | it | 第三人稱單數名詞 |

- **I don't** wash dishes.
  我不洗碗的。
- **They don't** play tennis.
  他們不打網球的。
- **My wife doesn't** cook dinner on Thursdays.
  我太太星期四都不做晚餐。

疑問句 —— **句首加上 do / does 且動詞用原形**

- Do I / you / we / they . . . ?
- Does he / she / it . . . ?

簡答句 —— 用 do / does

肯定簡答句型	否定簡答句型
Yes, **I/you/we/they do**.	No, **I/you/we/they don't**.
• Yes, **he/she/it does**.	No, **he/she/it doesn't**.

①
- I **often eat** squid. 我常吃烏賊。
- I **rarely eat** meat. 我很少吃肉。
- Peggy **drinks** coffee **every day**. 珮琪每天喝咖啡。

②
- Eve: **Do** you **like** cereal and milk for breakfast?
  Bob: **I do**.
  依芙：你早餐喜歡吃牛奶麥片嗎？
  鮑伯：喜歡。
- Jude: **Does** Wendy **drive** to work every day?
  Sid: Yes, **she does**.
  裘德：溫蒂每天開車上班嗎？
  席德：是的。

Practice

① 請寫出下列動詞的第三人稱單數動詞。

1. eat ....
2. cook ....
3. walk ....
4. run ....
5. brush ....

6. crunch ....
7. watch ....
8. box ....
9. marry ....
10. bury ....

② 下列是 Bobby 日常行程的描述，請分辨其中哪些動詞是現在簡單式，將它們畫上底線。

Bobby ▶ I <u>cook</u> simple food every day. I usually heat food in the microwave oven. I often make sandwiches. I sometimes pour hot water on fast noodles. However, I don't wash dishes.

③ 現在簡單式經常可以用來說明工具的功能。請依據圖示，自框中選用適當的動詞，用現在簡單式造句說明每個工具的功能。

move	tighten	cut

A wrench _____ bolts.

A wire cutter _____ wires.

A cart _____ boxes.

Unit 33 現在進行式

- I'm **making** a strawberry cake. 我正在做草莓蛋糕。
- The sun **is rising**. 旭日正在升起。
- Little Susie and Pinky **are playing** with their dolls. 小蘇西和蘋綺正在玩洋娃娃。
- Rick **is putting** a jigsaw puzzle together. 瑞克正在玩拼圖。

疑問句句型	肯定簡答句型	否定簡答句型
Am I thinking . . . ?	Yes, **I am**.	No, **I'm not**.
Are you/we/they thinking . . . ?	Yes, **you/we/they are**.	No, **you/we/they aren't**.
Is he/she/it thinking . . . ?	Yes, **he/she/it is**.	No, **he/she/it isn't**.

疑問／簡答句型

現在正在進行的動作 — be 動詞 + V-ing
- am making
- is rising

現在進行式 表示

肯定／否定句型

動詞字尾加上 ing

大多數直接加上 ing
- clean → cleaning 清掃
- study → studying 研讀
- walk → walking 走路

字尾 e （去 e 再加 ing）
- bake → baking 烘焙
- rise → rising 升起
- hope → hoping 希望

字尾 ie （ie 改成 y 再加 ing）
- die → dying 死亡
- lie → lying 說謊
- tie → tying 捆

字尾 單母音 + 單子音 （重複字尾子音 再加 ing）
- stop → stopping 停止
- hit → hitting 打

肯定句全形與縮寫	
I am thinking	**I'm** thinking
you/we/they are thinking	**you're/we're/they're** thinking
he/she/it is thinking	**he's/she's/it's** thinking

否定句全形與縮寫	
I am not thinking	**I'm not** thinking
you/we/they are not thinking	**you're/we're/they're not** thinking
he/she/it is not thinking	**he/she/it isn't** thinking

Practice

❶ 將下列動詞，加上 ing，並根據規則做必要的變化。

1. talk ....

2. care ....

3. stay ....

4. sleep ....

5. die ....

6. eat ....

7. make ....

8. rob ....

9. advise ....

10. jog ....

11. spit ....

12. jam ....

13. wait ....

14. clip ....

15. tie ....

16. compare ....

17. lie ....

18. plan ....

19. throw ....

20. speak ....

❷ 請依圖示，自框中選出適當的動詞，以現在進行式完成句子。

lie	walk
buy	run
picnic	sit
throw	play
shine	lie

1. The girl .... a dog.

2. The woman .... fruit.

3. The sun ....

4. The man .... garbage in the trash can.

5. The cat .... with a ribbon.

6. The girls ....

7. A surfboard .... on the beach.

8. They ....

9. The trash can .... on its side.

10. Mike .... on the lifeguard chair.

89

Unit 34 現在進行式和現在簡單式比較

現在進行式／現在簡單式

現在進行式 ─描述─
- 說話當下正在發生的事
  - 常搭配 now、right now
  - • Leslie is in the warehouse **now**. She**'s making** an inventory.
    雷思莉在倉庫裡，她正在開一張存貨清單。
- 問某人當下在做什麼
  - • Where is Leslie? **Is she working** in the warehouse?
    雷思莉在哪裡？她在倉庫裡工作嗎？

現在簡單式 ─描述─ 事實或習慣
常搭配 頻率副詞
不一定與說話當下有關
- every day
- usually
- often
- sometimes
- • Ian **checks** his email **every day**.
  伊恩每天都會收電子郵件。
- • **Does** Ivana **often update** her blog?
  伊凡娜有經常更新她的部落格嗎？

What are you doing? / **What do you do?**
- What are you doing? ─ 詢問正在做什麼
  - • Jay: What are you **doing**?
    Kay: I**'m playing** a computer game.
    杰：你在做什麼？
    凱：我正在玩電腦遊戲。
- What do you do? ─ 詢問職業
  - • Jay: What **do** you **do**?
    Kay: I **am** a computer game designer.
    杰：你是做什麼的？
    凱：我是電腦遊戲的設計師。

比較

現在進行式	現在簡單式
• I**'m listening** now. Please say it. 我正在聽，請說。	• I usually **listen to** heavy metal rock music. 我通常都聽重金屬搖滾樂。
• He**'s stealing** my bicycle! 他正在偷我的腳踏車！	• He frequently **steals** things, and sooner or later he will get caught and put into jail. 他慣性地偷竊，遲早會被抓去關的。

Practice

① 自框內選出適當的動詞,並正確使用現在簡單式或現在進行式,填空完成句子。

leave	drive
wish	drink
end	think
design	go

Bob Jones is stuck in traffic.
He's **①**_____ to work. Every day
he **②**_____ at 8:00 in the morning.
He is a microwave engineer.
He **③**_____ communication
systems for mobile phone operators. Whenever
he **④**_____ up sitting in a traffic jam,

he **⑤**_____ some coffee and listens
to music. Right now he **⑥**_____
about how fast microwaves travel and how slow
he **⑦**_____ in the traffic jam. He
⑧_____ he were a speedy little
microwave.

② 判斷以下句子應使用**現在簡單式**或**現在進行式**,利用題目詞彙組合造問句,根據事實簡答後,再寫出完整的句子描述事實。

	主詞	頻率副詞	動詞片語／形容詞	
1	you	often	listen to music	**Q** *Do you often listen to music?* **A** *Yes, I do. I often listen to music.*
2	you	at this moment	watch TV	**Q** **A**
3	it	now	hot	**Q** **A**
4	it	often / this time of year	hot	**Q** **A**
5	you	every day	drink coffee	**Q** **A**
6	you	right now	drink tea	**Q** **A**

Unit 35 不用進行式的動詞

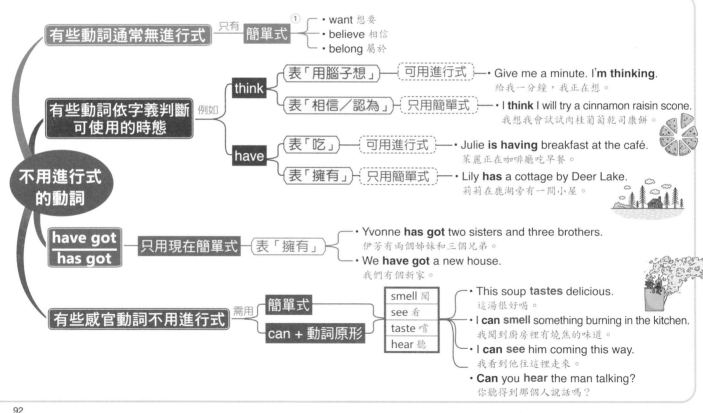

不用進行式的動詞

有些動詞通常無進行式 ── 只有 ─ 簡單式 ①
- want 想要
- believe 相信
- belong 屬於

有些動詞依字義判斷可使用的時態 ── 例如

think
- 表「用腦子想」── 可用進行式 ── • Give me a minute. I'm thinking.
  給我一分鐘，我正在想。
- 表「相信／認為」── 只用簡單式 ── • I think I will try a cinnamon raisin scone.
  我想我會試試肉桂葡萄乾司康餅。

have
- 表「吃」── 可用進行式 ── • Julie is having breakfast at the café.
  茱麗正在咖啡廳吃早餐。
- 表「擁有」── 只用簡單式 ── • Lily has a cottage by Deer Lake.
  莉莉在鹿湖旁有一間小屋。

have got / has got ── 只用現在簡單式 ── 表「擁有」
- Yvonne has got two sisters and three brothers.
  伊芳有兩個姊妹和三個兄弟。
- We have got a new house.
  我們有個新家。

有些感官動詞不用進行式 ── 需用

簡單式 / can + 動詞原形

smell 聞
see 看
taste 嚐
hear 聽

- This soup tastes delicious.
  這湯很好喝。
- I can smell something burning in the kitchen.
  我聞到廚房裡有燒焦的味道。
- I can see him coming this way.
  我看到他往這裡走來。
- Can you hear the man talking?
  你聽得到那個人說話嗎？

(1)

• want 想要	I **want** a notebook.
• believe 相信	I **believe** in you.
• belong 屬於	This bag **belongs** to you.
• forget 忘記	I **forget** things easily.
• hate 恨	I **hate** you.
• know 知道	I **know** the answer.
• like 喜歡	Dogs **like** meat.
• mean 意指	I **mean** what I say.
• need 需要	I **need** a dictionary.
• own 擁有	Jack **owns** a sports car.
• prefer 偏好	I **prefer** fish.
• realize 瞭解	Do you **realize** how difficult it will be to finish that project on time?
• recognize 認識	I don't **recognize** you.
• remember 記得	He **remembers** everything.
• seem 似乎	You **seem** tired.
• understand 瞭解	I **understand** you.

Practice

❶ 請用現在簡單式或現在進行式，填空完成下列句子。

1. I _____(eat) stewed prunes, but I really _____(hate) stewed prunes.

2. Harry _____(eat) a banana.

 He _____(like) bananas.

3. Ron _____(love) his weekend hiking trips.

4. The Jameson family _____(like) to barbeque.

5. Jack and Jane _____(make) sushi right now. They _____(know) how to make sushi.

6. _____ you _____(mean) we can leave now?

7. You _____(seem) very tired. What _____ you _____(do) right now?

❷ 下列句子，若動詞的用法正確，請在句後寫上 **OK**；若錯誤，請刪掉錯誤的用法並更正。

1. I am owning my own house. _____

2. This book belongs to Mary. _____

3. Mother is believing your story. _____

4. I often forget names. _____

5. I am having a snack. _____

6. The man is recognizing you. _____

Unit 32–33
重點複習

❶ 寫出下列動詞的第三人稱現在式和現在進行式。

1. change   *changes*   *changing*
2. visit
3. turn
4. jog
5. mix
6. cry
7. have
8. cut
9. fight
10. feel

11. tie
12. apply
13. jump
14. enjoy
15. steal
16. swim
17. send
18. taste
19. finish
20. study

Unit 29
重點複習

❷ 請用 **is** 或 **are** 以及題目所提供的字造問句；並根據事實回答。

1. What   your favorite TV show

   Q   What is your favorite TV show?

   A   The Simpsons.

2. What   your favorite movie

   Q

   A

3. Who   your favorite actor

   Q

   A

4. Who   your favorite actress

   Q

   A

5. What   your favorite food

   Q

   A

6. What   your favorite juice

   Q

   A

7. Who your parents

Q ....

A ....

8. Who your brothers and sisters

Q ....

A ....

Unit 29 重點複習

❸ 參考圖片回答問題。先用 is 或 are 完成問句，再依事實回答問題。

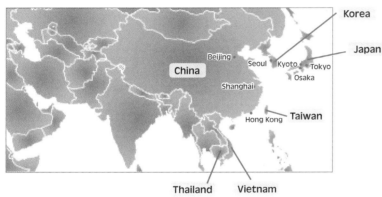

1. Q   *Is*   Seoul in Vietnam?

A   *No, Seoul is in Korea.*

2. Q .... Thailand and Vietnam in East Asia?

A ....

3. Q .... Hong Kong in Japan?

A ....

4. Q .... Beijing and Shanghai in China?

A ....

5. Q .... Osaka in Taiwan?

A ....

6. Q .... Tokyo, Osaka, and Kyoto in Japan?

A ....

Unit 30
重點複習

④ 依據上面圖示，利用框內提供的句型來完成下列問答。

1. Q: _Are there_ any men's shoe stores?
   A: _Yes, there are._

2. Q: _____ a wig（假髮）store?
   A: _____

3. Q: _____ a computer store?
   A: _____

4. Q: _____ two bookstores?
   A: _____

5. Q: _____ any women's clothing stores?
   A: _____

6. Q: _____ any women's shoe stores?
   A: _____

7. Q: _____ three music stores?
   A: _____

8. Q: _____ a jewelry store?
   A: _____

Is there

Are there

Yes, there is one.

No, there isn't.

Yes, there are.

No, there aren't.

Unit 29–33 重點複習

5 請正確填上 am、are、is、have 或 has。

1. My name _____ Leo.

2. I _____ a security guard at a bank.

3. I _____ got a gun.

4. There _____n't any bullets in my gun.

5. If the bank _____ a problem, I call the police.

6. Uh oh! There _____ two bank robbers.

7. I _____ moving closer to the robbers.

8. They _____ reaching out to grab something.

9. Hands up! Oops! I made a mistake. They _____ vice presidents.

10. I _____ sorry. I made a mistake.

Unit 29 重點複習

6 請用 is 或 are 以及題目所提供的字造問句；並根據事實，以肯定或否定句型簡答。

1. you   university student

   Q Are you a university student?

   A Yes, I am./No, I'm not.

2. you   big reader

   Q _____

   A _____

3. your birthday   coming soon

   Q _____

   A _____

4. your favorite holiday   Chinese New Year

   Q _____

   A _____

Unit 30 重點複習

7 看圖用 there is 或 there are 來描述圖中有什麼物品。

1. There is an alarm clock on the dresser.

2. _____

3. _____

4. _____

5. _____

8 用 do、does、don't、doesn't 和 work、works，填空完成句子。

Jasmine: ❶ _____ you **❷** _____ or go to school?

Anthone: I **❸** _____ go to school. I **❹** _____ at a bank.

Jasmine: ❺ _____ your friend George **❻** _____ too?

Anthone: Yes, he **❼** _____ at the same bank as I do.

Jasmine: ❽ _____ he **❾** _____ in the same department as you do?

Anthone: No, he **❿** _____. I **⓫** _____ in the trust department.

He **⓬** _____ in the foreign exchange department.

9 用 do 或 does 以及題目所提供的詞彙造問句，再依真實的情況簡答，並寫出完整句子描述事實。

1. you watch many movies

Q *Do you watch many movies?*

A *Yes, I do. I watch many movies.*

2. your mother work

Q _____

A _____

3. your father drive a car to work

Q _____

A _____

4. your family have a big house

Q _____

A _____

5. your neighbors have children

Q _____

A _____

6. you have a university degree

Q _____

A _____

Unit 32 重點複習

⑩ 閱讀 Annabelle 的自我介紹，並從框內選出適當的詞彙，造問句詢問她問題。

Hi, my name is Annabelle, but I like my friends to call me Annie. I am from Singapore. I am working at a junior high school in Hong Kong. After school at 4:00 I usually go to my favorite café. I have a cup of black coffee, read a newspaper, and grade some papers. About 6:00, I take the bus home, have dinner, and watch TV. I go to bed early because I have to get up early. I have to be at school by 6:45 a.m. During the school year I am busy every day.

| go home |
| go home |
| come from |
| like to be called |
| drink at the café |
| have to be at school |
| go to the café |

1. What _do you like to be called_ ?
2. Where _____ ?
3. What time _____ ?
4. What _____ ?
5. What time _____ ?
6. How _____ ?
7. What time _____ ?

Unit 31 重點複習

⑪ 用 have got 或 has got 改寫下列句子，若不能改寫，則劃上 ✕。

1. Peter has a good car.

→ _____

2. Paul is having a haircut right now.

→ _____

3. Wendy has a brother and a sister.

→ _____

4. The Hamiltons have two cars.

→ _____

5. Ken has a lot of good ideas.

→ _____

6. My sister is having dinner with her friend right now.

→ _____

12 請依圖示，自框中選出適當的動詞，以現在進行式完成句子。

deliver

use

fix

change

talk

work

1. Sam _____ the suspension.

2. Peter _____ packages.

3. Joe _____ the tire.

4. Bill _____ on the phone.

5. Chuck and Debbie _____ the computer.

6. They _____ in the car industry.

12 選出正確的答案。

1. **I am going/I go** to the store now.

2. I usually **stop/stopping** at the store on my way home from work.

3. Frank is working at the store. **He often has/He's often having** the afternoon shift.

4. The store **is having/is having got** a big sale on diapers.

5. Frank **wants/is wanting** a break from selling baby supplies.

6. Frank is taking a break now. He **is having/has** some cookies and a glass of milk.

7. "Be quiet," Frank says to Joe. "**I'm thinking/I think** about something."

8. "**I have got/I am having** an idea," says Frank.

9. "**I don't believe/I'm not believing** you," says Joe.

10. "You're not thinking. **I can hear/I'm hearing** you snoring."

14 請將下列句子改成否定句和疑問句。

1. We're tired.

→ *We aren't tired.*

→ *Are we tired?*

2. You're rich.

→

→

3. There's a message for Jim.

→

→

4. It is a surprise.

→

→

5. They have got tickets.

→

→

6. You have got electric power.

→

→

7. She works out at the gym.

→

→

8. He usually drinks a fitness shake for breakfast.

→

→

9. We are playing baseball this weekend.

→

→

10. He realizes this is the end of the vacation.

→

→

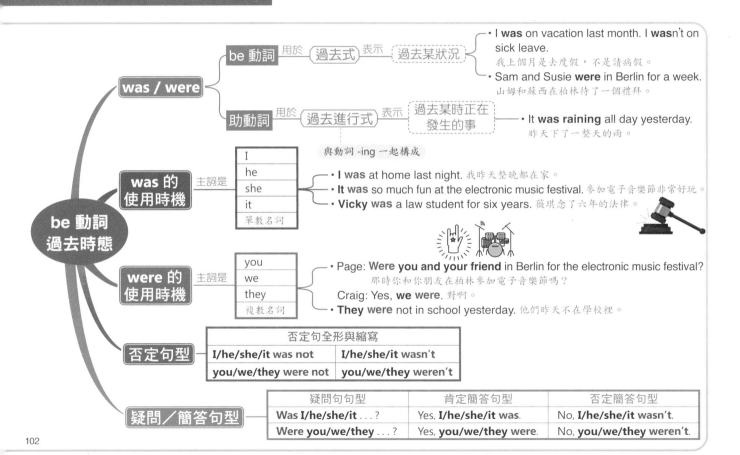

be 動詞過去時態

was / were

be 動詞 ─ 用於 過去式 ─ 表示 過去某狀況
- I **was** on vacation last month. I **was**n't on sick leave.
  我上個月是去度假，不是請病假。
- Sam and Susie **were** in Berlin for a week.
  山姆和蘇西在柏林待了一個禮拜。

助動詞 ─ 用於 過去進行式 ─ 表示 過去某時正在發生的事
- It **was raining** all day yesterday.
  昨天下了一整天的雨。

與動詞 -ing 一起構成

was 的使用時機 ─ 主詞是

| I |
| he |
| she |
| it |
| 單數名詞 |

- I **was** at home last night. 我昨天整晚都在家。
- It **was** so much fun at the electronic music festival. 參加電子音樂節非常好玩。
- Vicky **was** a law student for six years. 薇琪念了六年的法律。

were 的使用時機 ─ 主詞是

| you |
| we |
| they |
| 複數名詞 |

- Page: **Were you and your friend** in Berlin for the electronic music festival?
  那時你和你朋友在柏林參加電子音樂節嗎？
  Craig: Yes, **we were**. 對啊。
- **They were** not in school yesterday. 他們昨天不在學校裡。

否定句型

否定句全形與縮寫	
I/he/she/it was not	I/he/she/it wasn't
you/we/they were not	you/we/they weren't

疑問／簡答句型

疑問句句型	肯定簡答句型	否定簡答句型
Was I/he/she/it . . . ?	Yes, I/he/she/it was.	No, I/he/she/it wasn't.
Were you/we/they . . . ?	Yes, you/we/they were.	No, you/we/they weren't.

Practice

過
去
時
態

Unit
37
be
動
詞
過
去
時
態

❶ 請判斷句中的時態，自框內選用正確的 **be** 動詞完成句子。

is

are

was

were

1. Laura _____ a medical student for a long time. Now, she _____ a doctor.
2. Tammy _____ a cute little girl, and now she _____ a beautiful woman.
3. Today _____ a rainy day. Yesterday _____ a rainy day, too.
4. Today _____ January 1st, so yesterday _____ December 31st.
5. That _____ a big dog, but once it _____ a puppy.
6. Fluffy _____ such a busy little kitty, but now she _____ a lazy old cat.
7. The grapes _____ OK yesterday, but today they _____ overly ripe.
8. The new recruits _____ in Boot Camp last month. Now they _____ in technical school.
9. The thieves _____ in jail now. Last year they _____ not in jail.
10. We _____ so upset when we heard the news, but now we _____ feeling better.
11. Musicals _____ very popular in the past, and they _____ still popular today.
12. At one time, cell phones _____ uncommon, but now they _____ everywhere.

❷ 用 **was** 或 **were** 完成下列問句，依照實際情形做出簡答，並寫出完整句子描述事實。

1. → _Were_ you busy yesterday?
   → _Yes, I was. I was very busy yesterday._

2. → _____ you at school yesterday morning?
   → _____

3. → _____ yesterday the busiest day of the week?
   → _____

4. → _____ your father in the office last night?
   → _____

5. → _____ you at your friend's house last Saturday?
   → _____

6. → _____ your mother at home at 8 o'clock yesterday morning?
   → _____

7. → _____ you in bed at 11 o'clock last night?
   → _____

8. → _____ you at the bookstore at 6 o'clock yesterday evening?
   → _____

103

Unit 38 過去簡單式（1）

• Kelly: I **went** to Paris on vacation.
　　　我去了一趟巴黎度假。
　Sean: **Did** your boyfriend Andrew **go**?
　　　你的男友安德魯有一起去嗎？
• Kelly: Andrew **didn't go** with me.
　　　安德魯沒有和我一起去。
• Stella **called** a cab. The cab **drove** her home.
　　　史黛拉叫了一輛計程車。計程車載她回家。

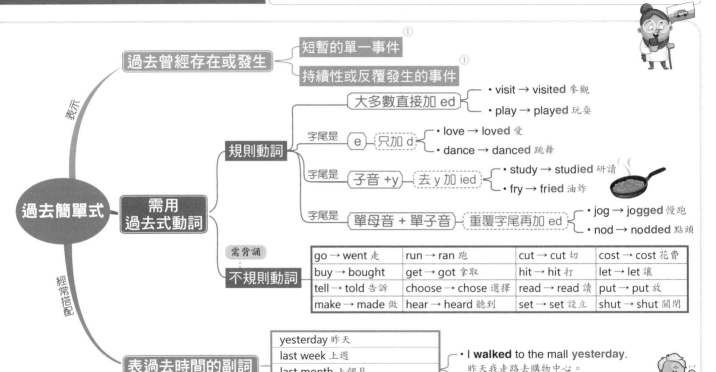

過去簡單式

表示 → 過去曾經存在或發生
- 短暫的單一事件
- 持續性或反覆發生的事件

需用過去式動詞
- 規則動詞
  - 大多數直接加 ed
    - visit → visited 參觀
    - play → played 玩耍
  - 字尾是 e → 只加 d
    - love → loved 愛
    - dance → danced 跳舞
  - 字尾是 子音 +y → 去 y 加 ied
    - study → studied 研讀
    - fry → fried 油炸
  - 字尾是 單母音 + 單子音 → 重覆字尾再加 ed
    - jog → jogged 慢跑
    - nod → nodded 點頭
- 不規則動詞（需背誦）

go → went 走	run → ran 跑	cut → cut 切	cost → cost 花費
buy → bought 買	get → got 拿取	hit → hit 打	let → let 讓
tell → told 告訴	choose → chose 選擇	read → read 讀	put → put 放
make → made 做	hear → heard 聽到	set → set 設立	shut → shut 關閉

經常搭配 → 表過去時間的副詞

| yesterday 昨天 |
| last week 上週 |
| last month 上個月 |
| in 2005 在 2005 年 |
| in the 20th century 在二十世紀 |

• I **walked** to the mall **yesterday**.
　昨天我走路去購物中心。
• Thomas Edison **invented** a lot of devices **in the 19th century**.
　愛迪生於十九世紀發明了許多裝置。

Practice

❶ 寫出下列動詞的過去式。

1. talk _____
2. plan _____
3. mail _____
4. hurry _____
5. date _____
6. eat _____
7. carry _____

8. note _____
9. show _____
10. clip _____
11. laugh _____
12. drink _____
13. marry _____
14. cook _____

15. write _____
16. come _____
17. drop _____
18. play _____
19. deliver _____
20. call _____
21. send _____

❷ 依據圖示，自框內選出適當的動詞，用過去式來描述圖中人物做過什麼。

| use | attend | receive | check | count | put |

He _____ the money.

They _____ a meeting.

She _____ some email.

She _____ a photocopier.

He _____ the products.

He _____ a box on the shelf.

Unit 39 過去簡單式（2）

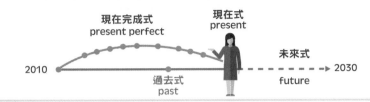

現在完成式 present perfect
現在式 present
未來式 future
過去式 past

2010 —— 2030

過去簡單式

did not 可縮寫為 didn't

否定句 — 主詞 + did not + 動詞原形
- She **did not arrive** on time. 她並未準時趕到。
- Mark and Tanya **didn't go** to the market yesterday morning. 馬克和譚雅昨天早上並沒有去市場。

疑問句 — 句首加 did 並用動詞原形
- **Did** you **call** me this morning? 你今天早上有打電話找我嗎？
- **Did** you **lock** Mr. Jones in his room? 你把瓊斯先生鎖在房間裡嗎？

簡答句
肯定簡答 — 主詞 + did
- A: Did your brother stay up late last night? 你哥哥昨晚是不是熬夜？
  B: Yes, **he did**. 是的，他是。

否定簡答 — 主詞 + didn't
- A: Did they lose the game? 他們輸掉比賽了嗎？
  B: No, **they didn't**. 沒有，他們沒輸。

經常用來說故事

- My drawing **was** not a picture of a hat. It **was** a picture of a boa constrictor digesting an elephant. But since the grown-ups **were** not able to understand it, I **made** another drawing: I **drew** the inside of the boa constrictor so that the grown-ups **could see** it clearly.

  我畫的可不是什麼帽子，是一條大蟒蛇正在消化牠肚裡的一頭大象。好吧，既然大人們看不懂這張圖，我又畫了一張：我把大蟒蛇肚子裡的東西也畫出來，這下大人們就看得懂了。

  —Antoine Saint-Exupery, *The Little Prince*

比較：過去簡單式 vs. 現在簡單式

- I am on vacation. I am in London now. Last night I **went** to the Tower of London. Last year I **visited** Paris. Two years ago I **stayed** in Rome for a week. I **like** Rome, but I **like** London better. I **like** vacations.

  我正在度假，我現在人在倫敦。昨晚我去了倫敦塔。去年我去巴黎參觀，兩年前則在羅馬待了一週。我喜歡羅馬，但更愛倫敦。我很喜歡度假。

Practice

❶ 用 did、didn't、have 或 had，完成下列句子。

1. Ken: .... Harry sleep late?

   Joe: Harry .... a late night, and he ....
   have to get up early, so he slept late.

2. Mia: .... you .... a lot of phone calls last
   night?

   Zoe: Yes, I .... Every time I put my head on
   the pillow the phone rang.

3. Bob: When .... you .... the time to read
   the book?

   Bell: I read it on the airplane. I .... it with me
   on my trip.

❷ 用 did 和題目提供的詞彙造問句，依照實際情況做出簡答，並寫
出完整句子來描述事實。

1. you | see your friends last night

   Q *Did you see your friends last night?*

   A *No, I didn't. I didn't see my friends last night.*

2. you | go to a movie last weekend

   Q ....

   A ....

3. you | play basketball yesterday

   Q ....

   A ....

4. you | graduate from university last year

   Q ....

   A ....

❸ 用過去式改寫括弧內的動詞，完成《小王子》的部分內容。

Once when I ❶ ....(be) six
years old I ❷ ....(see) a
magnificent picture in a book,
called True Stories from Nature,
about the primeval forest. It ❸ ....(be) a picture of
a boa constrictor in the act of swallowing an animal.
Here is a copy of the drawing.

I ❹ ....(ponder) deeply, then,
over the adventures of the jungle. And after
some work with a colored pencil I ❺
...............(succeed) in
making my first drawing. My drawing
Number One. It looked like this:

Unit 40　過去進行式

① ・ I **was watching** the movie **when** you **called**. 你打電話來的時候，我正在看電影。

② ・ I **called** when the movie **started**. 電影開始播放後，我就打了電話。

③ ・ The phone **rang** when he **was taking** a bath. 他在泡澡的時候，電話響了。

過去進行式

意涵 ── 過去某一時刻正在進行的事 ── ・ I **was watching** a vampire movie from 9:00 to 11:00 last night.
昨晚 9 點到 11 點之間，我在看一部吸血鬼的電影。

句式 ── be 動詞過去式 + V-ing ── ・ What **were** you **doing** at 8:00 last night?
昨晚 8 點你在做什麼？
・ At 8:00 last night I **was watching** the news. It was a slow news day. The newscasters **were talking** about turtles.
昨晚 8 點，我正在看新聞。那天的新聞很無聊，當時播報員正在談論烏龜。

過去簡單式 / 過去進行式 ── 與 when 連用

- 過去進行式 + when + 過去簡單式
  - 過去簡單式 ── 某個動作 ①
  - 過去進行式 ── 該動作發生時的背景 ①
- 過去簡單式 + when + 過去簡單式
  - 過去簡單式 ── 較短暫的動作 ②
- 過去簡單式 + when + 過去進行式
  - 過去進行式 ── 較長時間的動作 ③

否定句型

否定句全形與縮寫	
I/he/she/it was not watching	**I/he/she/it wasn't** watching
you/we/they were not watching	**you/we/they weren't** watching

疑問／簡答句型

疑問句句型	肯定簡答句型	否定簡答句型
Was I/he/she/it watching . . . ?	Yes, **I/he/she/it was**.	No, **I/he/she/it wasn't**.
Were you/we/they watching . . . ?	Yes, **you/we/they were**.	No, **you/we/they weren't**.

Practice

① 將括弧內的動詞以過去進行式填空。

We **①**＿＿＿＿＿＿＿＿＿＿(decorate) Debbie's apartment for her surprise birthday party when the door opened. Everybody froze. Trisha **②**＿＿＿＿＿＿＿＿＿＿(hang) balloons. Francine **③**＿＿＿＿＿＿＿＿＿＿(drape) streamers. Annabelle **④**＿＿＿＿＿＿＿＿＿＿(arrange) the forks and plates for the cake. Julie **⑤**＿＿＿＿＿＿＿＿(put) candles on the birthday cake.

Gina **⑥**＿＿＿＿＿＿＿＿＿＿(unpack) presents from the shopping bags. Cathy **⑦**＿＿＿＿＿＿＿＿＿＿(put) a bow and ribbon on Debbie's cat. Everybody looked at Debbie coming through the doorway. Debbie had arrived from work early. She walked in, looked around, and said, "Surprise! What are you doing?" I said, "We are preparing your surprise birthday party. Now go back outside and then come in so we can yell "'Surprise! Happy birthday!'"

② 用動詞 do 的過去進行式完成問句，詢問圖中人物在做什麼。
再依據圖示，自框內選出適當的動詞片語，用過去進行式造句回答問題。

| talk on the phone | drink a lot of coffee | try to fall asleep |

Q <u>What was he doing</u>　when the phone rang?

A <u>He was trying to fall asleep.</u>

＿＿＿＿＿＿＿＿＿＿＿＿＿＿＿

Q ＿＿＿＿＿＿＿＿＿＿ when the alarm clock went off?

A ＿＿＿＿＿＿＿＿＿＿＿＿＿＿＿

Q ＿＿＿＿＿＿＿＿＿ while watching TV during breakfast?

A ＿＿＿＿＿＿＿＿＿＿＿＿＿＿＿

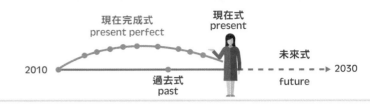

現在完成式
present perfect

現在式
present

未來式
future

2010   過去式   2030
              past

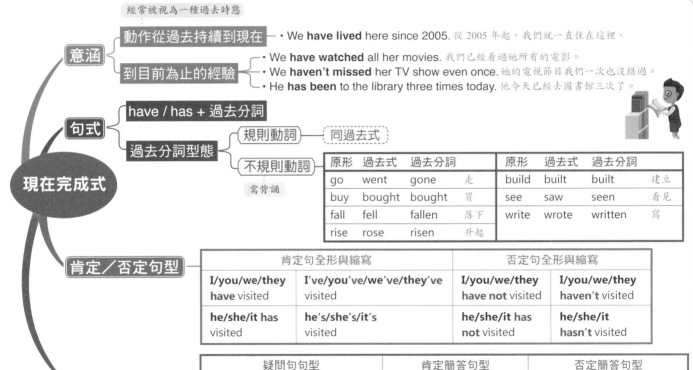

現在完成式

意涵

經常被視為一種過去時態

動作從過去持續到現在 — ・We **have lived** here since 2005. 從 2005 年起，我們就一直住在這裡。

到目前為止的經驗
- We **have watched** all her movies. 我們已經看過她所有的電影。
- We **haven't missed** her TV show even once. 她的電視節目我們一次也沒錯過。
- He **has been** to the library three times today. 他今天已經去圖書館三次了。

句式

have / has + 過去分詞

過去分詞型態

規則動詞 — 同過去式

不規則動詞 — 需背誦

原形	過去式	過去分詞		原形	過去式	過去分詞	
go	went	gone	走	build	built	built	建立
buy	bought	bought	買	see	saw	seen	看見
fall	fell	fallen	落下	write	wrote	written	寫
rise	rose	risen	升起				

肯定／否定句型

肯定句全形與縮寫		否定句全形與縮寫	
I/you/we/they **have** visited	**I've/you've/we've/they've** visited	**I/you/we/they** **have not** visited	**I/you/we/they** **haven't** visited
he/she/it has visited	**he's/she's/it's** visited	**he/she/it has** **not** visited	**he/she/it** **hasn't** visited

疑問／簡答句型

疑問句句型	肯定簡答句型	否定簡答句型
Have I/you/we/they visited . . . ?	Yes, **I/you/we/they have.**	No, **I/you/we/they haven't.**
Has he/she/it visited . . . ?	Yes, **he/she/it has.**	No, **he/she/it hasn't.**

Practice

❶ 寫出下列動詞的過去分詞。

1. talk   _talked_
2. go
3. drive
4. break
5. eat
6. think
7. shoot

8. buy
9. love
10. lose
11. smell
12. read
13. take
14. fall

15. drink
16. bring
17. swallow
18. write
19. leave
20. lie（躺）

❷ 從框內選出適當的動詞，以現在完成式填空，完成句子。

1. Colonel Sanders _____ fried chicken all his life.
2. Mrs. Fredericks _____ at this school for 25 years.
3. Johnny Baxter _____ at the airport.
4. Kathy Stein _____ another first place ribbon.
5. John Newman _____ money from his friends.
6. Sidney Green _____ three books.

> win
> steal
> arrive
> teach
> write
> eat

❸ 哪些動詞形式屬於現在完成式？將它們劃上底線。

Clive <u>grew up</u> in the country. He moved to the city in 2010. He has lived there since then.

He has worked in an Italian restaurant for a year and half. He met his wife in the restaurant. They got married last month, and she moved in to his apartment. They have become a happy couple, but they haven't had a baby yet.

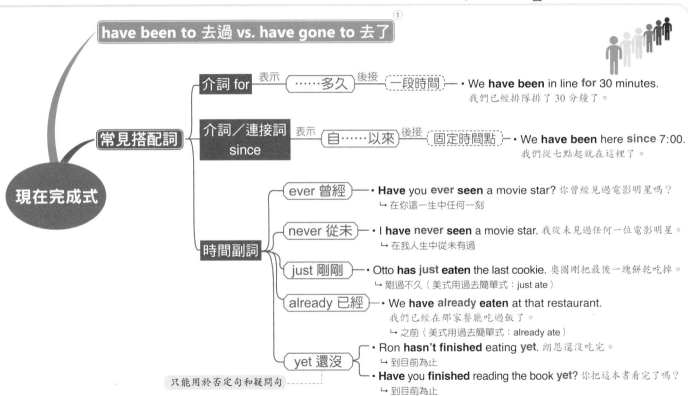

現在完成式

have been to 去過 **vs. have gone to** 去了

常見搭配詞

介詞 **for** ── 表示 ⋯⋯多久 ── 後接 一段時間 ── • We **have been** in line **for** 30 minutes.
我們已經排隊排了 30 分鐘了。

介詞／連接詞 **since** ── 表示 自⋯⋯以來 ── 後接 固定時間點 ── • We **have been** here **since** 7:00.
我們從七點起就在這裡了。

時間副詞

ever 曾經 ── • **Have** you **ever seen** a movie star? 你曾經見過電影明星嗎？
↳ 在你這一生中任何一刻

never 從未 ── • I **have never seen** a movie star. 我從未見過任何一位電影明星。
↳ 在我人生中從未有過

just 剛剛 ── • Otto **has just eaten** the last cookie. 奧圖剛把最後一塊餅乾吃掉。
↳ 剛過不久（美式用過去簡單式：just ate）

already 已經 ── • We **have already eaten** at that restaurant.
我們已經在那家餐廳吃過飯了。
↳ 之前（美式用過去簡單式：already ate）

yet 還沒 ── • Ron **hasn't finished** eating **yet**. 朗恩還沒吃完。
↳ 到目前為止
• **Have** you **finished** reading the book **yet**? 你把這本書看完了嗎？
↳ 到目前為止

只能用於否定句和疑問句

①

- **Have** you ever **been to** Brazil?
  你有去過巴西嗎？
  ↳ 詢問對方過去的經驗。

have been to
去過

- He **has been to** the library twice today.
  他今天去過圖書館兩次了。
  ↳ 他已經去過並回來了。

- I heard Teddy **has gone to** Rio
  for Carnival.
  我聽說泰迪到里約去參加嘉年華會了。
  ↳ 泰迪現在人還在那裡。

have gone to
去了

- He is not at home. He **has gone to** the library.
  他不在家，他去圖書館了。
  ↳ 他還沒回來。

Practice

❶ 請將括弧內的動詞以現在完成式來填空。沒有動詞提示的空格，請填上 **for** 或 **since**。

1. I am an airplane pilot. I _____*have been*_____ (be) a pilot
   _____*since*_____ I graduated from junior high school.

2. In high school I started making model airplanes.
   I _____(build) model airplanes _____
   25 years.

3. Ever since I was a kid, I _____
   (dream) about going to the moon.

4. _____ 2001, several companies _____
   (start) to offer space tourism.

❷ 利用題目提供的字彙造問句，依據實際情況做出簡答，並寫出完整的句子來描述事實。

1. eat a worm

   Q *Have you ever eaten a worm?*

   A *No, I haven't. I haven't eaten a worm.*

2. be to Japan

   Q _____

   A _____

3. swim in the ocean

   Q _____

   A _____

4. cheat on an exam

   Q _____

   A _____

Unit 43 現在完成式和過去簡單式比較

比較：現在完成式 vs. 過去簡單式
- **Have you ever been to** a baseball game?
  你去看過棒球比賽嗎？
- **Did you go to** the baseball game yesterday?
  你昨天有去看棒球賽嗎？

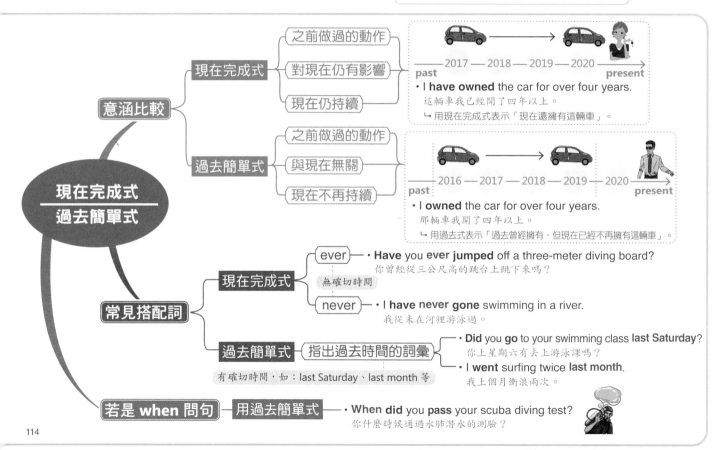

現在完成式 / 過去簡單式

意涵比較

現在完成式
- 之前做過的動作
- 對現在仍有影響
- 現在仍持續

- I **have owned** the car for over four years.
  這輛車我已經開了四年以上。
  ↳ 用現在完成式表示「現在還擁有這輛車」。

過去簡單式
- 之前做過的動作
- 與現在無關
- 現在不再持續

- I **owned** the car for over four years.
  那輛車我開了四年以上。
  ↳ 用過去式表示「過去曾經擁有，但現在已經不再擁有這輛車」。

常見搭配詞

現在完成式
無確切時間
- ever — **Have** you **ever jumped** off a three-meter diving board?
  你曾經從三公尺高的跳台上跳下來嗎？
- never — I **have never gone** swimming in a river.
  我從未在河裡游泳過。

過去簡單式 — 指出過去時間的詞彙
有確切時間，如：last Saturday、last month 等
- **Did** you **go** to your swimming class **last Saturday**?
  你上星期六有去上游泳課嗎？
- I **went** surfing twice **last month**.
  我上個月衝浪兩次。

若是 when 問句 — 用過去簡單式
- **When did** you **pass** your scuba diving test?
  你什麼時候通過水肺潛水的測驗？

Practice

1 請判斷動詞時態應該是現在完成式還是過去簡單式，將括弧內的動詞以正確時態填入空格中。

Jimmy Jones **1**_____(love) surfing since he was a teenager. He **2**_____(be) to Phuket Island in Thailand six times. On his first visit in 1999, he **3**_____(stay) at a popular beachfront hotel. He **4**_____(go surfing) at all the beaches on the west coast. He really **5**_____(like) the long white sand beaches on that side of the island. Later he **6**_____(discover) cheaper hotels in Phuket City. He **7**_____(rent) a small house in the city for a month on his last trip. He **8**_____(learn) how to drive a motorcycle. He **9**_____(visit) all the beaches along the southern coast. He also **10**_____(enjoy) fishing since he was a kid. He **11**_____(fish) all over Phuket and the outlying islands. He last **12**_____(visit) Phuket in 2010. Since then, he **13**_____(go) to Hawaii for all of his vacations. Recently, however, Jimmy Jones **14**_____(talk) about going back to Phuket one more time.

2 請根據上一題內容，以正確時態完成關於 Jimmy Jones 的問句。

1. Q How long _____ a surfer?
A Since he was a teenager.

2. Q When _____ his first trip to Phuket?
A His first trip was in 1999.

3. Q How many times _____ to Phuket?
A He has been to Phuket six times.

4. Q _____ to Phuket between 1999 and 2010?
A Yes, he did. He went to Phuket between 1999 and 2010.

5. Q _____ at a beachfront hotel in 1999?
A Yes, he did. He stayed at a beachfront hotel in 1999.

6. Q _____ all the beaches on the island since 1999?
A No, he hasn't visited all the beaches.

7. Q _____ Jimmy Jones' last trip to Phuket?
A His last trip was in 2010.

Unit 38,41
重點複習

1 寫出下列動詞的過去式和過去分詞。

1. mail ....

2. date ....

3. buy ....

4. go ....

5. do ....

6. eat ....

7. sing ....

8. write ....

9. drink ....

10. say ....

11. close ....

12. cry ....

13. think ....

14. read ....

15. meet ....

16. put ....

17. hit ....

18. shake ....

19. shut ....

20. ring ....

Unit 38,39
重點複習

2 將括弧內的動詞以過去簡單式完成句子。並分別將句子改寫為否定句及疑問句。

1. I ....(sail) on a friend's boat last weekend.

→ ....

→ ....

2. I ....(watch) the seals on the rocks.

→ ....

→ ....

3. We ....(feed) the seagulls.

→ ....

→ ....

4. The seagull ....(like) the bread we threw to it.

→ ....

→ ....

5. We ....(fish) for our dinner.

→ ....

→ ....

6. My friend ....(cook) our dinner in the galley of the boat.

→ ....

....

→ ....

....

7. We ....(eat) on deck.

→ ....

→ ....

8. We ....(pass) the time chatting and watching the water.

→ ....

....

→ ....

....

❸ 規則動詞的過去式，有 /ɪd/、/d/ 和 /t/ 三種字尾發音，請將框內單字改寫為過去式，並依照字尾發音，填至正確的欄位內。

part	march
play	shine
miss	deposit
push	mend
open	spray
cart	fish

① /d/

② /t/

③ /ɪd/

❹ Catherine 總是日復一日的做著同樣的事情。請閱讀以下文章，並以過去式改寫該文章的內容。

Catherine gets up every morning at 5:00. She takes a shower. Then she makes a cup of strong black coffee. She sits at her computer and checks her email. She answers her email and works on her computer until 7:30. At 7:30, she eats a light breakfast. After breakfast, she goes to work. She walks to work. She buys a cup of coffee and a newspaper on her way to work. She arrives promptly at 8:30 and is ready to start her day at the office.

Catherine got up at 5:00.

5 選出正確的答案。

1. It **snowed/was snowing** when I **went/was going** to bed last night.

2. After I **fell/was falling** asleep, I **had/was having** a dream.

3. We **walked/were walking** to the pet store when we **saw/were seeing** an elephant.

4. When we **saw/were seeing** the elephant, my brother John **said/was saying** he wanted to ride on it.

5. While John was riding the elephant, he **fell/was falling** off.

6. John **broke/was breaking** his glasses when he **fell/was falling** off the elephant.

7. I **fed/was feeding** the elephant when I **heard/was hearing**, "There's Jumbo."

8. When I **woke/was waking** up, I **realized/was realizing** it was only a dream.

9. As I was lying in bed, I **started/was starting** to think about going to the zoo.

6 曼果公司的銷售團隊,正在一項一項核對「應做事項表」,看看他們是否已為這次的貿易展做好了準備。
經理凱莉正在和約翰和喬安這兩名業務員說話。根據圖示,以**現在完成式**和「have . . . yet」的句型,
造問句並做出簡答,並以「they have already . . .」或「they haven't . . . yet」的句型完整描述事實。

1. **Q**　Have they picked up the flyers yet?

   A　Yes, they have. They have already picked up the flyers.

2. **Q**

   A

3. **Q**

   A

4. **Q**

   A

5. **Q**

   A

☑ pick up the flyers
☑ put out order pads
☐ get pens with our company logo
☐ set up the computer
☑ arrange flowers

❼ 回想你曾去過哪些地方度假？在哪一年？請依照範例，用**現在完成式** have been 的句型說出你去過的地方，再用過去式說明年分。

1. _I have been to Tokyo. I went to Tokyo in 2008._

2. _____

3. _____

4. _____

5. _____

6. _____

❽ 將括弧中提示的動詞，以正確的時態完成句子。

1. He _____ (be) sick yesterday, but he is feeling better today.

2. Today is Monday, and Jerry is at the office. Yesterday _____ (be) Sunday, and he _____ (be) at home.

3. Lydia _____ (have) a haircut yesterday, so she has short hair now.

4. Father _____ (buy) a new shirt yesterday, and he is wearing the new shirt today.

5. Sam _____ (sleep) well last night, so he is feeling energetic today.

6. Jill and Winnie _____ (go) to Canada. They are not at home now.

7. Uncle John _____ (keep) his dog for over ten years, but it _____ (die) of old age last month.

8. He _____ (register) for this school last week.

9. **Mom:** _____ you _____ (finish) your homework already?

   Tim: No, I _____ (finish) it yet.

10. She _____ (cook) dinner last night when the phone rang.

11. **Lily:** When _____ (do) you graduate from college?

    Sunny: In 2008.

9 選出正確的答案。

1. .... my new computer for one year.

    Ⓐ I had   Ⓑ I've had

2. .... my old cell phone two days ago.

    Ⓐ I've sold   Ⓑ I sold

3. .... at school last night.

    Ⓐ We've been   Ⓑ We were

4. The TV show .... about 30 minutes ago.

    Ⓐ ended   Ⓑ has ended

5. When did you .... that new hat?

    Ⓐ get   Ⓑ got

6. .... to Greece on vacation?

    Ⓐ Did you go   Ⓑ Did you went

7. Joey has worked in advertising .... ten years.

    Ⓐ for   Ⓑ since

8. Tommy has lived in Mumbai .... 1995.

    Ⓐ since   Ⓑ for

9. .... a painter since 1992.

    Ⓐ I'm   Ⓑ I've been

Unit 45 現在進行式表未來

未來計畫 ── 尤其是 ┬ 時間和地點已確定
└ 不具有正在進行的意味

- He **is going** to a board meeting on Monday.
  他星期一要參加董事會議。
- He **is meeting** with some international customers on Tuesday.
  他星期二要和國外客戶見面。
- He **is flying** to Moscow on Wednesday.
  他星期三要飛去莫斯科。

MOSCOW

- He **is visiting** an old friend in Moscow on Thursday.
  他星期四要去拜訪一位住在莫斯科的老友。
- He**'s returning** on Friday.
  他星期五會回來。

未來意圖 ── • I**'m not waiting** any longer.
我再也不等了。

**現在進行式
表未來**

表示

表示

表示

表示

正要發生的行為 ── • I **am going** for a walk. **Are** you **coming**?
我要去散步，你要來嗎？

詢問未來的狀況 ── • What **are** you **eating** for lunch tomorrow?
你明天午餐要吃什麼？

Practice

❶ 一對夫妻將要去度假。請利用圖片提供的資訊，以「現在進行式」完成問句，並回答問題。

Mark and Sharon

depart from Linz at 15:30

arrive in Budapest at 17:30

take Aeroflot Airlines, Flight 345

MAY
SUN MON TUE WED THU FRI SAT
1 2 3 4 5
6 7 8 9 10 11 12
13 14 15 16 17 18 19
20 21 22 23 24 25 26
27 28 29 30 31

May 18th, 2020

1. Who _____ *is going* _____ on vacation?

  → _Mark and Sharon are going on vacation._

2. When _____ Mark and Sharon _____ on vacation?

  → _____

3. Where _____ they _____ from?

  → _____

4. What time _____ they _____?

  → _____

5. Where _____ they _____ to?

  → _____

6. What time _____ they _____ at their destination?

  → _____

7. What airline _____ they _____?

  → _____

8. What flight _____ they _____?

  → _____

123

Unit 46 be going to 表未來

be going to 表未來

意涵

- 意圖 — • Are you **going to get** a job? 你要去找份工作嗎? JOB SEARCH
  ↳ 找工作的意圖

- 未來的決定 — • We **are going to eat** lunch in a few minutes. 我們馬上就要吃午餐了。
  ↳ 幾分鐘內的決定

- 預測未來即將發生的事 — • Be careful or you**'re going to get** hurt. 小心點,不然你會受傷。
  • It looks like we **are going to get** a visitor this evening.
    看來今晚我們可能會有訪客。

- 無法掌握而可能發生的事 — • It**'s going to rain** at any minute. 隨時會下雨。

be not going to

拒絕未來可能發生的事 — • I'm not **going to drive** you to the shopping mall.
我才不要載你去購物中心。

肯定／否定句型

肯定句全形與縮寫	
I am going to drive	I'm going to drive
you/we/they are going to drive	you're/we're/they're going to drive
he/she/it is going to drive	he's/she's/it's going to drive
否定句全形與縮寫	
I am not going to drive	I'm not going to drive
you/we/they are not going to drive	you're/we're/they're not going to drive
he/she/it is not going to drive	he's/she's/it's not going to drive

疑問／簡答句型

疑問句句型	肯定簡答句型	否定簡答句型
Am I going to drive?	Yes, I am.	No, I'm not.
Are you/we/they going to drive?	Yes, you/we/they are.	No, you/we/they aren't.
Is he/she/it going to drive?	Yes, he/she/it is.	No, he/she/it isn't.

Practice

❶ 請依圖示，對各個疑問句做出簡答，並用完整句子描述正確情況。

1. Is Santa Claus going to use a cell phone?

_____

2. Are the father and son going to buy some toys?

_____

3. Is the girl going to take a nap with her teddy bear?

_____

4. Are the grandparents going to drink some milk?

_____

5. Are the mother and daughter going to buy some toys, too?

_____

6. Is the salesperson going to give the customer a pen?

_____

❷ 依據事實，用 be going to 或 be not going to 描述你今晚會不會做這些事。

Tonight

1. eat at a restaurant

_____

2. watch a baseball game

_____

3. read a book

_____

4. play video games

_____

5. write an email

_____

Unit 47 未來簡單式 will

現在完成式 present perfect　現在式 present
2010　過去式 past　未來式 future　2030

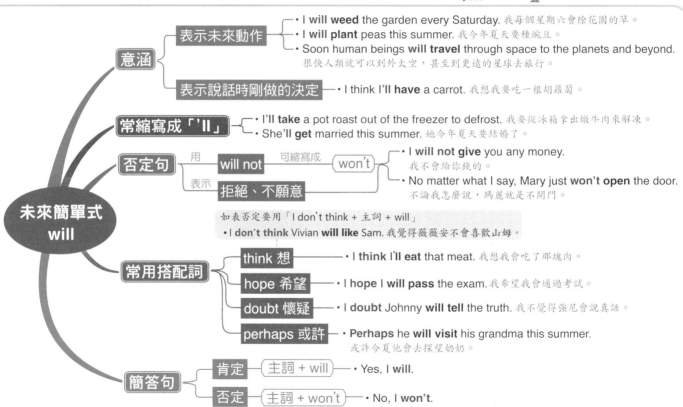

未來簡單式 will

意涵

- 表示未來動作
  - • I **will weed** the garden every Saturday. 我每個星期六會除花園的草。
  - • I **will plant** peas this summer. 我今年夏天要種豌豆。
  - • Soon human beings **will travel** through space to the planets and beyond.
    很快人類就可以到外太空，甚至到更遠的星球去旅行。

- 表示說話時剛做的決定
  - • I think I'll **have** a carrot. 我想我要吃一根胡蘿蔔。

常縮寫成「'll」
- • I'll **take** a pot roast out of the freezer to defrost. 我要從冰箱拿出燉牛肉來解凍。
- • She'll **get** married this summer. 她今年夏天要結婚了。

否定句
- 用 表示
  - will not 可縮寫成 won't
    - • I **will not give** you any money.
      我不會給你錢的。
    - • No matter what I say, Mary just **won't open** the door.
      不論我怎麼說，瑪麗就是不開門。
  - 拒絕、不願意

如表否定要用「I don't think + 主詞 + will」
• I **don't think** Vivian **will like** Sam. 我覺得薇薇安不會喜歡山姆。

常用搭配詞
- think 想 — • I **think** I'll **eat** that meat. 我想我會吃了那塊肉。
- hope 希望 — • I **hope** I **will pass** the exam. 我希望我會通過考試。
- doubt 懷疑 — • I **doubt** Johnny **will tell** the truth. 我不覺得強尼會說真話。
- perhaps 或許 — • **Perhaps** he **will visit** his grandma this summer.
  或許今夏他會去探望奶奶。

簡答句
- 肯定 — 主詞 + will — • Yes, I **will**.
- 否定 — 主詞 + won't — • No, I **won't**.

Practice

❶ 利用題目提供的主詞和動詞片語，以 will 分別造出疑問句、肯定句和否定句。

1. scientist　clone humans in 50 years
→ _Will scientists clone humans in 50 years?_
→ _Scientists will clone humans in 50 years._
→ _Scientists won't clone humans in 50 years._

2. robots　become family members in 80 years
→
→
→

3. doctors　insert memory chips behind our ears
→
→
→

4. police officers　scan our brains for criminal thoughts
→
→
→

❷ 將題目提供的文字，分別以 I think、perhaps 和 I doubt 造句，並視情況使用「'll」的縮寫形式。

1. I　live in another country
→ _I think I'll live in another country._
→ _Perhaps I'll live in another country._
→ _I doubt I'll live in another country._

2. my sister　learn how to drive
→
→
→

3. Jerry　marry somebody from another country
→
→
→

Part 5 未來時態

Unit **48** will、**be going to** 和現在進行式比較

比較：事件決定時間

- I'**ll make** a cup of coffee. 我來泡杯咖啡吧。
  ↳ 臨時做的決定
- I'm **going to make** a cup of coffee. 我要泡杯咖啡。
  ↳ 事先做好的決定

- **事件決定時間**
  - 突然決定的事件 〔will〕
    - I've got a good idea. I'**ll buy** her a baseball cap.
      我想到一個好點子了，我要買個棒球帽給她。
      ↳ 說話時刻做的決定
  - 事先決定的事件 〔be going to〕
    - I'm **going to drive** to the sporting goods store.
      我打算開車去運動用品店。
      ↳ 事前已做的決定
    - I **am going to buy** a present for Mom's birthday.
      我要去買我媽的生日禮物。
      ↳ 事前已做的決定

- **預測**
  - 預測可能會發生的事情 〔will〕
    - That guy looks like a thief. He'**ll steal** your wallet if you're not careful.
      那傢伙看起來像小偷。如果你不小心一點，他會偷走你的錢包。
  - 從目前狀況可立即預見的事情 〔be going to〕
    - Watch out. He **is going to steal** your wallet.
      小心，他打算要偷你的錢包。
    - Amy! You'**re going to crash** into the tree!
      艾美！你快撞到樹了！

- **事件性質**
  - 單純描述未來事件 〔will〕
    - I **will be** in Mexico next week. 我下星期人在墨西哥。
  - 強調意圖 〔be going to〕
    - I'm **going to meet** Mr. Simpson tomorrow night.
      我明天晚上打算與辛普森先生會面。
  - 強調一項安排 〔現在進行式〕
    - I'm **flying** to New York tomorrow morning.
      我明天早上就要飛去紐約。

比較：預測

• She'**ll fall** off the swivel chair. 她可能會從旋轉椅上跌下來。 ↳ 認為可能會發生的事	• She'**s going to fall** off the swivel chair. 她快要從旋轉椅上跌下來了。 ↳ 有徵兆已經可以預見

Practice

❶ 用括弧內提供的詞彙改寫句子。

1. Will you go to the bookstore tomorrow? (be going to)

→ _____

2. Janet will help Cindy move into her new house. (be going to)

→ _____

3. Are you going to play baseball this Saturday? (be + V-ing)

→ _____

4. He is going to cook dinner at 5:30. (will)

→ _____

5. She's going to fall into the water. (will)

→ _____

6. I will give him a call tonight. (be going to)

→ _____

7. When will you get up tomorrow morning? (be going to)

→ _____

8. I'll drive to Costco this afternoon. (be + V-ing)

→ _____

❷ 依提示用適當的動詞形式完成句子。

1. She _____ (leave) for Rome tomorrow. ▶ 安排

2. The ice cream _____ (melt) if you don't finish it soon. ▶ 可能

3. I _____ (quit) tomorrow! ▶ 臨時起意

4. I _____ (quit) next month. I've been admitted to the university. ▶ 事先決定

5. I think I _____ (eat) a sandwich. ▶ 臨時起意

6. Mr. Lee _____ (have) dinner with Mr. Sun on Friday night. ▶ 安排

7. I _____ (find) a good job, and I _____ (make) a lot of money. ▶ 意圖

8. It _____ (rain) tomorrow. ▶ 單純描述未來事件

❶ 根據題目提供的詞彙，以**現在進行式**完成肯定句，並將句子分別改寫為否定句和疑問句。

1. I _____(go) out for lunch tomorrow.

→ _____

→ _____

2. I _____(plan) a birthday party for my grandmother.

→ _____

→ _____

3. She _____(go) to take the dog for a walk after dinner.

→ _____

→ _____

4. Mike _____(plan) to watch a baseball game later tonight.

→ _____

→ _____

5. Dr. Johnson _____(meet) a patient at the clinic on Saturday.

→ _____

→ _____

6. Jack and Kim _____(apply) for admission to a technical college.

→ _____

→ _____

7. I _____(think) about having two kids after I get married.

→ _____

→ _____

Unit 45 重點複習

❷ 下列現在進行式的用法中，哪些是表示「正在進行的動作」？哪些是表示「未來已經計畫好的事」？
將表示正在進行的動作之句子寫上 C（continuous），表示未來計畫之句子寫上 F（future）。

.... **1.** I'm eating out on Saturday night.

.... **2.** Are you watching TV?

.... **3.** Jennifer is making a doll now.

.... **4.** Grandpa is watching a baseball game on TV at the moment.

.... **5.** What are you doing now?

.... **6.** I'm going downtown this Thursday.

.... **7.** He's going on a date with Paula tonight.

.... **8.** We're having dinner with the Smiths now.

Unit 46 重點複習

❸ 將提示的主詞和動詞 以「be going to」的句型完成問句，並依提示以「be going to」的句型回答問題。

1. What _are_ you _going to do_ (do) tomorrow night?

   I'm going to do some shopping tomorrow night. .... (do some shopping)

2. When .... you ....(leave)?

   .... (at 9 a.m.)

3. .... he ....(call) her later?

   .... (yes)

4. What .... you ....(say) when you see him?

   .... (tell him the truth)

5. .... they ....(study) British Literature in college?

   .... (Chinese Literature)

6. .... your family ....(have) a vacation in Hawaii?

   .... (Guam)

4 自 Solutions 中選出適當的片語，用「I think I'll」的句型寫出下列各項問題的解決方案。

Problems

1. I'm tired.
I think I'll take a nap.

2. It's too dark to see.
_____

3. I just missed a phone call.
_____

4. The grapes are ripe.
_____

5. I received my phone bill.
_____

6. It's my dad's birthday.
_____

7. Emma is sick.
_____

8. It's starting to rain.
_____

Solutions

buy him a gift

turn on a light

bring my umbrella

take a nap

visit her in the hospital

pay it at 7-Eleven

check the answering machine

eat them right away

5 判斷下列句子的用法是否正確，正確的請打 ✓，錯誤的請改寫出正確的句子。

1. Karl is working this weekend.

( )

2. I think it's raining soon.

( )

3. Harry is going to the grocery store later tonight.

( )

4. I'm sure you aren't getting called next week.

( )

5. Tina is going to write a screenplay.

( )

6. Is Laura going to working?

( )

7. I'll buy him a new bicycle.

( )

8. In the year 2100, people live on the moon.

( )

9. What are you do next week?

( )

6 選出正確的答案。

1. **Kelly:** What are you going to do today?

Sam: I think _____ my car.

Ⓐ I'll clean   Ⓑ I'm going to clean   Ⓒ I'm cleaning

2. Don't touch that pot. _____ .

Ⓐ You'll get burned   Ⓑ You're going to get burned   Ⓒ You're getting burned

3. **Tom:** It's time to pick up Ellen.

Larry: _____ right now.

Ⓐ I'll leave   Ⓑ I'm going to leave   Ⓒ I will be leaving

4. I have an idea for Janie's graduation present. I think _____ a briefcase for her.   .

Ⓐ I'll buy   Ⓑ I'm going to buy   Ⓒ I'm buying

❼ 將下列句子改寫為否定句和疑問句。

1. I'll be watching the game on Saturday afternoon.

→ I won't be watching the game on Saturday afternoon.

→ Will I be watching the game on Saturday afternoon?

2. You're going to visit Grandma Moses tomorrow.

→

→

3. She's planning to be on vacation next week.

→

→

4. We're going to take a trip to New Zealand next month.

→

→

5. He'll send the tax forms soon.

→

→

6. It'll be cold all next week.

→

→

❽ 判斷下列句子的未來形式屬於何種用法，選出正確答案。

........**1.** I'm thirsty. I'll get a drink.

  Ⓐ Sudden decision   Ⓑ Predictable future   Ⓒ Intention

........**2.** It will be winter soon.

  Ⓐ Simple future   Ⓑ Possibility   Ⓒ Plan in advance

........**3.** Be careful, or you will trip over a rock.

  Ⓐ Sudden decision   Ⓑ Possibility   Ⓒ Simple future

........**4.** There're only ten seconds left. We're going to lose the game.

  Ⓐ Simple future   Ⓑ Plan in advance   Ⓒ Predictable future

........**5.** I'm going to teach him a lesson.

  Ⓐ Intention   Ⓑ Simple future   Ⓒ Sudden decision

........**6.** All my friends will come to my birthday party.

  Ⓐ Predictable future   Ⓑ Simple future   Ⓒ Intention

........**7.** I'm going to buy a new car.

  Ⓐ Simple future   Ⓑ Intention   Ⓒ Sudden decision

........**8.** I'm visiting Mrs. Jones this afternoon.

  Ⓐ Fixed arrangement   Ⓑ Predictable future   Ⓒ Simple future

........**9.** Someone is knocking on the door. I'll see who it is.

  Ⓐ Intention   Ⓑ Possibility   Ⓒ Sudden decision

........**10.** The sky is dark. It's going to rain.

  Ⓐ Predictable future   Ⓑ Intention   Ⓒ Plan in advance

........**11.** I'm taking my dog to the vet on Saturday, so I can't go cycling with you.

  Ⓐ Sudden decision   Ⓑ Simple future   Ⓒ Fixed arrangement

........**12.** We will probably go to Greece for our honeymoon.

  Ⓐ Sudden decision   Ⓑ Possibility   Ⓒ Plan in advance

Unit 50 不定詞（1）

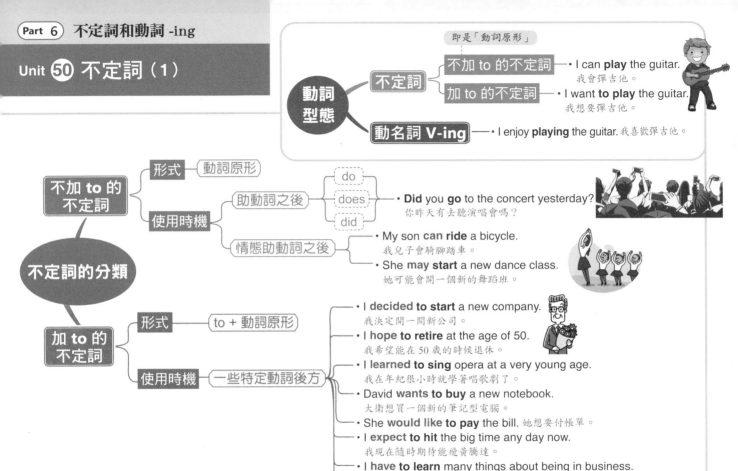

即是「動詞原形」

動詞型態 ─┬─ 不定詞 ─┬─ 不加 to 的不定詞 ── • I can **play** the guitar. 我會彈吉他。
          │   └─ 加 to 的不定詞 ── • I want **to play** the guitar. 我想要彈吉他。
          └─ 動名詞 V-ing ── • I enjoy **playing** the guitar. 我喜歡彈吉他。

不定詞的分類

不加 to 的不定詞 ─┬─ 形式 ── 動詞原形
                │
                └─ 使用時機 ─┬─ 助動詞之後 ── do / does / did ── • **Did** you **go** to the concert yesterday? 你昨天有去聽演唱會嗎？
                            │
                            └─ 情態助動詞之後 ── • My son **can ride** a bicycle. 我兒子會騎腳踏車。
                                                • She **may start** a new dance class. 她可能會開一個新的舞蹈班。

加 to 的不定詞 ─┬─ 形式 ── to + 動詞原形
              │
              └─ 使用時機 ── 一些特定動詞後方

• I **decided to start** a new company.
  我決定開一間新公司。
• I **hope to retire** at the age of 50.
  我希望能在 50 歲的時候退休。
• I **learned to sing** opera at a very young age.
  我在年紀很小時就學著唱歌劇了。
• David **wants to buy** a new notebook.
  大衛想買一個新的筆記型電腦。
• She **would like to pay** the bill. 她想要付帳單。
• I **expect to hit** the big time any day now.
  我現在隨時期待能飛黃騰達。
• I **have to learn** many things about being in business.
  關於生意方面的事，我有很多要學的。
• I **promise to remember** you when I'm rich and famous.
  我答應你，在我功成名就之後，還是會記得你。

Practice

❶ 將括弧內的動詞以正確的形式填空。

1. I may _____(watch) a football game this weekend.
2. I learned _____(play) baseball last summer.
3. I can't _____(fly) a kite.
4. He promised _____(give) me a call when he arrives in London.

5. Did you _____(hear) what she said?
6. I can _____(play) baseball.
7. I will _____(go) on an outing tomorrow.
8. I promise _____(be) a good guy.
9. I want _____(meet) your parents.

❷ 依據圖示，自框內選出適當的動詞片語，以正確的形式填空。

| pay the bill | look very happy | buy some red peppers | work 10 hours a day |
| quit drinking and smoking | wear clothes | make good coffee | |

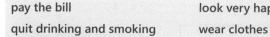

1. Help Joe decide _____.

2. Ms. Jones can _____.

3. Little Kuku does not _____.
   Maybe he doesn't want _____.

4. Jennifer has _____.

5. She would like _____.

137

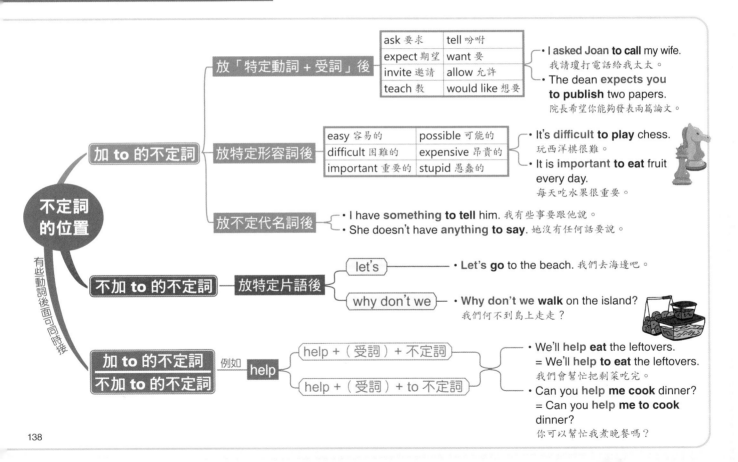

不定詞的位置

有些動詞後面可同時接

加 to 的不定詞

放「特定動詞 + 受詞」後

ask 要求	tell 吩咐
expect 期望	want 要
invite 邀請	allow 允許
teach 教	would like 想要

- I asked Joan **to call** my wife. 我請瓊打電話給我太太。
- The dean **expects you to publish** two papers. 院長希望你能夠發表兩篇論文。

放特定形容詞後

easy 容易的	possible 可能的
difficult 困難的	expensive 昂貴的
important 重要的	stupid 愚蠢的

- It's **difficult to play** chess. 玩西洋棋很難。
- It is **important to eat** fruit every day. 每天吃水果很重要。

放不定代名詞後

- I have **something to tell** him. 我有些事要跟他說。
- She doesn't have **anything to say**. 她沒有任何話要說。

不加 to 的不定詞

放特定片語後

let's

- **Let's go** to the beach. 我們去海邊吧。

why don't we

- **Why don't we walk** on the island? 我們何不到島上走走？

加 to 的不定詞 / 不加 to 的不定詞

例如 help

help +（受詞）+ 不定詞

help +（受詞）+ to 不定詞

- We'll **help eat** the leftovers. = We'll **help to eat** the leftovers. 我們會幫忙把剩菜吃完。
- Can you **help me cook** dinner? = Can you **help me to cook** dinner? 你可以幫忙我煮晚餐嗎？

Practice

❶ 請填入正確的動詞形態，有些動詞有二種正確的型態。

1. I want you _____(finish) cleaning the house in thirty minutes.

2. Let's _____(go) out to dinner.

3. Why don't we _____(sit) on the sofa?

4. Please teach me _____(fly) your airplane.

5. Let's invite your sister _____(join) the party.

6. I want you _____(call) her right now.

7. Would you like me _____(call) her for you?

8. Can I help you _____(make) some more phone calls?

❷ 依據圖示，自框內選出適當的詞彙，以正確的動詞型態填空。

make a cake	get the sausage on the plate
climb a wall	study for the exam
take a look at your answers	eat on a train

Is it possible _____ _____?

Let me _____ _____.

It's stupid _____ _____.

Am I allowed _____ _____?

It's easy _____ _____.

I'm too tired _____ _____.

139

Unit 52 動詞 -ing

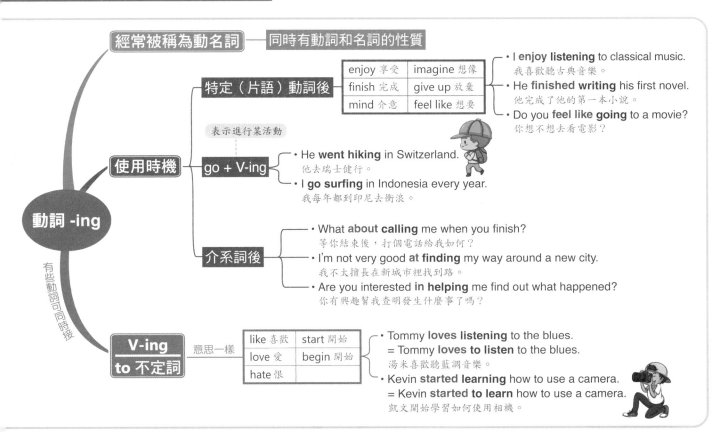

經常被稱為動名詞 —— 同時有動詞和名詞的性質

特定（片語）動詞後

enjoy 享受	imagine 想像
finish 完成	give up 放棄
mind 介意	feel like 想要

- I **enjoy listening** to classical music.
  我喜歡聽古典音樂。
- He **finished writing** his first novel.
  他完成了他的第一本小說。
- Do you **feel like going** to a movie?
  你想不想去看電影？

動詞 -ing

使用時機

表示進行某活動

go + V-ing

- He **went hiking** in Switzerland.
  他去瑞士健行。
- I **go surfing** in Indonesia every year.
  我每年都到印尼去衝浪。

介系詞後

- What **about calling** me when you finish?
  等你結束後，打個電話給我如何？
- I'm not very good **at finding** my way around a new city.
  我不太擅長在新城市裡找到路。
- Are you interested **in helping** me find out what happened?
  你有興趣幫我查明發生什麼事了嗎？

有些動詞可同時接

V-ing
to 不定詞

意思一樣

like 喜歡	start 開始
love 愛	begin 開始
hate 恨	

- Tommy **loves listening** to the blues.
  = Tommy **loves to listen** to the blues.
  湯米喜歡聽藍調音樂。
- Kevin **started learning** how to use a camera.
  = Kevin **started to learn** how to use a camera.
  凱文開始學習如何使用相機。

Practice

❶ 依據圖示，自框內選出適當的動詞，以 **V-ing** 的形式填空。

| play soccer | be high up on a tree | blow bubbles |
| sing a song | bike | make clothes |

 **1** He is good at
_____.

 **2** She is interested in
_____.

 **3** She loves
_____.

 4 He feels like
_____.

 **5** He enjoys _____
_____.

 **6** She went _____
with her friend yesterday.

❷ 請填入正確的動詞形態，有些動詞有兩種正確的形態。

1. Can I help you _____(call) your family?

2. It's possible _____(avoid) spending a lot of money.

3. I feel like _____(drink) a Coke now.

4. I hate _____(get up) early in the morning.

5. I'm not good at _____(swim).

6. Do you mind _____(share) the table with this lady?

7. How about _____(go) to Hong Kong with me?

8. He can't imagine _____(live) a life without her.

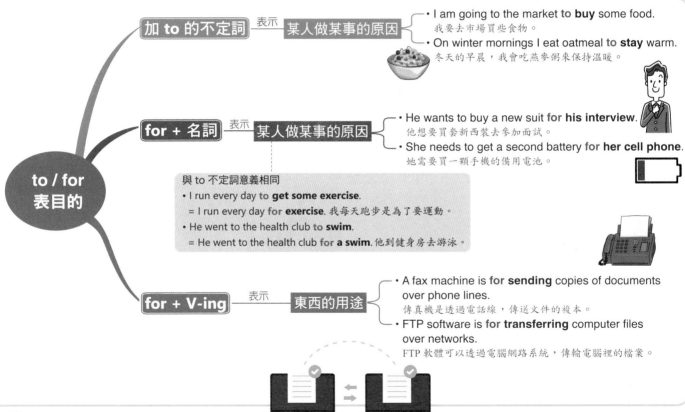

加 **to** 的不定詞 —— 表示 —— 某人做某事的原因

- I am going to the market **to buy** some food.
  我要去市場買些食物。
- On winter mornings I eat oatmeal **to stay** warm.
  冬天的早晨，我會吃燕麥粥來保持溫暖。

to / for 表目的

for + 名詞 —— 表示 —— 某人做某事的原因

- He wants to buy a new suit **for his interview**.
  他想要買套新西裝去參加面試。
- She needs to get a second battery **for her cell phone**.
  她需要買一顆手機的備用電池。

與 to 不定詞意義相同
- I run every day **to get some exercise**.
  = I run every day **for exercise**. 我每天跑步是為了要運動。
- He went to the health club **to swim**.
  = He went to the health club **for a swim**. 他到健身房去游泳。

for + **V-ing** —— 表示 —— 東西的用途

- A fax machine is **for sending** copies of documents over phone lines.
  傳真機是透過電話線，傳送文件的複本。
- FTP software is **for transferring** computer files over networks.
  FTP 軟體可以透過電腦網路系統，傳輸電腦裡的檔案。

Practice

❶ 自框內選出適當的詞彙來搭配題目地點，並正確選用「加 to 的不定詞」或「for + 名詞」的句型填空。

| fun | look at paintings | see the animals | see artifacts | borrow books | see the fish |

a library

1. You go to *a library to borrow books* ....

an art gallery

4. You go to ....
....

a history museum

2. You go to ....
....

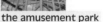
the amusement park

5. You go to ....
....

the aquarium

3. You go to ....
....

a zoo

6. You go to ....
....

❷ 自框內選出適當的動詞，用「for + V-ing」的形式說明下列交通工具的用途。

| tow cars and trucks | put out fires |
| take the wounded to the hospital | carry liquid cement （水泥） |

1. A cement truck is a vehicle
....

3. A tow truck is a vehicle
....

2. A fire truck is a vehicle
....

4. An ambulance is a vehicle
....

① 將提示動詞以正確動詞型態填空。

surf

1. I can _____ near my home in California.

2. I learned _____ during high school.

3. I love _____ and I go _____ every weekend.

ski

4. I might _____ this weekend.

5. I want _____ on Saturday afternoon.

6. We often go _____ on Mount Killington.

7. Let's _____ for a while.

drive

8. I'll help _____ if you get tired.

9. How about _____ into the city tomorrow?

10. It's easy _____ on the highway.

② 將下列句子以「加 **to** 的不定詞」或「**for** + 名詞」互相改寫。

1. My parents went out to walk.

→ *My parents went out for a walk.*

2. Mr. Lyle went to the front desk to pick up his package.

→ _____

3. I have to get everything ready to attend the meeting.

→ _____

4. I jog every day for my health.

→ _____

5. I walked into the McDonald's on Tenth Street for two cheeseburgers.

→ _____

❸ 選出正確的答案。

1. Do you enjoy _____ in cold water?
   Ⓐ swim　　Ⓑ to swim　　Ⓒ swimming

2. I don't _____ coffee at night.
   Ⓐ drink　　Ⓑ to drink　　Ⓒ drinking

3. Clive hopes _____ promoted in six months.
   Ⓐ get　　Ⓑ to get　　Ⓒ getting

4. Why don't we _____ the baseball game on channel 74?
   Ⓐ watch　　Ⓑ to watch　　Ⓒ watching

5. How about _____ a trip to France?
   Ⓐ take　　Ⓑ to take　　Ⓒ taking

6. Can you help me _____ the dishes?
   Ⓐ did　　Ⓑ to do　　Ⓒ doing

7. Do you mind _____ for fifteen minutes?
   Ⓐ wait　　Ⓑ to wait　　Ⓒ waiting

8. My father taught me _____ tennis when I was eight.
   Ⓐ play　　Ⓑ to play　　Ⓒ playing

9. He is depressed and wants to give up _____ to college.
   Ⓐ go　　Ⓑ to go　　Ⓒ going

10. Jessie told me _____ the secret.
    Ⓐ keep　　Ⓑ to keep　　Ⓒ keeping

11. It's difficult _____ Russian.
    Ⓐ learn　　Ⓑ to learn　　Ⓒ learning

12. I have nothing _____ at the moment.
    Ⓐ say　　Ⓑ to say　　Ⓒ saying

13. I would like you _____ the car on Monday.
    Ⓐ return　　Ⓑ to return　　Ⓒ returning

14. Do you want me _____ the window?
    Ⓐ open　　Ⓑ to open　　Ⓒ opening

15. Are you interested in _____ horror movies?
    Ⓐ watch　　Ⓑ to watch　　Ⓒ watching

④ 將右欄的詞彙與左欄的地點搭配，並正確選用「加 to 的不定詞」或「for + 名詞」的句型填空。

the beach

1. They went to _the beach to get some sun_.

get some sun

the water

2. The dog jumped into _____.

get the stick

the supermarket

3. They walked into _____.

some milk

the opera house

4. They went to _____.

a concert

the store

5. They went to _____.

buy a gift

the Starbucks

6. She went to _____.

a cup of latté

the stadium

7. Andy went to ....

....

watch a baseball game

the market

8. They went to ....

....

buy some pumpkins

Unit 50–53 重點複習

❺ 將錯誤的句子打 ✗，並寫出正確的句子。若句子無誤，則在括弧內打 ✓。

1. I might play basketball tonight.

( ) ....

2. I should to visit my sister.

( ) ....

3. Let's to go to the movies.

( ) ....

4. I'll help make dinner.

( ) ....

5. I'll help to make dinner.

( ) ....

6. I want you call me next week.

( ) ....

7. Would you like that me to call you next week?

( ) ....

8. Thank you for paying your rent on time.

( ) ....

9. Most people love to going on a vacation.

( ) ....

10. Ernie hates to eat liver and onions.

( ) ....

11. Kelly went to see the doctor for to have a checkup.

( ) ....

12. Kim went to the shop for some fresh sausages.

( ) ....

①
- My father used to **go fishing** with my uncle on the weekends.
  我父親過去經常在週末和我叔叔去釣魚。
- I'm **going shopping** with Lucy this Saturday.
  這個星期六，我要跟露西去逛街。

go 用法

從事某種活動

go + V-ing

go fishing 去釣魚	**go** camping 去露營
go shopping 去購物	**go** mountain climbing 去爬山
go jogging 去慢跑	**go** hiking 去健行

go for + 名詞

go for a walk 去散步
go for a swim 去游泳
go for a ride 去兜風
go for a jog 去慢跑

- Would you like to **go for a walk**?
  你想不想去散步？
- Liz and John **go for a swim** every Sunday.
  麗茲和約翰每週日都去游泳。

go on + 名詞

go on a trip 去旅行
go on (a) vacation 去度假
go on a picnic 去野餐

- Sam **went on a trip** to New Zealand by himself for two weeks.
  山姆獨自前往紐西蘭旅行了兩個禮拜。

go for
go on

| go for | 強調 go 的目的 |
| go on | 強調活動本身 |

- Who wants to **go for a picnic**?
  = Who wants to **go on a picnic**? 誰想去野餐？

變成某種狀態 — **go + 形容詞**

- Everything **went wrong**! I don't know what to do. 什麼事都不對了！我不知道該怎麼辦。
- The milk **has gone sour**. Don't drink it. 牛奶酸掉了，不要喝了。

常用片語

go crazy 發瘋
go bad 腐壞
go by 時間過去
go on 發生
go Dutch 各自付帳

- I'm **going crazy** with this project. 這個案子真是令我抓狂。
- Tofu **goes bad** easily if you don't put it in the refrigerator.
  如果你不把豆腐放進冰箱，它很容易就會壞掉。
- His memories of the old days faded as time **went by**.
  隨著時光流逝，他的往日回憶也逐漸模糊。
- What's **going on**? 發生什麼事了？
- Let's **go Dutch**. 我們各付各的吧。

Practice

❶ 依據圖示，自框中選出正確的動詞，寫出「go + V-ing」的句型。

bowl

skate

ski

camp

sail

swim

go bowling

❷ 自框內選出適當的詞彙，以正確的形式填空。

1. The leftover soup .... bad. Don't eat it.

2. The weather is good. Let's .... a ride.

3. Seven years .... since his wife died, and he still strongly misses her.

4. There's too much homework. I'm .... crazy.

5. How about .... a jog tomorrow morning?

6. Philip and Linda .... a vacation in Belgium last month.

7. Tony .... boating with his brother yesterday.

go

go on

go for

go by

Unit 56 get / take 用法

① · Please **get somebody to fix** the toilet. 請找個人來修理馬桶

② · I'll **get everything done** as soon as possible. 我會盡快把所有的事情辦好。

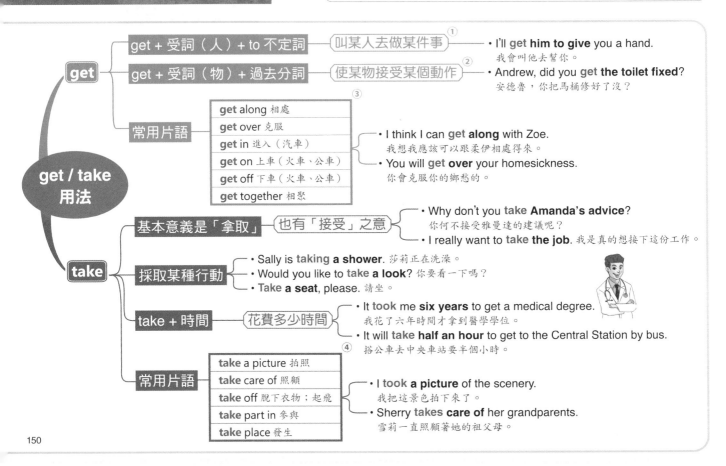

get / take 用法

get

- get + 受詞（人）+ to 不定詞 — ① 叫某人去做某件事 — · I'll **get him to give** you a hand.
  我會叫他去幫你。
- get + 受詞（物）+ 過去分詞 — ② 使某物接受某個動作 — · Andrew, did you **get the toilet fixed**?
  安德魯，你把馬桶修好了沒？

常用片語 ③

| get along 相處 |
| get over 克服 |
| get in 進入（汽車）|
| get on 上車（火車、公車）|
| get off 下車（火車、公車）|
| get together 相聚 |

- · I think I can **get along** with Zoe.
  我想我應該可以跟柔伊相處得來。
- · You will **get over** your homesickness.
  你會克服你的鄉愁的。

take

基本意義是「拿取」 — 也有「接受」之意
- · Why don't you **take Amanda's advice**?
  你何不接受雅曼達的建議呢？
- · I really want to **take the job**. 我是真的想接下這份工作。

採取某種行動
- · Sally is **taking a shower**. 莎莉正在洗澡。
- · Would you like to **take a look**? 你要看一下嗎？
- · **Take a seat**, please. 請坐。

take + 時間 — 花費多少時間
- · It **took** me **six years** to get a medical degree.
  我花了六年時間才拿到醫學學位。
- · It will **take half an hour** to get to the Central Station by bus. ④
  搭公車去中央車站要半個小時。

常用片語

| take a picture 拍照 |
| take care of 照顧 |
| take off 脫下衣物；起飛 |
| take part in 參與 |
| take place 發生 |

- · I **took a picture** of the scenery.
  我把這景色拍下來了。
- · Sherry **takes care of** her grandparents.
  雪莉一直照顧著她的祖父母。

(3)

- **get in** 上車
  Get in the car now.
  快上車。

- **get on** 上車
  You can **get on** a No. 16 bus at the bus stop two blocks away.
  你可以在兩個路口之後的公車站搭 16 路公車。

- **get off** 下車
  Get off the train at the Central Station.
  在中央車站就要下車。

- **get together** 相聚
  Ben and Tommy **get together** twice a month.
  班和湯米每個月要聚會兩次。

(4)

- **take off** 脫下
  Please **take off** your shoes before entering the house.
  進屋子前請先脫鞋。
  Our flight will **take off** in thirty minutes.
  我們的班機將在 30 分鐘後起飛。

- **take part in** 參與
  Will you **take part in** the basketball game?
  你會參加這場籃球賽嗎？

- **take place** 發生
  The accident **took place** in the middle of the night.
  這場意外於夜半發生。

Practice

❶ 將括弧內的動詞以正確的形式填空。

1. Marty, will you get Sam _____ (finish) his dinner?
2. I can't get my students _____ (listen) to me. I'm so upset.
3. I'll get my hair _____ (cut) tonight.
4. Are you going to get your car _____ (wash) tomorrow?

❷ 哪些名詞經常搭配 take 組成固定片語？請在框內打 ✓。

take _____

☐ a walk ☐ a sleep ✓ a shower ☐ a nap ☐ a jog ☐ a look

❸ 選出正確的答案。

1. **Get on/Get in** the bus here, and **get out/get off** at the fifth stop.
2. It **got/took** me five hours to finish this report.
3. Let's work together and **get over/get away** this problem.
4. **Get off/Take off** your dirty clothes and throw them in the laundry basket.
5. We're eager to **get part in/take part in** this reconstruction project.

Unit 57 do / make 用法

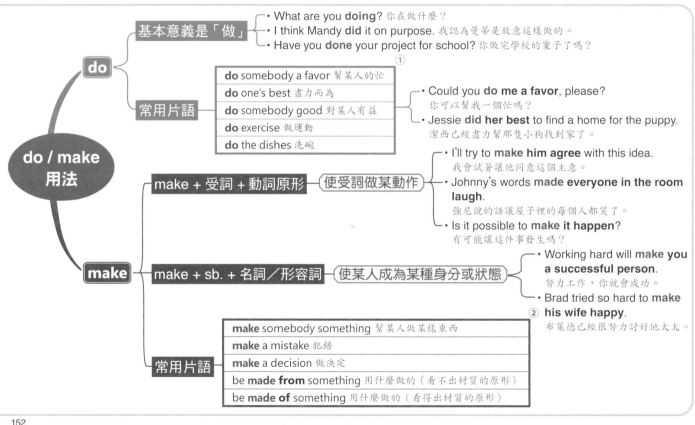

do / make 用法

do

基本意義是「做」
- What are you **doing**? 你在做什麼？
- I think Mandy **did** it on purpose. 我認為曼蒂是故意這樣做的。
- Have you **done** your project for school? 你做完學校的案子了嗎？
  ①

常用片語

| **do** somebody a favor 幫某人的忙 |
| **do** one's best 盡力而為 |
| **do** somebody good 對某人有益 |
| **do** exercise 做運動 |
| **do** the dishes 洗碗 |

- Could you **do me a favor**, please?
  你可以幫我一個忙嗎？
- Jessie **did her best** to find a home for the puppy.
  潔西已經盡力幫那隻小狗找到家了。

make

make + 受詞 + 動詞原形 —— 使受詞做某動作
- I'll try to **make him agree** with this idea.
  我會試著讓他同意這個主意。
- Johnny's words made **everyone in the room laugh**.
  強尼說的話讓屋子裡的每個人都笑了。
- Is it possible to **make it happen**?
  有可能讓這件事發生嗎？

make + sb. + 名詞／形容詞 —— 使某人成為某種身分或狀態
- Working hard will **make you a successful person**.
  努力工作，你就會成功。
- Brad tried so hard to **make his wife happy**.
  ② 布萊德已經很努力討好他太太。

常用片語

| **make** somebody something 幫某人做某樣東西 |
| **make** a mistake 犯錯 |
| **make** a decision 做決定 |
| be **made from** something 用什麼做的（看不出材質的原形） |
| be **made of** something 用什麼做的（看得出材質的原形） |

①
- **do somebody good** 對某人有益
  Try to eat some fruit. It'll **do you good**.
  吃點水果吧，那對身體好。
- **do exercise** 做運動
  My grandfather **does exercise** every morning.
  我爺爺每天早上做運動。
- **do the dishes** 洗碗
  Andy, will you **do the dishes** tonight?
  安迪，今晚你洗碗好嗎？

②
- **making somebody something** 幫某人做某樣東西
  I'm **making my sister a wedding dress**.
  我在幫我姊姊做一件結婚禮服。
- **make a mistake** 犯錯
  Don't blame yourself too much. Everyone **makes mistakes**.
  別太自責了，人人都會犯錯。
- **make a decision** 做決定
  You have to **make the decision** right now.
  你現在就必須做出決定。
- **be made from something** 用什麼做的（看不出材質的原形）
  Paper **is made from** wood.
  紙是用木材做的。

- **be made of something** 用什麼做的（看得出材質的原形）
  This table **is made of** wood.
  這張桌子是木製的。

Practice

❶ 自框內選出適當的詞彙，搭配 do 或 make 填空。

a wish	a favor	a mistake	his best

1. Johnny, will you do me _____ by helping me move this box away, please?
2. He made _____ by sending the package to the wrong person.
3. Don't blame him. He has already done _____.
4. After everyone sang Happy Birthday, she made _____ and blew out the candles.

❷ 選出正確的答案。

1. Amy, can you **do/make** the dishes right now?

2. Years of practice has **done/made** him a good snowboard player.

3. Does Kim **do/make** exercise every morning?

4. Cheese is **made of/made from** milk.

5. Reading every day will do you **good/well**.

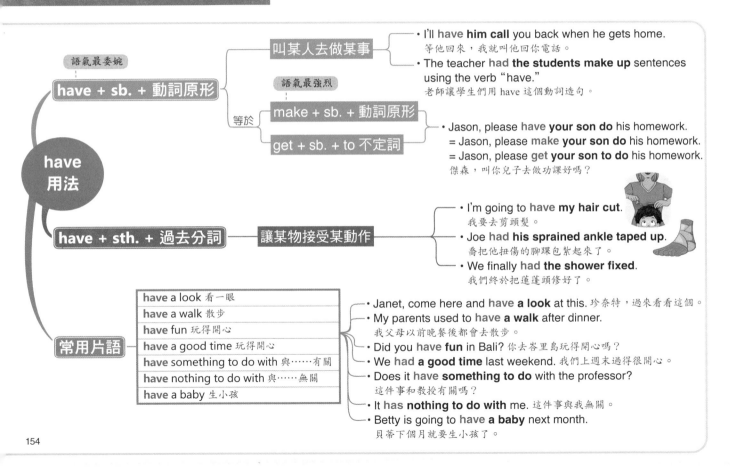

have 用法

have + sb. + 動詞原形 (語氣最委婉)

叫某人去做某事

- I'll **have him call** you back when he gets home.
  等他回來，我就叫他回你電話。
- The teacher **had the students make up** sentences using the verb "have."
  老師讓學生們用 have 這個動詞造句。

等於 (語氣最強烈)

make + sb. + 動詞原形

get + sb. + to 不定詞

- Jason, please **have your son do** his homework.
  = Jason, please **make your son do** his homework.
  = Jason, please **get your son to do** his homework.
  傑森，叫你兒子去做功課好嗎？

have + sth. + 過去分詞

讓某物接受某動作

- I'm going to **have my hair cut**.
  我要去剪頭髮。
- Joe **had his sprained ankle taped up**.
  喬把他扭傷的腳踝包紮起來了。
- We finally **had the shower fixed**.
  我們終於把蓮蓬頭修好了。

常用片語

have a look 看一眼	
have a walk 散步	
have fun 玩得開心	
have a good time 玩得開心	
have something to do with 與……有關	
have nothing to do with 與……無關	
have a baby 生小孩	

- Janet, come here and **have a look** at this. 珍奈特，過來看看這個。
- My parents used to **have a walk** after dinner.
  我父母以前晚餐後都會去散步。
- Did you **have fun** in Bali? 你去峇里島玩得開心嗎？
- We **had a good time** last weekend. 我們上週末過得很開心。
- Does it **have something to do** with the professor?
  這件事和教授有關嗎？
- It **has nothing to do with** me. 這件事與我無關。
- Betty is going to **have a baby** next month.
  貝蒂下個月就要生小孩了。

Practice

❶ 將下列句子以「have + sb. + 動詞原形」或「have + sth. + 過去分詞」的形式改寫。

1. He shortened the pants.

→ ....

2. Yvonne got her son to mop the floor.

→ ....

3. She washed the car.

→ ....

4. She asked her husband to replace the light bulb.

→ ....

5. He folded the paper.

→ ....

6. She packed the box with the books and sent it to the professor.

→ ....

7. He made his students read thirty pages of the book a day.

→ ....

8. I'm going to wrap this gift.

→ ....

❷ 自框內選出正確的片語，填空完成句子。

1. When are you going to .... ?

2. Does it .... Jeff? I saw him leaving the building yesterday.

3. No, it .... Jeff. The police suspect someone else.

4. Can I .... at your new cell phone?

5. Did you .... on your last trip to New Zealand?

6. I'm thinking about .... tomorrow.

have a look
have a good time
have your baby
have a haircut
have something to do with
have nothing to do with

1 選出正確的答案。

1. George and Lulu _____ shopping yesterday.
   Ⓐ went   Ⓑ did   Ⓒ made

2. It will _____ 45 minutes to get to the airport.
   Ⓐ have   Ⓑ get   Ⓒ take

3. You should _____ your fear of water.
   Ⓐ get over   Ⓑ get alone   Ⓒ get off

4. Would you like to _____ a swim this afternoon?
   Ⓐ go   Ⓑ go for   Ⓒ go on

5. The festival will _____ in Shanghai next month.
   Ⓐ take place   Ⓑ get together   Ⓒ have fun

6. I'll _____ your advice and give it another try.
   Ⓐ get   Ⓑ take   Ⓒ have

7. The plane is going to _____ in fifteen minutes.
   Please fasten your seatbelts.
   Ⓐ take place   Ⓑ take off   Ⓒ take over

8. Father _____ a business trip to Hong Kong.
   Ⓐ has made   Ⓑ has gone for   Ⓒ has gone on

9. Why don't you _____ his job offer?
   Ⓐ do   Ⓑ make   Ⓒ take

10. What's _____ here?
    Ⓐ going on
    Ⓑ getting on
    Ⓒ taking off

11. The teacher wants us to _____.
    Ⓐ do a favor
    Ⓑ do our good
    Ⓒ do our best

12. He is a weird guy. I can't _____ with him at all.
    Ⓐ get over
    Ⓑ get together
    Ⓒ get along

13. The shirt is _____ 100% cotton.
    Ⓐ made of
    Ⓑ made from
    Ⓒ made on

14. This matter _____ Jenny.
    Ⓐ doesn't have something to do with
    Ⓑ has anything to do with
    Ⓒ has nothing to do with

❷ 看圖自框內選出正確的片語，以正確的形式填空。

is made of	is made from	go for	go on
get along	get over	take part in	take place

1. Cheese .... milk.

2. My parents and I .... a walk this afternoon.

3. Lucky and Puffy cannot .... with each other.

4. Jessica .... the play last week.

5. My family decided to .... a vacation in Europe.

6. The music festival .... in August, 2020.

7. .... your fear and try parachuting.

8. This vase .... glass.

3 將括弧內的動詞以正確形式填空。

1. My brother made me _____ (finish) all the leftovers on the table.

2. Could you please get somebody _____ (change) the sheets and pillowcases?

3. Will you have everything _____ (finish) in twenty minutes?

4. Father had me _____ (clean) the bathroom on Sunday.

5. I'll have David _____ (apologize) to you.

6. The boss had everyone _____ (work) overtime last weekend.

7. I just want to get things _____ (do) as soon as possible.

8. Jason had his house _____ (paint).

9. Please get someone _____ (remove) the stain on the wall.

10. I'll have him _____ (explain) to you in person.

11. I'll get my bicycle _____ (repair) tomorrow.

4 在問句的空格內填上正確的動詞，並依據事實，用完整的句子回答問題。

1. Did you _____ your hair cut last week?

→ _____

2. Do you have to _____ a lot of homework tonight?

→ _____

3. Does your family _____ on a picnic every weekend?

→ _____

4. Do you like to _____ pictures of dogs and cats?

→ _____

5. Do you _____ care of your little sister when your parents are out?

→ _____

6. Do you like to _____ camping on your summer vacation?

→ _____

7. Do you _____ a shower in the morning?

→ _____

8. Do you _____ crazy with your homework every day?

→ _____

9. Do you _____ a lot of mistakes?

→ _____

10. Have you ever _____ the dentist fill a cavity?

→ _____

Unit 56–57 重點複習

5 將下列圖中所代表的名詞，依據其前面該用的動詞，填到正確的框內。

do

exercise

a nap

exercise

friends

take

the laundry

a bath

a wish

make

a break

money

the shopping

159

Unit 60 can 用法

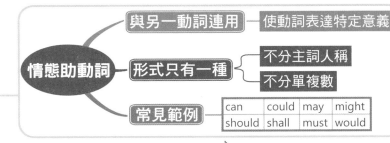

情態助動詞 ─── 與另一動詞連用 ── 使動詞表達特定意義

情態助動詞 ─── 形式只有一種 ── 不分主詞人稱 / 不分單複數

常見範例

can	could	may	might
should	shall	must	would

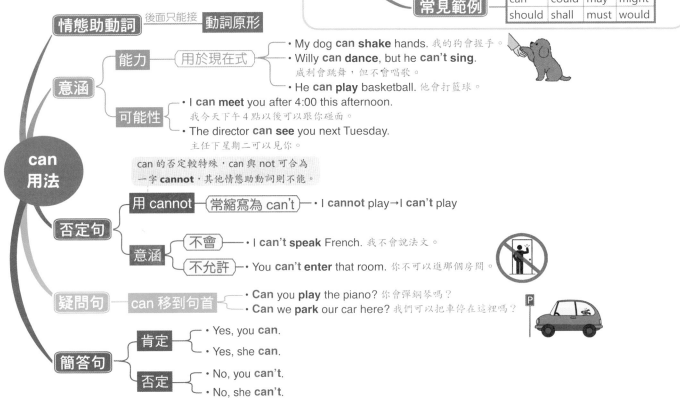

can 用法

情態助動詞 ─ 後面只能接 ─ 動詞原形

意涵
- 能力 ─ 用於現在式
  - My dog **can shake** hands. 我的狗會握手。
  - Willy **can dance**, but he **can't sing**. 威利會跳舞,但不會唱歌。
  - He **can play** basketball. 他會打籃球。
- 可能性
  - I **can meet** you after 4:00 this afternoon. 我今天下午4點以後可以跟你碰面。
  - The director **can see** you next Tuesday. 主任下星期二可以見你。

can 的否定較特殊,can 與 not 可合為一字 **cannot**,其他情態助動詞則不能。

否定句
- 用 cannot ─ 常縮寫為 can't ─ I **cannot** play→I **can't** play
- 意涵
  - 不會 ─ I **can't speak** French. 我不會說法文。
  - 不允許 ─ You **can't enter** that room. 你不可以進那個房間。

疑問句 ─ can 移到句首
- **Can** you **play** the piano? 你會彈鋼琴嗎?
- **Can** we **park** our car here? 我們可以把車停在這裡嗎?

簡答句
- 肯定
  - Yes, you **can**.
  - Yes, she **can**.
- 否定
  - No, you **can't**.
  - No, she **can't**.

Practice

1 在各個圖示中，**Y** 表示 Chris 會演奏這種樂器，**N** 表示他不會。
用 can 或 can't 造句，描述 Chris 會的樂器和不會的樂器。框內有提示的樂器名稱。

flute
violin
guitar
piano
drums

1. *Chris can play the guitar.*

2. _____

3. _____

4. _____

5. _____

6. _____

2 依據事實，用 can 或 can't 回答問題。

1. Can you speak English?

→ *Yes, I can. I can speak English.*

2. Can you read German?

→ _____

3. Can you hang out with your friends on the weekend?

→ _____

4. Can you run very fast?

→ _____

5. Can your mother cook Mexican food?

→ _____

6. Can a dog fly?

→ _____

7. Can a pig climb a tree?

→ _____

8. Can we speak loudly in the museum?

→ _____

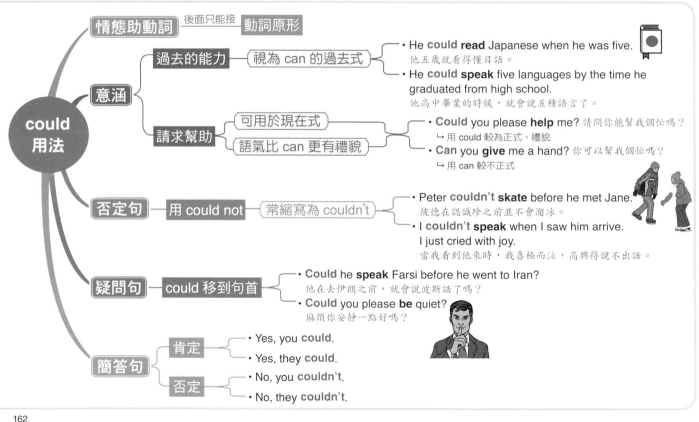

could 用法

- **情態助動詞** — 後面只能接 — **動詞原形**

- **意涵**
  - **過去的能力** — **視為 can 的過去式**
    - He **could read** Japanese when he was five.
      他五歲就看得懂日語。
    - He **could speak** five languages by the time he graduated from high school.
      他高中畢業的時候，就會說五種語言了。
  - **請求幫助**
    - **可用於現在式**
    - **語氣比 can 更有禮貌**
    - **Could** you please **help** me? 請問你能幫我個忙嗎？
      ↳ 用 could 較為正式、禮貌
    - **Can** you **give** me a hand? 你可以幫我個忙嗎？
      ↳ 用 can 較不正式

- **否定句** — 用 could not — 常縮寫為 couldn't
  - Peter **couldn't skate** before he met Jane.
    彼德在認識珍之前並不會溜冰。
  - I **couldn't speak** when I saw him arrive. I just cried with joy.
    當我看到他來時，我喜極而泣，高興得說不出話。

- **疑問句** — could 移到句首
  - **Could** he **speak** Farsi before he went to Iran?
    他在去伊朗之前，就會說波斯話了嗎？
  - **Could** you please **be** quiet?
    麻煩你安靜一點好嗎？

- **簡答句**
  - **肯定**
    - Yes, you **could**.
    - Yes, they **could**.
  - **否定**
    - No, you **couldn't**.
    - No, they **couldn't**.

Practice

❶ 請依圖示，自框內選出正確的片語，
用 could 的句型填空。

make pots	sculpt figures	write calligraphy
paint landscapes	shoot photographs	paint pictures

Lucy _____ when _____ she was 10 years old.

Johnny _____ when _____ he was 5 years old.

Sandra _____ when she was 15 years old.

Kelly _____ when _____ she was 10 years old.

Laura _____ when she was 65 years old.

Jane _____ when she was 18 years old.

❷ 當你 12 歲的時候，你已經會做哪些事？還不會做哪些事？請依據事實，用 could 的肯定或否定句型，寫出完整句子回答問題。

1. Could you play the piano when you were twelve?

→ _____

2. Could you swim when you were twelve?

→ _____

3. Could you use a computer when you were twelve?

→ _____

4. Could you read novels in English when you were twelve?

→ _____

5. Could you ride a bicycle when you were twelve?

→ _____

① • He **can't be** at his office. I saw him in the grocery store just ten minutes ago.
他不可能在辦公室呀，因為我十分鐘前才在雜貨店看到他。
• **Can** it be Jessica at the door?
門外會是潔西卡嗎？

情態助動詞 — 後面只能接 — 動詞原形

must 用法

意涵
- 必要性
  - • My passport is about to expire. I **must renew** my passport. 我的護照快要過期了，我必須更換新護照。
  - • I have a problem with my tooth. I **must go** to the dentist tomorrow.
  我的牙齒有毛病，我明天得去看牙醫。
- 極有可能
  - 可譯為 — 一定是 / 一定要 — • You **must be** Mrs. Smith. Your daughter has told me many good things about you.
  你一定是史密斯太太，你女兒跟我提起很多關於你的好事。
  - 只能用於肯定句
  如要表達否定意義「極不可能」，或疑問意義「有可能嗎」，則必須用 **can**。①

否定句
- 用 must not — 常縮寫為 mustn't — • they **must not use** → they **mustn't use**
- 意涵 — 不可以 — • You **must not miss** the Autumn Festival. 你不可以錯過秋季嘉年華。
  • You **mustn't forget** your mother's birthday. 你不可以忘記你媽媽的生日。

疑問句
- • **Must you use** . . . ?
- • **Must they use** . . . ?

簡答句
- 肯定
  - • Yes, I **must**.
  - • Yes, you **must**.
- 否定
  - • No, I **mustn't**.
  - • No, you **mustn't**.

時態 — 無過去式 — 若要表達過去必做之事 — 用 had to — • As a child growing up on a farm, I **had to milk** the cows every morning.
身為農場長大的小孩，我以前每天早上都得擠牛奶。

164

Practice

1 哪些是該做或不該做的事？請將括弧內的動詞以 **must**、**mustn't** 或 **had to** 的句型來填空。

1. You <u>must finish</u> (finish) your homework before watching TV.
2. You _____ (smoke) cigarettes.
3. We _____ (clean) the house before the party started.
4. You _____ (fight) with your sisters or brothers.
5. Tell Billy that he _____ (come) home before dinner.

6. You _____ (finish) your dinner before eating dessert.
7. Tony forgot to bring his keys, so he _____ (break) the window to get into the house.
8. You _____ (eat) too much fast food.
9. Marie _____ (behave) herself at school.
10. I overslept yesterday so I _____ (run) to catch the bus.

2 自框內選出適當詞彙，用 **must** 或 **mustn't** 的句型回應各個句子。

| lose it |
| hurry |
| go to bed |
| be careful |
| eat something |
| fight with them |
| drink something |

1. I'm late.
   → <u>You must hurry.</u>
2. I'm very tired.
   → _____
3. I'm starving.
   → _____
4. I'm extremely dehydrated.
   → _____
5. I'm cutting glass all day.
   → _____
6. I'm having a fight with my parents.
   → _____
7. I'm carrying a large amount of money in my wallet.
   → _____

Unit 63 have to 用法

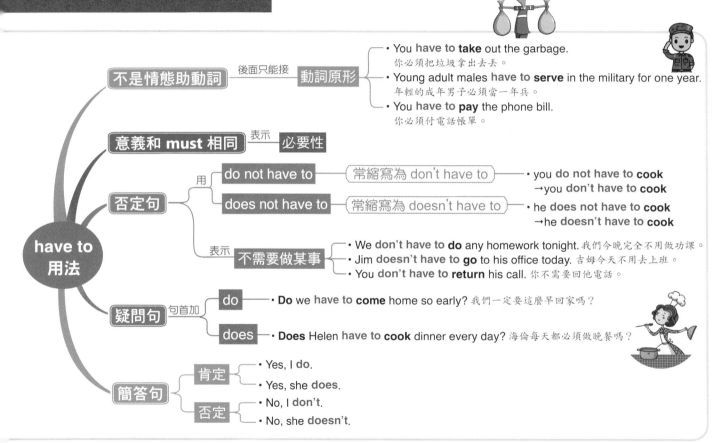

have to 用法

- **不是情態助動詞** — 後面只能接 — 動詞原形
  - You **have to take** out the garbage.
    你必須把垃圾拿出去丟。
  - Young adult males **have to serve** in the military for one year.
    年輕的成年男子必須當一年兵。
  - You **have to pay** the phone bill.
    你必須付電話帳單。

- **意義和 must 相同** — 表示 — 必要性

- **否定句**
  - 用
    - **do not have to** — 常縮寫為 don't have to
      - you **do not have to cook**
        →you **don't have to cook**
    - **does not have to** — 常縮寫為 doesn't have to
      - he **does not have to cook**
        →he **doesn't have to cook**
  - 表示 — 不需要做某事
    - We **don't have to do** any homework tonight. 我們今晚完全不用做功課。
    - Jim **doesn't have to go** to his office today. 吉姆今天不用去上班。
    - You **don't have to return** his call. 你不需要回他電話。

- **疑問句** — 句首加
  - **do** — **Do** we **have to come** home so early? 我們一定要這麼早回家嗎?
  - **does** — **Does** Helen **have to cook** dinner every day? 海倫每天都必須做晚餐嗎?

- **簡答句**
  - 肯定
    - Yes, I **do**.
    - Yes, she **does**.
  - 否定
    - No, I **don't**.
    - No, she **doesn't**.

Practice

1 自框內選出與圖片相符的片語，用 **have to** 或 **has to** 的句型，描述圖中這些辦公室職員每天必須做的事。

pack products

answer the phone

make copies

work on the computer

She has to pack products.

_____

_____

_____

_____

_____

_____

_____

2 那麼，通常主管級的人物不需要自己做一些事，有哪些事呢？請依提示，用 **don't have to** 或 **doesn't have to** 描述這些事。

deliver the mail

1. Judy _____

_____

2. Mr. Taylor and Mr. Watson

_____

_____

make coffee

show up every day

3. James _____

_____

4. Ms. Keaton _____

_____

fax documents

167

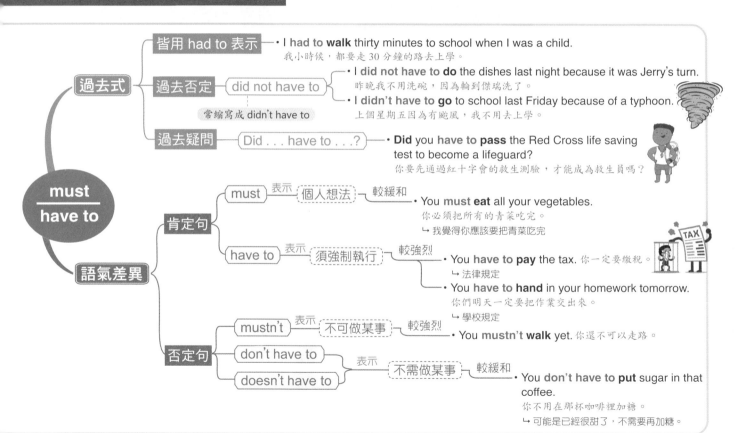

must / have to

過去式

皆用 had to 表示 ── • I **had to walk** thirty minutes to school when I was a child.
我小時候，都要走 30 分鐘的路去上學。

過去否定 ── did not have to
常縮寫成 didn't have to
• I **did not have to do** the dishes last night because it was Jerry's turn.
昨晚我不用洗碗，因為輪到傑瑞洗了。
• I **didn't have to go** to school last Friday because of a typhoon.
上個星期五因為有颱風，我不用去上學。

過去疑問 ── Did . . . have to . . .?
• **Did** you **have to pass** the Red Cross life saving test to become a lifeguard?
你要先通過紅十字會的救生測驗，才能成為救生員嗎？

語氣差異

肯定句

must ── 表示 個人想法 ── 較緩和
• You **must eat** all your vegetables.
你必須把所有的青菜吃完。
↳ 我覺得你應該要把青菜吃完

have to ── 表示 須強制執行 ── 較強烈
• You **have to pay** the tax. 你一定要繳稅。
↳ 法律規定
• You **have to hand** in your homework tomorrow.
你們明天一定要把作業交出來。
↳ 學校規定

否定句

mustn't ── 表示 不可做某事 ── 較強烈
• You **mustn't walk** yet. 你還不可以走路。

don't have to
doesn't have to ── 表示 不需做某事 ── 較緩和
• You **don't have to put** sugar in that coffee.
你不用在那杯咖啡裡加糖。
↳ 可能是已經很甜了，不需要再加糖。

Practice

❶ 說說看，你上個星期有哪些必須做的事？又有哪些不必做的事？用 **had to** 或 **didn't have to** 來造句。

1. I had to go to school from Monday to Friday.

2. ....

3. ....

4. ....

5. ....

6. ....

❷ 根據圖示中的標示，並利用括弧提供的動詞或片語，用「**You mustn't . . .**」或「**You don't have to . . .**」的句型造句。

1. ....

(smoke) in the café.

2. ....

.... (pay cash) in this shop.

3. ....

.... (skateboard) in the park.

4. ....

.... (talk on a cell phone) in the movie theater.

5. ....

.... (pay full price) during a sale.

Unit 65 may / might 用法

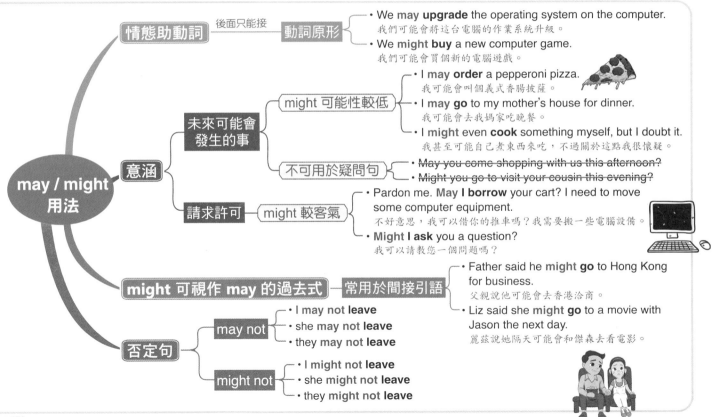

may / might 用法

- 情態助動詞 — 後面只能接 — 動詞原形
  - We **may upgrade** the operating system on the computer.
    我們可能會將這台電腦的作業系統升級。
  - We **might buy** a new computer game.
    我們可能會買個新的電腦遊戲。

- 意涵
  - 未來可能會發生的事
    - might 可能性較低
      - I **may order** a pepperoni pizza.
        我可能會叫個義式香腸披薩。
      - I **may go** to my mother's house for dinner.
        我可能會去我媽家吃晚餐。
      - I **might** even **cook** something myself, but I doubt it.
        我甚至可能自己煮東西來吃，不過關於這點我很懷疑。
    - 不可用於疑問句
      - ~~May you come shopping with us this afternoon?~~
      - ~~Might you go to visit your cousin this evening?~~
  - 請求許可 — might 較客氣
    - Pardon me. **May I borrow** your cart? I need to move some computer equipment.
      不好意思，我可以借你的推車嗎？我需要搬一些電腦設備。
    - **Might I ask** you a question?
      我可以請教您一個問題嗎？

- **might 可視作 may 的過去式** — 常用於間接引語
  - Father said he **might go** to Hong Kong for business.
    父親說他可能會去香港洽商。
  - Liz said she **might go** to a movie with Jason the next day.
    麗茲說她隔天可能會和傑森去看電影。

- 否定句
  - may not
    - I **may not leave**
    - she **may not leave**
    - they **may not leave**
  - might not
    - I **might not leave**
    - she **might not leave**
    - they **might not leave**

Practice

❶ 自框內選出適當的動詞片語，自由以 **may** 或 **might** 的句型填空。

win the set 贏下這局	
win the race 贏得賽事	
clear the bar 跳過這一杆	
hit a home run 擊出全壘打	
block the shot 守住對方射門	
score a touchdown 達陣	

1. This goalie ___*may*___
   ___*block the shot*___.

2. This batter _____
   _____.

3. This tennis player _____
   _____.

4. This football player _____
   _____.

5. Horse No. 3 _____
   _____.

6. This pole vaulter _____
   _____.

❷ 利用括弧裡的 **may** 或 **might** 改寫句子。

1. Perhaps we will go to the seashore tomorrow. (may)

   → _We may go to the seashore tomorrow._

2. Perhaps I will take you on a trip to visit my hometown.

   (might)

   → _____

3. Maybe we can pick up Grandpa on the way. (may)

   → _____

4. Perhaps we can visit my sister in Sydney next year. (might)

   → _____

5. Perhaps my sister will bring her husband and baby to visit

   us instead. (may)

   → _____

6. Maybe we can go to Hong Kong for the weekend. (might)

   → _____

7. Perhaps you will go to a boarding school in Switzerland. (may)

   → _____

8. Or maybe you will go to live with your grandparents. (might)

   → _____

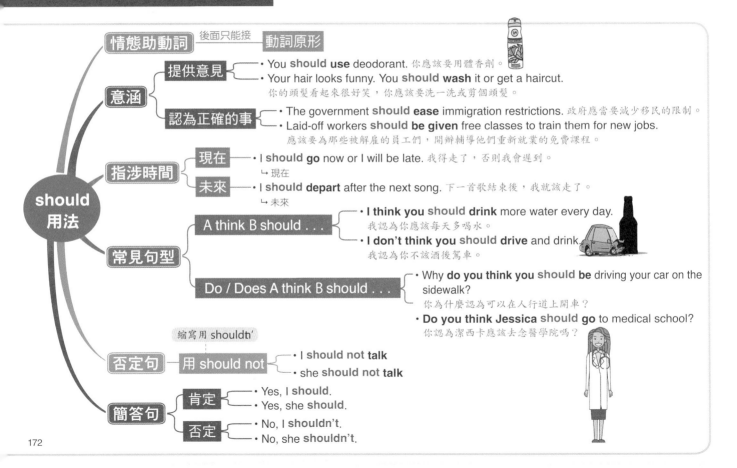

情態助動詞 ── 後面只能接 ── 動詞原形

意涵
- 提供意見
  - You **should use** deodorant. 你應該要用體香劑。
  - Your hair looks funny. You **should wash** it or get a haircut.
    你的頭髮看起來很好笑，你應該要洗一洗或剪個頭髮。
- 認為正確的事
  - The government **should ease** immigration restrictions. 政府應當要減少移民的限制。
  - Laid-off workers **should be given** free classes to train them for new jobs.
    應該要為那些被解雇的員工們，開辦輔導他們重新就業的免費課程。

should 用法

指涉時間
- 現在
  - I **should go** now or I will be late. 我得走了，否則我會遲到。
    ↳ 現在
- 未來
  - I **should depart** after the next song. 下一首歌結束後，我就該走了。
    ↳ 未來

常見句型
- A think B should . . .
  - **I think you should drink** more water every day.
    我認為你應該每天多喝水。
  - **I don't think you should drive** and drink.
    我認為你不該酒後駕車。
- Do / Does A think B should . . .
  - Why **do you think you should be** driving your car on the sidewalk?
    你為什麼認為可以在人行道上開車？
  - **Do you think Jessica should go** to medical school?
    你認為潔西卡應該去念醫學院嗎？

否定句 ── 縮寫用 shouldn'
- 用 should not
  - I **should not talk**
  - she **should not talk**

簡答句
- 肯定
  - Yes, I **should**.
  - Yes, she **should**.
- 否定
  - No, I **shouldn't**.
  - No, she **shouldn't**.

Practice

❶ 自框內選用適當的動詞，分別以 should 和 shouldn't 造句。

| arrive | work | eat | yield | feed | take | cheat | respect |

1. We _____ on a subway train.
2. We _____ seats to the elderly on a subway train.

3. Students _____ on an exam.
4. Students _____ their teachers.

5. You _____ late.
6. You _____ hard.

7. You _____ your dog French fries.
8. You _____ your dog out for a run.

❷ 利用題目提供的詞彙，分別用「Should . . . ?」和「Do you think . . . should . . . ?」的句型造句。

1. I call the director about the résumé I sent
   → *Should I call the director about the résumé I sent?*
   → *Do you think I should call the director about the résumé I sent?*

2. I bring a gift with me
   → _____
   → _____

3. Mike go on a vacation once in a while
   → _____
   → _____

4. we visit our grandma more often
   → _____
   → _____

5. I ask Nancy out for a date
   → _____
   → _____

6. Sally apply for that job in the restaurant
   → _____
   → _____

Unit **67** may / could / can 表請求

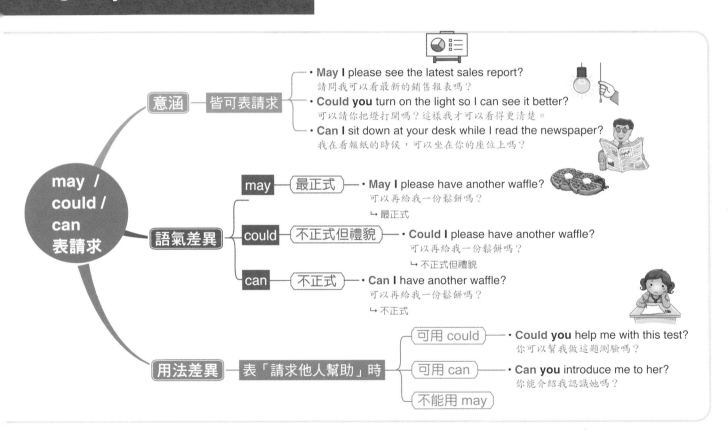

意涵 — 皆可表請求

- **May I** please see the latest sales report?
  請問我可以看最新的銷售報表嗎?
- **Could you** turn on the light so I can see it better?
  可以請你把燈打開嗎?這樣我才可以看得更清楚。
- **Can I** sit down at your desk while I read the newspaper?
  我在看報紙的時候,可以坐在你的座位上嗎?

may / could / can 表請求

語氣差異

- may — 最正式
  - **May I** please have another waffle?
    可以再給我一份鬆餅嗎?
    ↳ 最正式
- could — 不正式但禮貌
  - **Could I** please have another waffle?
    可以再給我一份鬆餅嗎?
    ↳ 不正式但禮貌
- can — 不正式
  - **Can I** have another waffle?
    可以再給我一份鬆餅嗎?
    ↳ 不正式

用法差異 — 表「請求他人幫助」時

- 可用 could
  - **Could you** help me with this test?
    你可以幫我做這題測驗嗎?
- 可用 can
  - **Can you** introduce me to her?
    你能介紹我認識她嗎?
- 不能用 may

Practice

1 服飾店裡有名男子正在挑選衣物，請按物品編號，依序寫出他會問的問題。
從框內挑選適當的詞彙，並用「May I...?」、「Could I...?」和「Can I...?」造問句。

- pay with a credit card
- get two more shirts just like this one
- have three pairs of socks similar to these
- have a tie that goes with my shirt

1. → *May I get two more shirts just like this one?*
   → *Could I get two more shirts just like this one?*
   → *Can I get two more shirts just like this one?*

2. → _____
   → _____
   → _____

3. → _____
   → _____
   → _____

4. → _____
   → _____
   → _____

2 自框中選出正確的用語，以提示的情態助動詞造句完成對話。

- speak to Dennis
- borrow your father's drill
- move these boxes for me
- turn up the heat
- put my files here

1. _____ (may)
   Hang on, please. I'll get him on the phone.

2. _____ (may)
   I'm not sure. I'll ask him about it.

3. _____ (could)
   I'm sorry, but I think they're too heavy for me, too.

4. _____ (could)
   No problem. Is it warmer now?

5. _____ (can)
   Yes, of course. That shelf belongs to you.

Unit 68 would like / will / shall 表提供和邀請

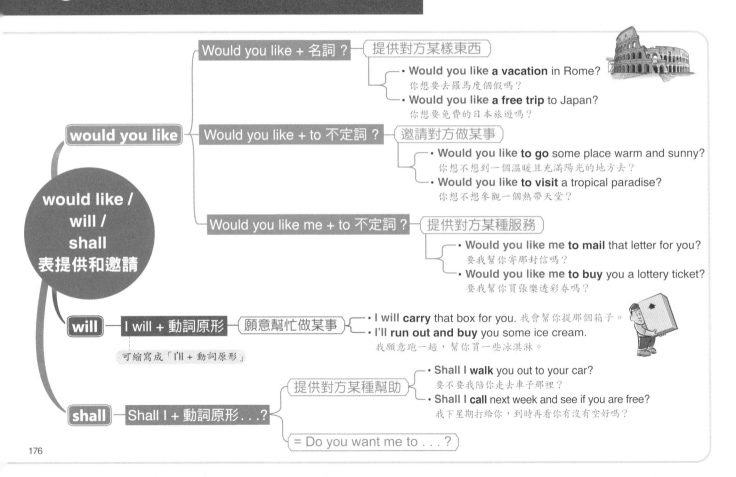

would like / will / shall 表提供和邀請

would you like

Would you like + 名詞？ —— 提供對方某樣東西
- **Would you like a vacation** in Rome?
  你想要去羅馬度個假嗎？
- **Would you like a free trip** to Japan?
  你想要免費的日本旅遊嗎？

Would you like + to 不定詞？ —— 邀請對方做某事
- **Would you like to go** some place warm and sunny?
  你想不想到一個溫暖且充滿陽光的地方去？
- **Would you like to visit** a tropical paradise?
  你想不想參觀一個熱帶天堂？

Would you like me + to 不定詞？ —— 提供對方某種服務
- **Would you like me to mail** that letter for you?
  要我幫你寄那封信嗎？
- **Would you like me to buy** you a lottery ticket?
  要我幫你買張樂透彩券嗎？

will —— I will + 動詞原形 —— 願意幫忙做某事
- **I will carry** that box for you. 我會幫你提那個箱子。
- I'll **run out and buy** you some ice cream.
  我願意跑一趟，幫你買一些冰淇淋。

可縮寫成「I'll + 動詞原形」

shall —— Shall I + 動詞原形 . . . ? —— 提供對方某種幫助
- **Shall I walk** you out to your car?
  要不要我陪你走去車子那裡？
- **Shall I call** next week and see if you are free?
  我下星期打給你，到時再看看你有沒有空好嗎？

= Do you want me to . . . ?

Practice

❶ 依照範例，利用題目提示的詞彙，分別用框內的四種句型，造出表示提供某樣東西的問句。

- **Would you like + 名詞 . . . ?** • **Would you like me to . . . ?** • **I'll . . .** • **Shall I . . . ?**

1. make some fruit salad

→ *Would you like some fruit salad?*

→ *Would you like me to make some fruit salad?*

→ *I'll make some fruit salad for you.*

→ *Shall I make some fruit salad for you?*

2. make some tea

→ _____

→ _____

→ _____

→ _____

3. squeeze some orange juice

→ _____

→ _____

→ _____

→ _____

4. make some pudding

→ _____

→ _____

→ _____

→ _____

❷ 依據圖示，自框內選出正確的片語，以「 Would you like to . . . ?」的句型完成句子。

go hiking

go fishing

go to the beach

play basketball

have some pizza

Would you like to go fishing ___ this Saturday?

___ tomorrow?

___ on Sunday?

___ next Tuesday?

___ for lunch?

Unit 69 shall we / let's / why don't we / how about　表提議

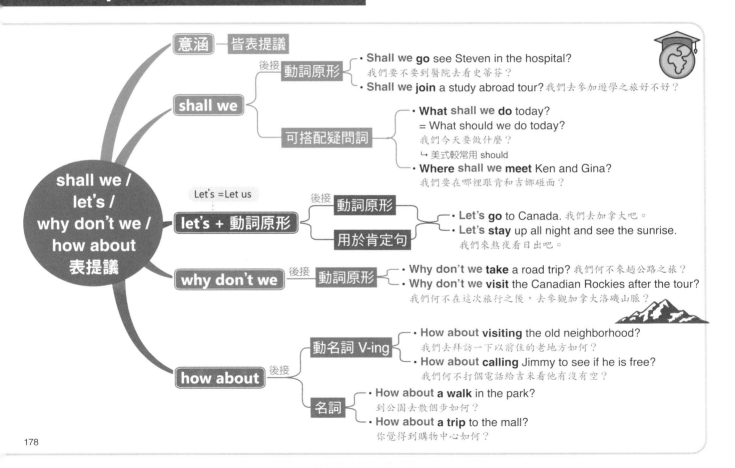

- 意涵 ── 皆表提議

shall we
- 後接 動詞原形
  - • **Shall we go** see Steven in the hospital?
    我們要不要到醫院去看史蒂芬？
  - • **Shall we join** a study abroad tour? 我們去參加遊學之旅好不好？
- 可搭配疑問詞
  - • **What shall we do** today?
    = What should we do today?
    我們今天要做什麼？
    ↳ 美式較常用 should
  - • **Where shall we meet** Ken and Gina?
    我們要在哪裡跟肯和吉娜碰面？

let's + 動詞原形　Let's =Let us
- 後接 動詞原形
- 用於肯定句
  - • **Let's go** to Canada. 我們去加拿大吧。
  - • **Let's stay** up all night and see the sunrise.
    我們來熬夜看日出吧。

why don't we
- 後接 動詞原形
  - • **Why don't we take** a road trip? 我們何不來趟公路之旅？
  - • **Why don't we visit** the Canadian Rockies after the tour?
    我們何不在這次旅行之後，去參觀加拿大洛磯山脈？

how about
- 後接 動名詞 V-ing
  - • **How about visiting** the old neighborhood?
    我們去拜訪一下以前住的老地方如何？
  - • **How about calling** Jimmy to see if he is free?
    我們何不打個電話給吉米看他有沒有空？
- 名詞
  - • **How about a walk** in the park?
    到公園去散個步如何？
  - • **How about a trip** to the mall?
    你覺得到購物中心如何？

Part
8

情態助動詞

Unit
69
shall we / let's /
why don't we / how about 表提議

Practice

1 依照範例，利用各題目提示的動詞，分別用框內的四種句型造句。

Shall we . . . ?

Why don't we . . . ?

How about . . . ?

Let's . . . .

1. play another volleyball game
   - → _Shall we play another volleyball game?_
   - → _Why don't we play another volleyball game?_
   - → _How about playing another volleyball game?_
   - → _Let's play another volleyball game._

2. go on a picnic
   - → ....
   - → ....
   - → ....
   - → ....

4. take a walk
   - → ....
   - → ....
   - → ....
   - → ....

3. eat out tonight
   - → ....
   - → ....
   - → ....
   - → ....

5. go to Bali this summer
   - → ....
   - → ....
   - → ....
   - → ....

Unit 60
重點複習

① 依據圖示，自框內選出正確的動詞，用 can 寫出問句詢問是否會烹調圖中的食物。
依據實際情況做出簡答後，再以完整句子描述事實。

① tea eggs　② tomatoes　③ French fries　④ hamburgers

⑤ muffins　⑥ coffee　⑦ an egg　⑧ buns

fry 油炸
make 煮
bake 烘烤
purée 製漿
boil 水煮
deep-fry 油炸
grill 燒烤
steam 蒸

1. **Q** *Can you boil tea eggs?*
   A *No, I can't. I can't boil tea eggs.*

2. **Q**
   A

3. **Q**
   A

4. **Q**
   A

5. **Q**
   A

6. **Q**
   A

7. **Q**
   A

8. **Q**
   A

Unit 63 重點複習

❷ 請用「do . . . have to」或「does . . . have to」填空完成下列問句。

1. How old _____ you _____ be to get a motorcycle driver's license?

2. _____ every person in a car _____ wear a seatbelt?

3. _____ you _____ take a written test and a road test to get an automobile driver's license?

4. _____ you _____ pass an entrance exam to go to college?

5. _____ every adult citizen _____ pay income tax?

6. How old _____ you _____ be to vote for the President?

Unit 67–68 重點複習

❸ 自框內選出適當的句型來完成下列餐廳與飯店內的對話，並且注意要用禮貌的語氣。

Can I

May I

I'll

Could you

Shall I

How about

Would you

1. **Waiter:** _____ take your order?

   Guest: Yes, I'll have a fish fillet and a bowl of onion soup.

2. **Guest:** _____ have the table by the window?

   Waiter: I'm afraid it's reserved.

3. **Guest:** _____ send someone to fix the towel rod in my bathroom?

   Receptionist: I'll send someone up right away.

4. **Guest:** It's a little stuffy in the room.

   Bellboy: _____ turn on the air conditioner for you?

5. **Waiter:** _____ like a tomato salad or a chicken salad?

   Guest: A chicken salad, please.

6. **Guest:** I didn't order fruit tea. I ordered a pot of milk tea.

   Waiter: I'm terribly sorry. _____ bring your milk tea right away.

7. **Guest:** I want to have something light.

   Waiter: _____ the chicken soup? It's popular among our guests.

8. **Guest:** I don't like chicken. Do you have anything else?

   Waiter: _____ like to try Today's Special? It's steamed fish. It's a light dish, too.

181

4 從圖中選出適當的詞彙，用「Would you like . . . ?」的句型造問句，
完成下列空服員（**F** Flight Attendant）與乘客（**P** Passenger）間的對話。

1. **F** *Would you like something to drink?*

   P Yes, please. What do you have?

2. **F** _____

   P No, thanks. I don't drink beer or wine.

3. **F** _____

   P No, thanks. It's too sweet. Do you have anything hot?

4. **F** _____

   P A cup of tea would be great.

5. **F** _____

   P No, thank you. I'm not hungry.

   F Enjoy your tea.

a bag of nuts

some juice

an alcoholic beverage

a cup of coffee or tea

something to drink

5 將下列句子改寫為否定句。

1. I can walk to work.

   → _____

2. Susie could dance all night.

   → _____

3. I have to go to Joe's house tonight.

   → _____

4. I have to go to see the doctor tomorrow.

   → _____

5. I may go on a vacation in August.

   → _____

My dog can sing!

My dog can't sing.

6. I might go see the Picasso exhibit at the museum.

→

7. My friend can sit in the full lotus position.

→

8. I can finish all my homework this weekend.

→

9. I must stop eating beans.

→

10. John has to see Joseph.

→

11. The turtle may win the race against the rabbit.

→

12. My friend Jon should get a different job.

→

Unit 60–64 重點複習

6 將下列句子改寫為疑問句。

1. You can fry an egg.
   → *Can you fry an egg?*

2. Paul could swim out to the island.
   →

3. John must go to Japan.
   →

4. Abby has to go to the studio.
   →

5. George can play the guitar.
   →

6. David must finish his homework before he goes outside to play.
   →

7. I have to give away my concert tickets.
   →

8. Joan has to stay at home tomorrow night.
   →

❼ 選出正確的答案。

1. **Bob:** I'm bored. _____
   _____ go somewhere?
   Ⓐ Why don't we
   Ⓑ Shall we
   Ⓒ Both A and B

2. **Stan:** _____ taking a ride on
   the subway?
   Ⓐ How about
   Ⓑ Why don't we
   Ⓒ Shall we

3. **Bob:** Great. _____ go.
   Ⓐ Why don't we
   Ⓑ Shall we
   Ⓒ Let's

4. **Stan:** _____ go to Forest Park?
   Ⓐ Shall we
   Ⓑ How about
   Ⓒ Let's

5. **Bob:** _____ do at Forest Park?
   Ⓐ What shall we
   Ⓑ Shall we
   Ⓒ Both A and B

6. **Stan:** _____ taking a walk in the park?
   Bob: No. That's boring.
   Ⓐ How about
   Ⓑ Shall we
   Ⓒ Let's

7. **Stan:** In that case, _____ do?
   Bob: I want to go home and watch TV.
   Ⓐ what shall we
   Ⓑ let's
   Ⓒ why don't we

8. **Stan:** _____ forget about it.
   You go home. I'm going for a walk in the park.
   Ⓐ How about
   Ⓑ Shall we
   Ⓒ Let's

9. **Bob:** OK. _____ take a walk in Forest Park.
   Ⓐ How about
   Ⓑ Let's
   Ⓒ Why don't we

10. **Stan:** _____ hop the next train?
    Ⓐ Let's
    Ⓑ Shall we
    Ⓒ What shall we

8 請將各個句子依據情態助動詞的作用，填入適當的分類編號。

A Asking for something 請求得到某物

B Asking permission 請求允許

C Asking someone to do something 請求他人幫忙

D Offering something 供應物品

E Inviting someone 邀請他人

F Offering to do something 願意幫忙做某事

G Asking for a suggestion 徵求意見

H Making a suggestion 提議

1. Can I have a cookie, please? (A)

2. Would you like one more croissant? ( )

3. Why don't we visit Sam tomorrow? ( )

4. Can you call the police for me? ( )

5. I'll go get a bandage for you. ( )

6. May I try on this shirt? ( )

7. What should I do with my parents? ( )

8. Would you like to play badminton? ( )

9 依據對話的意思，用 **must** 或 **mustn't** 搭配括弧中的動詞完成對話。

1. Jack: Susan has been working for six hours.

   Olive: She _____(be) very tired. She should take a break.

2. Eddie: Ken has gone to Japan for a vacation. It's his mother's birthday today.

   Yvonne: His mother says he _____ (visit) her in Tokyo.

3. Ada: Bob hasn't eaten anything the whole day.

   Tim: He _____(be) starving. He _____(eat) something.

4. Billy: Cindy's phone bill is due today.

   Zoe: She _____(pay) the bill right now, or she can't call anyone with her phone.

5. Rick: My little brother was taken to the hospital last night. He burned his fingers.

   Heather: He _____(pay) with matches any more.

10 依據對話的意思，用 **may** 或 **should not / may not / must not** 搭配括弧中的動詞完成對話。

1. You _____(have) one more piece of the pizza, but you _____(eat) all of it.

2. You _____(listen) to music on an authorized website, but you _____(download) music from an illegal site.

3. You _____(have) a cup of coffee a day, but you _____(put) too much sugar in it.

4. You _____(drive) to the bank, but you _____ (find) a parking space anywhere near the bank.

5. You _____(call) her in the middle of the night, but she _____(answer) the phone.

6. You _____(watch) the lions in the zoo, but you _____ (try) to touch them.

⓫ 依據對話的意思，用 should 或 shouldn't 搭配括弧中的動詞完成對話。

1. Peggy: My dog Momo has been playing with his toy for twenty minutes.
James: You ＿＿＿＿＿＿＿＿＿＿＿＿＿(give) Momo some water to drink.

2. James: Snowbell is too fat.
Anne: You ＿＿＿＿＿＿＿＿＿＿＿＿＿(feed) her so much food.

3. Joanne: She looks so cute and friendly.
David: I think we ＿＿＿＿＿＿＿＿＿＿＿＿＿(adopt) her.

4. Erica: Ted had a diarrhea this morning.
Pete: You ＿＿＿＿＿＿＿＿＿＿＿＿＿(give) him any more ice cream.

5. Amy: Jimmy doesn't look happy today.
Lucas: He just wants to play. You ＿＿＿＿＿＿＿＿＿＿＿ (spend) more time with him.

6. Diana: Kiki is losing a lot of hair.
Jacky: That's not good. You ＿＿＿＿＿＿＿＿＿＿＿ (take) her to a vet.

Unit 71 肯定句／否定句

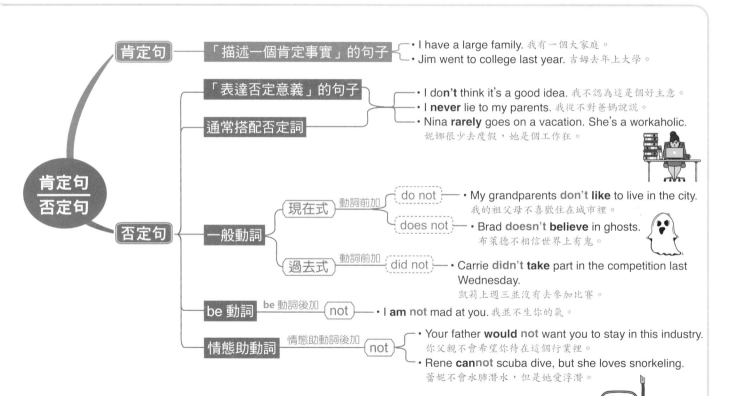

肯定句
- 「描述一個肯定事實」的句子
  - I have a large family. 我有一個大家庭。
  - Jim went to college last year. 吉姆去年上大學。

否定句
- 「表達否定意義」的句子
- 通常搭配否定詞
  - I **don't** think it's a good idea. 我不認為這是個好主意。
  - I **never** lie to my parents. 我從不對爸媽說謊。
  - Nina **rarely** goes on a vacation. She's a workaholic.
    妮娜很少去度假，她是個工作狂。

- 一般動詞
  - 現在式 動詞前加 do not
    - My grandparents **don't like** to live in the city.
      我的祖父母不喜歡住在城市裡。
  - does not
    - Brad **doesn't believe** in ghosts.
      布萊德不相信世界上有鬼。
  - 過去式 動詞前加 did not
    - Carrie **didn't take** part in the competition last Wednesday.
      凱莉上週三並沒有去參加比賽。

- be 動詞 **be 動詞後加** not
  - I **am not** mad at you. 我並不生你的氣。

- 情態助動詞 情態助動詞後加 not
  - Your father **would not** want you to stay in this industry.
    你父親不會希望你待在這個行業裡。
  - Rene **cannot** scuba dive, but she loves snorkeling.
    蕾妮不會水肺潛水，但是她愛浮潛。

Practice

❶ 將下列肯定句改寫為否定句。

1. James is playing with his new iPhone.

→ ....

2. Vincent owns a shoe factory.

→ ....

3. They went to a concert last night.

→ ....

4. I enjoy reading.

→ ....

5. I can ride a unicycle.

→ ....

6. Summer vacation will begin soon.

→ ....

7. I had a nightmare last night.

→ ....

8. I am from Vietnam.

→ ....

❷ 將下列否定句改寫為肯定句。

1. Sue didn't watch the football game on TV last night.

→ ....

2. Rick can't speak Japanese.

→ ....

3. Phil and Jill weren't at the office yesterday.

→ ....

4. I couldn't enter the house this morning.

→ ....

5. Joseph doesn't like spaghetti.

→ ....

6. They aren't drinking apple juice.

→ ....

7. She isn't going shopping tomorrow.

→ ....

8. I won't tell Sandy.

→ ....

Unit 72 疑問句（1）

> ① **Do** you spend your summer on a tropical island every year?
> 你每年夏天都去熱帶島嶼度假嗎？

疑問句

- 提出疑問的句子 — 以問號「？」結尾
  - Are you satisfied with the results? 你對這結果滿意嗎？
  - Did he apologize for being rude? 他為他的無禮表示歉意了嗎？

- 一般動詞
  - 現在式 — 句首加 do / does ① / 動詞用原形 ①
    - **Does** he jog for fifty minutes every day? 他每天慢跑五十分鐘嗎？
  - 過去式 — 句首加 did
    - **Did** I tell you that I had passed the exam? 我有沒有告訴你我已經通過考試了？

- be 動詞 — 將 be 動詞移至句首
  - **Is** there anything wrong? 有什麼不對勁嗎？

- 情態助動詞 — 將情態助動詞移至句首
  - **Shall** we set off for the train station? 我們是不是該出發去火車站了？
  - **Will** you keep the secret? 你會保密嗎？

- 疑問詞在句首 — 常見疑問詞

what 什麼	when 何時	who 誰	which 哪個
where 哪裡	why 為什麼	how 如何	whose 誰的

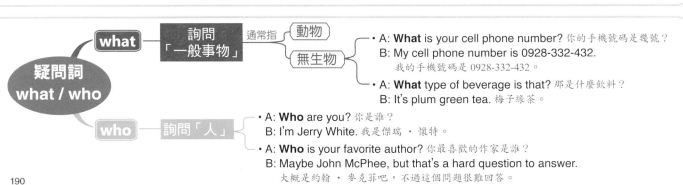

疑問詞 what / who

- **what** — 詢問「一般事物」 — 通常指 動物 / 無生物
  - A: **What** is your cell phone number? 你的手機號碼是幾號？
    B: My cell phone number is 0928-332-432. 我的手機號碼是 0928-332-432。
  - A: **What** type of beverage is that? 那是什麼飲料？
    B: It's plum green tea. 梅子綠茶。

- **who** — 詢問「人」
  - A: **Who** are you? 你是誰？
    B: I'm Jerry White. 我是傑瑞・懷特。
  - A: **Who** is your favorite author? 你最喜歡的作家是誰？
    B: Maybe John McPhee, but that's a hard question to answer.
    大概是約翰・麥克菲吧，不過這個問題很難回答。

Practice

① 將下列句子改寫為疑問句。

1. Jerry is good at photography.

→ *Is Jerry good at photography?*

2. Jane doesn't believe what he said.

→ ....

3. He never showed up at the party.

→ ....

4. Johnny gets up early every day.

→ ....

5. I will remember you.

→ ....

6. Julie asked me to give her a ride yesterday.

→ ....

7. She was surprised when he called.

→ ....

8. He's going to buy a gift tomorrow.

→ ....

② 依據粗體字的提示，將句子以 who 或 what 造出問句。

1. **Q** *What are you watching on TV?*

A I'm watching **the news** on TV.

2. **Q** ....

A I'm interested in **painting scenery**.

3. **Q** ....

A **That man** is the vice president of the company.

4. **Q** ....

A My favorite musician is **Bach**.

5. **Q** ....

A He is looking at **a cat on the roof**.

6. **Q** ....

A **Jude** is writing an email.

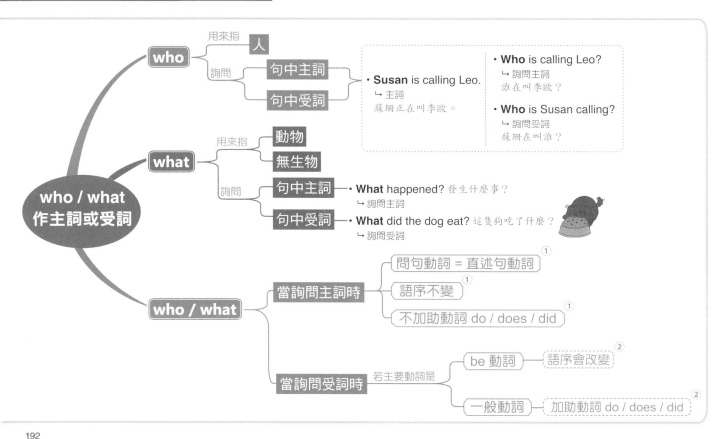

- **who** ─ 用來指 **人**
  - 詢問 ─ 句中主詞
          └ 句中受詞

  - **Susan** is calling Leo.
    └ 主詞
    蘇珊正在叫李歐。

  - **Who** is calling Leo?
    └ 詢問主詞
    誰在叫李歐？
  - **Who** is Susan calling?
    └ 詢問受詞
    蘇珊在叫誰？

- **what** ─ 用來指 ─ 動物
                    無生物
  - 詢問 ─ 句中主詞 • **What** happened? 發生什麼事？
            └ 詢問主詞
          句中受詞 • **What** did the dog eat? 這隻狗吃了什麼？
            └ 詢問受詞

who / what 作主詞或受詞

- **who / what**
  - 當詢問主詞時 ─ 問句動詞＝直述句動詞 ①
                 語序不變 ①
                 不加助動詞 do / does / did ①
  - 當詢問受詞時 ─ 若主要動詞是 ─ be 動詞 ─ 語序會改變 ②
                              一般動詞 ─ 加助動詞 do / does / did ②

①

直述句	用 who 或 what 詢問主詞
• **Willy** is eating a sandwich. 威利正在吃三明治。	• **Who** is eating a sandwich? 誰正在吃三明治？
• **Debbie** likes mountain climbing. 黛比喜歡爬山。	• **Who** likes mountain climbing? 誰喜歡爬山？
• **Something** has happened to Jim. 吉姆發生了一些事。	• **What** has happened to Jim? 吉姆發生了什麼事？

②

直述句	用 who 或 what 詢問受詞
• Willy is eating **a sandwich**. 威利正在吃三明治。	• **What** is Willy eating? 威利正在吃什麼？
• Debbie likes **mountain climbing**. 黛比喜歡爬山。	• **What** does Debbie like? 黛比喜歡什麼？
• The vase is made of **plastic**. 這個花瓶是塑膠做的。	• **What** is the vase made of? 這個花瓶是什麼做的？

Practice

❶ 用 who 或 what 分別寫出詢問主詞和受詞的問句。

1. Johnny ate my slice of pizza.
→ *Who ate my slice of pizza?*

→ *What did Johnny eat?*

2. The boss consulted Lauren first.
→ ....

→ ....

3. Tom helped cook the fish.
→ ....

→ ....

4. My dog broke the vase.
→ ....

→ ....

5. Mom is feeding the baby.
→ ....

→ ....

6. Denise is standing next to Allen.
→ ....

→ ....

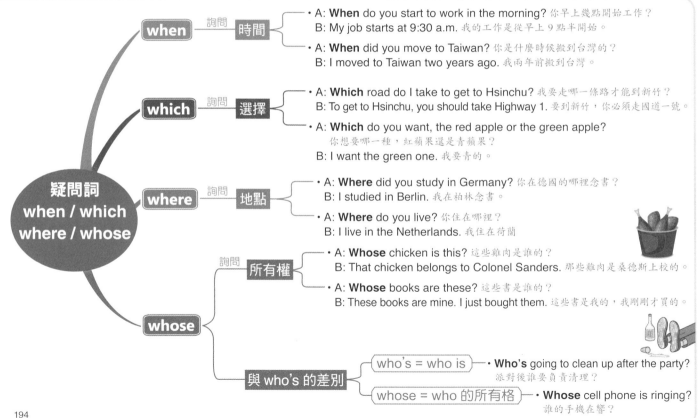

when ──詢問── 時間

- A: **When** do you start to work in the morning? 你早上幾點開始工作？
  B: My job starts at 9:30 a.m. 我的工作是從早上 9 點半開始。

- A: **When** did you move to Taiwan? 你是什麼時候搬到台灣的？
  B: I moved to Taiwan two years ago. 我兩年前搬到台灣。

which ──詢問── 選擇

- A: **Which** road do I take to get to Hsinchu? 我要走哪一條路才能到新竹？
  B: To get to Hsinchu, you should take Highway 1. 要到新竹，你必須走國道一號。

- A: **Which** do you want, the red apple or the green apple?
  你想要哪一種，紅蘋果還是青蘋果？
  B: I want the green one. 我要青的。

where ──詢問── 地點

- A: **Where** did you study in Germany? 你在德國的哪裡念書？
  B: I studied in Berlin. 我在柏林念書。

- A: **Where** do you live? 你住在哪裡？
  B: I live in the Netherlands. 我住在荷蘭

whose ──詢問── 所有權

- A: **Whose** chicken is this? 這些雞肉是誰的？
  B: That chicken belongs to Colonel Sanders. 那些雞肉是桑德斯上校的。

- A: **Whose** books are these? 這些書是誰的？
  B: These books are mine. I just bought them. 這些書是我的，我剛剛才買的。

疑問詞
when / which
where / whose

與 who's 的差別

who's = who is ─ **Who's** going to clean up after the party?
派對後誰要負責清理？

whose = who 的所有格 ─ **Whose** cell phone is ringing?
誰的手機在響？

Practice

❶ 下列詞彙適合做哪一個疑問詞的回答？將它們填入正確的空格內。

| this one | my sister's | in 2006 | London | tomorrow | the garage | Ms. Lee's | the mall |
| the blue shirt | the large one | the cat's | the taller man | last June | the office | next month | Vicky's |

which

this one

where

when

whose

❷ 自框中選出正確的疑問詞填空。

where

when

whose

which

1. _____ was the Meiji Restoration in Japan?

2. _____ is Gary going to meet his client, in a café or in his office?

3. _____ city, Kyoto or Osaka, has the most beautiful temples?

4. _____ invention was the Walkman?

5. _____ is the British Museum located?

6. _____ was the steam train invented?

7. _____ bicycle is this?

8. _____ did you last see him?

9. _____ do you like better on pasta, olive oil or butter?

10. _____ does your school begin?

① · A: **How** do you get to the zoo? 你是怎麼去動物園的？
　　 B: Take the train to the last stop, and then walk past the mall to the zoo.
　　　　搭火車到最後一站，然後再經過大賣場走到動物園。

疑問詞
how / why

how ─ 詢問 ─ 方法 ①

　　　　　　　程度 ─ 常與特定字詞連用

how old（年紀）多大

how tall 多高 ─ · A: **How tall** was that dinosaur?
　　　　　　　　　　那隻恐龍有多高？
　　　　　　　　　　B: That dinosaur was 10 meters tall.
　　　　　　　　　　那隻恐龍有 10 公尺高。

how long 多長 ─ · A: **How long** was that dinosaur?
　　　　　　　　　　那隻恐龍有多長？
　　　　　　　　　　B: That dinosaur was 30 meters long.
　　　　　　　　　　那隻恐龍有 30 公尺長。

how much 多少　不可數 ─ · A: **How much** did that dinosaur weigh?
　　　　　　　　　　那隻恐龍有多重？
　　　　　　　　　　B: That dinosaur weighed over 2,500 kilograms.
　　　　　　　　　　那隻恐龍重達 2,500 公斤以上。

how many 多少　可數 ─ · A: **How many** animal species have survived from the time of the dinosaurs?
　　　　　　　　　　有幾種動物從恐龍時代存活下來？
　　　　　　　　　　B: Only a few, such as sharks.
　　　　　　　　　　只有非常少數，像是鯊魚。

how often 多常

why ─ 詢問 ─ 理由

· A: **Why** did that chicken cross the road?
　　為什麼那隻雞要過馬路？
　 B: That chicken crossed the road to get to the other side.
　　過馬路是因為牠要到路的另一邊。

· A: **Why** are you going to school?
　　你為什麼要上學？
　 B: I am going to school to study animal behavior.
　　我上學校為了研究動物行為。

Practice

1 自框內選出適當的疑問詞彙來完成句子。

How	How much	How old	How long	How many	How tall	How often

1. **A:** _____ is your brother?
   B: He is 25 years old.

2. **A:** _____ is your sister?
   B: She is 160 centimeters tall.

3. **A:** _____ money do you have in your wallet?
   B: I have about 500 dollars in my wallet.

4. **A:** _____ times were you late for work this week?
   B: I was late three times this week.

5. **A:** _____ do I operate this machine?
   B: You can follow the instruction manual.

6. **A:** _____ do you see your boyfriend?
   B: I see him every weekend.

7. **A:** _____ is your winter break from school?
   B: My winter break is about three weeks.

8. **A:** _____ was your hamster when it ran away?
   B: It was over two years old.

9. **A:** This building is tightly guarded. _____ could he enter the manager's room?
   B: He must be a smart thief.

10. **A:** _____ is Taipei 101?
    B: It is about 100 stories tall.

11. **A:** _____ does a cup of pearl milk tea cost?
    B: It usually costs 25 dollars.

12. **A:** _____ do you go to Chicago to visit your relatives?
    B: I usually go to Chicago to visit my relatives twice a year.

13. **A:** _____ do you stay when you visit your family in Chicago?
    B: I usually stay a week or so.

14. **A:** _____ do I get to the airport?
    B: Use a map.

Unit 76 附加問句

①
- Tina is single, **isn't she?** 蒂娜還是單身，對嗎？
- Jerry doesn't have a girlfriend, **does he?** 傑瑞沒有女朋友，對嗎？
- I can introduce them to each other, **can't I?** 我可以介紹他們兩個認識，不是嗎？

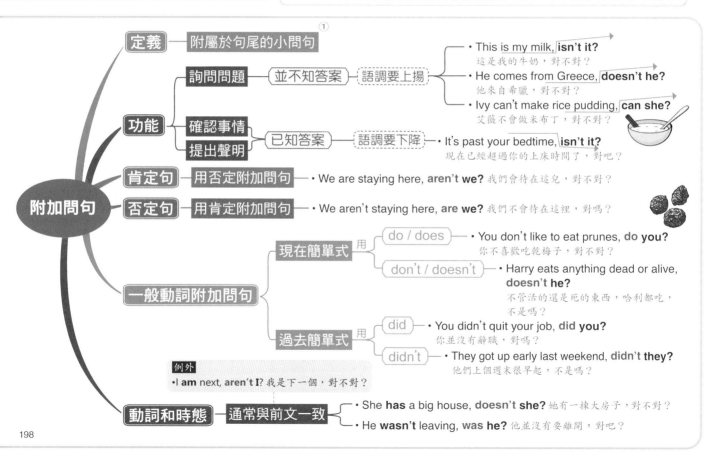

附加問句

定義 — 附屬於句尾的小問句

功能
- 詢問問題 — 並不知答案 — 語調要上揚
  - This is my milk, **isn't it?** 這是我的牛奶，對不對？
  - He comes from Greece, **doesn't he?** 他來自希臘，對不對？
  - Ivy can't make rice pudding, **can she?** 艾薇不會做米布丁，對不對？
- 確認事情 / 提出聲明 — 已知答案 — 語調要下降
  - It's past your bedtime, **isn't it?** 現在已經超過你的上床時間了，對吧？

肯定句 — 用否定附加問句
- We are staying here, **aren't we?** 我們會待在這兒，對不對？

否定句 — 用肯定附加問句
- We aren't staying here, **are we?** 我們不會待在這裡，對嗎？

一般動詞附加問句
- 現在簡單式 用
  - do / does
    - You don't like to eat prunes, **do you?** 你不喜歡吃乾梅子，對不對？
  - don't / doesn't
    - Harry eats anything dead or alive, **doesn't he?** 不管活的還是死的東西，哈利都吃，不是嗎？
- 過去簡單式 用
  - did
    - You didn't quit your job, **did you?** 你並沒有辭職，對嗎？
  - didn't
    - They got up early last weekend, **didn't they?** 他們上個週末很早起，不是嗎？

例外
- I **am** next, **aren't I?** 我是下一個，對不對？

動詞和時態 — 通常與前文一致
- She **has** a big house, **doesn't she?** 她有一棟大房子，對不對？
- He **wasn't** leaving, **was he?** 他並沒有要離開，對吧？

Practice

1 摔角選手 Hulk（HH）正在接受脫口秀主持人 DL 的訪問，請根據訪問內容，寫出正確的附加問句。

DL: Hello, Hulk. I can call you Hulk, **①** _____?

HH: I prefer Mr. Hooligan.

DL: You're joking, **②** _____?

HH: Of course. I don't look like a guy who stands on formality, **③** _____?

DL: You look like a guy who stands on other people's heads. I can say that, **④** _____?

HH: Sure. I'm proud of crushing my opponents under the heels of my boots.

DL: When you stand on your opponents, you don't hurt them, **⑤** _____?

HH: Hey! I haven't killed anybody yet, **⑥** _____?

DL: Let's go back to the beginning. You started wrestling as a child, **⑦** _____?

HH: My first real opponent was my older brother.

DL: You didn't fight with your sister, **⑧** _____?

HH: She was stronger than my brother, so I left her alone.

DL: You didn't wrestle with anybody else, **⑨** _____?

HH: We had a pet alligator.

DL: You have wrestled with alligators, **⑩** _____?

HH: Yeah, but my sister was tougher than any alligator.

DL: Who was uglier, your sister or the alligator?

HH: You don't want to make me mad, **⑪** _____?

DL: No! You don't want to talk about that, **⑫** _____? Let's talk about your new TV show . . .

2 寫出下列句子的附加問句。

1. You're going to adopt a stray cat, _____?

2. He is not going abroad to study the law, _____?

3. You can't run fast, _____?

4. She will come to the class, _____?

5. I passed the exam, _____?

6. She doesn't believe me, _____?

7. The gift is for me, _____?

8. I'm chosen, _____?

9. It's midnight, _____?

10. Sam didn't cook dinner last night, _____?

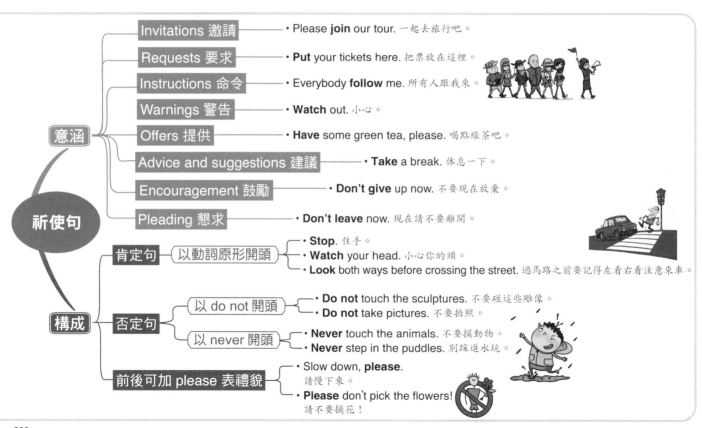

意涵

祈使句

- Invitations 邀請 —— · Please **join** our tour. 一起去旅行吧。
- Requests 要求 —— · **Put** your tickets here. 把票放在這裡。
- Instructions 命令 —— · Everybody **follow** me. 所有人跟我來。
- Warnings 警告 —— · **Watch** out. 小心。
- Offers 提供 —— · **Have** some green tea, please. 喝點綠茶吧。
- Advice and suggestions 建議 —— · **Take** a break. 休息一下。
- Encouragement 鼓勵 —— · **Don't give** up now. 不要現在放棄。
- Pleading 懇求 —— · **Don't leave** now. 現在請不要離開。

構成

- 肯定句 — 以動詞原形開頭
  - · **Stop**. 住手。
  - · **Watch** your head. 小心你的頭。
  - · **Look** both ways before crossing the street. 過馬路之前要記得左看右看注意來車。
- 否定句
  - 以 do not 開頭
    - · **Do not** touch the sculptures. 不要碰這些雕像。
    - · **Do not** take pictures. 不要拍照。
  - 以 never 開頭
    - · **Never** touch the animals. 不要摸動物。
    - · **Never** step in the puddles. 別踩進水坑。
- 前後可加 please 表禮貌
  - · Slow down, **please**. 請慢下來。
  - · **Please** don't pick the flowers! 請不要摘花！

Practice

1 下列句子哪些屬於祈使句？請在祈使句前面打 ✓。

.... **1.** Help yourself to that egg.

.... **2.** You must talk to your teacher right away.

.... **3.** Do not touch the stove.

.... **4.** Can't you be honest?

.... **5.** Please sit down.

.... **6.** Tie your shoes this way.

.... **7.** Nobody trusts Jason.

.... **8.** Go back to bed now.

.... **9.** I won't let you leave home.

.... **10.** Don't feed your brother worms.

2 將下列句子改寫為祈使句。

1. Paul, I want you to close that door.

→ ....

2. You should not go out at midnight.

→ ....

3. You can't throw garbage into the toilet.

→ ....

4. Can you go buy some eggs now?

→ ....

5. I hope you're not mad at me.

→ ....

6. You can take a No. 305 bus to the city hall.

→ ....

7. You should be careful not to wake up the baby.

→ ....

8. You don't have to worry about so many things.

→ ....

9. You should relax.

→ ....

10. Why don't you do your homework right now?

→ ....

Unit 71-75
重點複習

1 分辨下列句子是肯定句、否定句還是疑問句。
在肯定句的前面寫上 A（affirmative），在否定句的前面寫上 N（negative），在疑問句的前面寫上 Q（question）。

1. You can't get into that room.
2. That is the best movie I've ever watched.
3. Betty is never late for work.
4. Am I wrong about him?
5. They're not from Peru.
6. Did he make these cookies by himself?
7. Timmy bought two boxes of chocolate in the store.
8. Have you ever seen a whale?
9. What happened last night?
10. I'll come back in fifteen minutes.

Unit 72-75
重點複習

2 用 Who、What、Where、When、Why、How、Which 或 Whose 等疑問詞，完成填空。

1. _____ can I pick up my dry cleaning? Tonight or tomorrow morning?
2. _____ can I get new sports shoes?
3. _____ is the most famous Japanese musician?
4. _____ much does a lottery ticket cost?
5. _____ left the refrigerator door open?
6. _____ do you want to go on a vacation? Guam?
7. _____ does the plane leave for Bali?
8. _____ many brothers and sisters do you have?
9. _____ did you hit your sister?
10. _____ should people eat a balanced diet?
11. _____ train did you take on Friday night, the 9:30 p.m. train or the one at 11:30 p.m.?
12. _____ is the name of the tallest mountain in the world?

13. _____ of these novels did you enjoy reading the most?

14. _____ are the names of the movies you have seen this month?

15. _____ scooter is blocking my car?

16. _____ turn is it to use the bathroom?

Unit 73 重點複習

❸ 依據底線的提示，將句子以 who 或 what 造出問句。

1. **Eve** is visiting Charles.

    → _Who is visiting Charles?_

2. Eve is visiting **Charles**.

    → _____

3. **Edward** wants to meet Cathy.

    → _____

4. Cathy wants to meet **Edward**.

    → _____

5. He took the **birthday cake** with him.

    → _____

6. Keith is dating **someone**.

    → _____

7. **Something** crashed.

    → _____

8. **Dad** answered the phone.

    → _____

9 **Someone** wants to marry Jenny.

    → _____

10. Dennis wants to buy **a new cell phone**.

    → _____

11. **Dennis** wants to buy a new cell phone.

    → _____

12. **Sylvia** wants to eat peanuts.

    → _____

13. Sylvia wants to eat **peanuts**.

    → _____

4 請在每一句的後面，加上正確的附加問句。

1. Sightseeing is fun, _____isn't it?_____

2. Working 60 hours a week isn't good for you,

_____

3. Chocolate chip cookies are tasty, _____

4. We aren't too old to have a good time,

_____

5. You did a good job on the report, _____

6. You didn't get the letter in the mail, _____

7. The meeting was boring, _____

8. The project wasn't finished on time, _____

9. You liked the lentils, _____

5 請將下列錯誤的句子，更正重寫。

1. Who Chris is calling?

→ _Who is Chris calling?_

2. What Irene wants to do?

→ _____

3. Who does want to stay for dinner?

→ _____

4. Who the last piece of cake finished?

→ _____

5. Who did invented the automobile?

→ _____

6. Who's dirty dishes are these on the table?

→ _____

7. What side of the road do you drive on?

→ _____

8. Rupert likes history, does he?

→ _____

9. They drive a minivan, don't it?

→ _____

Unit 77 重點複習

❻ 找出下列對話中屬於**祈使句**的用法，劃上底線。

Bob: How can I get to the station?

Eve: <u>Go</u> straight down this road. Walk for fifteen minutes and you will see a park.

Bob: So, the station is near the park.

Eve: Yes. Turn right at the park and walk for another five minutes.
Cross the main road. The station will be at your left. You won't miss it.

Bob: That's very helpful of you.

Eve: Be sure not to take any small alleys on the way.

Bob: I won't. Thank you very much.

Eve: You're welcome.

Unit 71–75 重點複習

❼ 將下列句子分別改寫為否定句和疑問句。

1. Eddie is a naughty boy.

→ *Eddie isn't a naughty boy.*

→ *Is Eddie a naughty boy?*

2. Jack walks to work every morning.

→

→

3. Sammi visited Uncle Lu last Saturday.

→

→

4. She will be able to finish the project next week.

→

→

5. My boss is going to Beijing tomorrow.

→

→

6. Joe has already seen the show.

→

→

Unit 79　片語動詞（1）

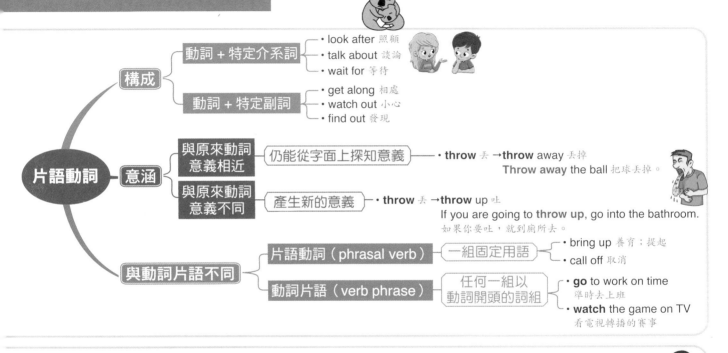

片語動詞

- **構成**
  - 動詞 + 特定介系詞
    - look after 照顧
    - talk about 談論
    - wait for 等待
  - 動詞 + 特定副詞
    - get along 相處
    - watch out 小心
    - find out 發現
- **意涵**
  - 與原來動詞意義相近 ── 仍能從字面上探知意義
    - **throw** 丟 →**throw** away 丟掉
      Throw away the ball 把球丟掉。
  - 與原來動詞意義不同 ── 產生新的意義
    - **throw** 丟 →**throw** up 吐
      If you are going to **throw up**, go into the bathroom. 如果你要吐，就到廁所去。
- **與動詞片語不同**
  - 片語動詞（phrasal verb）── 一組固定用語
    - bring up 養育；提起
    - call off 取消
  - 動詞片語（verb phrase）── 任何一組以動詞開頭的詞組
    - **go** to work on time 準時去上班
    - **watch** the game on TV 看電視轉播的賽事

片語動詞單獨存在

- 為「動詞 + 副詞」組合時
  - stand up 起立
  - take off 起飛
- 後面不需再加受詞
  - When you hear your name, please **stand up**. 叫到你的名字時請站起來。
  - Don't **take off** until I get back. 我還沒回去前請先別出發。

片語動詞單獨存在

- **watch out** 小心
  Watch out! There's a car coming.
  小心！有車子來了。
- **shut up** 閉嘴
  Will you please **shut up**?
  拜託你閉嘴好嗎？
- **show up** 出現
  Jason promised to come to the meeting, but he never **showed up**.
  傑森答應要來開會，但一直沒出現。
- **go off** 響起
  The alarm clock **went off** while I was having a sweet dream.
  我好夢正甜時，鬧鐘就響了。
- **calm down** 冷靜
  Calm down. I'll help you go through all this.
  冷靜點，我會幫你度過這一切。
- **hang out** 在某地逗留；與某人相處
  We should **hang out** together at the mall sometime next week.
  我們下星期找個時間在購物中心聚聚。
- **give up** 放棄
  Don't **give up**.
  不要放棄。

Practice

1 自框內選出正確的片語動詞填空，並做出適當的變化，完成句子。

come along	take off	stay up	work out
move in	hang out	come in	

1. My wife didn't _____ on the trip to Egypt.
2. Curtis needs to _____ at the gym more often.
3. Why don't we _____ together next week?
4. The plane has _____. You're too late.
5. You look tired. Did you _____ late last night?
6. Another family is _____ to the neighborhood.

2 選出正確的答案。

1. Are we going to eat **up/out** tonight?
2. I think I'll try to encourage him. He shouldn't give **up/off**.
3. Did he show **up/down** at the party? I didn't see him.
4. I'm moving **in/out** tomorrow. We'll soon become roommates.
5. Don't stand there. Sit **up/down**.
6. I'm sorry for being late. The alarm clock didn't go **on/off** this morning.
7. Fay fell **out/down** and got hurt.
8. Can I have a plastic bag? I feel like throwing **out/up**.

Unit **80** 片語動詞（2）

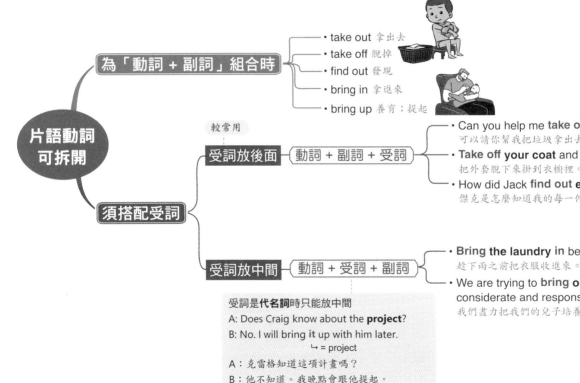

片語動詞可拆開

為「動詞 + 副詞」組合時
- take out 拿出去
- take off 脫掉
- find out 發現
- bring in 拿進來
- bring up 養育；提起

須搭配受詞

受詞放後面 （較常用）　動詞 + 副詞 + 受詞
- Can you help me **take out the garbage**?
  可以請你幫我把垃圾拿出去丟嗎？
- **Take off your coat** and hang it in the closet.
  把外套脫下來掛到衣櫥裡。
- How did Jack **find out everything about me**?
  傑克是怎麼知道我的每一件事情的？

受詞放中間　動詞 + 受詞 + 副詞
- **Bring the laundry in** before it rains.
  趁下雨之前把衣服收進來。
- We are trying to **bring our son up** to be considerate and responsible.
  我們盡力把我們的兒子培養得既體貼又有責任感。

受詞是**代名詞**時只能放中間
A: Does Craig know about the **project**?
B: No. I will bring **it** up with him later.
　　↳ = project
A：克雷格知道這項計畫嗎？
B：他不知道。我晚點會跟他提起。

片語動詞可拆開

- **look up** 查閱
  Pan **looked up** the word in the dictionary.
  = Pan **looked** the word **up** in the dictionary.
  潘在字典裡查了這個字。

- **fill out** 填寫
  Please **fill out** the form. → Please **fill it out**.
  請填妥這張表格。

- **call off** 取消
  They **called off** the game because of rain.
  → They **called it off** because of rain.
  他們因雨取消了這場比賽。

- **turn up/down** 調大聲／調小聲
  Turn down the volume. → **Turn it down**.
  把聲音調小一點。

- **turn on/off** 打開／關閉
  He **turned on** the light and started to read.
  = He **turned** the light **on** and started to read.
  他開燈開始看書。

- **put out** 撲滅
  The firefighter **put out** the fire within an hour.
  = The firefighter **put** the fire **out** within an hour.
  消防人員在一小時內撲滅了火勢。

- **set off** 點燃
  They **set off** the fireworks.
  = They **set** the fireworks **off**.
  他們點燃爆竹。

- **turn down** 拒絕
  The manager **turned down** his proposal.
  = The manager **turned** his proposal **down**.
  經理推翻了他的提議。

Practice

❶ 自框內選出正確的片語動詞來填空，並依照範例，用另外兩種句型來改寫句子。

set off	turn down	try on
take off	fill out	throw away

1. Dick and Byron ___*set off*___ the fire crackers.
   → *Dick and Byron set the fire crackers off.*
   → *Dick and Byron set them off.*

2. Don't _____ the price tag in case we have to return the sweater.
   → _____
   → _____

3. Don't _____ the offer right away.
   → _____
   → _____

4. We don't _____ bottles if they can be recycled.
   → _____
   → _____

5. You need to _____ the form and attach two photos.
   → _____
   → _____

6. Would you like to _____ these shoes?
   → _____
   → _____

片語動詞
不可拆開

為「動詞 + 介系詞」組合時
- take after 與……相似
- pull for 支持

須搭配受詞 —— 只能放最後 —— 動詞 + 介系詞 + 受詞
- Your daughter **takes after your wife**.
  你女兒很像你太太。
- The crowd is **pulling for the home team**.
  群眾全力支持地主隊。

較長片語
動詞

組成較長 —— 為「動詞 + 副詞 + 介系詞」組合時
- look forward to 期待
- move away from 搬離

須搭配受詞 —— 只能放最後 —— 動詞 + 副詞 + 介系詞 + 受詞
- Walter is **looking forward to a break** after finishing the IPO.
  在完成公司初次公開上市的工作之後，華特很期待能小休一下。
- Nicole is **moving away from home** for the first time.
  這是妮可第一次離開家。

- **apply for** 申請
  I have already **applied for** the job.
  我已經去應徵這份工作了。
- **arrive in** 抵達
  Gina **arrived in** Athens on Saturday.
  吉娜於星期六抵達了雅典。
- **depend on** 依靠
  Success **depends on** hard work.
  成功端賴努力。
- **look after** 照顧
  Could you **look after** the baby on weekends?
  你可以每個週末照顧寶寶嗎？
- **look for** 尋找
  Scientists are **looking for** some rare elements.
  科學家們在尋找一些稀有元素。
- **run into** 遇見
  I **ran into** an old friend on my way home.
  我在回家的路上遇到一位老朋友。

- **keep away from** 遠離
  Keep away from the broken windows. 遠離碎裂的窗戶。
- **catch up with** 趕上
  You should study hard to **catch up with** your classmates.
  你要用功才能趕上你同學。
- **get along with** 與……相處
  I can't **get along with** Susan. 我跟蘇珊無法相處。
- **put up with** 忍受
  I can't **put up with** him anymore. 我再也受不了他了。
- **be fed up with** 受夠
  Shut up. I'm **fed up with** your lies.
  不要再說了，我聽夠了你的謊言。

Practice

❶ 自框內選出正確的片語動詞填空，完成句子。

catch up with	come across	watch out for
put up with	look after	

1. It's hard to _____ other people's kids.
2. _____ the bucket on the floor.
3. You can leave now, and I will _____ you later.
4. I can _____ almost anything except screaming babies.
5. If you _____ any wooden napkin rings, please let me know.

❷ 自框內選出適當的介系詞填空，完成句子。

on	of	into	to	off	for

1. I got _____ the train at Angel Street and got _____ at the main station.
2. I ran _____ Jack this morning. He was in a hurry, so we didn't talk.
3. Thank you for coming. I look forward _____ seeing you next time.
4. We ran out _____ toilet paper. I'll buy some this afternoon.
5. Winnie applied _____ the scholarship last week.

1 自框內選出適當的片語動詞，填空完成句子。

1. Please _____ me _____ at seven tomorrow morning. I don't want to sleep late.

2. Alison is going to _____ with her friends at the Internet café tonight.

3. The plane is going to _____ soon. We have to _____ the plane right away.

4. When are we going to _____ this report?

5. Sam _____ his old cell phone and bought a new one.

6. When are you going to _____ to your new apartment?

7. _____ the car now.

8. _____ the grass. Don't step on it.

9. Please _____ the registration form.

10. We are _____ each other very well.

11. She walks so fast. I can hardly _____ her.

12. Could you _____ Janet on your way to the office?

13. I _____ in the country, but I'm living in the city now.

14. Aunt Sally _____ her two kids all by herself.

15. **Pete:** Where is Tony?
    Ron: He is _____ at the gym.

16. The vice president is not available tomorrow. We'll have to _____ the meeting.

17. He finished the conversation with Zoe and _____ the phone.

18. May I _____ this coat?

get in
throw away
take off
hang out
wake up
pick up
work out
call off
get on
hand in
grow up
fill out
get along with
bring up
move in
keep away from
hang up
keep up with
try on

❷ 自框內選出適當的副詞或介系詞，搭配句中的動詞構成片語動詞，填空完成句子。

look

up	down	in
out	on	off
after	away	for

1. I'm .... my wallet. Did you see it?

2. .... the meaning of this phrasal verb in your electronic dictionary.

3. I have to .... my little brother on Saturday.

4. ....! Don't trip over that wire.

turn

5. Could you .... the heat, please? It's too hot.

6. Why not .... the TV and relax?

7. Don't .... this offer, because it's the best you are going to get.

8. Make sure you .... the lights before going to bed.

take

9. Could you .... the garbage now?

10. .... your sunglasses so that I can see your eyes.

11. The plane will .... in a few minutes.

12. I don't .... my father. I look like my mother.

put

13. It's cold outside. You should .... a coat.

14. We .... the campfire and left the park.

15. Don't .... the plan until tomorrow.

16. He .... his toys and went to bed.

go

17. I'm back. Please .... with the story.

18. The fire alarm .... at midnight.

19. They .... for a date.

213

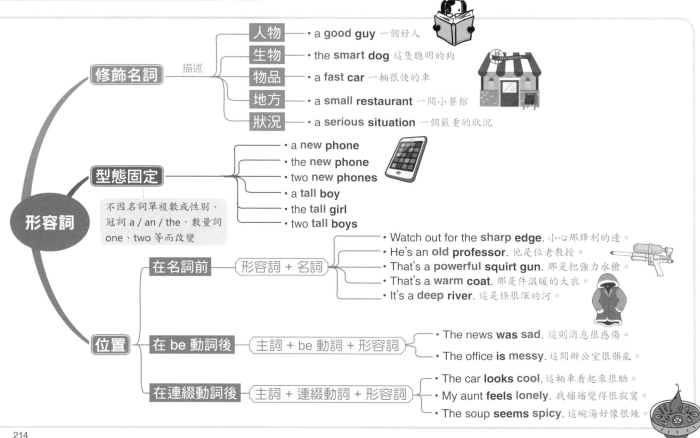

形容詞

修飾名詞 ──描述──
- 人物 ── • a **good** guy 一個好人
- 生物 ── • the **smart** dog 這隻聰明的狗
- 物品 ── • a **fast** car 一輛很快的車
- 地方 ── • a **small** restaurant 一間小餐館
- 狀況 ── • a **serious** situation 一個嚴重的狀況

型態固定
- • a **new** phone
- • the **new** phone
- • two **new** phones
- • a **tall** boy
- • the **tall** girl
- • two **tall** boys

不因名詞單複數或性別、冠詞 a / an / the、數量詞 one、two 等而改變

位置
- **在名詞前** ─（形容詞 + 名詞）
  - • Watch out for the **sharp edge**. 小心那鋒利的邊。
  - • He's an **old professor**. 他是位老教授。
  - • That's a **powerful squirt gun**. 那是把強力水槍。
  - • That's a **warm coat**. 那是件溫暖的大衣。
  - • It's a **deep river**. 這是條很深的河。
- **在 be 動詞後** ─（主詞 + be 動詞 + 形容詞）
  - • The news **was sad**. 這則消息很感傷。
  - • The office **is messy**. 這間辦公室很髒亂。
- **在連綴動詞後** ─（主詞 + 連綴動詞 + 形容詞）
  - • The car **looks cool**. 這輛車看起來很酷。
  - • My aunt **feels lonely**. 我嬸嬸覺得很寂寞。
  - • The soup **seems spicy**. 這碗湯好像很辣。

Practice

1 自框內選出適當的形容詞，搭配圖片的名詞完成填空。

big	small	old	new
soft	hard	curved	straight

pants

his <u>old pants</u>

pants

my _____

chair

a _____

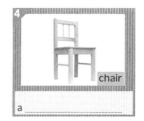
chair

a _____

dog

her _____

dog

his _____

road

a _____

road

a _____

2 將下列各組詞彙重組，以正確語序完成句子。

1. he in lives town small a

   → _____

2. eyes blue she has

   → _____

3. smells the lamb stew good

   → _____

4. two I have kids lovely

   → _____

5. cute is my teddy bear

   → _____

①
· It was an **easy** job. 這是個輕鬆的工作。
　　　↳ 形容詞
· We finished the job **easily**.
　　　　　　↳ 副詞
我們很輕鬆地完成工作。

②
· He has **clean** forgotten it.
　　　↳ 副詞
他完全忘記這件事了。
· He got away **cleanly**. 他逃得無影無蹤。
　　　　　↳ 副詞

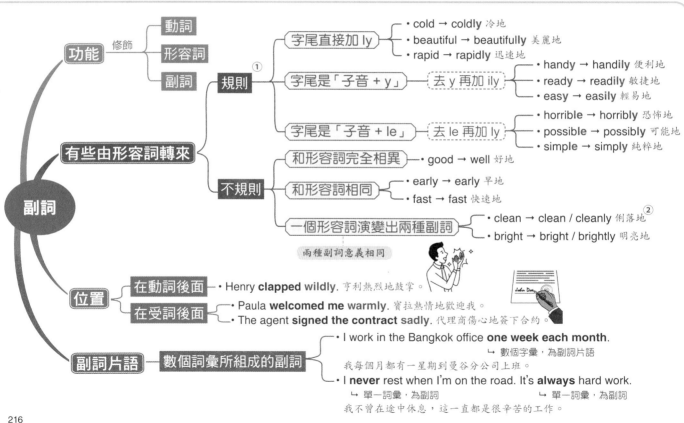

副詞

功能 — 修飾 — 動詞 / 形容詞 / 副詞

有些由形容詞轉來

規則 ①
- 字尾直接加 ly
  - cold → cold**ly** 冷地
  - beautiful → beautiful**ly** 美麗地
  - rapid → rapid**ly** 迅速地
- 字尾是「子音 + y」— 去 y 再加 ily
  - handy → handily 便利地
  - ready → readily 敏捷地
  - easy → easily 輕易地
- 字尾是「子音 + le」— 去 le 再加 ly
  - horrible → horribly 恐怖地
  - possible → possibly 可能地
  - simple → simply 純粹地

不規則
- 和形容詞完全相異
  - good → well 好地
- 和形容詞相同
  - early → early 早地
  - fast → fast 快速地
- 一個形容詞演變出兩種副詞
  - clean → clean / cleanly 俐落地 ②
  - bright → bright / brightly 明亮地

兩種副詞意義相同

位置
- 在動詞後面
  - Henry **clapped wildly**. 亨利熱烈地鼓掌。
- 在受詞後面
  - Paula **welcomed me warmly**. 寶拉熱情地歡迎我。
  - The agent **signed the contract sadly**. 代理商傷心地簽下合約。

副詞片語 — 數個詞彙所組成的副詞
- I work in the Bangkok office **one week each month**.
  　　　　　　　　　　　↳ 數個字彙，為副詞片語
  我每個月都有一星期到曼谷分公司上班。
- I **never** rest when I'm on the road. It's **always** hard work.
  　↳ 單一詞彙，為副詞　　　　　　　　　↳ 單一詞彙，為副詞
  我不曾在途中休息，這一直都是很辛苦的工作。

Practice

❶ 寫出下列形容詞所對應的副詞。

1. careful _____
2. possible _____
3. merry _____
4. usual _____
5. entire _____
6. cheerful _____
7. real _____

8. quick _____
9. honest _____
10. silent _____
11. fast _____
12. early _____
13. strange _____
14. calm _____

15. angry _____
16. good _____
17. final _____
18. slow _____
19. wise _____
20. deep _____

❷ 運用粗體字的副詞形式，搭配括弧內提示的動詞，改寫各個句子。

1. He gave a **clear** answer. (answer)
   → *He answered clearly.*

2. He's a **bad** singer. (sing)
   → _____

3. He was **late** for school. (arrive)
   → _____

4. She's a **good** painter. (paint)
   → _____

5. She's a **fast** learner. (learn)
   → _____

6. He's a **noisy** worker. (work)
   → _____

7. She's a **professional** translator. (translate)
   → _____

8. It was a **terrible** earthquake. (tremble)
   → _____

9. She's a **fast** reader. (read)
   → _____

10. She's a **frequent** shopper. (shop)
    → _____

Unit 85 時間副詞／地方副詞

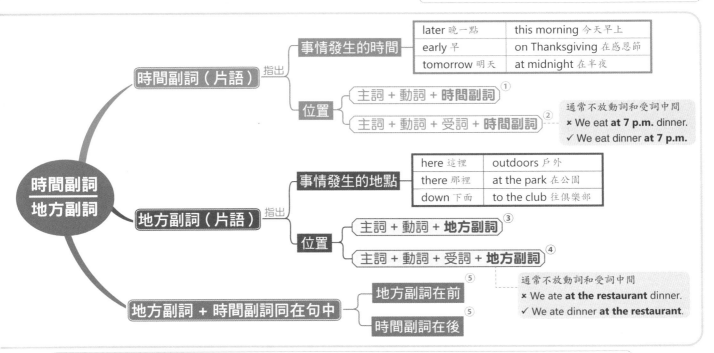

主詞	➕ 動詞	➕ 時間副詞	
• The plane	arrived	**late**.	這班飛機誤點了。
• Ladies	go	**first**.	女士優先。

時間副詞 地方副詞

時間副詞（片語） — 指出

事情發生的時間

later 晚一點	this morning 今天早上
early 早	on Thanksgiving 在感恩節
tomorrow 明天	at midnight 在半夜

位置
- 主詞 + 動詞 + **時間副詞** ①
- 主詞 + 動詞 + 受詞 + **時間副詞** ②

通常不放動詞和受詞中間
✗ We eat **at 7 p.m.** dinner.
✓ We eat dinner **at 7 p.m.**

地方副詞（片語） — 指出

事情發生的地點

here 這裡	outdoors 戶外
there 那裡	at the park 在公園
down 下面	to the club 往俱樂部

位置
- 主詞 + 動詞 + **地方副詞** ③
- 主詞 + 動詞 + 受詞 + **地方副詞** ④

通常不放動詞和受詞中間
✗ We ate **at the restaurant** dinner.
✓ We ate dinner **at the restaurant**.

地方副詞 + 時間副詞同在句中
- 地方副詞在前 ⑤
- 時間副詞在後 ⑤

主詞	➕ 動詞（片語）➕	地方副詞	➕	時間副詞	
• Ronald	ate his lunch	**behind the store**		**after the delivery truck left**.	貨車離開後，雷諾在商店吃午餐。
• Judy	walked	**to Suzy's house**		**on Saturday afternoon**.	茱蒂在星期六下午走路到蘇西家。
• Trent	had a party	**in his house**		**on Christmas day**.	聖誕節那天，崔特在他家舉辦派對。

②

主詞 ⊕	動詞 ⊕	受詞 ⊕	時間副詞	
• He	brushes	his teeth	**in the morning**.	他早上刷牙。
• She	baked	the cake	**before the party**.	她在派對開始前烤了一個蛋糕。

③

主詞	⊕ 動詞 ⊕	地方副詞	
• He	lives	**in the suburbs**.	他住在郊外。
• The newspaper	was	**in the mailbox**.	報紙在信箱裡。

④

主詞 ⊕	動詞 ⊕	受詞 ⊕	地方副詞	
• Wally	parked	the car	**in the driveway**.	華利把車子停在車道上。
• Erica	took	the box	**to the post office**.	艾麗卡把箱子拿去郵局。

Practice

❶ 將下列各組詞彙重組，以正確的語序完成句子。

1. over there　my parents　live

   → *My parents live over there.*

2. they bought　over 20 years ago　the house

   → ....

3. pays the mortgage　on the first day of each month　my dad

   to the bank

   → ....

   ....

4. to Wendy's house　were delivered　this morning　no packages

   → ....

5. Jack and Jimmy　at the café　are going to meet

   this afternoon

   → ....

❷ 依提示回答問題。

1. When and where did you leave the bag?

   (in the cloakroom / at 4:30 yesterday)

   → ....

   ....

2. When and where did you last see him?

   (on January 22nd / at Teresa's birthday party)

   → ....

   ....

3. When and where did you buy that book?

   (last week / at the bookstore around the corner)

   → ....

   ....

4. When and where do you go swimming?

   (at the health club / on Sundays)

   → ....

   ....

5. When and where did you learn to dive?

   (three years ago / at the Pacific Diving Club)

   → ....

   ....

①
- Morty **always eats** lunch at his desk.
  莫提總是在他的辦公桌吃午餐。
- I **rarely drink** coffee at night.
  我晚上很少喝咖啡。
- We **often develop** plans as a team.
  我們通常團隊一起構思企畫。
- David **never remembers** his dreams.
  大衛從來不記得他做過的夢。

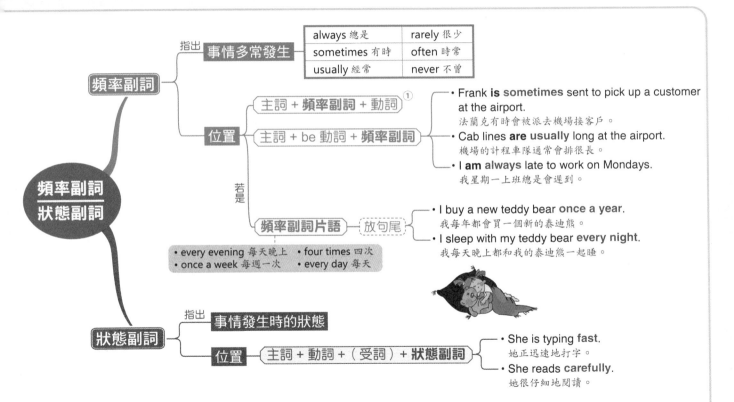

頻率副詞 / 狀態副詞

頻率副詞
— 指出 → 事情多常發生

always 總是	rarely 很少
sometimes 有時	often 時常
usually 經常	never 不曾

— 位置
- 主詞 + **頻率副詞** + 動詞 ①
  - • Frank **is sometimes** sent to pick up a customer at the airport.
    法蘭克有時會被派去機場接客戶。
- 主詞 + be 動詞 + **頻率副詞**
  - • Cab lines **are usually** long at the airport.
    機場的計程車隊通常會排很長。
  - • I **am always** late to work on Mondays.
    我星期一上班總是會遲到。

若是
頻率副詞片語 — 放句尾
- • I buy a new teddy bear **once a year**.
  我每年都會買一個新的泰迪熊。
- • I sleep with my teddy bear **every night**.
  我每天晚上都和我的泰迪熊一起睡。

- every evening 每天晚上　• four times 四次
- once a week 每週一次　• every day 每天

狀態副詞
— 指出 → 事情發生時的狀態
— 位置 — 主詞 + 動詞 + （受詞）+ **狀態副詞**
  - • She is typing **fast**.
    她正迅速地打字。
  - • She reads **carefully**.
    她很仔細地閱讀。

Practice

① 將下列各組詞彙重組，以正確的語序完成句子。

1. he   misses   never   the mortgage payment

    → ....

2. is   in the morning   always   the first customer   he

    → ....

3. he   to work   walks   every day

    → ....

4. the water   quickly   overflowed

    → ....

5. exploded   suddenly   the volcano

    → ....

6. many burglaries   lately   have been   there

    → ....

7. entirely   their minds   that   changed

    → ....

② 依據事實，使用頻率副詞回答下列問題。

1. How often do you go to school?

    → ....

2. How often do you exercise?

    → ....

3. How often do you go on a trip to a foreign country?

    → ....

4. How often do you go to a movie?

    → ....

5. How often do you do the dishes?

    → ....

6. How often do you visit your grandparents?

    → ....

7. How often do you eat fast food?

    → ....

8. How often do you work on Saturdays?

    → ....

形容詞型態

- 原級
- 比較級 — 比較兩個事物
- 最高級 — 比較三個以上的事物

表示 → 修飾的程度

原級	比較級	最高級
young 年輕的	younger 較年輕的	youngest 最年輕的
big 大的	bigger 較大的	biggest 最大的
beautiful 美的	more beautiful 較美的 less beautiful 較不美的	most beautiful 最美的 least beautiful 最不美的

- Look at that **old** ship.
  看那艘老舊的船。
- That ship is as **old** as my great grandfather.
  那艘船就跟我的曾祖父一樣老。
- If there is an **older** one, I don't see it.
  我還沒看過比這更舊的船。

- That is the **oldest** ship at the dock.
  那是碼頭裡最舊的一艘船。
- Your kite is **higher** than my kite, but his kite is the **highest**.
  你的風箏飛得比我的高，但是他的風箏飛得最高。

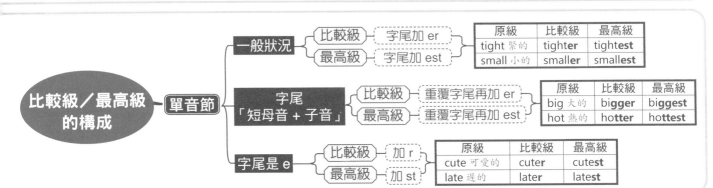

比較級／最高級的構成

單音節

一般狀況
- 比較級 — 字尾加 er
- 最高級 — 字尾加 est

原級	比較級	最高級
tight 緊的	tighter	tightest
small 小的	smaller	smallest

字尾「短母音＋子音」
- 比較級 — 重覆字尾再加 er
- 最高級 — 重覆字尾再加 est

原級	比較級	最高級
big 大的	bigger	biggest
hot 熱的	hotter	hottest

字尾是 e
- 比較級 — 加 r
- 最高級 — 加 st

原級	比較級	最高級
cute 可愛的	cuter	cutest
late 遲的	later	latest

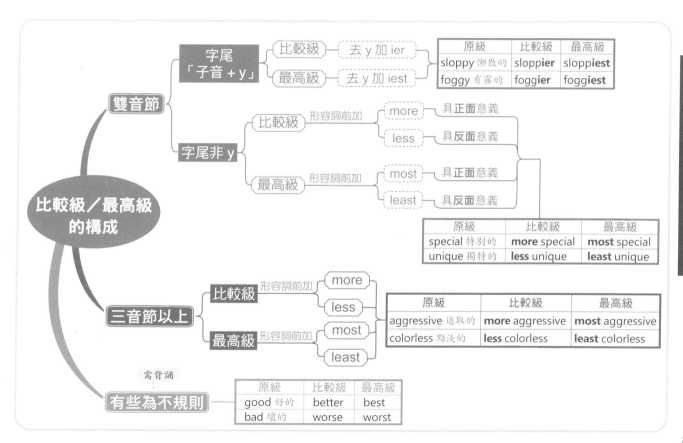

原級	比較級	最高級
sloppy 懶散的	sloppier	sloppiest
foggy 有霧的	foggier	foggiest

原級	比較級	最高級
special 特別的	more special	most special
unique 獨特的	less unique	least unique

原級	比較級	最高級
aggressive 進取的	more aggressive	most aggressive
colorless 黯淡的	less colorless	least colorless

需背誦

原級	比較級	最高級
good 好的	better	best
bad 壞的	worse	worst

比較級／最高級的構成

雙音節
　字尾「子音＋y」
　　比較級 → 去 y 加 ier
　　最高級 → 去 y 加 iest
　字尾非 y
　　比較級　形容詞前加
　　　more　具正面意義
　　　less　具反面意義
　　最高級　形容詞前加
　　　most　具正面意義
　　　least　具反面意義

三音節以上
　比較級　形容詞前加
　　more
　　less
　最高級　形容詞前加
　　most
　　least

有些為不規則

Practice

1 寫出下列形容詞的比較級和最高級。

1. tall ....
2. long ....
3. short ....
4. fine ....
5. spicy ....
6. big ....
7. close ....
8. slim ....
9. thin ....
10. late ....

11. bad ....
12. many ....
13. fat ....
14. tiny ....
15. pale ....
16. bright ....
17. sappy ....
18. slimy ....
19. thick ....
20. calm ....

❷ 將括弧內的形容詞以「最高級」的形式填空，來詢問「誰是最⋯⋯的人」，並依據事實回答問題。

1. Who is _____(cute) in your class?

→ _____

2. Who is _____(hardworking) in your class?

→ _____

3. Who is _____(funny) in your class?

→ _____

4. Who is _____(boring) in your class?

→ _____

5. Who is _____(friendly) in your class?

→ _____

6. Who is _____(tall) in your class?

→ _____

7. Who is _____(smart) in your class?

→ _____

8. Who is _____(creative) in your class?

→ _____

Unit 88 表「比較」的句型

①
- That is **the tallest** building in the city. 那是這座城市最高的大樓。
  ↳ 這城市有三座以上的高樓
- She is **the most amazing** woman I have ever met. 她是我見過最不可思議的女子。
  ↳ 我見過三個以上令人驚嘆的女子

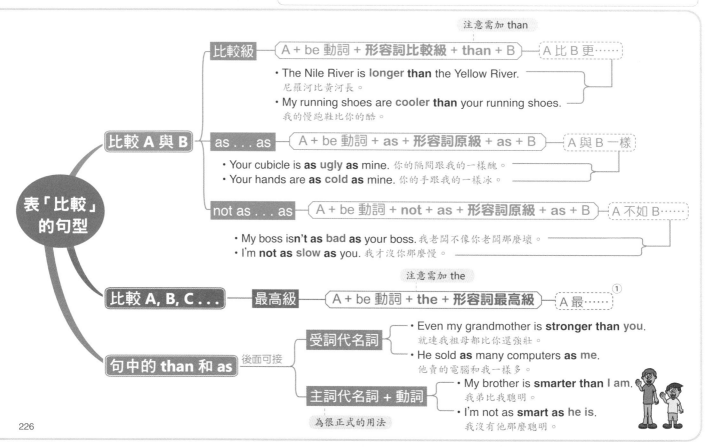

表「比較」的句型

比較 A 與 B

比較級 — A + be 動詞 + **形容詞比較級** + **than** + B — A 比 B 更……
注意需加 than
- The Nile River is **longer than** the Yellow River.
  尼羅河比黃河長。
- My running shoes are **cooler than** your running shoes.
  我的慢跑鞋比你的酷。

as . . . as — A + be 動詞 + **as** + **形容詞原級** + **as** + B — A 與 B 一樣
- Your cubicle is **as ugly as** mine. 你的隔間跟我的一樣醜。
- Your hands are **as cold as** mine. 你的手跟我的一樣冰。

not as . . . as — A + be 動詞 + **not** + **as** + **形容詞原級** + **as** + B — A 不如 B
- My boss isn't **as bad as** your boss. 我老闆不像你老闆那麼壞。
- I'm **not as slow as** you. 我才沒你那麼慢。

比較 A, B, C . . .

最高級 — A + be 動詞 + **the** + **形容詞最高級** — A 最……①
注意需加 the

句中的 than 和 as

後面可接

受詞代名詞
- Even my grandmother is **stronger than you**.
  就連我祖母都比你還強壯。
- He sold **as** many computers **as me**.
  他賣的電腦和我一樣多。

主詞代名詞 + 動詞
- My brother is **smarter than I am**.
  我弟比我聰明。
- I'm not as **smart as he is**.
  我沒有他那麼聰明。

為很正式的用法

Practice

❶ 依據圖示，用框內的詞彙，以「A is . . . than B」的句型來描述 Jim 和 Ken 的不同。

Jim

Ken

1. Ken is shorter than Jim.
2. _____
3. _____
4. _____
5. _____
6. _____
7. _____
8. _____

short
professional
fat
tall
casual
business-like
intense
lighthearted

❷ 將錯誤的句子打 ✗，並改寫為正確的句子。若句子無誤，則打 ✓。

★ Labrador：拉布拉多，一種獵犬。

1. Mt. Everest is highest mountain in the world.

   (✗) _Mt. Everest is the highest mountain in the world._

2. The Japan Trench is deeper the Java Trench, but the Mariana Trench is deepest.

   ( ) _____

   _____

3. Africa is not as large than Asia.

   ( ) _____

4. Blue whales are the larger animal in the world.

   ( ) _____

5. A giant rabbit can grow as big as a Labrador.

   ( ) _____

6. China is not as more democratic as the United States.

   ( ) _____

7. The Burj Dubai is tallest than Taipei 101.

   ( ) _____

8. The Pacific Ocean is larger than the Indian Ocean.

   ( ) _____

Unit 89 too 和 enough 搭配形容詞或副詞

too 搭配形容詞或副詞

too + 形容詞 — 太…… — • I can't see. It's **too foggy**. 我看不見，霧太濃了。

too + 副詞 — 太…… — • Hurry up. You're walking **too slow**. 快一點，你走得太慢了。

too + 形容詞／副詞 + for + 受詞 — 對受詞太…… — • I found a studio apartment, but it was **too expensive** for you.
我找到一間公寓套房，但對你而言太貴了。

too + 形容詞／副詞 + to V — 太……而無法…… — • This bar is **too noisy to hold** a conversation.
酒吧太吵了，無法談話。

too + 形容詞／副詞 + for + 受詞 + to V — 對受詞太……而無法…… — • It was **too noisy for me to read**.
太吵了，我無法看書。

與 very 同為程度副詞 —差異—

too 表「超過需要」 — • Larry is not a good swimmer, and he has been underwater **too long**.
賴瑞不太會游泳，他已經待在水底太久了。
↳ too 表示已超過他應該待在水底的時間

very 用來強調形容詞 — • Terry is a fast swimmer. She swims **very fast**.
泰芮是位游泳健將，她游得非常快。
↳ very 用來強調她游得多快

形容詞 + enough ── 表「足夠的」── • You can't wear my clothes. You aren't **big** enough.
你不能穿我的衣服，你的體型不夠大。

副詞 + enough ── 表「足夠地」── • I can't read your phone number. You're not writing **clearly** enough.
我看不到你的電話號碼，你寫得不夠清楚。

形容詞／副詞 + enough + for + 受詞 ── 對受詞夠……
• The apartment is **cheap** enough **for me**.
這間公寓對我而言夠便宜了。

**enough
搭配形容詞
或副詞**

形容詞／副詞 + enough + to V ── 夠……而可以……── • This café is **quiet** enough **to read**.
這家咖啡廳夠安靜，可以讀書。

形容詞／副詞 + enough + for + 受詞 + to V ── 對受詞夠……而可以……
• It wasn't **quiet** enough **for him to read**.
不夠安靜，他無法看書。

❶ 這些工作場合有什麼問題？請依據圖示，自框內選出適當的形容詞或副詞，用「too...」的句型造句，描述圖片中狀況。

| noisy | dark | busy | talkative | many |

1. Charlie couldn't talk on the phone because it was _____.

2. Amy couldn't take a coffee break because there were _____ phone calls.

3. Andrew couldn't see the keyboard very well because it was _____.

4. Jessica couldn't help her colleagues with their work because she was _____.

5. Tony couldn't concentrate on his work because his colleagues were _____.

❷ 使用框內的句型，改寫上一大題的句子。　　**too . . . (for sb.) to . . .**

1. *It was too noisy for Charlie to talk on the phone.*

2. _____

3. _____

4. _____

5. _____

Unit 83
重點複習

❶ 依據圖示，自框內選出適當的詞彙，用 **is** 或 **look** 來造句。

| fat | healthy and quick | tall | short | strong | weak | happy | thoughtful |

He is/looks strong.

Unit 83–84
重點複習

❷ 選出正確的答案。

1. It was a **clear/clearly** day.

2. He loved her **dear/dearly**.

3. It was a **fair/fairly** shot.

4. The decision was **just/justly**.

5. It was a **wide/widely** river.

6. The bunny ran **quick/quickly**.

7. He was **wrong/wrongly** accused.

8. The balloon drifted **slow/slowly**.

9. She drove home **careful/carefully**.

❸ 將下列詞彙依正確的語序重組，並在結尾加上句號或問號，完成句子。

1. guy | handsome | a | is | He
→ *He is a handsome guy.*

2. to his office | takes the subway | Ned
→

3. to take a break | ready | Penny | is | always
→

4. terrible | is | driver | a | Dennis
→

5. Dennis | terribly | drives
→

6. I'm | to | excited | too | wait
→

7. these gifts | for | big | enough | isn't | This bag
→

8. Do you | here | work | in this building
→

9. Does Larry | with his brother | fight | every day
→

10. Did we | at the Italian restaurant | meet | last Monday night
→

④ 依據圖示，自框內選出適當的頻率副詞填空。

Mon. Tue. Wed. Thur. Fri. Sat. Sun.

1. Meg reads books _____.

Mon. Tue. Wed. Thur. Fri. Sat. Sun.

2. Tom drives to work _____.

Mon. Tue. Wed. Thur. Fri. Sat. Sun.

3. Luke _____ drinks coffee.

Mon. Tue. Wed. Thur. Fri. Sat. Sun.

4. Jason _____ eats French fries.

Mon. Tue. Wed. Thur. Fri. Sat. Sun.

5. Steve _____ takes vitamins.

| never |
| often |
| twice a week |
| every day |
| sometimes |

⑤ 依據圖示，自框內選出適當的頻率副詞填空，完成句子。

| every week | always | six times a month | every Sunday |

FEBRUARY ● ● ●

SUN	MON	TUE	WED	THU	FRI	SAT
						1
2	3	4	5	6	7	8
9	10	11	12	13	14	15
16	17	18	19	20	21	22
23	24	25	26	27	28	29

1. Jason goes to church _____.

● ● ● **MAY**

SUN	MON	TUE	WED	THU	FRI	SAT
				1	2	3
4	5	6	7	8	9	10
11	12	13	14	15	16	17
18	19	20	21	22	23	24
25	26	27	28	29	30	31

2. Lily goes to the gym _____.

JULY

SUN	MON	TUE	WED	THU	FRI	SAT
		1	2	3	4	5
6	7	8	9	10	11	12
13	14	15	16	17	18	19
20	21	22	23	24	25	26
27	28	29	30	31		

3. Kate _____ goes swimming on Tuesday.

DECEMBER

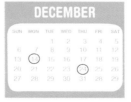

SUN	MON	TUE	WED	THU	FRI	SAT
	1	2	3	4	5	
6	7	8	9	10	11	12
13	14	15	16	17	18	19
20	21	22	23	24	25	26
27	28	29	30	31		

4. Timmy doesn't wash his laundry _____.

Unit 83—84, 87-88 重點複習

6 將下列錯誤的句子打 ✗，並寫出正確的句子。若句子無誤，則在括弧內打 ✓。

1. I see two talls guys.
   (✗) *I see two tall guys.*

2. That is a tall guy.
   (　)

3. Tony is tallest than David.
   (　)

4. Who is the most tall guy in the room?
   (　)

5. John is taller than Sam.
   (　)

6. James is gooder at math than Robert.
   (　)

7. Irving is a happily guy.
   (　)

8. Janice speaks English very good.
   (　)

Unit 84, 86 重點複習

7 依據圖示，自框內選出適當的副詞填空，完成句子。

quietly
slowly
joyfully
eagerly

Kitty is sleeping _____ on the ground.

Dori is chewing the bone _____.

The sisters are pillow fighting _____.

My turtle swims _____.

235

❽ 用「not as ... as」的句型，來比較圖中這些地方。

Canada
Area: 836,109 sq mi

Greenland
Area: 674,843 km²

Iceland

Germany

Sweden
Area: 41,285 km²

Switzerland

Russia
Area: 6,592,800 sq mi

Mt. Everest
Height: 8,848 m

Seoul
Per Capita Income: 39,786 US dollars

France

Spain

Italy

Mexico

Mt. Fuji
Height: 3,776 m

Tokyo
Population: 13,742,906

Egypt

Brazil
Area: 3,287,597 sq mi

Madagascar
Area: 226,597 sq mi

Jakarta
Per Capita Income: 17,374 US dollars

Manila
Population: 1,500,000

1. Mt. Fuji and Mt. Everest (tall)

→ *Mt. Fuji isn't as tall as Mt. Everest.*

2. Brazil and Russia (big)

→ ....

3. Madagascar and Greenland (big)

→ ....

4. Jakarta and Seoul (prosperous)

→ ....

5. Manila and Tokyo (densely populated)

→ ....

6. France and Switzerland (small)

→ ....

7. Iceland and Spain (far south)

→ ....

8. Italy and Germany (far north)

→ ....

9. Canada and Mexico (hot)

→ ....

10. Egypt and Sweden (cold)

→ ....

9 自框內選出適當的形容詞，用題目指定的句型寫出「表示比較」的句子。

| big | high | terrible | tall | fast | hot | warm | sweet | cold |

. . . than

1. An orange is _____ a lemon.
2. A coat is _____ a shirt.
3. Florida is _____ Michigan.

as . . . as

7. Earthquakes are _____ typhoons.
8. Can a horse run _____ a train?
9. Can a kite fly _____ an eagle?

the . . .

4. The Antarctica is _____ place on earth.
5. The Jupiter is _____ planet in our solar system.
6. Taipei 101 is _____ building in Taiwan.

Unit 89 重點複習

10 依據題意，將括弧裡的單字搭配 **too** 或 **enough** 填空。有些題目可有兩種寫法。

1. You have worked _____. (hard)
2. Don't work _____. (late)
3. This soup is _____. (salty)
4. This curry isn't _____. (spicy)

5. The way you speak is _____. (blunt)
6. Your music is _____. (loud)
7. This cell phone is _____. (expensive)
8. This computer is _____. (slow)

Unit 91 介系詞 in / on / at 表地點(1)

in the box

on the box

at the bottom of the pole

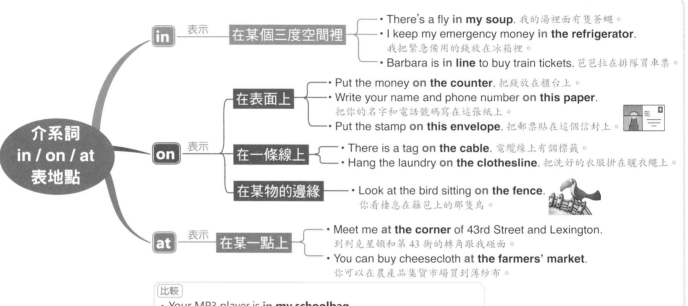

介系詞 in / on / at 表地點

in 表示 在某個三度空間裡
- There's a fly **in my soup**. 我的湯裡面有隻蒼蠅。
- I keep my emergency money **in the refrigerator**. 我把緊急備用的錢放在冰箱裡。
- Barbara is **in line** to buy train tickets. 芭芭拉在排隊買車票。

on 表示
- 在表面上
  - Put the money **on the counter**. 把錢放在櫃台上。
  - Write your name and phone number **on this paper**. 把你的名字和電話號碼寫在這張紙上。
  - Put the stamp **on this envelope**. 把郵票貼在這個信封上。
- 在一條線上
  - There is a tag **on the cable**. 電纜線上有個標籤。
  - Hang the laundry **on the clothesline**. 把洗好的衣服掛在曬衣繩上。
- 在某物的邊緣
  - Look at the bird sitting **on the fence**. 你看棲息在籬笆上的那隻鳥。

at 表示 在某一點上
- Meet me **at the corner** of 43rd Street and Lexington. 到列克星頓和第 43 街的轉角跟我碰面。
- You can buy cheesecloth **at the farmers' market**. 你可以在農產品集貨市場買到薄紗布。

比較
- Your MP3 player is **in my schoolbag**. 你的 MP3 隨身聽在我的書包裡。
- My schoolbag is **on the table** by the door. 我的書包擺在門邊的桌上。
- I paused the MP3 player **at the beginning** of the fourth song. 我把 MP3 隨身聽暫停在第四首歌一開始的地方。

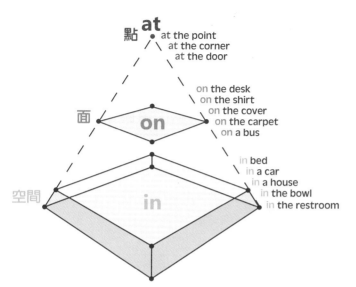

at 點

- at the point
- at the corner
- at the door

on 面

- on the desk
- on the shirt
- on the cover
- on the carpet
- on a bus

in 空間

- in bed
- in a car
- in a house
- in the bowl
- in the restroom

Practice

① 根據圖示，用 in、on 或 at 填空，完成句子。

1. This dog is _____ the sofa.

2. This dog is _____ the dog house.

3. Jack is _____ the end of the line.

4. Mavis is _____ the middle of the line.

5. This cat is _____ the cup.

6. I'd like some whipped cream _____ my coffee.

7. There's a magazine _____ the table.

8. Ben is jumping _____ the bed.

9. The geese are standing _____ the edge of a river.

Unit 92　介系詞 in / on / at 表地點（2）

①
- There is an elevator **in the Eiffel Tower**. 艾菲爾鐵塔裡有電梯。
- There are spas in the rooms **in the Hot Spring Hotel**. 溫泉旅館的房間裡有溫泉水療。

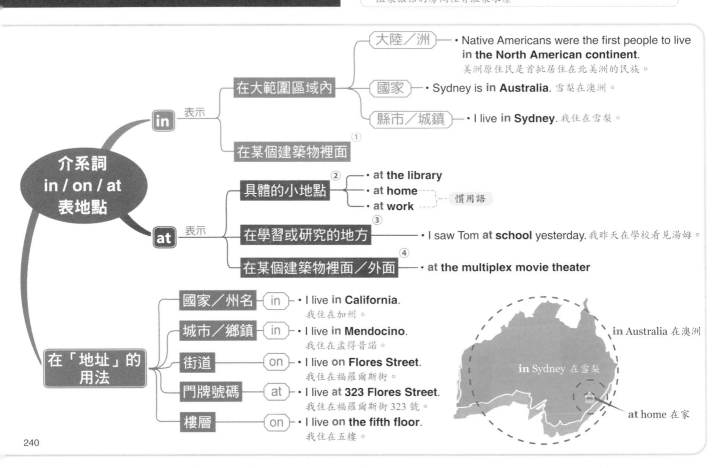

介系詞 in / on / at 表地點

in 表示
- 在大範圍區域內
  - 大陸／洲 · Native Americans were the first people to live **in the North American continent**. 美洲原住民是首批居住在北美洲的民族。
  - 國家 · Sydney is **in Australia**. 雪梨在澳洲。
  - 縣市／城鎮 · I live **in Sydney**. 我住在雪梨。
- 在某個建築物裡面 ①

at 表示
- 具體的小地點 ②
  - · **at the library**
  - · **at home** ⎫ 慣用語
  - · **at work** ⎭
- 在學習或研究的地方 ③ · I saw Tom **at school** yesterday. 我昨天在學校看見湯姆。
- 在某個建築物裡面／外面 ④ · **at the multiplex movie theater**

在「地址」的用法
- 國家／州名 ⟨in⟩ · I live **in California**. 我住在加州。
- 城市／鄉鎮 ⟨in⟩ · I live **in Mendocino**. 我住在孟得昔諾。
- 街道 ⟨on⟩ · I live **on Flores Street**. 我住在福羅爾斯街。
- 門牌號碼 ⟨at⟩ · I live **at 323 Flores Street**. 我住在福羅爾斯街 323 號。
- 樓層 ⟨on⟩ · I live **on the fifth floor**. 我住在五樓。

in Australia 在澳洲
in Sydney 在雪梨
at home 在家

②
- Otto is **at the library**, but he will be back for dinner.
  奧圖現在在圖書館，但是他會回來吃晚餐。
- I'll be **at home** if you need me.
  如果你需要我，我會在家裡。
- I'll be **at work** this afternoon from 1:00 to 5:00.
  今天下午 1 點到 5 點，我要上班。

③
- She is a kindergarten teacher **at Tiny Tots Language School**.
  她是 Tiny Tots 語言學校的幼稚園老師。

④
- He met her **at the multiplex movie theater**. 他和她在電影城見面。
  ↳ inside or outside

3. There are some people .... the train station.

4. Vicky is .... the library.

Practice

❶ 用 in 或 at 填空，完成句子。

1. There are many people .... the airport.

2. The kids are .... school.

❷ 依據圖示，用 in、on 或 at 填空，完成句子。

To: Sherman Johnson
Apt. 3F, 223 Oak Street
Evansville, Indiana, 56082, U.S.A.

1. Sherman Johnson lives .... the U.S.A.
2. He lives .... the third floor.
3. He lives .... Oak Street.
4. He lives .... 223 Oak Street.
5. He lives .... Evansville.
6. He lives .... Indiana.

Unit 93 其他表地點的介系詞

❶ in 在……之內

in the box

❷ on 在……之上
↳ 有接觸到

on the box

❸ over 在……之上
↳ 正上方
↳ 沒接觸到

over the box

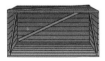

❹ under 在……之下
↳ 正下方

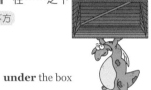

under the box

❺ in front of 在……前面

in front of the box

❻ behind 在……後面

behind the box

❼ near 在……附近
next to 緊鄰著……

near / next to the box

❽ between 在……之間

between the boxes

❾ across 在……對面

across the line

❿ against 倚靠著……

against the box

Practice

❶ 根據圖示，自框內選出適當的介系詞填空，完成句子。可重複選取。

in	on	near	next to	in front of	behind	between	over	under	against

1. The frog is .... the leaf.

2. The woman is standing .... the bicycle.

3. The boy is sleeping .... the car.

4. The man is sitting .... the bicycle.

5. The woman is resting .... a tree and .... a bike.

6. The girl is sleeping .... the teddy bear.

7. The taxi stopped .... the hotel.

8. The car is driving .... the highway.

9. The man is hiding .... the desk.

10. The seagull is flying .... the ocean.

11. The dog is .... the boys.

12. The white-headed cat is leaning .... the black-headed cat.

❶ into 到⋯⋯之內

into the
telephone booth

❹ off 離開⋯⋯

off the box

❾ across 橫越／跨越　　**❿ along** 沿著／順著

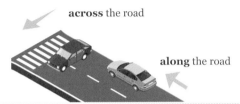

across the road

along the road

❷ out of 到⋯⋯之外

out of the
telephone booth

❺ up 往⋯⋯上　　**❻ down** 往⋯⋯下

up the hill　　　　**down** the hill

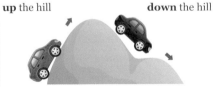

⓫ past 經過

past a traffic light

❸ onto 到⋯⋯之上

onto the box

❼ to 往⋯⋯　　**❽ from** 從⋯⋯

from the city

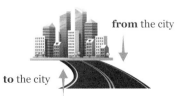

to the city

⓬ through 穿越／通過

through the
tunnel

⓭ around 圍繞

around the traffic circle

Practice

❶ 根據圖示，自框內選出適當的介系詞填空，完成句子。可重複選取。

| into | out of | on | off | up | around | through | across | along | past | down |

1. The kids are partially
_____ the car.

2. The man is throwing
garbage _____ the
trash can.

3. The man is walking
_____ the hill.

4. Someone is pouring water
_____ the instant
noodles.

5. You need to drive
_____ the traffic circle.

6. The dolphin is jumping
_____ the water.

7. These taxis are driving
_____ the road.

8. The pedestrians are walking
_____ the street.

9. Are we going to drive
_____ the tunnel?

10. The kayaker in the yellow
boat went _____ the
other kayaker.

11. Gordon is looking
_____ at Marty.

12. The woman fell _____
the bike.

Unit 95 介系詞 in / on / at 表時間（1）

但「在晚上」會用 at night
- He always gets lost **at night**.
  他晚上老是迷路。

in — 一天中的某個時段
- I like to drink coffee and read the newspaper **in the afternoon**.
  我喜歡在下午喝咖啡看報紙。
- Breakfast restaurants are only open **in the morning**.
  早餐店只有早上營業。

介系詞 in / on / at 表時間

on — 星期
- We are going to meet at the night market **on Friday**. 我們星期五約在夜市見面。
- **On Saturdays** I always sleep late. 星期六我總是睡到很晚。

星期幾的某個時段
- I like to watch movies **on Friday nights** after the kids go to bed.
  我喜歡在星期五晚上孩子們都上床後看電影。
- Let's go to the farmers' market **on Saturday morning**.
  我們星期六上午到農產品集散市場去吧。

週末
- Are you going to the Music Festival **on the weekend**? ---- 英式用 **at** the weekend
  你週末要去參加音樂慶典嗎？
- **On weekends** I catch up with all my housework. 我都在週末把所有的家事做完。

假日當天
- I love to eat turkey and stuffing **on Thanksgiving Day**.
  我很喜歡在感恩節那天吃火雞肉和火雞裡的填料。
- We stay up to see in the new year **on New Year's Eve**.
  我們會在除夕夜徹夜不眠迎接新年。

at — 一天中特定的時間
- I have to turn in this report **at 3:00**. 我必須在 3 點交出這份報告。
- **At 5:00** I leave the office no matter what is happening.
  不管發生什麼事，我都會在 5 點下班。

假期期間
- We visit her every year **at Thanksgiving**. 我們每年感恩節都會去看她。
- I always gain weight **at Christmas**. 我一到聖誕節就會變胖。

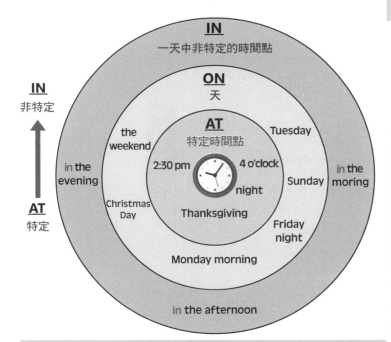

IN
非特定

↑

AT
特定

IN
一天中非特定的時間點

ON
天

AT
特定時間點

the weekend
Tuesday
2:30 pm　4 o'clock
in the evening
night　Sunday
in the morning
Christmas Day
Thanksgiving
Friday night
Monday morning
in the afternoon

7. I need to get up _____ 6:20 tomorrow morning.

8. We usually go to the traditional market _____ weekends.

❷ 將框內這些表示時間的詞彙，依據其應該搭配的介系詞，填入正確的空格內。

Saturdays

6 o'clock

night

Monday

Christmas

the evening

the weekend

the afternoon

Christmas Day

Tuesday afternoons

Thanksgiving Day

_____ in

_____ on

_____ at

Practice

❶ 用 in、on 或 at 填空，完成句子。

1. Meet me _____ 5:00.

2. Let's go to a baseball game _____ Saturday.

3. The store isn't open _____ the morning.

4. I only play online games _____ night.

5. I do my laundry _____ Sunday afternoons.

6. The best time to go there is _____ Independence Day.

Unit 96 介系詞 in / on / at 表時間（2）

比較
- Let's go **in September**. 我們九月去吧。
- I am free **on September 26th**. 我 9 月 26 日那天有空。
- Are you free **on that day**? 那你那天有空嗎？

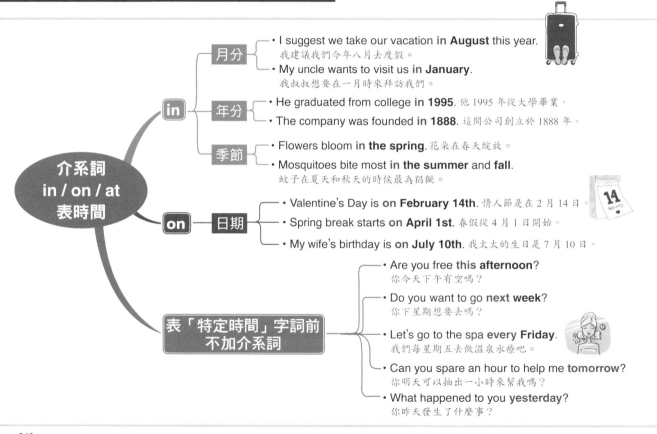

介系詞 in / on / at 表時間

in

月分
- I suggest we take our vacation **in August** this year.
  我建議我們今年八月去度假。
- My uncle wants to visit us **in January**.
  我叔叔想要在一月時來拜訪我們。

年分
- He graduated from college **in 1995**. 他 1995 年從大學畢業。
- The company was founded **in 1888**. 這間公司創立於 1888 年。

季節
- Flowers bloom **in the spring**. 花朵在春天綻放。
- Mosquitoes bite most **in the summer** and **fall**.
  蚊子在夏天和秋天的時候最為猖獗。

on

日期
- Valentine's Day is **on February 14th**. 情人節是在 2 月 14 日。
- Spring break starts **on April 1st**. 春假從 4 月 1 日開始。
- My wife's birthday is **on July 10th**. 我太太的生日是 7 月 10 日。

表「特定時間」字詞前不加介系詞
- Are you free **this afternoon**?
  你今天下午有空嗎？
- Do you want to go **next week**?
  你下星期想要去嗎？
- Let's go to the spa **every Friday**.
  我們每星期五去做溫泉水療吧。
- Can you spare an hour to help me **tomorrow**?
  你明天可以抽出一小時來幫我嗎？
- What happened to you **yesterday**?
  你昨天發生了什麼事？

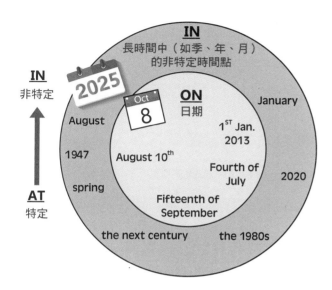

❷ 將框內這些表示時間的詞彙，依據其應該搭配的介系詞，或者是不需要介系詞，填入正確的空格內。

this weekend	winter	March 3ʳᵈ
next summer	February	1500
last month	the fall	July 13ᵗʰ
yesterday morning	tomorrow afternoon	

__in__

__on__

__×__

this weekend

Practice

❶ 用 in 或 on 填空，完成句子。若不需要介系詞，請劃上「×」。

1. He was born _____ 1971.

2. She was born _____ December 22, 1975.

3. The school basketball season is _____ the winter.

4. Edward is leaving this country _____ July 1ˢᵗ.

5. This book will be in print _____ April.

6. Jenny does her laundry _____ every Saturday.

7. We need to hand in this report _____ next Tuesday.

8. The museum is free _____ Sunday.

Unit 97 介系詞 **for / since** 表時間（與 **ago** 比較）

for two months

December
two months ago

Now
since December

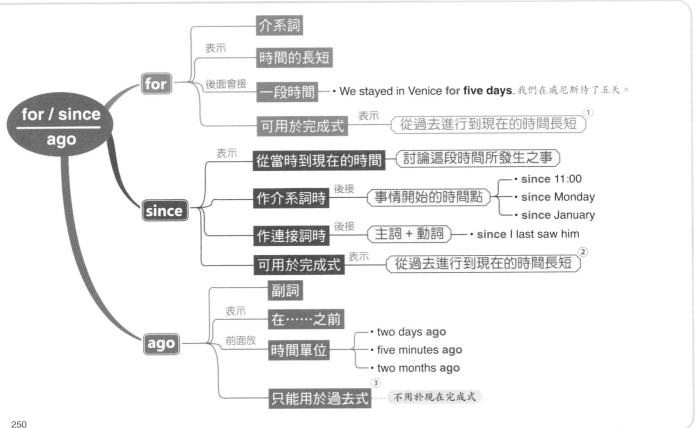

for / since ago

for
- 表示 → 介系詞
- 表示 → 時間的長短
- 後面會接 → 一段時間 — • We stayed in Venice for **five days**. 我們在威尼斯待了五天。
- 可用於完成式 — 表示 → 從過去進行到現在的時間長短 ①

since
- 表示 → 從當時到現在的時間 — 討論這段時間所發生之事
- 作介系詞時 — 後接 → 事情開始的時間點
  - • since 11:00
  - • since Monday
  - • since January
- 作連接詞時 — 後接 → 主詞 + 動詞 — • since I last saw him
- 可用於完成式 — 表示 → 從過去進行到現在的時間長短 ②

ago
- 表示 → 副詞
- 表示 → 在……之前
- 前面放 → 時間單位
  - • two days **ago**
  - • five minutes **ago**
  - • two months **ago**
- 只能用於過去式 ③ ---- 不用於現在完成式

Practice

① 依據事實，用 ago 回答問題。

1. When did you move to your current apartment?

→ _____

2. When did you buy your cell phone?

→ _____

3. When did you have your last vacation?

→ _____

② 下列表示時間的詞彙，應該搭配 for 還是 since 使用？請在空格內填入正確的介系詞。

1. _____ Friday   **4.** _____ 20 minutes

2. _____ last year   **5.** _____ 1 o'clock

3. _____ one week

③ 依據事實，分別用 for 或 since 的兩種句型回答問題。

1. How long have you been learning English?

→ _____

→ _____

2. How long have you lived in your current apartment?

→ _____

→ _____

3. How long have you had your own computer?

→ _____

→ _____

---

①
- We **have been working for hours**.
  我們已經工作好幾個小時了。
- I **haven't seen** him **for three years**.
  我已經三年沒見到他了。
- He **has waited for one hour**.
  他已經等了一個鐘頭了。

②
- I **haven't talked** to him **since 2008**.
  從 2008 年之後，我就沒和他說過話了。
- He **has been waiting since 10:00**.
  他從 10 點等到現在。
- It **has been** two years **since I last saw him**.
  從我上次見到他到現在已經兩年了。

③
- Steve left **ten minutes ago**.
  史帝夫 10 分鐘前離開了。
  ↳ 從現在算起的 10 分鐘前
- He graduated from Central University **ten years ago**.
  他 10 年前從中央大學畢業。
  ↳ 從現在算起的 10 年前
- I climbed the mountain **three months ago**.
  我三個月前去爬過山。
- I saw him **five minutes ago**.
  我五分鐘前見過他。

Unit 93–94 重點複習

❶ 寫出下列詞彙的反義詞。

1. in front of ↔ _____
2. to ↔ _____
3. over ↔ _____
4. up ↔ _____
5. onto ↔ _____
6. into ↔ _____

Unit 91–94 重點複習

❷ 依據圖示，自框內選出適當的表示地點或位置的介系詞來填空，完成句子。

in	on	past	against
over	under	to	along
into	out of	down	behind
near	between		

1. The strawberries are _____ the box.

2. The blueberry tarts are _____ the plate.

3. I put some peanut butter _____ the toast.

4. The apple is _____ the books.

5. I poured some coffee _____ the cup.

6. She is taking a jar of pickles _____ the refrigerator.

7. She is putting some chicken _____ her mouth.

8. These pieces of ice are floating _____ the sea.

9. The cheese is _____ the two halves of the bun.

10. Sheep B is standing _____ Sheep A.

11. The bee is flying _____ the flower.

12. These camels are walking _____ the desert.

13. The crab is moving _____ the beach.

14. This turtle is swimming _____ a group of fish.

15. The dog has a tennis ball _____ his mouth.

16. She is sitting _____ her suitcase.

17. The lion is _____ a car.

18. She is staying _____ the surface of the water.

19. The man is walking _____ his room.

20. She is walking _____ the stairs.

❸ 請用 at、in 或 on 填空，完成句子。

1. The box is _____ the table by the door.

2. His office is _____ your bus route.

3. He is expecting you _____ 9 a.m.

4. He says he will be _____ work all day.

5. Are you going to be _____ school all day today?

6. I need you to get some tickets_____ the lobby of the station.

7. Take the tickets to Tony's house _____ Glendale.

8. She is living _____ 109 Spring Street.

9. She is _____ the first floor.

10. She is _____ Apartment 110.

❹ 請用 in、on 或 at 填空，完成句子。

1. My family always gets together _____ Thanksgiving Day.

2. My class starts _____ 8:10.

3. What are you going to do _____ Tuesday?

4. I'm going jogging with my wife _____ the morning.

5. He usually watches sports games on TV _____ night.

6. Aunt Betty goes to church _____ Sunday mornings.

7. Uncle Bob goes fishing _____ the weekend.

8. We get together with our grandparents _____ Christmas. We always have a feast _____ Christmas Day.

9. Mr. and Mrs. Smith are going on a vacation _____ July. They will leave for Australia _____ July 5th.

10. The restaurant was founded _____ 1977.

11. Jeff always goes surfing _____ the summer.

Unit 93 重點複習

⑤ 依據圖示，自框內選出正確的介系詞填空，完成句子。

1. The ball is .... his foot. His foot is .... the ball.

2. The ball is .... the net.

between	behind
near	opposite
next to	in front of
in	on
under	

3. Player A is .... Player B.

4. Player B is .... Player A.

5. Player A is .... Player B.

6. Player A is .... Player B.

7. Player A is running .... Player B.

8. Player B is .... Players A and C.

6 以下內容是關於一名男子和他擁有車子的經歷，請用 **ago**、**for** 或 **since** 填空，完成句子。

1. I drove my first car _____ four years.

2. I crashed it while I was a college student, and I couldn't afford to buy another car _____ a long time.

3. My father told me to save my money and buy a used car. I have owned several used cars _____ then.

4. I bought my first used car 16 years _____.

5. It was a piece of junk, and I only drove it _____ two months before it broke down.

6. I drove my second used car _____ three months, and then the transmission broke.

7. I bought my third "good" used car about 15 years _____ . I loved that car very much.

8. It lasted _____ five years, and then the cost of repairs forced me to get rid of it. I decided to buy another "good" used car.

9. I have gone through five more used cars _____ I got rid of my third used car. I'm still driving a used car, and I will probably continue to do so until I can't drive any more.

7 根據題目的內容，用 **ago** 重新造句。

1. It's 4:00 now. Dana left the office at 3:00.

→ _Dana left an hour ago._

2. It's 4:35 now. Nancy walked out of the office at 4:00.

→ ....

3. It's 9:00 now. Victor called at 6:00.

→ ....

4. Today is Friday. Julie came on Monday morning.

→ ....

5. This is July. It happened last month on the same date.

→ ....

6. It's 2014. We saw her last year.

→ ....

8 選出正確的答案。

1. It's 6:00. The 5:00 bus left an hour **ago/since**.

2. My sister **left/has left** to go home two days ago.

3. We walked along the beach **for/since** three hours.

4. I have been visiting my grandparents **for/since** a week.

5. She has been visiting her grandparents **for/since** Saturday.

6. I have had this car **since/for** I was 21 years old.

Unit 99 連接詞 and / but / or / because / so

可連接句中個別部分

and ──連接── 同類型的字

- My grandmother has two cats **and** two dogs.
  我奶奶有兩隻貓和兩隻狗。
- We have salty **and** sweet bread.
  我們有鹹的和甜的麵包。

連接詞
and / but / or

but ──連接── 相反概念

- I went to his office, **but** he wasn't there.
  我到他的辦公室去，可是他不在。
- I tried to call him, **but** his voice mail kept picking up the call.
  我打電話給他，但一直轉到語音信箱。

or ──連接── 多者擇一的可能性

- We could go on a vacation to Hong Kong **or** Macau.
  我們可以到香港或澳門度假。
- Are you married **or** single? 你已婚還是單身？

連接詞

連接對象 ┬ 兩個詞彙
        ├ 兩個片語
        └ 兩個句子

範例

and	so	if
but	because	before
or	when	after

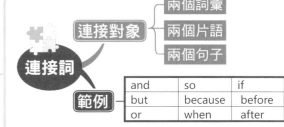

- I'll take a hamburger **and** French fries.
  我要一個漢堡和薯條。
- I love fries, **but** I hate ketchup.
  我喜歡薯條，可是我討厭番茄醬。
- Sometimes I have a cola **or** a lemon drink.
  有時我會喝可樂或檸檬飲料。
- I eat fast food **because** it tastes good.
  我吃速食是因為它好吃。
- I know it's not healthy, **so** I don't eat it often.
  我知道它不健康，所以我不常吃。

後方接子句

連接詞
because / so

because ──描述── 原因
- I can't go **because** my wife won't let me. 我不能去，因為我太太不讓我去。
- I can go **because** my wife is out of town. 我可以去，因為我太太出城去了。

so ──描述── 結果
- The meeting is cancelled, **so** you don't have to go now. 會議取消，所以你現在不用去了。
- They want to meet you right now, **so** you have to come as soon as you can.
  他們想馬上見你，所以你得儘快趕來。

Practice

① 請用 and、but 或 or 連接下列句子。

1. I like soda. I like potato chips.

→ *I like soda and potato chips.*

2. Do you want to leave at night? Do you want to leave in the morning?

→

3. I can't cook. I can barbecue.

→

4. I have been to Switzerland. I have been to New Zealand.

→

5. She isn't a ballet dancer. She is a great hip hop dancer.

→

6. Tom says he is rich. He always borrows money from me.

→

7. Will you come this week? Will you come next week?

→

8. Shall we sit in the front? Shall we sit in the back?

→

9. I read comic books. I read novels.

→

10. Do you like to eat German food? Do you like to eat French food?

→

連接子句

連接詞 when / if

when 表示 將來確定會發生的事
- You can talk to him **when** he gets here.
  當他到這裡時，你可以跟他談談。
- I'll be your best man **when** you get married.
  你結婚時，我會當你的伴郎。

if 表示 不確定是否會發生的事
- We'll talk about buying you a scooter **if** your grades improve.
  如果你的成績進步，我們再談買機車給你的事。
- We'll find the money **if** you get into UCLA.
  假如你申請上加州大學洛杉磯分校，我們就出錢供你念。

when / if 後面不可用 will

後面用 現在簡單式表未來
- I will call you **when** I **am** free. 我有空的時候會打給你。
- I will come **if** you **invite** me. 如果你邀請我，我就會來。

放句首時 句中需加逗號
- **When** you need a ride, give me a call. 當你需要人來載你時，打個電話給我。
- **If** you come back to Taipei, give me a call. 如果你回來台北，打電話給我。

連接子句

連接詞 before / after

before 表示 發生在某事之前
- I have to finish this project **before** the manager comes back.
  我要在經理回來之前完成這件案子。
- Everybody left the party **before** Jacky arrived.
  傑克還沒到，大家就已經走光了。

after 表示 發生在某事之後
- I'll meet you at the basketball court **after** I finish cleaning my room.
  等我整理完房間，我就去籃球場找你。
- He set out for Paris right **after** he came back from Tokyo.
  他從東京回來，旋即又前往巴黎。

before　　　　after

Practice

❶ 依據圖示，分別自兩個框內選出適當的片語，用「if . . ., . . . will . . .」的句型造句。

lift weights	read widely	practice writing
practice public speaking	skip dessert	often go jogging

learn lots of things	become self-confident
increase her stamina	build up his muscles
stay slim	improve his communication skills

1 If he lifts weights, he will build up his muscles.

2 ....

3 ....

❷ 利用題目給的片語，用「when she . . ., she'll . . .」的句型造句。

1. start jogging   finish stretching
   → ....

2. rest on a bench   get tired
   → ....

3 get home   eat breakfast
   → ....

Unit 99
重點複習

1 以「**I missed our date . . .**」做句首，用 because 或 so 完成句子。

1. my car broke down

→ I missed our date *because my car broke down* .

2. my boss needed me to work late in the office

→ I missed our date _____ .

3. I could finish my report

→ I missed our date _____ .

4. I had to bake cookies

→ I missed our date _____ .

5. my dog was sick

→ I missed our date _____ .

6. I could see my favorite TV show

→ I missed our date _____ .

7. I had to take a sick friend to the hospital

→ I missed our date _____ .

8. I had to help my mom clean the house

→ I missed our date _____ .

Unit 99
重點複習

2 請用 and、but 或 or 填空，完成句子。

1. I love to eat pepperoni pizza _____ watch TV.

2. I like action movies, _____ my husband likes romantic comedies.

3. Are you going to see a doctor _____ not?

4. My mother _____ father want to come over this weekend.

5. You can quit school, _____ it's not a good idea.

6. Do you want to stay single _____ get married?

7. He has a double major in law _____ accounting.

8. I haven't graduated yet, _____ I will soon.

9. You can come with our group _____ go with the other group.

10. He will join the Army _____ go to graduate school.

Part 13 連接詞

❸ 請用 **when** 或 **if** 填空，完成句子。

1. I want to be in the delivery room in the hospital ＿＿＿＿＿＿ the baby is born.
2. I will buy pink baby clothes ＿＿＿＿＿＿ it is a girl.
3. My brother will drive us home ＿＿＿＿＿＿ we leave the hospital.
4. I will take care of the baby ＿＿＿＿＿＿ it cries between feedings at night.
5. The baby will have a nice new crib ＿＿＿＿＿＿ it comes home from the hospital.
6. I can't wait to find out ＿＿＿＿＿＿ it is a boy or a girl.
7. ＿＿＿＿＿＿ the baby is two years old, I want to have a second child.
8. ＿＿＿＿＿＿ the first child is a boy, then I want a second boy.
9. Two boys can play together ＿＿＿＿＿＿ they are young.
10. ＿＿＿＿＿＿ we have a boy and a girl, I am worried they won't play together.

❹ 請依據題意，在第一格填入 **when** 或 **if**，並在第二格用簡單現在式或 **will** 的句型完成句子。

1. ＿＿＿＿＿＿ I get dressed tomorrow morning, I ＿＿＿＿＿＿ (wear) my holiest jeans.
2. Perhaps Linda will be at the party. ＿＿＿＿＿＿ I see her, I ＿＿＿＿＿＿ (ask) her out on a date.
3. I'm definitely going to do it next time I see her. I'll give her my business card ＿＿＿＿＿＿ I ＿＿＿＿＿＿ (ask) her out.
4. I hope she says yes. ＿＿＿＿＿＿ she agrees, I ＿＿＿＿＿＿ (take) her to the aquarium to see the new killer whales.
5. Maybe that's too weird. She will probably think I am strange ＿＿＿＿＿＿ I ＿＿＿＿＿＿ (tell) her we are going the aquarium.
6. I know what I will do. ＿＿＿＿＿＿ I ask her out, I ＿＿＿＿＿＿ (give) her the choice of where to go.

❺ 請用 **before** 或 **after** 填空，完成句子。

1. Spring comes ＿＿＿＿＿＿ winter and ＿＿＿＿＿＿ summer.
2. The lightning came ＿＿＿＿＿＿ the thunder.
3. It began to rain ＿＿＿＿＿＿ the thunder.
4. It rained heavily ＿＿＿＿＿＿ the sky turned bright.
5. Sometimes there will be a rainbow ＿＿＿＿＿＿ the rain.

Unit 102 數字（1）

數字的三種形式

- 基數
  - one 一
  - two 二
  - three 三
- 序數
  - first 第一
  - second 第二
  - third 第三
- 分數
  - one-third 三分之一
  - two-thirds 三分之二
  - one-fourth 四分之一

基數

0 到 29 寫法					
zero	0	ten	10	twenty	20
one	1	eleven	11	twenty-one	21
two	2	twelve	12	twenty-two	22
three	3	thirteen	13	twenty-three	23
four	4	fourteen	14	twenty-four	24
five	5	fifteen	15	twenty-five	25
six	6	sixteen	16	twenty-six	26
seven	7	seventeen	17	twenty-seven	27
eight	8	eighteen	18	twenty-eight	28
nine	9	nineteen	19	twenty-nine	29

21 到 99 之間的複合數字，中間都要加連字號。
- twenty-one　　• ninety-nine

10, 20, ... 90 寫法			
ten	10	sixty	60
twenty	20	seventy	70
thirty	30	eighty	80
forty	40	ninety	90
fifty	50		

100 以上寫法：百位數和十位數之間需加 and	
one hundred	100
one hundred and one	101
one hundred and ten	110
one hundred and twenty	120
one hundred and twenty-one	121
one hundred and ninety-nine	199
two hundred	200

1,000 以上寫法		
one thousand	1,000	一千
ten thousand	10,000	一萬
one hundred thousand	100,000	十萬
one million	1,000,000	一百萬
one billion	1,000,000,000	十億
one trillion	1,000,000,000,000	一兆

有些不可加 s 表複數	
hundred（百）	→three hundred 三百
thousand（千）	→three thousand 三千
million（百萬）	→three million 三百萬
billion（十億）	→three billion 三十億

電話號碼唸法：每個數字個別唸	
電話號碼	5236-8813 five two three six eight eight one three
台灣地區電話號碼 （含國碼與區碼）	886-2-7612-0096 eight eight six, dash, two, dash, seven six one two zero zero nine six
含通行密碼、國碼、區碼和分機號碼	001-1-202-347-1000 Ext. 2022 zero zero one, dash, one, dash, two zero two, dash, three four seven one zero zero zero, extension two zero two two

Practice

❶ 請用英文寫出下列數字的唸法。

1. 7 _____

2. 67 _____

_____

3. 5,694 _____

_____

4. 1,000,022 _____

_____

❷ 請用英文寫出下列電話號碼的唸法。

1. 911

→ _____

2. 8823-1462

→ _____

_____

3. 001-1-847-864-2303

→ _____

_____

4. 0928-053-253

→ _____

_____

5. 2365-9739 Ext. 33

→ _____

_____

Unit 103 數字（2）

| 用途 | 指出先後順序 |

規則	大多數 ── 在數字後加 th ── 1、2、3 例外
	0 沒有序數
	前方需加 the

- He was **the first** prize winner.
  他是第一特獎的贏家。
- The door to his office is **the third** one on the left.
  他的辦公室在左邊第三個門。

序數

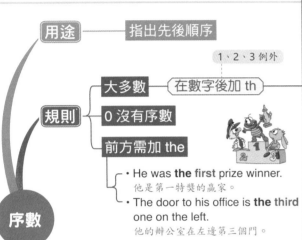

1	1st	first	21	21st	twenty-first
2	2nd	second	22	22nd	twenty-second
3	3rd	third	23	23rd	twenty-third
4	4th	fourth	24	24th	twenty-fourth
5	5th	fifth	25	25th	twenty-fifth
6	6th	sixth	26	26th	twenty-sixth
7	7th	seventh	27	27th	twenty-seventh
8	8th	eighth	28	28th	twenty-eighth
9	9th	ninth	29	29th	twenty-ninth
10	10th	tenth	30	30th	thirtieth
11	11th	eleventh	40	40th	fortieth
12	12th	twelfth	50	50th	fiftieth
13	13th	thirteenth	60	60th	sixtieth
14	14th	fourteenth	70	70th	seventieth
15	15th	fifteenth	80	80th	eightieth
16	16th	sixteenth	90	90th	ninetieth
17	17th	seventeenth	100	100th	one hundredth
18	18th	eighteenth	200	200th	two hundredth
19	19th	nineteenth	1,000	1,000th	one thousandth
20	20th	twentieth	1,000,000	1,000,000th	one millionth

| 經常描述事物 | 樓層 |
| | 日期 |

樓層
- I bought the lipstick on **the second floor** of the department store. 我在百貨公司的二樓買了這條口紅。
- I live on **the fifth floor** of this apartment building. 我住在這棟公寓的五樓。

日期
- Are you free on **the fifteenth of November**? 你 11 月 15 日有沒有空？
- Our flight departs on **the second of May**. 我們的班機 5 月 2 日起飛。

Practice

Part
14
數字、時間和日期

Unit
103
數字（2）

267

❶ 根據右列的美國歷任總統表，依範
例用序數來描述各任美國總統。

1. George Washington was ___*the first*___
   President of the United States.

2. Thomas Jefferson was ___
   President of the United States.

3. James Madison was ___
   President of the United States.

4. Abraham Lincoln was ___
   President of the United States.

5. Warren Harding was ___
   President of the United States.

6. Franklin Roosevelt was ___
   President of the United States.

7. John Kennedy was ___
   President of the United States.

8. Richard Nixon was ___
   President of the United States.

9. Barack Obama is ___
   President of the United States.

10. Donald Trump is ___
    President of the United States.

1	1789–1797	George Washington
2	1797–1801	John Adams
3	1801–1809	Thomas Jefferson
4	1809–1817	James Madison
5	1817–1825	James Monroe
6	1825–1829	John Quincy Adams
7	1829–1837	Andrew Jackson
8	1837–1841	Martin Van Buren
9	1841	William Harrison
10	1841–1845	John Tyler
11	1845–1849	James Polk
12	1849–1850	Zachary Taylor
13	1850–1853	Millard Fillmore
14	1853–1857	Franklin Pierce
15	1857–1861	James Buchanan
16	1861–1865	Abraham Lincoln
17	1865–1869	Andrew Johnson
18	1869–1877	Ulysses Grant
19	1877–1881	Rutherford Hayes
20	1881	James Garfield
21	1881–1885	Chester Arthur
22	1885–1889	Grover Cleveland

23	1889–1893	Benjamin Harrison
24	1893–1897	Grover Cleveland
25	1897–1901	William McKinley
26	1901–1909	Theodore Roosevelt
27	1909–1913	William Taft
28	1913–1921	Woodrow Wilson
29	1921–1923	Warren Harding
30	1923–1929	Calvin Coolidge
31	1929–1933	Herbert Hoover
32	1933–1945	Franklin Roosevelt
33	1945–1953	Harry S. Truman
34	1953–1961	Dwight Eisenhower
35	1961–1963	John Kennedy
36	1963–1969	Lyndon Johnson
37	1969–1974	Richard Nixon
38	1974–1977	Gerald Ford
39	1977–1981	Jimmy Carter
40	1981–1989	Ronald Reagan
41	1989–1992	George Bush
42	1993–2001	Bill Clinton
43	2001–2009	George Walker Bush
44	2009–2017	Barack Obama
45	2017	Donald Trump

Unit 104 年分／月分／星期／日期

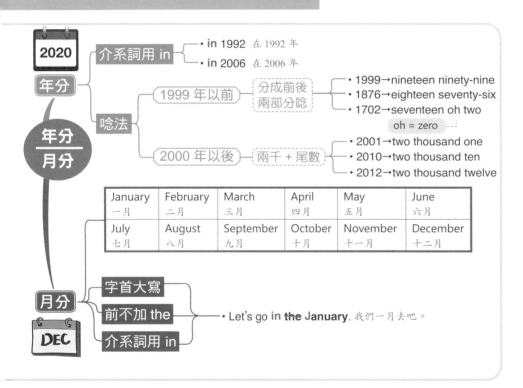

年分

2020 年分

介系詞用 in
- in 1992 在 1992 年
- in 2006 在 2006 年

唸法

1999 年以前 — 分成前後兩部分唸
- 1999→nineteen ninety-nine
- 1876→eighteen seventy-six
- 1702→seventeen oh two
  - oh = zero

2000 年以後 — 兩千 + 尾數
- 2001→two thousand one
- 2010→two thousand ten
- 2012→two thousand twelve

年分／月分

January 一月	February 二月	March 三月	April 四月	May 五月	June 六月
July 七月	August 八月	September 九月	October 十月	November 十一月	December 十二月

月分 DEC

- 字首大寫
- 前不加 the
- 介系詞用 in

- Let's go ~~in the~~ January. 我們一月去吧。

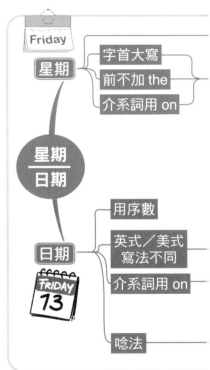

Friday

星期

- 字首大寫
- 前不加 the
- 介系詞用 on

星期／日期

日期 FRIDAY 13

- 用序數
- 英式／美式寫法不同
- 介系詞用 on
- 唸法

| Monday 星期一 |
| Tuesday 星期二 |
| Wednesday 星期三 |
| Thursday 星期四 |
| Friday 星期五 |
| Saturday 星期六 |
| Sunday 星期日 |

- Call me **on ~~the~~ Friday**.
  星期五打電話給我。

英式	美式
15th January, 2010	January 15th, 2010
15 January, 2010	January 15, 2010
15.1.2010	1-15-2010
15.1.10	1-15-10

- We leave **on** January 10th.
  我們 1 月 10 號出發。
- Meet me **on** December 31st.
  12 月 31 號來找我。

1 月 4 日
- **the fourth** of January
- January (the) **fourth**

Practice

❶ 依據 Mr. Simpson 的行事曆，
造句描述他的行程。

1. *Mr. Simpson is meeting*
   Ms. Miller on Monday.

2. _____

   _____

3. _____

   _____

4. _____

   _____

5. _____

   _____

6. _____

   _____

7. _____

Appointment Book

Mon.
meet Mr. Miller

Tue.
visit his grandma

Wed.
go shopping

Thur.
have dinner with Tom

Fri.
pick up Peter at the airport

Sat.
play basketball

Sun.
go to the movies

❷ 用英文寫出下列日期的唸法。

1. 21. 4. 01

   → _____

   _____

2. 13. 8. 1999

   → _____

   _____

3. 12-31-2004

   → _____

   _____

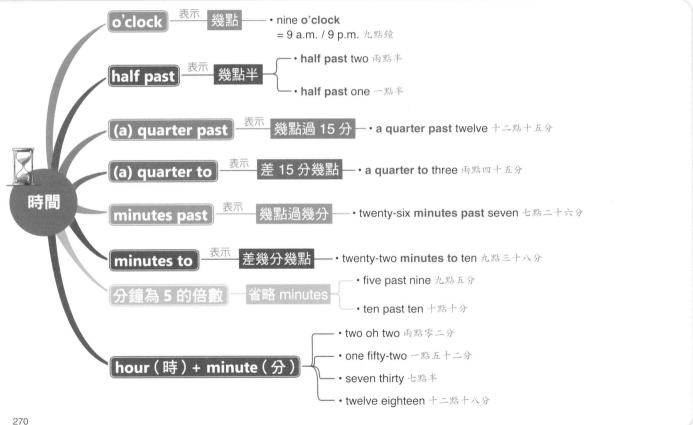

o'clock ——表示—— 幾點 —— • nine o'clock
= 9 a.m. / 9 p.m. 九點鐘

half past ——表示—— 幾點半 —— • half past two 兩點半
• half past one 一點半

(a) quarter past ——表示—— 幾點過 15 分 —— • a quarter past twelve 十二點十五分

(a) quarter to ——表示—— 差 15 分幾點 —— • a quarter to three 兩點四十五分

minutes past ——表示—— 幾點過幾分 —— • twenty-six minutes past seven 七點二十六分

minutes to ——表示—— 差幾分幾點 —— • twenty-two minutes to ten 九點三十八分

分鐘為 5 的倍數 —— 省略 minutes —— • five past nine 九點五分
• ten past ten 十點十分

hour（時）+ minute（分）—— • two oh two 兩點零二分
• one fifty-two 一點五十二分
• seven thirty 七點半
• twelve eighteen 十二點十八分

時間

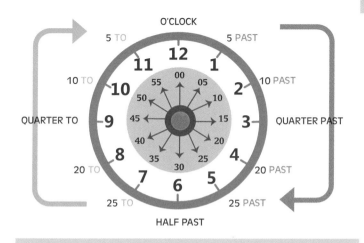

O'CLOCK

5 TO   5 PAST

10 TO   10 PAST

QUARTER TO   QUARTER PAST

20 TO   20 PAST

25 TO   25 PAST

HALF PAST

❶ 依據圖示，自框內選出正確的時間填空。

A half past eleven   **B** five o'clock

C ten to twelve   **D** two minutes to twelve

1   B

2

3

4

❷ 依據圖示，分別用兩種方式，以完整句子描述時間。

1.   It's a quarter past nine.
     It's nine fifteen.

2.

3.

4.

271

Unit 104
重點複習

❶ 在空格內填入正確的星期或月分。

1. The Chinese New Year is always in _____ or _____.

2. Easter always falls on a _____.

3. _____ is the third month.

4. _____ is the eighth month.

5. Mother's Day is on the second _____ of May.

6. _____ comes after Wednesday.

7. _____ the 13th occurs when the 13th day of a month falls on a Friday.

8. In Taiwan, typhoons occur mostly in _____, _____, and _____.

9. Thanksgiving Day falls on the fourth _____ of _____.

10. People born from late _____ to late _____ are Geminis（雙子座）.

Unit 104
重點複習

❷ 用「the . . . of . . .」的形式，在空格內填入正確的日期。

1. Christmas Day is on _____.

2. New Year's Eve falls on _____.

3. New Year's Day falls on _____.

4. Valentine's Day is on _____.

5. The Dragon Boat Festival is on _____
   of the Chinese lunar calendar.

6. The Chinese Valentine's Day falls on _____
   of the Chinese lunar calendar.

7. The Autumn Festival is on _____ of the Chinese lunar calendar.

8. Halloween is celebrated on _____.

9. Is that true people born on _____ can only celebrate their
   birthday once every four years?

❸ 寫出下列各項資訊的唸法。

電話號碼　**1.** 2300-1235 → ⋯⋯⋯⋯⋯⋯⋯⋯⋯⋯⋯⋯⋯⋯⋯⋯⋯⋯⋯

2. 02-2579-4581 → ⋯⋯⋯⋯⋯⋯⋯⋯⋯⋯⋯⋯⋯⋯⋯⋯⋯

3. 886-7-215-5748 → ⋯⋯⋯⋯⋯⋯⋯⋯⋯⋯⋯⋯⋯⋯⋯⋯

4. 5578-2641 Ext. 109 → ⋯⋯⋯⋯⋯⋯⋯⋯⋯⋯⋯⋯⋯⋯⋯

5. 0935-233-010 → ⋯⋯⋯⋯⋯⋯⋯⋯⋯⋯⋯⋯⋯⋯⋯⋯⋯

日期　**6.** 四月三日 → ⋯⋯⋯⋯⋯⋯⋯⋯⋯⋯⋯⋯⋯⋯⋯⋯⋯⋯

7. 六月二十五日 → ⋯⋯⋯⋯⋯⋯⋯⋯⋯⋯⋯⋯⋯⋯⋯⋯

8. 一月十一日 → ⋯⋯⋯⋯⋯⋯⋯⋯⋯⋯⋯⋯⋯⋯⋯⋯⋯

9. 九月二十二日 → ⋯⋯⋯⋯⋯⋯⋯⋯⋯⋯⋯⋯⋯⋯⋯

年分　**10.** 1435 → ⋯⋯⋯⋯⋯⋯⋯⋯⋯⋯⋯⋯⋯⋯⋯⋯⋯⋯⋯⋯

11. 1948 → ⋯⋯⋯⋯⋯⋯⋯⋯⋯⋯⋯⋯⋯⋯⋯⋯⋯⋯⋯⋯

12. 2003 → ⋯⋯⋯⋯⋯⋯⋯⋯⋯⋯⋯⋯⋯⋯⋯⋯⋯⋯⋯⋯

Answer Key

Unit 1
P. 11

1 1. cats 2. cars 3. losses 4. taxes 5. flushes
6. matches 7. tuxes 8. pushes 9. punches 10. stars
11. groups 12. pictures 13. oranges 14. hikes 15. kicks
16. dives 17. trees 18. branches 19. ticks 20. clocks

2 1. trees 2. plants 3. hands 4. shirts
5. shoes 6. legs 7. paths

3 1. aunts, roofs, parks, shops
2. brothers, cards, jobs, ideas
3. wishes, classes, boxes, watches

Unit 2
P. 13

1 1. kitties 2. cargoes 3. calves 4. pianos
5. strawberries 6. flies 7. wolves 8. heroes
9. scarves 10. doggies

2 1. jeans 2. glasses 3. x 4. shorts 5. x

3 1. ✓ 2. ✓ 3. ✓
4. x Leaves keep falling from the trees.
5. x People say cats have nine lives.
6. x I can't find the clothes I wore yesterday.
7. x I'd like to express my thanks to every one of you.
8. x You can find three libraries in this city.

Unit 3
P. 15

1 1. bison 2. geese 3. reindeer
4. goldfish / goldfishes 5. mice

2 1. C 2. B 3. C 4. A 5. C 6. A 7. B 8. A

Unit 4
P. 17

1 **Lydia bought:** a newspaper, an ice cube tray, a candle, an orange
Trent bought: a lightbulb, a fish, an umbrella

2 1. a cab 2. a glass of beer 3. a cup of coffee
4. an art museum 5. an opera 6. a restaurant 7. an owl

Unit 5
P. 19

1 1. a, the 2. the, The, the, the, The, the
3. The, a 4. the, the, a 5. a, the

2 1. ⓐ the channel ⓑ a channel
2. ⓐ a movie ⓑ the movie
3. ⓐ a sandwich ⓑ the sandwich
4. ⓐ a soda ⓑ the soda

Unit 6 — P. 21

❶ 可數：an electric razor, a hairdryer, a mirror
不可數：shampoo, toilet paper, toothpaste

❷ **1**. is, **x**　**2**. is, **x**　**3**. is, a　**4**. are, **x**　**5**. is, a
6. is, a　**7**. is, an　**8**. is, a

❸ **1**. hair　**2**. jewelry　**3**. makeup　**4**. OK
5. courage　**6**. OK

Unit 7 — P. 23

❶ **1**. two bottles of　　**2**. two bars of
3. three jars of　　**4**. a tube of
5. some　　**6**. a bowl of
7. two cartons of　　**8**. five sticks of

❷ **1**. Where can I buy some chocolate?
2. How much luggage do you have? / How many pieces of luggage do you have?
3. It's too quiet. I need some music.
4. How many bottles of perfume did you get?
5. Can you buy me two pieces of / some bread?
6. My brother wants to buy a piece of / some new furniture.

Unit 8 — P. 25

❶ **1**. Dogs like dogs.　**2**. Dogs like water.
3. Dogs like balls.　**4**. Dogs don't like cats.
5. Dogs don't like showers.
6. Dogs don't like vets.

❷ **1**. ⓐ Coffee　　ⓑ The coffee
2. ⓐ money　　ⓑ the money
3. ⓐ Rice　　ⓑ The rice
4. ⓐ attendance　　ⓑ the class attendance

Unit 9 — P. 27

❶ **1**. the　**2**. x　**3**. x　**4**. x　**5**. the　**6**. x　**7**. x
8. the　**9**. x　**10**. the　**11**. x　**12**. x　**13**. the　**14**. the
15. the　**16**. x　**17**. the　**18**. x　**19**. x

❷ **1**. "What are you reading?" "I'm reading **the China Post**."
2. Is **Mary** going to **Japan** with you?
3. **Jane** has a project due in **October**.
4. Why don't we see the latest movie in **the Miramar Cinema**?
5. Is the **Yellow River** the longest river in **China**?
6. Excuse me, how do I get to **Maple Street**?

Unit **1** | Unit **9**

Unit 10
— P. 29

❶ **1**. the radio　**2**. the theater　**3**. foot
　4. breakfast　**5**. the rain　**6**. plane
❷ **1**. the　**2**. the　**3**. x　**4**. the　**5**. x, x　**6**. x

Unit 11
— P. 31

❶ **1**. the sea　**2**. the flute　**3**. the city　**4**. school　**5**. prison
　6. hospital（美式：the hospital）
❷ **1**. the　**2**. x　**3**. the, the, the　**4**. x　**5**. x, x
　6. the　**7**. the　**8**. x

Unit 12
— P. 33

❶ **1**. work　**2**. ping-pong　**3**. winter　**4**. bed　**5**. home
❷ **1**. x　**2**. x, the　**3**. x, x　**4**. x　**5**. x　**6**. x
❸（答案略）

Unit 13
— P. 35

❶ **1**. Jody's key, Jody's　**2**. Momo's collar, Momo's
　3. my father's briefcase, my father's
　4. the wizard's magic wand, the wizard's
　5. Vince Carters' basketball, Vince Carter's

❷ **1**. ant's, ape's, Frank's, Jeff's
　2. Michael's, teacher's, lion's, kid's
　3. brush's, Alice's, mouse's, ox's

Unit 14
— P. 37

❶ **1**. the teacher's pen　**2**. Jennifer's iPod
　3. Grandpa's umbrella　**4**. Jane's lunch
　5. my mother's pillow　**6**. the manager's telephone
　7. my brothers' PlayStation　**8**. Liz's purse
❷ **1**. the light of the sun　**2**. the pile of trash
　3. the keyboard of the computer
　4. the speech of the president
　5. the ninth symphony of Beethoven

Unit 15 Review Test
— P. 38

❶ **1**. C　**2**. C　**3**. U　**4**. U　**5**. U　**6**. C　**7**. C　**8**. C　**9**. U
　10. C　**11** U　**12**. C　**13**. C　**14**. C　**15**. U
❷ **1**. rats　**2**. dishes　**3**. branches　**4**. jelly candies
　5. calves　**6**. Elves　**7**. teeth　**8**. fish
❸ **1**. a carrot　**2**. a carrot　**3**. Carrots　**4**. a lion
　5. the lion　**6**. Lions　**7**. sugar　**8**. the sugar
　9. a banana　**10**. the banana　**11**. a video
　12. the video　**13**. Music　**14**. the music

❹ **1.** the suburbs   **2.** car   **3.** football   **4.** TV

5. home   **6.** dinner   **7.** bed   **8.** an Egyptian

9. the Nile River   **10.** Egyptians   **11.** Brazil

12. the Amazon River   **13.** scientists   **14.** tourists

❺ **1.** a camera   **2.** potatoes   **3.** hair   **4.** a box

5. a loaf   **6.** lots of snow   **7.** is   **8.** are   **9.** Is

❻ **1.** ⓐ Ned's suitcase   ⓑ the suitcase of Ned

2. ⓐ my father's jacket

    ⓑ the jacket of my father

3. ⓐ my sisters' room

    ⓑ the room of my sisters

4. ⓐ x   ⓑ the corner of the bathroom

5. ⓐ Edward's brother

    ⓑ the brother of Edward

6. ⓐ x   ⓑ the end of the vacation

❼ **1. a bottle of:** soy sauce, alcohol, lotion

2. a can of: sardine, shaving cream, soda

3. a bowl of: cherries, salad, soup

4. a piece of: baggage, cheese, jewelry

5. a tube of: cleansing foam, watercolor, ointment

6. a jar of: pickles, peanut butter, facial cream

7. a pot of: tea, coffee, boiling water

8. a packet of: potato chips, ketchup, cookies

❽ （參考答案）

1. ✓ the Shed Aquarium, the Field Museum

2. ✓ the Hilton Hotel, the Metro Café

3. x Monday, Tuesday

4. ✓ the Village Playhouse, the Civic Center Theater

5. ✓ the Pacific Ocean, the Aegean Sea

6. x Sri Lanka, Europe, Eurasia

7. ✓ the New Wave Cinema, the Varsity Multiplex

8. x Madison Avenue, Hollywood Boulevard

9. x March, May

10. x Spaniards, Japanese

11. ✓ the Concord River, the River Thames

12. x Mt. Kisco, Long Island City

Unit 16 ———————————————————— P. 45

❶ **1.** I   **2.** You   **3.** She   **4.** It

5. I   **6.** They   **7.** She   **8.** He

❷ **1.** They   **2.** He   **3.** She   **4.** He   **5.** She

6. He   **7.** It   **8.** We

Unit 10

Unit 16

Unit 17
P. 47

❶ **1**. I like him. / I don't like him.

2. I like it. / I don't like it.

3. I like it. / I don't like it.

4. I like it. / I don't like it.

5. I like them. / I don't like them.

6. I like her. / I don't like her.

❷ **1**. us   **2**. us   **3**. him   **4**. me   **5**. him   **6**. her

7. them   **8**. it   **9**. him   **10**. us   **11**. him   **12**. us

Unit 18
P. 49

❶ **1**. My   **2**. our   **3**. his   **4**. her

5. their   **6**. their   **7**. Our   **8**. his, her, their

❷ **1**. your, hers   **2**. my, your   **3**. your, mine   **4**. its   **5**. Yours

Unit 19
P. 51

❶ **1**. There aren't any eggs.

2. There're some leeks.

3. There isn't any ice.

4. There's some kiwi juice.

5. There're some lemons.

6. There's some wine.

❷ **1**. There's no space.

2. We haven't got any newspapers.

3. She's got no money.

4. There aren't any boxes.

5. I haven't got any blank disks.

6. He doesn't have any bonus points.

❸ **1**. some   **2**. any   **3**. some

4. no   **5**. some   **6**. any

Unit 20
P. 54

❶ **1**. How many televisions do you want?

2. How many microphones do you want?

3. How many cellphone batteries do you want?

4. How many cameras do you want?

5. How much detergent do you want?

6. How many lightbulbs do you want?

7. How many air conditioners do you want?

8. How many water filters do you want?

❷ **1**. too much   **2**. too much   **3**. too many

4. too many   **5**. too much   **6**. too many

7. too much   **8**. enough   **9**. too many

Unit 21 ———————————— P. 57

❶ （參考答案）

1. There are a lot of bananas.
2. There are a few lemons.
3. There are a lot of watermelons.
4. There are a few guavas.
5. There are many pears.
6. There isn't much orange juice. /
   There's a little orange juice.

❷ **1**. much　**2**. a few　**3**. Little / A little
　4. much　**5**. many　**6**. a little

Unit 22 ———————————— P. 59

❶ **1**. one, one, one　**2**. one, one, one
　3. ones, ones, one, ones, one

Unit 23 ———————————— P. 61

❶ **1**. someone, anyone, anyone
　2. anyone, someone
　3. someone, anyone / someone, someone

❷ **1**. go　**2**. to talk　**3**. Someone　**4**. anyone
　5. anyone　**6**. to keep　**7**. someone

Unit 24 ———————————— P. 63

❶ **1**. anything to eat　**2**. anything to drink
　3. anywhere to go　**4**. something to do

❷ **1**. anything, anything　**2**. to hide
　3. somewhere　**4**. something　**5**. anywhere

Unit 25 ———————————— P. 67

❶ **1**. There is nobody at the office.
　2. There is no one leaving today.
　3. There is nothing to feed the fish.
　4. There is nowhere to buy stamps around here.
　5. There isn't anybody here who can speak Indonesian.
　6. There isn't anyone that can translate your letter.
　7. There isn't anything that will change the director's mind.
　8. There isn't anywhere we can go to get out of the rain.

❷ **1**. I have nowhere to go. / I don't have anywhere to go.
　2. No one believed me.
　3. Everything is ready. Let's go.

Unit
17
|
Unit
25

4. There is nothing to eat.

5. I never want to hurt anybody.

6. Everyone in this room will vote for me.

7. Did you see my glasses? I can't find it anywhere.

8. Anyone who doesn't support this idea please raise your hand.

Unit 26 ———————————— P. 69

❶ **1**. This **2**. Those **3**. This **4**. These

❷ **1**. this **2**. that **3**. those **4**. these **5**. that
6. this **7**. Those **8**. these **9**. That **10**. those

Unit 27 ———————————— P. 71

❶ **1**. myself **2**. yourself **3**. itself **4**. himself
5. herself **6**. yourself **7**. ourselves **8**. themselves

❷ **1**. each other **2**. themselves **3**. themselves

Unit 28 Review Test ———————————— P. 72

❶ **1**. my **2**. I **3**. mine **4**. me
5. My **6**. I **7**. me **8**. mine

❷ **1**. My, your **2**. I, Our **3**. her **4**. my .
5. he, her **6**. I, mine, you, mine / it **7**. their, ours **8**. it
9. It, them **10**. Their, They, it **11**. your, It, mine

❸ **1**. wine / green peppers **2**. bread / cookies
3. sugar **4**. toothpaste **5**. candy **6**. grapes
7. fish / goats **8**. medicine **9**. fruit tarts
10. soup / juice **11**. garlic **12**. notebooks

❹ **1**. We have ~~any~~ rice. **<u>some</u>**

2. Are there any spoons in the drawer? **<u>OK</u>**

3. There isn't ~~some~~ orange juice in the refrigerator. **<u>any</u>**

4. Are there any cookies in the box? **<u>OK</u>**

5. Could I have ~~any~~ coffee, please? **<u>some</u>**

6. Would you like some ham? **<u>OK</u>**

7. We have lots of fruit. Would you like ~~any~~? **<u>some</u>**

8. I already had ~~some~~ fruit at home. I don't need some now.
<u>any</u>

9. There aren't ~~some~~ newspapers. **<u>any</u>**

10. There are ~~any~~ magazines. **<u>some</u>**

❺ **1**. Who are these boxes for, the **ones** you are carrying?

2. Do you like the red socks or the white **ones**?

3. My cubicle is the **one** next to the manager's office.

4. I like the pink hat. Which **one** do you like?

5. Our racquets are the **ones** stored over there.

❻ **1**. B **2**. B **3**. B **4**. A **5**. B
6. A **7**. A **8**. A **9**. A **10**. B

❼ 1. everywhere 2. nowhere 3. anywhere 4. somewhere

5. no one 6. anyone 7. Someone 8. Everyone

9. something 10. anything 11. nothing 12. everything

13. everybody 14. anybody 15. somebody 16. nobody

❽ 1. someone 2. No one 3. anyone

4. Everyone 5. No one 6. somewhere

7. anywhere 8. nowhere 9. everywhere

10. somewhere 11. something 12. anything

13. nothing 14. everything

❾ 1. A 2. A 3. C 4. B 5. B 6. A

❿ 1. My brother made himself sick by eating too much ice cream. **OK**

2. My sister made ~~himself~~ sick by eating two big pizzas. **herself**

3. The dog is scratching itself. **OK**

4. I jog every morning by ~~me~~. **myself**

5. You have only yourself to blame. **OK**

6. We would have gone there ~~us~~ but we didn't have time. **ourselves**

7. He can't possibly lift that sofa all by himself. **OK**

8. Do you want to finish this project by yourself or do you need help? **OK**

9. I helped him. He helped me. We helped ~~ourselves~~. **each other**

10. Don't fight about it. You two need to talk to each other if you are going to solve this problem. **OK**

⓫ 1. a little 2. a few 3. enough 4. a lot of

5. enough 6. a lot 7. little 8. Few

9. enough 10. many 11. a few 12. a lot of

13. too many 14. enough

Unit 29 ———————————— P. 81

❶ 1. is 2. am 3. is 4. is 5. is 6. is 7. are

8. are 9. am 10. is 11. are 12. are 13. is 14. are

❷ 1. Karl is Canadian. He is a violinist.

2. Dominique is Russian. He is a chef.

3. Huyuki is Japanese. He is a drummer.

4. Lino is Italian. He is a waiter.

5. Jane is Chinese. She is a singer.

6. Mike is American. He is a policeman.

Unit 30 ———————————— P. 83

❶ 1. There isn't 2. There are 3. There isn't 4. There are

5. There is 6. There is 7. There is 8. There isn't

9. There isn't 10. There are 11. There isn't 12. There are

13. There aren't 14. There is 15. There isn't 16. There are

❷ 1. is, It is 2. isn't, it 3. is, It is

4. are, They are 5. are, They are 6. is, It is

Unit 31

P. 85

❶ 1. She's got a hamster. 2. She's got a parrot.
3. They've got a cat. 4. He's got a big dog.
5. She's got a snake. 6. He's got a pig.

❷ 1. Has your family got a cottage on Lake Michigan?
2. Have you got your own room?
3. Have you got your own closet?
4. How many pets have you got?
5. How many TVs has your family got?
6. How many cars has your brother got?

Unit 32

P. 87

❶ 1. eats 2. cooks 3. walks 4. runs 5. brushes
6. crunches 7. watches 8. boxes 9. marries 10. buries

❷ Bobby: I **cook** simple food every day. I usually **heat** food in the microwave oven. I often **make** sandwiches. I sometimes **pour** hot water on fast noodles. However, I **don't wash** dishes.

❸ 1. tightens 2. cuts 3. moves

Unit 33

P. 89

❶ 1. talking 2. caring 3. staying 4. sleeping
5. dying 6. eating 7. making 8. robbing

9. advising 10. jogging 11. spitting
12. jamming 13. waiting 14. clipping
15. tying 16. comparing 17. lying
18. planning 19. throwing 20. speaking

❷ 1. is walking 2. is buying 3. is shining
4. is throwing 5. is playing 6. are picnicking
7. is lying 8. are running 9. is lying 10. is sitting

Unit 34

P. 91

❶ 1. driving 2. leaves 3. designs 4. ends
5. drinks 6. is thinking 7. is going 8. wishes

❷ 1. Q: Do you often listen to music?
A: Yes, I do. I often listen to music.
2. Q: Are you watching TV at this moment?
A: Yes, I am. I'm watching TV at this moment. /
No, I'm not. I'm not watching TV at this moment.
3. Q: Is it hot now?
A: Yes, it is. It is hot now. / No, it isn't. It isn't hot now.
4. Q: Is it often hot this time of year?
A: Yes, it is. It is often hot this time of year. /
No, it isn't. It isn't often hot this time of year.
5. Q: Do you drink coffee every day?
A: Yes, I do. I drink coffee every day. /
No, I don't. I don't drink coffee every day.

6. Q: Are you drinking tea right now?

A: Yes, I am. I'm drinking tea right now. /

No, I'm not. I'm not drinking tea right now.

Unit 35 ——————————————— P. 93

❶ **1.** am eating, hate   **2.** is eating, likes   **3.** loves   **4.** like

5. are making, know   **6.** Do, mean   **7.** seem, are, doing

❷ **1.** I ~~am owning~~ my own house. **own**

2. This book belongs to Mary. **OK**

3. Mother is ~~believing~~ your story. **believes**

4. I often forget names. **OK**

5. I am having a snack. **OK**

6. The man is ~~recognizing~~ you. **recognizes / recognized**

Unit 36 Review Test ——————————— P. 94

❶ **1.** changes, changing   **2.** visits, visiting

3. turns, turning   **4.** jogs, jogging

5. mixes, mixing   **6.** cries, crying

7. has, having   **8.** cuts, cutting

9. fights, fighting   **10.** feels, feeling

11. ties, tying   **12.** applies, applying

13. jumps, jumping   **14.** enjoys, enjoying

15. steals, stealing   **16.** swims, swimming

17. sends, sending   **18.** tastes, tasting

19. finishes, finishing   **20.** studies, studying

❷ **1.** Q: What is your favorite TV show?

A: The Simpsons.（參考答案）

2. Q: What is your favorite movie?

A: The Godfather.（參考答案）

3. Q: Who is your favorite actor?

A: Johnny Depp.（參考答案）

4. Q: Who is your favorite actress?

A: Nicole Kidman.（參考答案）

5. Q: What is your favorite food?

A: Hamburgers.（參考答案）

6. Q: What is your favorite juice?

A: Orange juice.（參考答案）

7. Q: Who are your parents?

A: Mike and Jennifer.（參考答案）

8. Q: Who sare your brothers and sisters?

A: James, David, and Alice.（參考答案）

❸ **1.** Q: **Is** Seoul in Vietnam?

A: **No, Seoul is in Korea.**

2. Q: **Are** Thailand and Vietnam in East Asia?

A: **No, they are in Southeast Asia.**

3. Q: **Is** Hong Kong in Japan?

A: **No, Hong Kong is in China.**

4. **Q: Are** Beijing and Shanghai in China?

   A: Yes, they are in China.

5. **Q: Is** Osaka in Taiwan?

   A: No, Osaka is in Japan.

6. **Q: Are** Tokyo, Osaka, and Kyoto in Japan?

   A: Yes, they are in Japan.

❹ 1. **Q: Are there** any men's shoe stores?

   A: Yes, there are. / Yes, there is one.

2. **Q: Is there** a wig store?

   A: No, there isn't.

3. **Q: Is there** a computer store?

   A: No, there isn't.

4. **Q: Are there** two bookstores?

   A: Yes, there are.

5. **Q: Are there** any women's clothing stores?

   A: Yes, there are. / Yes, there is one.

6. **Q: Are there** any women's shoe stores?

   A: Yes, there are. / Yes, there is one.

7. **Q: Are there** three music stores?

   A: No, there aren't.

8. **Q: Is there** a jewelry store?

   A: Yes, there is one.

❺ 1. is   **2.** am   **3.** have   **4.** are   **5.** has

  6. are   **7.** am   **8.** are   **9.** are   **10.** am

❻ 1. **Q:** Are you a university student?

   A: Yes, I am. / No, I'm not.

2. **Q:** Are you a big reader?

   A: Yes, I am. / No, I'm not.

3. **Q:** Is your birthday coming soon?

   A: Yes, it is. / No, it isn't.

4. **Q:** Is your favorite holiday Chinese New Year?

   A: Yes, it is. / No, it isn't.

❼ （參考答案）

· There is an alarm clock on the dresser.

· There are two pillows on the bed.

· There is a chair in the room.

· There is a candle on the dresser.

· There is a pen and a bottle of ink on the dresser.

· There are some books on the shelf.

· There is a light hanging from the ceiling.

· There is a dresser in the room.

· There is a bed in the room.

❽ 1. Do   **2.** work   **3.** don't   **4.** work   **5.** Does

  6. work   **7.** works   **8.** Does   **9.** work

  10. doesn't   **11.** work   **12.** works

❾ 1. **Q:** Do you watch many movies?

   A: Yes, I do. I watch many movies. /

     No, I don't. I don't watch many movies.

2. Q: Does your mother work?

A: Yes, she does. She works. /

No, she doesn't. She doesn't work.

3. Q: Does your father drive a car to work?

A: Yes, he does. He drives a car to work. /

No, he doesn't. He doesn't drive a car to work.

4. Q: Does your family have a big house?

A: Yes, we do. My family has a big house. /

Yes, we do. We have a big house. /

No, we don't. We don't have a big house. /

No, we don't. My family doesn't have a big house.

5. Q: Do your neighbors have children?

A: Yes, they do. They have children. /

No, they don't. They don't have children.

6. Q: Do you have a university degree?

A: Yes, I do. I have a university degree. /

No, I don't. I don't have a university degree.

 1. do you like to be called

2. do you come from   **3**. do you go to the café

4. do you drink at the café   **5**. do you go home

6. do you go home   **7**. do you have to be at school

 1. Peter has got a good car.   **2. x**

3. Wendy has got a brother and a sister.

4. The Hamiltons have got two cars.

5. Ken has got a lot of good ideas.   **6. x**

 1. is fixing   **2**. is delivering   **3**. is changing

4. is talking   **5**. are using   **6**. are working

❸ 1. I am going   **2**. stop   **3**. He often has

4. is having   **5**. wants   **6**. is having

7. I'm thinking   **8**. I have got

9. I don't believe   **10**. I can hear

❹ 1. We aren't tired.

Are we tired?

2. You aren't rich.

Are you rich?

3. There isn't a message for Jim.

Is there a message for Jim?

4. It isn't a surprise.

Is it a surprise?

5. They haven't got tickets.

Have they got tickets?

6. You haven't got electric power.

Have you got electric power?

7. She doesn't work out at the gym.

Does she work out at the gym?

8. He doesn't usually drink a fitness shake for breakfast.

Does he usually drink a fitness shake for breakfast?

9. We aren't playing baseball this weekend.

Are we playing baseball this weekend?

10. He doesn't realize this is the end of the vacation.

Does he realize this is the end of the vacation?

Unit 37 ──────────────── P. 103

❶ 1. was, is   2. was , is   3. is, was   4. is, was

5. is, was   6. was, is   7. were, are   8. were, are

9. are, were   10. were, are   11. were, are   12. were, are

❷ 1. → **Were** you busy yesterday?

→ **Yes, I was. I was very busy yesterday. /**

No, I wasn't. I wasn't very busy yesterday.

2. → **Were** you at school yesterday morning?

→ **Yes, I was. I was at school yesterday morning. /**

No, I wasn't. I wasn't at school yesterday morning.

3. → **Was** yesterday the busiest day of the week?

→ **Yes, it was. It was the busiest day of the week. /**

No, it wasn't. It wasn't the busiest day of the week.

4. → **Was** your father in the office last night?

→ **Yes, he was. He was in the office last night. /**

No, he wasn't. He wasn't in the office last night.

5. → **Were** you at your friend's house last Saturday?

→ **Yes, I was. I was at my friend's house last Saturday. /**

No, I wasn't. I wasn't at my friend's house last

Saturday.

6. → **Was** your mother at home at 8 o'clock yesterday morning?

→ **Yes, she was. She was at home at 8 o'clock yesterday morning. / No, she wasn't. She wasn't at home at 8 o'clock yesterday morning.**

7. → **Were** you in bed at 11 o'clock last night?

→ **Yes, I was. I was in bed at 11 o'clock last night. / No, I wasn't. I wasn't in bed at 11 o'clock last night.**

8. → **Were** you at the bookstore at 6 o'clock yesterday evening?

→ **Yes, I was. I was at the bookstore at 6 o'clock yesterday evening. / No, I wasn't. I wasn't at the bookstore at 6 o'clock yesterday evening.**

Unit 38 ──────────────── P. 105

❶ 1. talked   2. planned   3. mailed   4. hurried   5. dated

6. ate   7. carried   8. noted   9. showed   10. clipped

11. laughed   12. drank   13. married   14. cooked

15. wrote   16. came   17. dropped   18. played

19. delivered   20. called   21. sent

❷ 1. counted   2. attended   3. received

4. used   5. checked   6. put

Unit 39 ———————————————— P. 107

❶ **1.** Did, had, didn't have   **2.** Did, have, did

3. did, have, had

❷ **1.** Q: Did you see your friends last night?

A: Yes, I did. I saw my friends last night. /

No, I didn't. I didn't see my friends last night.

2. Q: Did you go to a movie last weekend?

A: Yes, I did. I went to a movie last weekend. /

No, I didn't. I didn't go to a movie last weekend.

3. Q: Did you play basketball yesterday?

A: Yes, I did. I played basketball yesterday. /

No, I didn't. I didn't play basketball yesterday.

4. Q: Did you graduate from university last year?

A: Yes, I did. I graduated from university last year. /

No, I didn't. I didn't graduate from university last year.

❸ **1.** was   **2.** saw   **3.** was   **4.** pondered   **5.** succeeded

Unit 40 ———————————————— P. 109

❶ **1.** were decorating   **2.** was hanging

3. was draping   **4.** was arranging

5. was putting   **6.** was unpacking   **7.** was putting

❷ **1.** Q: **What was he doing** when the phone rang?

A: **He was trying to fall asleep.**

2. Q: **What was he doing** when the alarm clock went off?

A: **He was talking on the phone.**

3. Q: **What was he doing** while watching TV during breakfast?

A: **He was drinking a lot of coffee.**

Unit 41 ———————————————— P. 111

❶ **1.** talked   **2.** gone   **3.** driven   **4.** broken

5. eaten   **6.** thought   **7.** shot   **8.** bought

9. loved   **10.** lost   **11.** smelled   **12.** read

13. taken   **14.** fallen   **15.** drunk   **16.** brought

17. swallowed   **18.** written   **19.** left   **20.** lain

❷ **1.** has eaten   **2.** has taught   **3.** has arrived

4. has won   **5.** has stolen   **6.** has written

❸ Clive grew up in the country. He moved to the city in 2010. He **has lived** there since then. He **has worked** in an Italian restaurant for a year and half. He met his wife in the restaurant. They got married last month, and she moved in to his apartment. They **have become** a happy couple, but they **haven't had** a baby yet.

Unit
36
|
Unit
41

Unit 42

P. 113

❶ **1**. have been, since   **2**. have built, for

3. have dreamed   **4**. Since, have started

❷ **1**. Q: Have you ever eaten a worm?

A: Yes, I have. I have eaten a worm. /

No, I haven't. I haven't eaten a worm.

2. Q: Have you ever been to Japan?

A: Yes, I have. I have been to Japan. /

No, I haven't. I haven't been to Japan.

3. Q: Have you ever swum in the ocean?

A: Yes, I have. I have swum in the ocean. /

No, I haven't. I haven't swum in the ocean.

4. Q: Have you ever cheated on an exam?

A: Yes, I have. I have cheated on an exam. /

No, I haven't. I haven't cheated on an exam. /

No, I haven't. I have never cheated on an exam.

Unit 43

P. 115

❶ **1**. has loved   **2**. has been   **3**. stayed

4. went surfing   **5**. liked   **6**. discovered

7. rented   **8**. learned   **9**. visited

10. has enjoyed   **11**. has fished   **12**. visited

13. has gone   **14**. has talked

❷ **1**. has he been   **2**. was   **3**. has he been

4. Did he go   **5**. Did he stay

6. Has he visited   **7**. When was

Unit 44 Review Test

P. 116

❶ **1**. mailed, mailed   **2**. dated, dated

3. bought, bought   **4**. went, gone

5. did, done   **6**. ate, eaten   **7**. sang, sung

8. wrote, written   **9**. drank, drunk

10. said, said   **11**. closed, closed

12. cried, cried   **13**. thought, thought

14. read, read   **15**. met, met   **16**. put, put

17. hit, hit   **18**. shook, shaken

19. shut, shut   **20**. rang, rung

❷ **1**. I **sailed** on a friend's boat last weekend.

→ **I didn't sail on a friend's boat last weekend.**

→ **Did I sail on a friend's boat last weekend?**

2. I **watched** the seals on the rocks.

→ **I didn't watch the seals on the rocks.**

→ **Did I watch the seals on the rocks?**

3. We **fed** the seagulls.

→ **We didn't feed the seagulls.**

→ **Did we feed the seagulls?**

4. The seagull **liked** the bread we threw to it.

   → **The seagull didn't like the bread we threw to it.**

   → **Did the seagull like the bread we threw to it?**

5. We **fished** for our dinner.

   → **We didn't fish for our dinner.**

   → **Did we fish for our dinner?**

6. My friend **cooked** our dinner in the galley of the boat.

   → **My friend didn't cook our dinner in the galley of the boat.**

   → **Did my friend cook our dinner in the galley of the boat?**

7. We **ate** on deck.

   → **We didn't eat on deck.**

   → **Did we eat on deck?**

8. We **passed** the time chatting and watching the water.

   → **We didn't pass the time chatting and watching the water.**

   → **Did we pass the time chatting and watching the water?**

❸ **1**. played, opened, shined, sprayed

   2. missed, pushed, marched, fished

   3. parted, carted, deposited, mended

❹ Catherine **got** up at 5:00. She **took** a shower. Then she **made** a cup of strong black coffee. She **sat** at her computer and **checked** her email. She **answered** her email and **worked** on her computer until 7:30. At 7:30, she **ate** a light breakfast. After breakfast, she **went** to work. She **walked** to work. She **bought** a cup of coffee and a newspaper on her way to work. She **arrived** promptly at 8:30 and **was** ready to start her day at the office.

❺ **1**. was snowing, went   **2**. fell, had

   3. were walking, saw   **4**. saw, said   **5**. fell

   6. broke, fell   **7**. was feeding, heard

   8. woke, realized   **9**. started

❻ **1**. Q: Have they picked up the flyers yet?

   A: Yes, they have. They have already picked up the flyers.

   2. Q: Have they put out order pads yet?

   A: Yes, they have. They have already put out order pads.

   3. Q: Have they gotten pens with our company logo yet?

   A: No, they haven't. They haven't gotten pens with our company logo yet.

   4. Q: Have they set up the computer yet?

   A: No, they haven't. They haven't set up the computer yet.

   5. Q: Have they arranged flowers yet?

   A: Yes, they have. They have already arranged flowers.

Unit | Unit

❼ （答案略）

❽ **1**. was **2**. was, was **3**. had **4**. bought

 5. slept **6**. have gone **7**. kept, died **8**. registered

 9. Have, finished, haven't finished

 10. was cooking **11**. did

❾ **1**. B **2**. B **3**. B **4**. A **5**. A **6**. A **7**. A **8**. A **9**. B

Unit 45 ———————————————— P. 123

❶ **1**. Who **is going** on vacation?

 → **Mark and Sharon are going on vacation.**

 2. When **are** Mark and Sharon **going** on vacation?

 → **They are going on vacation on May 18th.**

 3. Where **are** they **departing** from?

 → **They are departing from Linz.**

 4. What time **are** they **departing**?

 → **They are departing at 15:30.**

 5. Where **are** they **flying** to?

 → **They are flying to Budapest.**

 6. What time **are** they **arriving** at their destination?

 → **They are arriving at their destination at 17:30.**

 7. What airline **are** they **taking**?

 → **They are taking Aeroflot Airlines.**

 8. What flight **are** they **taking**?

 → **They are taking Flight 345.**

Unit 46 ———————————————— P. 125

❶ **1**. No, he isn't. He is going to use a laptop.

 2. Yes, they are. They're going to buy some toys.

 3. Yes, she is. She's going to take a nap with her teddy bear.

 4. No, they aren't. They're going to drink some orange juice.

 5. No, they aren't. They are going to buy some clothes.

 6. No, she isn't. She's going to give the customers a key.

❷ **1**. I'm going to eat at a restaurant. /

 I'm not going to eat at a restaurant.

 2. I'm going to watch a baseball game. /

 I'm not going to watch a baseball game.

 3. I'm going to read a book. /

 I'm not going to read a book.

 4. I'm going to play video games. /

 I'm not going to play video games.

 5. I'm going to write an email. /

 I'm not going to write an email.

Unit 47 ———————————————— P. 127

❶ **1**. Will scientists clone humans in 50 years?

 Scientists will clone humans in 50 years.

 Scientists won't clone humans in 50 years.

2. Will robots become family members in 80 years?

Robots will become family members in 80 years.

Robots won't become family members in 80 years.

3. Will doctors insert memory chips behind our ears?

Doctors will insert memory chips behind our ears.

Doctors won't insert memory chips behind our ears.

4. Will police officers scan our brains for criminal thoughts?

Police officers will scan our brains for criminal thoughts.

Police officers won't scan our brains for criminal thoughts.

❷ 1. I think I'll live in another country.

Perhaps I'll live in another country.

I doubt I'll live in another country.

2. I think my sister will learn how to drive.

Perhaps my sister will learn how to drive.

I doubt my sister will learn how to drive.

3. I think Jerry will marry somebody from another country.

Perhaps Jerry will marry somebody from another country.

I doubt Jerry will marry somebody from another country.

Unit 48 ———————————————— P. 129

❶ 1. Are you going to the bookstore tomorrow?

2. Janet is going to help Cindy move into her new house.

3. Are you playing baseball this Saturday?

4. He will cook dinner at 5:30.

5. She will fall into the water.

6. I'm going to give him a call tonight.

7. When are you going to get up tomorrow morning?

8. I'm driving to Costco this afternoon.

❷ 1. is leaving   2. will melt   3. will quit

4. am going to quit   5. will eat   6. is having

7. am going to find, am going to make   8. will rain

Unit 49 Review Test ———————————— P. 130

❶ 1. I **am going** out for lunch tomorrow.

→ **I am not going out for lunch tomorrow.**

→ **Am I going out for lunch tomorrow?**

2. I **am planning** a birthday party for my grandmother.

→ **I'm not planning a birthday party for my grandmother.**

→ **Am I planning a birthday party for my grandmother?**

3. She **is going** to take the dog for a walk after dinner.

→ **She isn't going to take the dog for a walk after dinner.**

→ **Is she going to take the dog for a walk after dinner?**

4. Mike **is planning** to watch a baseball game later tonight.

→ **Mike isn't planning to watch a baseball game later tonight.**

Unit
44
|
Unit
49

→ **Is Mike planning to watch a baseball game later tonight?**

5. Dr. Johnson **is meeting** a patient at the clinic on Saturday.

→ **Dr. Johnson isn't meeting a patient at the clinic on Saturday.**

→ **Is Dr. Johnson meeting a patient at the clinic on Saturday?**

6. Jack and Kim **are applying** for admission to a technical college.

→ **Jack and Kim aren't applying for admission to a technical college.**

→ **Are Jack and Kim applying for admission to a technical college?**

7. I **am thinking** about having two kids after I get married.

→ **I'm not thinking about having two kids after I get married.**

→ **Am I thinking about having two kids after I get married?**

❷ 1. F   2. C   3. C   4. C   5. C   6. F   7. F   8. C

❸ 1. What **are** you **going to do** tomorrow night?

I'm going to do some shopping tomorrow night.

2. When **are** you **going to leave**?

I'm going to leave at 9 a.m.

3. **Is** he **going to call** her later?

Yes, he is going to call her later.

4. What **are** you **going to say** when you see him?

I'm going to tell him the truth.

5. **Are** they **going to study** British Literature in college?

No, they are going to study Chinese Literature in college.

6. **Is** your family **going to have** a vacation in Hawaii?

No, my family is going to have a vacation in Guam.

❹ 1. I think I'll take a nap.

2. I think I'll turn on a light.

3. I think I'll check the answering machine.

4. I think I'll eat them right away.

5. I think I'll pay it at 7-Eleven.

6. I think I'll buy him a gift.

7. I think I'll visit her in the hospital.

8. I think I'll bring my umbrella.

❺ 1. ✓   2. ✗ I think it'll rain soon.   3. ✓

4. ✗ I'm sure you won't get called next week.

5. ✓   6. ✗ Is Laura going to work?   7. ✓

8. ✗ In the year 2100, people will live on the moon.

9. ✗ What are you doing next week?

❻ 1. A   2. A   3. A   4. A

❼ 1. I won't be watching the game on Saturday afternoon.

Will I be watching the game on Saturday afternoon?

2. You aren't going to visit Grandma Moses tomorrow.

Are you going to visit Grandma Moses tomorrow?

3. She isn't planning to be on vacation next week.

Is she planning to be on vacation next week?

4. We aren't going to take a trip to New Zealand next month.

Are we going to take a trip to New Zealand next month?

5. He won't send the tax forms soon.

Will he send the tax forms soon?

6. It won't be cold all next week.

Will it be cold all next week?

❽ **1.** A   **2.** A   **3.** B   **4.** C   **5.** A   **6.** B

7. B   **8.** A   **9.** C   **10.** A   **11.** C   **12.** B

Unit 50 ———————————————— P. 137

❶ **1.** watch   **2.** to play   **3.** fly   **4.** to give

5. hear   **6.** play   **7.** go   **8.** to be   **9.** to meet

❷ **1.** to quit drinking and smoking   **2.** make good coffee

3. look very happy; to wear clothes

4. to work 10 hours a day

5. to buy some red peppers

Unit 51 ———————————————— P. 139

❶ **1.** to finish   **2.** go   **3.** sit   **4.** to fly   **5.** to join

6. to call   **7.** to call   **8.** make / to make

❷ **1.** to get the sausage on the plate

2. take a look at your answers

3. to climb a wall   **4.** to eat on a train

5. to make a cake   **6.** to study for the exam

Unit 52 ———————————————— P. 141

❶ **1.** playing soccer   **2.** making clothes

3. blowing bubbles   **4.** singing a song

5. being high up on a tree   **6.** biking

❷ **1.** call / to call   **2.** to avoid   **3.** drinking

4. getting up / to get up   **5.** swimming

6. sharing   **7.** going   **8.** living

Unit 53 ———————————————— P. 143

❶ **1.** a library to borrow books

2. a history museum to see artifacts

3. the aquarium to see the fish

4. an art gallery to look at paintings

5. the amusement park for fun

6. a zoo to see the animals

❷ **1.** for carrying liquid cement

2. for putting out fires

Unit 49 | Unit 53

3. for towing cars and trucks

4. for taking the wounded to the hospital

Unit 54 Review Test

❶ **1**. surf   **2**. to surf   **3**. to surf / surfing

   4. ski   **5**. to ski   **6**. skiing   **7**. drive

   8. drive / to drive   **9**. driving   **10**. to drive

❷ **1**. My parents went out for a walk.

   2. Mr. Lyle went to the front desk for his package.

   3. I have to get everything ready for the meeting.

   4. I jog every day to stay healthy.

   5. I walked into the McDonald's on Tenth Street to buy two cheeseburgers.

❸ **1**. C   **2**. A   **3**. B   **4**. A   **5**. C

   6. B   **7**. C   **8**. B   **9**. C   **10**. B

   11. B   **12**. B   **13**. B   **14**. B   **15**. C

❹ **1**. the beach to get some sun

   2. the water to get the stick

   3. the supermarket for some milk

   4. the opera house for a concert

   5. the store to buy a gift

   6. the Starbucks for a cup of latté

   7. the stadium to watch a baseball game

   8. the market to buy some pumpkins

❺ **1**. ✓   **2**. ✗ I should visit my sister.

   3. ✗ Let's go to the movies.   **4**. ✓   **5**. ✓

   6. ✗ I want you to call me next week.

   7. ✗ Would you like me to call you next week?

   8. ✓

   9. ✗ Most people love to go on a vacation. / Most people love going on a vacation.

   10. ✓

   11. ✗ Kelly went to see the doctor to have a checkup / Kelly went to see the doctor for a checkup.

   12. ✓

Unit 55

❶ **1**. go bowling   **2**. go swimming   **3**. go skiing

   4. go sailing   **5**. go camping   **6**. go skating

❷ **1**. has gone   **2**. go for   **3**. have gone by

   4. going   **5**. going for   **6**. went on   **7**. went

Unit 56

❶ **1**. to finish   **2**. to listen   **3**. cut   **4**. washed

❷ a shower, a walk, a nap, a look

❸ 1. Get on, get off   **2**. took   **3**. get over
4. Take off   **5**. take part in

Unit 57 ———————————————— P. 153

❶ 1. a favor   **2**. a mistake   **3**. his best   **4**. a wish
❷ 1. do   **2**. made   **3**. do   **4**. made from   **5**. good

Unit 58 ———————————————— P. 155

❶ 1. He had the pants shortened.
  2. Yvonne had her son mop the floor.
  3. She had the car washed.
  4. She had her husband replace the light bulb.
  5. He had the paper folded.
  6. She had the box packed with books and sent to the
    professor.
  7. He had his students read thirty pages of the book a day.
  8. I'm going to have this gift wrapped.
❷ 1. have your baby   **2**. have something to do with
  3. has nothing to do with   **4**. have a look
  5. have a good time   **6**. having a haircut

Unit 59 Review Test ———————————— P. 156

❶ 1. A   **2**. C   **3**. A   **4**. B   **5**. A   **6**. B   **7**. B
  8. C   **9**. C   **10**. A   **11**. C   **12**. C   **13**. A   **14**. C
❷ 1. is made from   **2**. went for   **3**. get along
  4. took part in   **5**. go on   **6**. took place
  7. Get over   **8**. is made of
❸ 1. finish   **2**. to change   **3**. finished   **4**. clean
  5. apologize   **6**. work   **7**. done   **8**. painted
  9. to remove   **10**. explain   **11**. repaired
❹ 1. Did you **have** your hair cut last week?
  → **Yes, I did. I had my hair cut last week. /**
    No, I didn't. I didn't have my hair cut last week.
  2. Do you have to **do** a lot of homework tonight?
  → **Yes, I do. I have to do a lot of homework tonight. /**
    No, I don't. I don't have to do a lot of homework
    tonight.
  3. Does your family **go** on a picnic every weekend?
  → **Yes, we do. We go on a picnic every weekend. /**
    No, we don't. We don't go on a picnic every weekend.
  4. Do you like to **take** pictures of dogs and cats?
  → **Yes, I do. I like to take pictures of dogs and cats. /**
    No, I don't. I don't like to take pictures of dogs and
    cats.

Unit

53

Unit

59

5. Do you **take** care of your little sister when your parents are out?

→ **Yes, I do. I take care of my little sister when my parents are out. / No, I don't. I don't take care of my little sister when my parents are out.**

6. Do you like to **go** camping on your summer vacation?

→ **Yes, I do. I like to go camping on my summer vacation. / No, I don't. I don't like to go camping on my summer vacation.**

7. Do you **take** a shower in the morning?

→ **Yes, I do. I take a shower in the morning. / No, I don't. I don't take a shower in the morning.**

8. Do you **go** crazy with your homework every day?

→ **Yes, I do. I go crazy with my homework every day. / No, I don't. I don't go crazy with my homework every day.**

9. Do you **make** a lot of mistakes?

→ **Yes, I do. I make a lot of mistakes. / No, I don't. I don't make a lot of mistakes.**

10. Have you ever **had** the dentist fill a cavity?

→ **Yes, I have. I have had the dentist fill a cavity. / No, I haven't. I haven't had the dentist fill a cavity.**

❺ **do:** exercise, the laundry, the shopping

take: a nap, a bath, a break

make: friends, a wish, money

296

❶ 1. Chris can play the guitar.

2. Chris can't play the drums.

3. Chris can't play the piano.

4. Chris can play the flute.

5. Chris can play the violin.

6. Chris can't play the saxophone.

❷ 1. Yes, I can. I can speak English. /
No, I can't. I can't speak English.

2. Yes, I can. I can read German. /
No, I can't. I can't read German.

3. Yes, I can. I can hang out with my friends on the weekend. /
No, I can't. I can't hang out with my friends on the weekend.

4. Yes, I can. I can run very fast. /
No, I can't. I can't run very fast.

5. Yes, she can. She can cook Mexican food. /
No, she can't. She can't cook Mexican food.

6. No, it can't. A dog can't fly.

7. No, it can't. A pig can't climb a tree.

8. No, we can't. We can't speak loudly in the museum.

Unit 61 P. 163

❶ 1. could paint pictures
2. could write calligraphy
3. could sculpt figures
4. could shoot photographs
5. could make pots
6. could paint landscapes

❷ 1. Yes, I could. I could play the piano when I was twelve. /
No, I couldn't. I couldn't play the piano when I was twelve.
2. Yes, I could. I could swim when I was twelve. /
No, I couldn't. I couldn't swim when I was twelve.
3. Yes, I could. I could use a computer when I was twelve. /
No, I couldn't. I couldn't use a computer when I was twelve.
4. Yes, I could. I could read novels in English when I was twelve. / No, I couldn't. I couldn't read novels in English when I was twelve.
5. Yes, I could. I could ride a bicycle when I was twelve. /
No, I couldn't. I couldn't ride a bicycle when I was twelve.

Unit 62 P. 165

❶ 1. must finish   2. mustn't smoke
3. had to clean   4. mustn't fight

5. must come   6. must finish   7. had to break
8. mustn't eat   9. must behave   10. had to run

❷ 1. You must hurry.
2. You must go to bed.
3. You must eat something.
4. You must drink something.
5. You must be careful.
6. You mustn't fight with them.
7. You mustn't lose it.

Unit 63 P. 167

❶ 1. She has to pack products.
2. She has to work on the computer.
3. She has to answer the phone.
4. She has to make copies.

❷ 1. doesn't have to deliver the mail.
2. don't have to make coffee.
3. doesn't have to show up every day.
4. doesn't have to fax documents.

Unit 64

P. 169

❶ （答案略）

❷ 1. You mustn't smoke

2. You don't have to pay cash

3. You mustn't skateboard

4. You mustn't talk on a cell phone

5. You don't have to pay full price

Unit 65

P. 171

❶ 1. may / might block the shot

2. may / might hit a home run

3. may / might win the set

4. may / might score a touchdown

5. may / might win the race

6. may / might clear the bar

❷ 1. We may go to the seashore tomorrow.

2. I might take you on a trip to visit my hometown.

3. We may pick up Grandpa on the way.

4. We might visit my sister in Sydney next year.

5. My sister may bring her husband and baby to visit us instead.

6. We might go to Hong Kong for the weekend.

7. You may go to a boarding school in Switzerland.

8. Or you might go to live with your grandparents.

Unit 66

P. 173

❶ 1. shouldn't eat   2. should yield

3. shouldn't cheat   4. should respect

5. shouldn't arrive   6. should work

7. shouldn't feed   8. should take

❷ 1. → Should I call the director about the resume I sent?

→ Do you think I should call the director about the resume I sent?

2. → Should I bring a gift with me?

→ Do you think I should bring a gift with me?

3. → Should Mike go on a vacation once in a while?

→ Do you think Mike should go on a vacation once in a while?

4. → Should we visit our grandma more often?

→ Do you think we should visit our grandma more often?

5. → Should I ask Nancy out for a date?

→ Do you think I should ask Nancy out for a date?

6. → Should Sally apply for that job in the restaurant?

→ Do you think Sally should apply for that job in the restaurant?

Unit 67
P. 175

❶ 1. → May I get two more shirts just like this one?

→ Could I get two more shirts just like this one?

→ Can I get two more shirts just like this one?

2. → May I have three pairs of socks similar to these?

→ Could I have three pairs of socks similar to these?

→ Can I have three pairs of socks similar to these?

3. → May I have a tie that goes with my shirt?

→ Could I have a tie that goes with my shirt?

→ Can I have a tie that goes with my shirt?

4. → May I pay with a credit card?

→ Could I pay with a credit card?

→ Can I pay with a credit card?

❷ 1. May I speak to Dennis?

2. May I borrow your father's drill?

3. Could you move these boxes for me?

4. Could you turn up the heat?

5. Can I put my files here?

Unit 68
P. 177

❶ 1. → Would you like some fruit salad?

→ Would you like me to make some fruit salad?

→ I'll make some fruit salad for you.

→ Shall I make some fruit salad for you?

2. → Would you like some tea?

→ Would you like me to make some tea?

→ I'll make some tea for you.

→ Shall I make some tea for you?

3. → Would you like some orange juice?

→ Would you like me to squeeze some orange juice?

→ I'll squeeze some orange juice for you.

→ Shall I squeeze some orange juice for you?

4. → Would you like some pudding?

→ Would you like me to make some pudding?

→ I'll make some pudding for you.

→ Shall I make some pudding for you?

❷ 1. Would you like to go fishing

2. Would you like to play basketball

3. Would you like to go hiking

4. Would you like to go to the beach

5. Would you like to have some pizza

Unit 64 | Unit 68

❶ 1. → Shall we play another volleyball game?

→ Why don't we play another volleyball game?

→ How about playing another volleyball game?

→ Let's play another volleyball game.

2. → Shall we go on a picnic?

→ Why don't we go on a picnic?

→ How about going on a picnic?

→ Let's go on a picnic.

3. → Shall we eat out tonight?

→ Why don't we eat out tonight?

→ How about eating out tonight?

→ Let's eat out tonight.

4. → Shall we take a walk?

→ Why don't we take a walk?

→ How about taking a walk?

→ Let's take a walk.

5. → Shall we go to Bali this summer?

→ Why don't we go to Bali this summer?

→ How about going to Bali this summer?

→ Let's go to Bali this summer.

❶ 1. Q: Can you boil tea eggs?

A: Yes, I can. I can boil tea eggs. /

No, I can't. I can't boil tea eggs.

2. Q: Can you purée tomatoes?

A: Yes, I can. I can purée tomatoes. /

No, I can't. I can't purée tomatoes.

3. Q: Can you deep-fry French fries?

A: Yes, I can. I can deep-fry French fries. /

No, I can't. I can't deep-fry French fries.

4. Q: Can you grill hamburgers?

A: Yes, I can. I can grill hamburgers. /

No, I can't. I can't grill hamburgers.

5. Q: Can you bake muffins?

A: Yes, I can. I can bake muffins. /

No, I can't. I can't bake muffins.

6. Q: Can you make coffee?

A: Yes, I can. I can make coffee. /

No, I can't. I can't make coffee.

7. Q: Can you fry an egg?

A: Yes, I can. I can fry an egg. /

No, I can't. I can't fry an egg.

8. Q: Can you steam buns?

A: Yes, I can. I can steam buns. /

No, I can't. I can't steam buns.

❷ 1. do, have to   2. Does, have to   3. Do, have to

4. Do, have to   5. Does, have to   6. do, have to

❸ 1. May I   2. Can I / May I   3. Could you

4. Shall I   5. Would you   6. I'll

7. How about   8. Would you

❹ 1. Would you like something to drink?

2. Would you like an alcoholic beverage?

3. Would you like some juice?

4. Would you like a cup of coffee or tea?

5. Would you like a bag of nuts?

❺ 1. I can't walk to work.

2. Susie couldn't dance all night.

3. I don't have to go to Joe's house tonight.

4. I don't have to go to see the doctor tomorrow.

5. I may not go on a vacation in August.

6. I might not go see the Picasso exhibit at the museum.

7. My friend can't sit in the full lotus position.

8. I can't finish all my homework this weekend.

9. I don't have to stop eating beans.

10. John doesn't have to see Joseph.

11. The turtle may not win the race against the rabbit.

12. My friend Jon shouldn't get a different job.

❻ 1. Can you fry an egg?

2. Could Paul swim out to the island?

3. Must John go to Japan?

4. Does Abby have to go to the studio?

5. Can George play the guitar?

6. Must David finish his homework before he goes outside to play?

7. Do I have to give away my concert tickets?

8. Does Joan have to stay at home tomorrow night?

❼ 1. C   2. A   3. C   4. A   5. A

6. A   7. A   8. C   9. B   10. B

❽ 1. A   2. D   3. H   4. C   5. F   6. B   7. G   8. E

❾ 1. must be   2. must visit   3. must be, must eat

4. must pay   5. mustn't play

❿ 1. may have, should not eat / must not eat

2. may listen, should not download / must not download

3. may have, should not put / must not put

4. may drive, may not find

5. may call, may not answer

6. may watch, should not try / must not try

⓫ 1. should give   2. shouldn't feed

3. should adopt   4. shouldn't give

5. should spend   6. should take

Unit

69
|
Unit

70

Unit 71
P. 189

❶ 1. James is not / isn't playing with his new iPhone.

2. Vincent doesn't own a shoe factory.

3. They didn't go to a concert last night.

4. I don't enjoy reading.

5. I can't ride a unicycle.

6. Summer vacation won't begin soon.

7. I didn't have a nightmare last night.

8. I am not / I'm not from Vietnam.

❷ 1. Sue watched the football game on TV last night.

2. Rick can speak Japanese.

3. Phil and Jill were at the office yesterday.

4. I could enter the house this morning.

5. Joseph likes spaghetti.

6. They are drinking apple juice.

7. She is going shopping tomorrow.

8. I will tell Sandy.

Unit 72
P. 191

❶ 1. Is Jerry good at photography?

2. Doesn't Jane believe what he said?

3. Did he ever show up at the party?

4. Does Johnny get up early every day?

5. Will I remember you?

6. Did Julie ask me to give her a ride yesterday?

7. Was she surprised when he called?

8. Is he going to buy a gift tomorrow?

❷ 1. What are you watching on TV?

2. What are you interested in?

3. Who is that man?

4. Who is your favorite musician?

5. What is he looking at?

6. Who is writing an email?

Unit 73
P. 193

❶ 1. → Who ate my slice of pizza?

→ What did Johnny eat?

2. → Who consulted Lauren first?

→ Who did the boss consult first?

3. → Who helped cook the fish?

→ What did Tom help cook?

4. → Who broke the vase?

→ What did my dog break?

5. → Who is feeding the baby?

→ Who is Mom feeding?

6. → Who is standing next to Allen?

→ Who is Denise standing next to?

Unit 74 ── P. 195

❶ **which:** this one, the blue shirt, the large one, the taller man
where: London, the mall, the office, the garage
when: in 2006, last June, tomorrow, next month
whose: my sister's, the cat's, Vicky's, Ms. Lee's
❷ **1**. When **2**. Where **3**. Which **4**. Whose **5**. Where
6. When **7**. Whose **8**. When **9**. Which **10**. When

Unit 75 ── P. 197

❶ **1**. How old **2**. How tall **3**. How much
4. How many **5**. How **6**. How often
7. How long **8**. How old **9**. How
10. How tall **11**. How much **12**. How often
13. How long **14**. How

Unit 76 ── P. 199

❶ **1**. can't I **2**. aren't you **3**. do I **4**. can't I
5. do you **6**. have I **7**. didn't you **8**. did you
9. did you **10**. haven't you **11**. do you **12**. do you
❷ **1**. aren't you **2**. is he **3**. can you
4. won't she **5**. didn't I **6**. does she
7. isn't it **8**. aren't I **9**. isn't it **10**. did he

Unit 77 ── P. 201

❶ **1**. ✓ **2**. - **3**. ✓ **4**. - **5**. ✓
6. ✓ **7**. - **8**. ✓ **9**. - **10**. ✓
❷ **1**. Paul, close that door.
2. Don't go out at midnight.
3. Don't throw garbage into the toilet.
4. Go buy some eggs now.
5. Don't be mad at me.
6. Take a No. 305 bus to the city hall.
7. Be careful not to wake up the baby.
8. Don't worry about so many things.
9. Relax.
10. Do your homework right now.

Unit 78 Review Test ── P. 202

❶ **1**. N **2**. A **3**. N **4**. Q **5**. N
6. Q **7**. A **8**. Q **9**. Q **10**. A
❷ **1**. When **2**. Where **3**. Who **4**. How
5. Who **6**. Where **7**. When **8**. How
9. Why **10**. Why **11**. Which **12**. What
13. Which **14**. What **15**. Whose **16**. Whose
❸ **1**. Who is visiting Charles?
2. Who is Eve visiting?

3. Who wants to meet Cathy?

4. Who does Cathy want to meet?

5. What did he take with him?

6. Who is Keith dating?

7. What crashed?

8. Who answered the phone?

9. Who wants to marry Jenny?

10. What does Dennis want to buy?

11. Who wants to buy a new cell phone?

12. Who wants to eat peanuts?

13. What does Sylvia want to eat?

❹ 1. isn't it?   2. is it?   3. aren't they?

4. are we?   5. didn't you?   6. did you?

7. wasn't it   8. was it?   9. didn't you?

❺ 1. Who is Chris calling?

2. What does Irene want to do?

3. Who wants to stay for dinner?

4. Who finished the last piece of cake?

5. Who invented the automobile?

6. Whose dirty dishes are these on the table?

7. Which side of the road do you drive on?

8. Rupert likes history, doesn't he?

9. They drive a minivan, don't they?

❻ Bob: How can I get to the station?

Eve: **Go** straight down this road. **Walk** for fifteen minutes and you will see a park.

Bob: So the station is near the park?

Eve: Yes. **Turn** right at the park and **walk** for another five minutes. **Cross** the main road. The station will be at your left. You won't miss it.

Bob: That's very helpful of you.

Eve: **Be** sure not to take any small alleys on the way.

Bob: I won't. Thank you very much.

Eve: You're welcome.

❼ 1. → Eddie isn't a naughty boy.

→ Is Eddie a naughty boy?

2. → Jack doesn't walk to work every morning.

→ Does Jack walk to work every morning?

3. → Sammi didn't visit Uncle Lu last Saturday.

→ Did Sammi visit Uncle Lu last Saturday?

4. → She won't be able to finish the project next week.

→ Will she be able to finish the project next week?

5. → My boss isn't going to Beijing tomorrow.

→ Is my boss going to Beijing tomorrow?

6. → Joe hasn't seen the show yet.

→ Has Joe already seen the show?

Unit 79 ————————————— P. 207

❶ **1.** come along   **2.** work out   **3.** hang out
4. taken off   **5.** stay up   **6.** moving in
❷ **1.** out   **2.** up   **3.** up   **4.** in
5. down   **6.** off   **7.** down   **8.** up

Unit 80 ————————————— P. 209

❶ **1. set off**
  → Dick and Byron set the fire crackers off.
  → Dick and Byron set them off.

2. take off
  → Don't take the price tag off in case we have to return the sweater.
  → Don't take it off in case we have to return the sweater.

3. turn down
  → Don't turn the offer down right away.
  → Don't turn it down right away.

4. throw away
  → We don't throw bottles away if they can be recycled.
  → We don't throw them away if they can be recycled.

5. fill out
  → You need to fill the form out and attach two photos.
  → You need to fill it out and attach two photos.

6. try on
  → Would you like to try these shoes on?
  → Would you like to try them on?

Unit 81 ————————————— P. 211

❶ **1.** look after   **2.** Watch out for   **3.** catch up with
4. put up with   **5.** come across
❷ **1.** on, off   **2.** into   **3.** to   **4.** of   **5.** for

Unit 82 Review Test ————————————— P. 212

❶ **1.** wake, up   **2.** hang out   **3.** take off, get on   **4.** hand in
5. threw away   **6.** move in   **7.** Get in   **8.** Keep away from
9. fill out   **10.** getting along with   **11.** keep up with
12. pick up   **13.** grew up   **14.** brought up
15. working out   **16.** call off   **17.** hung up   **18.** try on
❷ **1.** looking for   **2.** Look up   **3.** look after   **4.** Look out
5. turn down   **6.** turn on   **7.** turn down   **8.** turn off
9. take out   **10.** Take off   **11.** take off   **12.** take after
13. put on   **14.** put out   **15.** put off   **16.** put away
17. go on   **18.** went off   **19.** went out

Unit 78

Unit 82

Unit 83 P. 215

❶ 1. old pants　2. new pants　3. soft chair　4. hard chair

5. big dog　6. small dog　7. curved road　8. straight road

❷ 1. He lives in a small town.

2. She has blue eyes.

3. The lamb stew smells good.

4. I have two lovely kids.

5. My teddy bear is cute.

Unit 84 P. 217

❶ 1. carefully　2. possibly　3. merrily　4. usually　5. entirely

6. cheerfully　7. really　8. quickly　9. honestly　10. silently

11. fast　12. early　13. strangely　14. calmly　15. angrily

16. well　17. finally　18. slowly　19. wisely　20. deeply

❷ 1. He answered clearly.

2. He sings badly.

3. He arrived at school late. / He arrived late for school.

4. She paints well.

5. She learns fast.

6. He works noisily.

7. She translates professionally.

8. The earth trembled terribly.

9. She reads fast.

10. She shops frequently.

Unit 85 P. 219

❶ 1. My parents live over there.

2. They bought the house over 20 years ago.

3. My dad pays the mortgage to the bank on the first day of each month.

4. No packages were delivered to Wendy's house this morning.

5. Jack and Jimmy are going to meet at the café this afternoon.

❷ 1. I left the bag in the cloakroom at 4:30 yesterday.

2. I last saw him at Teresa's birthday party on January 22nd.

3. I bought that book at the bookstore around the corner last week.

4. I go swimming at the health club on Sundays.

5. I learned to dive at the Pacific Diving Club three years ago.

Unit 86 P. 221

❶ 1. He never misses the mortgage payment.

2. He is always the first customer in the morning.

3. He walks to work every day.

4. The water overflowed quickly.

5. The volcano exploded suddenly.

6. There have been many burglaries lately.

7. That changed their minds entirely.

❷ （答案略）

Unit 87
——————————— P. 224

❶ **1**. taller, tallest   **2**. longer, longest

3. shorter, shortest   **4**. finer, finest

5. spicier, spiciest   **6**. bigger, biggest

7. closer, closest   **8**. slimmer, slimmest

9. thinner, thinnest   **10**. later, latest

11. worse, worst   **12**. more, most

13. fatter, fattest   **14**. tinier, tiniest

15. paler, palest   **16**. brighter, brightest

17. sappier, sappiest   **18**. slimier, slimiest

19. thicker, thickest   **20**. calmer, calmest

❷ （答句之答案略）

1. the cutest   **2**. the most hardworking

3. the funniest   **4**. the most boring

5. the most friendly   **6**. the tallest

7. the smartest   **8**. the most creative

Unit 88
——————————— P. 227

❶ **1**. Ken is shorter than Jim.

2. Ken is more professional than Jim.

3. Ken is fatter than Jim.

4. Jim is taller than Ken.

5. Jim is more casual than Ken.

6. Ken is more business-like than Jim.

7. Ken is more intense than Jim.

8. Jim is more lighthearted than Ken.

❷ **1**. x   Mt. Everest is the highest mountain in the world.

2. x   The Japan Trench is deeper than the Java Trench, but the Mariana Trench is the deepest.

3. x   Africa is not as large as Asia.

4. x   Blue whales are the largest animal in the world.

5. ✓

6. x   China is not as democratic as the United States.

7. x   The Burj Dubai is taller than Taipei 101.

8. ✓

Unit 83 — Unit 89

Unit 89
——————————— P. 230

❶ **1**. too noisy   **2**. too many   **3**. too dark

4. too busy   **5**. too talkative

❷ **1**. It was too noisy for Charlie to talk on the phone.

2. There were too many phone calls for Amy to take a coffee break.

3. It was too dark for Andrew to see the keyboard very well.

4. Jessica was too busy to help her colleagues with their work.

5. Tony's colleagues were too talkative for him to concentrate on his work.

Unit 90 Review Test

P. 232

❶ **1.** He is / looks strong.   **2.** He is / looks weak.

3. She is / looks tall.   **4.** She is / looks short.

5. He is / looks fat.   **6.** She is / looks healthy and quick.

7. She is / looks happy.   **8.** She is / looks thoughtful.

❷ **1.** clear   **2.** dearly   **3.** fair   **4.** just   **5.** wide

6. quickly   **7.** wrongly   **8.** slowly   **9.** carefully

❸ **1.** He is a handsome guy.

2. Ned takes the subway to his office.

3. Penny is always ready to take a break.

4. Dennis is a terrible driver.

5. Dennis drives terribly.

6. I'm too excited to wait.

7. This bag isn't big enough for these gifts.

8. Do you work here in this building?

9. Does Larry fight with his brother every day?

10. Did we meet at the Italian restaurant last Monday night?

❹ **1.** every day   **2.** twice a week   **3.** often

4. sometimes   **5.** never

❺ **1.** every Sunday   **2.** six times a month

3. always   **4.** every week

❻ **1.** x I see two tall guys.

2. ✓

3. x Tony is taller than David.

4. x Who is the tallest guy in the room?

5. ✓

6. x James is better at math than Robert.

7. x Irving is a happy guy.

8. x Janice speaks English very well.

❼ **1.** quietly   **2.** joyfully   **3.** eagerly   **4.** slowly

❽ **1.** Mt. Fuji isn't as tall as Mt. Everest.

2. Brazil isn't as big as Russia.

3. Madagascar isn't as big as Greenland.

4. Jakarta isn't as prosperous as Seoul.

5. Manila isn't as densely populated as Tokyo.

6. France isn't as small as Switzerland.

7. Iceland isn't as far south as Spain.

8. Italy isn't as far north as Germany.

9. Canada isn't as hot as Mexico.

10. Egypt isn't as cold as Sweden.

❾ **1.** sweeter than   **2.** warmer than   **3.** hotter than

4. the coldest   **5.** the biggest   **6.** the tallest

7. as terrible as   **8.** as fast as   **9.** as high as

❿ **1.** too hard / hard enough

2. too late

3. too salty / salty enough

4. too spicy / spicy enough

5. too blunt / blunt enough

6. too loud / loud enough

7. too expensive

8. too slow

Unit 91 ——————————— P. 239

❶ **1.** on **2.** in **3.** at **4.** in **5.** in
   6. on **7.** on **8.** on **9.** on

Unit 92 ——————————— P. 241

❶ **1.** in / at **2.** at **3.** in / at **4.** in

❷ **1.** in **2.** on **3.** on **4.** at **5.** in **6.** in

Unit 93 ——————————— P. 243

❶ **1.** behind **2.** next to **3.** in **4.** on
   5. against, near **6.** next to **7.** in front of **8.** on
   9. under **10.** over **11.** between **12.** against

Unit 94 ——————————— P. 245

❶ **1.** out of **2.** into **3.** up **4.** on **5.** around
   6. out of **7.** along **8.** across **9.** through
   10. past **11.** down **12.** off

Unit 95 ——————————— P. 247

❶ **1.** at **2.** on **3.** in **4.** at
   5. on **6.** on **7.** at **8.** on

❷ **in:** the afternoon, the evening
   on: Tuesday afternoons, Thanksgiving Day, Christmas Day,
   Saturdays, Monday, the weekend
   at: 6 o'clock, night, Christmas

Unit 96 ——————————— P. 249

❶ **1.** in **2.** on **3.** in **4.** on
   5. in **6.** x **7.** x **8.** on

❷ **in:** winter, February, 1500, the fall
   on: March 3rd, July 13th
   x : this weekend, tomorrow afternoon, next summer, yesterday
   morning, last month

Unit 97 ——————————— P. 251

❶ （答案略）

❷ **1.** since **2.** since **3.** for **4.** for **5.** since

❸ （答案略）

Unit 98 Review Test

❶ **1**. behind **2**. from **3**. under **4**. down **5**. off **6**. out of

❷ **1**. in **2**. on **3**. on **4**. on **5**. into **6**. out of

7. into **8**. on **9**. between **10**. behind

11. over **12**. in **13**. along **14**. past **15**. in **16**. against

17. near **18**. under **19**. to **20**. down

❸ **1**. on **2**. on **3**. at **4**. at **5**. at

6. in **7**. in **8**. at **9**. on **10**. in

❹ **1**. on **2**. at **3**. on **4**. in **5**. at **6**. on

7. on **8**. at, on **9**. in, on **10**. in **11**. in

❺ **1**. under, on **2**. in **3**. in front of

4. behind **5**. near / next to **6**. opposite

7. near / next to **8**. between

❻ **1**. for **2**. for **3**. since **4**. ago **5**. for

6. for **7**. ago **8**. for **9**. since

❼ **1**. Dana left an hour ago.

2. Nancy walked out of the office thirty-five minutes ago.

3. Victor called three hours ago.

4. Julie came four days ago.

5. It happened a month ago.

6. We saw her a year ago.

❽ **1**. ago **2**. left **3**. for **4**. for **5**. since **6**. since

Unit 99

P. 259

❶ **1**. I like soda and potato chips.

2. Do you want to leave at night or in the morning?

3. I can't cook, but I can barbecue.

4. I have been to Switzerland and New Zealand.

5. She isn't a ballet dancer, but she is a great hip hop dancer.

6. Tom says he is rich, but he always borrows money from me.

7. Will you come this week or next week?

8. Shall we sit in the front or in the back?

9. I read comic books and novels.

10. Do you like to eat German food or French food?

Unit 100

P. 261

❶ **1**. If he lifts weights, he will build up his muscles.

2. If she skips dessert, she will stay slim.

3. If she often goes jogging, she will increase her stamina.

4. If she reads widely, she will learn lots of things.

5. If he practices writing, he will improve his writing skills.

6. If he practices public speaking, he will become self-confident.

❷ **1**. When she finishes stretching, she will start jogging.

2. When she gets tired, she'll rest on a bench.

3. When she gets home, she'll eat breakfast.

Unit 101 Review Test
— P. 262

❶ 1. because my car broke down

2. because my boss needed me to work late in the office

3. so I could finish my report

4. because I had to bake cookies

5. because my dog was sick

6. so I could see my favorite TV show

7. because I had to take a sick friend to the hospital

8. because I had to help my mom clean the house

❷ 1. and 2. but 3. or 4. and 5. but

6. or 7. and 8. but 9. or 10. or

❸ 1. when 2. if 3. when 4. if 5. when

6. if 7. When 8. If 9. when 10. If

❹ 1. When, will wear 2. If, will ask 3. when, ask

4. If, will take 5. if, tell 6. When, will give

❺ 1. after, before 2. before 3. after 4. before 5. after

Unit 102
— P. 265

❶ 1. seven 2. sixty-seven

3. five thousand, six hundred and ninety-four

4. one million and twenty-two

❷ 1. nine one one

2. eight eight two three, one four six two

3. zero zero one, dash, one, dash, eight four seven, dash, eight six four two three zero three

4. zero nine two eight zero five three two five three

5. two three six five nine seven three nine, extension three three

Unit 103
— P. 267

❶ 1. the first 2. the third 3. the fourth 4. the sixteenth

5. the twenty-ninth 6. the thirty-second 7. the thirty-fifth

8. the thirty-seventh 9. the forty-fourth 10. the forty-fifth

Unit 104
— P. 269

❶ 1. Mr. Simpson is meeting Ms. Miller on Monday.

2. Mr. Simpson is visiting his grandma on Tuesday.

3. Mr. Simpson is going shopping on Wednesday.

4. Mr. Simpson is having dinner with Tom on Thursday.

5. Mr. Simpson is picking up Peter at the airport on Friday.

6. Mr. Simpson is playing basketball on Saturday.

7. Mr. Simpson is going to the movies on Sunday.

❷ 1. the twenty-first of April, two thousand one

2. the thirteenth of August, nineteen ninety-nine

3. the thirty-first of December, two thousand four

Unit 98 | Unit 104

Unit 105

P. 271

❶ 1. B   2. C   3. A   4. D

❷ 1. It's a quarter past nine.

It's nine fifteen.

2. It's half past three.

It's three thirty.

3. It's a quarter to three.

It's fifteen minutes to three.

It's two forty-five.

4. It's seven oh two.

It's two minutes past seven.

Unit 106 Review Test

P. 272

❶ 1. January, February   2. Sunday   3. March

4. August   5. Sunday   6. Thursday   7. Friday

8. July, August, September

9. Thursday, November   10. May, June

❷ 1. the twenty-fifth of December

2. the thirty-first of December

3. the first of January

4. the fourteenth of February

5. the fifth of May   6. the seventh of July

7. the fifteenth of August

8. the thirty-first of October

9. the twenty-ninth of February

❸ 1. two three zero zero one two three five

2. zero two, dash, two five seven nine four five eight one

3. eight eight six, dash, seven, dash, two one five five seven four eight

4. five five seven eight two six four one, extension one zero nine

5. zero nine three five two three three zero one zero

6. the third of April / April (the) third

7. the twenty-fifth of June / June (the) twenty-fifth

8. the eleventh of January / January (the) eleventh

9. the twenty-second of September / September (the) twenty-second

10. fourteen thirty-five

11. nineteen forty-eight

12. two thousand three

13. two thousand ten